THE REALM OF OBLIVION

MARAE GOOD

The Realm of Oblivion

ISBN 979-8-9870986-1-5

Cover design by Kody Taylor

Developmental Edit by Liz Lowham

Line Edit/ Proofreading by Kara Aisenbrey

This is a work of fiction. Names, characters, businesses, events, and incidents are the products of the author's imagination or are used fictitiously. Any resemblance to actual persons, living or dead, or actual events is purely coincidental.

For Brody,

Thank you for seeing me.

I love you.

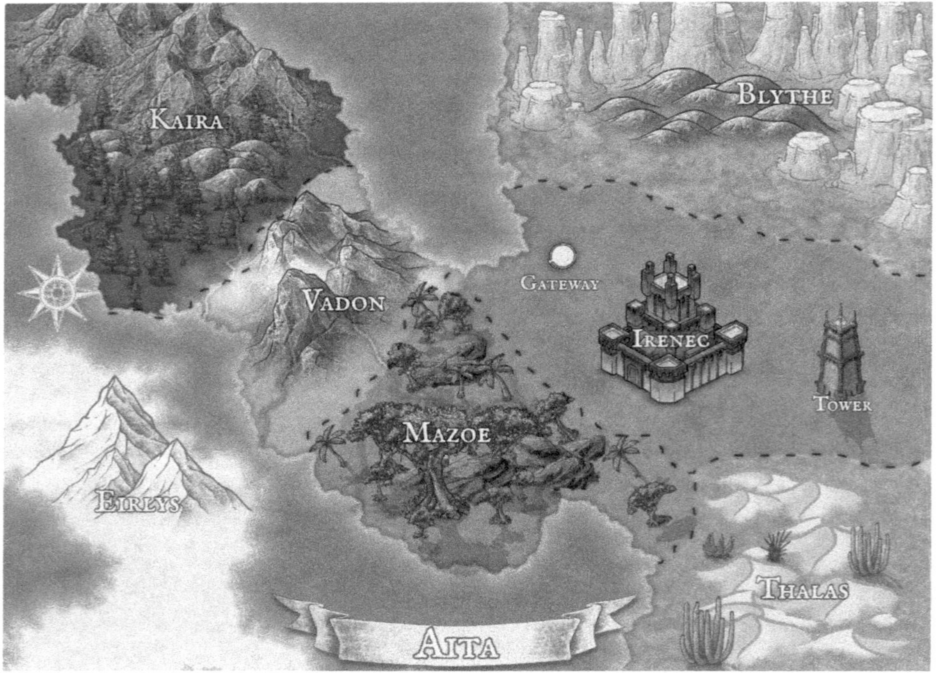
Kaira
Blythe
Vadon
Gateway
Irenec
Tower
Mazoe
Eirlys
Thalas
Aita

Pronunciation Guide

People

Collins: CALL-ins

Iveh: i-VEH

Aramis: air-UH-miss

Aideen: a-DEEN

Vidaar: VA-dar

Hekate: HEH-kate

Conon: CON-in

Caelum: KAY-lum

Akira: UH-ke-ruh

Alderick: ALL-drick

Sander: San-DER

Ashula: uh-SHU-la

Weylin: WAY-lin

Drystan: DRY-stin

Alois: Al-OH-is

Selene: SEE-lean

Places

Aita: i-EE-tah

Kaira: cah-RR-AH

Mazoe: MAH-zo

Irenec: EAR-ah-nic

Blythe: B-lithe

Eirlys: I-ER-liss

Vadon: VA-don

Elysia: e-LIE-sia

Pronunciation Guide

<u>Other</u>

Cyrbus: SEER-bus

Caelitis: cal-LA-e-tis

Vimniran: VIM-ner-in

Kefi: KEF-e

Verda: VER-dah

Eunioa: yoo-NOH-uh

Saudade: sow-dah-dE

Drifting Guide

<u>Clicks</u>

Aita/Gateway**:** Three clicks to the right.

Kaira: One click to the left.

Eirlys: Two clicks to the left.

Vadon: Three clicks to the left.

Blythe: Four clicks to the left.

Thalas: Five clicks to the left.

Mazoe: Six clicks to the left.

Irenec: Seven clicks to the left.

Chapter One

One tiny lightning bolt. That was all I wanted.

There was an inkling in my mind—a survival instinct—whispering to avoid the lightning storm, to flee into the false security of my home, certain the sturdy walls would detain the barreling winds. But cowering to the storm beyond my windowpane wasn't an option. I faced it, hand pressed to the glass, pleading one of its sparks would perhaps reach me. Bring something back to life that had long been asleep.

I couldn't remember the last time I was truly awake.

My hand was steady, even when no thrum of electricity fired through my nerves with the boisterous rumble filling the void in my mind. Flashes of light washed over the once-clear sky, but nothing was quite as frightening as the piercing gaze from the strange woman behind me.

The chair beneath me creaked as I shifted closer to my wooden desk, so my finger might properly race the dwindling drops down the window. I ran a nail along the cool glass as her voice scraped the drafty air. "I wasn't aware you'd lost your ability to speak."

I wasn't aware I was permitted to speak—much less to a stranger.

I wanted to talk. My throat ached with the need to engage in meaningful conversation, to release the thoughts I'd long piled up. But it wasn't clear why she was here, why someone was in my room to begin with, asking questions of a time long forgotten. Perhaps because of the upcoming election Father was running in.

She sucked in a tight breath. "Have you regained your memories from before your accident?"

"No." My freckled hand accepted defeat to the racing drops and lowered back to the desk. Another loss, just like the memories stolen in a tragic car accident, a result of a brain injury. Doctors' predictions were worthless, given as weeks became months and then years. But my brain was as empty as before. Despite Iveh's crude observation, I was very much capable of speaking. But I'd learned long ago my thoughts weren't welcomed.

The fact my parents hired Iveh was as strange as her name. Even more so that this interview was taking place in my bedroom, rather than her office. But it shouldn't serve as a surprise I wasn't permitted to leave, not even for this.

I wrapped a copper strand around my finger, no sign of the unruly curls I loved. I braced my spine while I turned in my chair to face her, if only so this would end sooner. Envy wove through me at the sight of her raven hair and beautiful chestnut skin, rich and full of color. A stark contrast to my dull, hollow complexion.

Was hers a mirror to her soul, much like mine?

My gaze retreated to the spotless wooden floor when her striking blue eyes flicked up. "Have you tried to end your life since the accident?"

I pulled my knees to my chest and stared at the bookcase behind her, wishing I could disappear into the worlds woven with words. Reading was one of the only factors that led me to answer honestly, "No, I haven't."

Shuffling pages in her notebook interrupted the consuming silence, doing little to slow the walls that pressed closer each day. Besides the bookcase, this room contained nothing of real value. Not even the pristine artwork layered on the gray walls, nor the gold-rimmed oval mirror above the vanity, containing an assortment of jewelry and fine sprays.

I looked back out the window—the only other item of value—before Iveh said, "It says here you used to suffer from recurring nightmares. Are those still appearing?"

I rubbed my temple, where that very dream lay. "No."

To be fair, this wasn't an outright lie. I'd never considered it a nightmare and it was only one consistent dream. But I wouldn't reveal that. Not when the last time I had, my parents handed me a bottle of pills that made me too drowsy to think, much less dream.

It was a dream I never wanted to escape.

I leaned back and stared up at the attic latch, as if it acted as a portal to another world. I closed my eyes and plunged into the world painted in fire, a smokeless, beautiful fire. Not one of flame, but in essence and hue. A time of purging and growth. The forest was changing, transitioning into the next season. No longer solely green and lush but greeted with licks of orange and yellow. A layer of fog settled over the forest, thick enough to cut with a knife. No matter how deep I ventured, the fog lingered, never allowing a clear view. It was the same each time I visited, unchanged. Haunting and teasing me with its beauty, but never allowing a full taste. I blindly followed the path as the wind tousled my wild hair. Rocks shifted beneath my feet as I wound through the fog—

"Collins." Iveh's scowl welcomed me when I emerged from the dream. She cocked her head as she studied me, as if she could see the imagery hiding in my mind.

My chest squeezed, tightening with every breath. "Why are you here?" I blurted, fearful she could somehow crumble my treasured dream with her tiny fist.

"It's only a routine checkup to see if you've made any progress."

Why were we checking for progress? This incident had long been swept from the minds of those who also occupied this house, as if they too had forgotten. Other than allowing me to see a psychologist for a few short weeks, my parents never made any real effort to regain my memories. The only consistent effort was insisting I focus on the present. Put the past behind me. If you ignore things long enough, they vanish and lose their power.

How long until I simply vanish?

But still, a glimmer of hope rippled through me, giving me the strength to speak again. "My last psychologist mentioned a spot for me in a clinical trial to help with amnesia. Would you know if that's still a possibility?"

Something unreadable flickered across her face, so quickly I couldn't decipher it. Her voice was sharp, slicing through any hope. "No, you wouldn't be a good candidate." She gifted me a smile, though it was a cruel one. "Someone with your range of damage is too far gone."

Any flicker of hope faded away and transformed into a fiery sensation, as if the storm outside had at last jolted my nerves. My eyes burned as I blinked, shuddering a breath. "A word of advice: you could at least wait until you've left to relish in my devastation. You're a terrible psychologist."

Her smile grew. "It's a good thing I'm not one, then."

Then why was she here? She hadn't introduced herself as one, but what purpose would she have in searching the rubble remnants in my mind? Why would my parents allow such a violation?

My self-control snapping, I stood, my chair thudding against the floor. "As much as I'd love to be your entertainment for the day, I'll have to ask you to leave." I grasped the door handle, left unlocked for Iveh's convenience. "You can take your smile and shove it back into whatever hole you crawled out of." I forced my hand to remain steady as I gestured out the door.

Chills coiled through me when she laughed, a sound I was certain would haunt my dreams. She crossed her legs, clearly not done just yet.

"I'll have to report back to your parents it appears you're still unfit to have a say in your own life." She clicked her tongue as she stood, her eyes leering over me as she walked. "Pity."

The handle shook beneath my hand, unable to move as she passed, her cackle trailing down the stairs. I didn't dare close it, if only so I wouldn't suffocate in my mistake. Of course this was a test. A test I'd clearly failed. Wobbly legs and shallow breaths carried me to the comfort of my bed. I hoped the cloudlike cream bedspread could perhaps carry me out of here. I didn't know why this gutted me; I hadn't truly lost anything.

My voice had been silenced the moment I woke up.

Chapter Two

Remorse and panic fully settled into my bones when I padded down the stairs and saw Father perched on the sitting room sofa. Had Iveh informed him of my behavior? Why else would he be home? He never returned until long after the sun went to rest. Even as a retired lawyer, he had plenty to occupy his time. Most of which was consumed with being a prospect for a Texas senator.

My bare foot hovered on the last step as I hesitated, unsure of the best strategy. The silence was typical, leaving me without a clue as to what he knew. The wooden banister dug into my palm as the television filled the silence, a news segment about a possible tropical storm hitting the coast of Texas tomorrow. The dwindling rainstorm of this morning was only the beginning.

I bit my lip as I crossed the hardwood floor, careful to not make the slightest noise when I sat beside the glass coffee table. He didn't so much as look up from his phone, not even as I began the puzzle I'd been working on to pass the time.

I loved puzzles. I liked the way they challenged me. Within my grasp, I held the possibility of creating worlds. I could create an exquisite alternate reality with my own hands as there was nothing I could do about the bare, colorless walls pressing in on me. And if I sought further liberation, I'd dive into one of my many books. I'd lose myself for hours in enchanting worlds, full of possibilities and dreams.

I didn't devour this puzzle as quickly as the others, cherishing the gift from Father. One evening he'd caught me staring up at the night sky, and the next, there was a puzzle outside my door. A man standing on an ocean, not afraid of the deep, inky sea beneath his feet while he stared up into the violet night of endless stars. It was a kind gesture, but I would've preferred to experience it beyond my fingertips. The chance to breathe in the humid air and lie among the grass and lose myself in the soulful stars. And if I dared, I'd invite him to stay with me. Allow me the chance to share a frail, intimate piece of myself.

But he'd have to look at me first, something he hardly ever did. Sena—my past psychologist—had assured me it was because of his grief, that in some way he believed his daughter died when I lost the understanding of who I was. But if he'd truly open his eyes, he'd see I was right here. That I was alive. I'd do anything to stop being a ghost.

Remaining in this house was one of them.

His wrinkled face was relaxed as he looked at his phone, oblivious to my staring. He and I couldn't be more different. His skin was nicely bronzed from the sun, while my pale, freckled skin would surely burn. He adored the limelight, while I fumbled with any attention. His eyes were dark as mud—much like Mother's—lacking the freckle I strangely inherited in one of my green eyes, along with the golden ring encompassing them both. Like whoever created me knew I would never experience the sun's rays embracing fresh, rich grass and instead placed it within me. The only similarity I could possibly find would be our hair, but his red had faded to a dull, lifeless gray.

I huffed a breath and ran a hand across my chest, a weak attempt to soothe the ache. "Did you have a good day?"

His russet eyes widened when he glanced up, stretching his wrinkles. I didn't know if he was shocked I'd spoken or was unaware I was in his presence. "It was fine." His voice was toneless, uninterested. The usual.

I hid my burning cheeks and stared at the puzzle, wishing I could dive into the dark, unending sea. Perhaps if I could walk on water, he'd finally talk to me. I didn't know what else to do.

But still, I tried. "Is there anything I could assist you with while you're here? The election?" I didn't know what I was capable of offering, but I'd lick envelopes late into the night if it got me out of this house. If it persuaded him to look at me.

But only my aching throat and teetering heart accompanied the silence.

If I understood who I'd been before, I could replicate myself. Become the acceptable and ideal daughter they longed for. Then I could finally stop tripping on the scraps of my past and seize the reins to my life. No longer would they choose who I was, what I wore, even what I ate. They didn't believe I was mentally capable of making my own choices yet. Hence why my highest degree of education was high school and I was jobless and living under their roof, despite being a legal adult.

Entirely dependent on them.

But it would get better. They promised once I slipped into who I used to be, they'd let up. I didn't pretend to understand why they pushed me to let go of the past, when they couldn't offer the same. I'd listen to Reed's—my supposed boyfriend—words, his reminders to trust them. This was out of love. For now, I'd stay in line and play the role they wanted. Someday I'd be released from the acting, and it would simply be me.

I flinched, shocked to find Father's hand on my shoulder. My heart pounded beneath my loose lavender sundress as he stared at the puzzle. "You're still working on this?"

I slowly nodded, so as to not appear overeager. Should I be thrilled he noticed or nervous he was unsatisfied with the time I'd spent on it? "It's been difficult," I mumbled as I pulled the hem of my dress over my knees. I cleared my throat, aware of his hand tightening on my shoulder, remembering they hated when I mumbled. "I've thought about cutting off a few edges to make the lost pieces fit." I forced a laugh, exposing my hope. "Did you want to help? A fresh set of eyes could be the solution."

If not for the hand on my shoulder, I'd believe I was alone. I wasn't bothered by the silence; it was a constant companion. My stomach wrenched when his touch faded, along with his eyes. He was almost to the kitchen when he said, "You can try to alter the pieces all you like. It doesn't change the fact they're useless."

His bitter, unsensible words stung more than they should. Perhaps because it felt like they were directed at me and not the puzzle. No matter how hard I tried to fit, I'd always be without a spot.

Useless.

The remainder of my solitude was served in my room, my legs tangled in ivory sheets as I gobbled up a novel. I wondered if once upon a time, in a different time, Mother and Father shared whimsical tales with me as I lost myself in the story. So much so I lost track of time and failed to notice the orange glare against the window, forcing me to rush and get ready for dinner. A meal I usually ate alone. Tonight, however, Reed and our parents would grace me with their presence.

My stomach churned while I fussed with my appearance in front of the cream vanity. My copper hair was neatly pressed, exactly how Mother liked it. I coated another layer of powder over my scattered freckles, ensuring I covered the scar etched along the tail of my right brow, its jagged line running across my temple. Besides the lack of memories, it was the only evidence of the accident. It wasn't longer than two inches, but after a few more laser treatments—per Mother's request—it would be as if it never happened.

I flinched, my ribs hitting the edge of the vanity when the door jiggled, the lock still tightly in place. Because of the automatic lock, I usually left the door open. But it was Father who'd closed it this afternoon, after I scurried up here to hide. Another small detail arranged by my parents, so they needn't worry for my safety when they left me here alone.

But I couldn't hide any longer when Mother pulled open the door, somehow leaving me lonelier than before. She strode in, radiant and confident in a rust dress that complimented her onyx hair in a way that made her even more intimidating.

I looked down at the variety of rouges and balms scattered about my vanity as she said, "They'll be here in ten minutes. Let's have a look at you." She motioned for me to stand before the mirror with a hint of shakiness in her tone, nerves I assumed were for her guests.

Even in her heels, I stood at least an inch taller while I awkwardly spun, letting her see every inch of the black A-line dress. She rolled her eyes before she stalked to the closet and retrieved a glistening navy silk gown. I wasn't sure if I was more unfit for this casual dinner or the dress was, but I bit my tongue and slipped it on, the material clinging to my thin curves with a slit exposing my long legs. Her thin lips stretched out as she examined me for any flaws. I didn't protest when she slipped up my hair, no doubt to reveal the low cut in the back. As if I wasn't vulnerable enough.

Her words were chilling, much like her fingers as she tightened the strings at my waist. "Your father and I were more than generous to arrange that visit, yet you treated her poorly. Would you care to explain yourself?"

My throat clammed up—I'd somehow forgotten about Iveh until now. I didn't know how to proceed; this was a trap regardless. My shoulders dipped as I whispered, "Is it truly so bad I wish to remember?"

There was no warmth or endearment when her chestnut eyes found mine in the mirror, as she motioned for me to sit. She applied a deep-plum stain to my lips. "We have told you everything you need to remember. Do I really need to remind you whose fault it was that the accident occurred in the first place?" She clicked her tongue while she rummaged through a drawer in the vanity. "Learn from your mistakes, Collins. Don't disobey us again."

My eyes burned as I stared at her incredulously through the mirror, flinching when she fastened a gold chain around my neck. She held my gaze as her fingers leisurely lingered, taunting me with the control she so clearly held. I dared to loosen it a fraction as I asked, "How long will you continue to punish me? How long until I can begin to live my life?" I looked down, certain her glare was capable of shattering glass.

"Your father and I setting your life up for success isn't a punishment. Perhaps if you could look past yourself, you would realize that."

I wanted to demand the purpose behind locking me up each day. Why she felt it was acceptable to suffocate me, to only allow me flimsy breaths of fresh air when she willed it. How she believed this life was sustainable. My lungs urgently burned, begging to scream for their permission to be my own person. I didn't know what dreams or desires I wished for myself, but I desperately needed to find out. Was it wrong to believe there was more to life than this?

Any sign of rebellion retreated when she pushed against my shoulders, holding me down with a strength I didn't know her frail frame possessed. "You will not embarrass us tonight. You will sit there and be the daughter we've raised. You might find your life restrictive now, but so help me, Collins. If you do not stay in place tonight, I will show you how much worse it can be." Her hold loosened, and with one quick glance over my appearance she was gone, pleased with her work.

I'd yet to decide if I preferred Father pretending I didn't exist or Mother hating my existence.

Chapter Three

Mother's gag order firmly held the reins, making it difficult to choke down my salad while I sat with Reed and his family. I'd been with Reed almost half of my new existence, though I didn't know why. Much like anything else, this was simply how things were done. My parents liked him and that was that. He was fine. Probably exactly the type of man most parents dreamed of their daughter dating. If you could look past his wandering eyes to my chest, you'd see a successful, educated, wealthy man. I'd never cared to ask what occupied his time; all I knew was there was talk of him someday running for government, much to Father's delight.

He wasn't horrible. Nothing like the valiant men carved from words, their souls pressed neatly to paper-thin worlds. But he was plenty attractive, with his cropped golden hair and sun-kissed sculpted frame. But his welcoming chocolate eyes couldn't distract me from the fact he was a bore and nearly ten years older than me. He was ready to settle down, and I simply wanted to live. I didn't love him and I never would. I was, however, grateful for his presence, if only so I could escape my parents' snares for a moment.

I stared beyond Mother's plastered-on smile and looked through the grand French doors, teasing me with the outside world. I half-heartedly sucked on a crouton, savoring the stale bread, when Reed rested his hand beside mine, tracing a finger across my wrist. "I'll miss you when I leave next month."

I clenched my hand, resisting the urge to hide it under the table. "Where are you going?" I scanned through our previous one-sided conversations, hoping he hadn't already told me.

"Italy. I need to meet with a potential client."

I bit my lip when he grabbed my hand. I stared at it, willing the fingers lying limply in his hold not to shake. "Italy? That sounds wonderful. How long are you gone?"

"A week." I sucked on a tasteless leaf, holding in my drool while he finished the last of his lobster. "I figured I'd take some time to see a bit of the culture. Perhaps visit the island of Capri."

No longer was I envious of his devoured lobster. I forced a smile, hiding how badly I'd love to see the sight. Even my dreams were incapable of doing the stunning island justice. "I hope you travel safely. Make sure to take pictures to show me when you return."

His chocolate eyes scanned our parents, both sets engaged in their own conversations. "You should come with me," he whispered.

"What?" I asked, certain I'd heard him incorrectly.

His chair screeched against the tile as he scooted closer with a grin I'd never seen before. "Come with me. I'll work for a few days and then we can visit wherever you'd like. I'll even extend the trip an extra week."

"Really?" It came out strained. I didn't know how to properly speak with the strange feeling building inside of me. Reed knew how much this meant to me, as he was aware I only left the house with my parents' permission. Which was little to none. I didn't care if it meant two weeks alone with his unwelcomed looks and wandering hands—maybe this was exactly what I needed. If I could experience him away from the pressure of my parents, maybe I could see him in a new light. Could he be my way out? "I'd love to." I failed to bite back my smile.

He smiled beautifully, and for once, I wondered what it might be like to kiss that mouth. Really kiss him, more than the chaste ones I so seldomly offered.

"Consider it done. I'll have my assistant book our trip in the morning."

"Thank you." I twined my fingers through his, giddy and confident for the future. So much so, I ignored the ache in my chest when he dropped my hand and rested it atop my thigh. If I kept trying, I could be happy and satisfied with this lifestyle. Maybe my parents truly knew best.

I eagerly grasped onto every word as he listed destinations we could visit, until Mother interrupted us. Reed cleared his throat and looked at me, as if he thought I'd caught what she said. "Sorry, could you repeat yourself?" He smiled, oblivious to the displeasure seeping from her pores.

"I asked what plans you and Collins made." Her smile was tight, on the edge of snapping the mask she carefully adopted in front of guests.

"Oh." His smile worsened the ache in my chest. "I'll be traveling to Italy in a few weeks. I asked Collins to join me."

Her mask broke for only a moment before she looked at Father, sharing silent words as Reed's parents remained oblivious. The glass edge of the table dug into my ribs as I sat on the tip of my seat, the silence threatening to smother my hope.

Father stared at his disassembled lobster. "I'm afraid that won't be possible."

"Why?" I dared ask as I leaned closer into the table.

Mother shrugged while she wiped her mouth, a shallow attempt to hide her scowl. "You have an appointment."

I choked on a laugh, stifling the urge to ask if I was meeting with Iveh again. Reed spared me a glance and ran a hand through his straw-like hair, grasping for a solution. "Is there no way you could reschedule it?"

Her smile was bogus, much like her words. "I'm sorry. I'm afraid she can't miss this one. Perhaps another time."

There wouldn't be another time. It was nothing but an excuse—they had no intention of releasing me from their grasp. I stared at my silver heels, my breaths sharpening with every intake. Reed leaned in, placing a hand on my knee. "I will take you another time."

I couldn't blame him for giving in so easily. How could I expect him to fight for me when I was a coward myself?

My salad somehow tasted blander while I finished it, blocking out their chatter and the clanking of silver dishes. Even Reed joined in with our fathers, giving up after several failed attempts to converse with me. I didn't have the energy to try any longer. I poked and probed at a grape tomato with a fork as their voices rose, coming to some sort of agreement over something I didn't bother to listen to.

"Did you hear the news, Collins?" Mother's voice was as strangely bubbly as the shimmering champagne she poured into five glasses. Something I wouldn't be participating in.

I rolled my eyes as I snapped, "What?" Reed's hand tightened, but I brushed it off. I had no interest in pretending any longer.

She smiled behind her glass. "Arden has agreed to endorse your father's campaign. Isn't that wonderful?"

"Wonderful." Why the hell would I care? It did, however, confirm my suspicion as to why they pushed me toward Reed, no doubt needing his father's influence and money. While my family was wealthy, the Amberwoods were beyond the term. They were from old money, an amount that was likely limitless and passed down from each generation. I doubted there was a business in town Arden wasn't tied to.

I also doubted his generosity was from the goodness of his heart; he'd have some form of opinion on Father's agenda. Arden might be powerful, but he was unlikable. Versus my father, who was well accustomed to adjusting his mask to the liking of others. They were the perfect pair. Had Reed known he was likely a pawn in this as well?

"It really is." Reed's mother, Miriam, joined in. I didn't dislike her. Most of our encounters were brief, but always on good terms. She'd probably instilled what good qualities Reed possessed, spending most of her time doing charity work with her society group—yet she didn't seem concerned with my lack of freedom. "So, Collins." She smiled as she brushed a golden curl over her shoulder. "That leaves us to discuss your future plans."

My nerves worked on their own accord, rebelling when I raised a brow and smirked. "I wasn't aware I had any plans."

Miriam might be beautiful, but her words certainly weren't when she casually said, "Well, with you and Reed getting married. Your mother and I believe it would be a great time to start introducing you—"

"What?" I choked, steel digging into my palm as I clenched my fork. "Married?"

Besides Reed, everyone erupted into an unsettling bout of laughter. I stared at him for any sort of explanation, but he refused to meet my eye. My fork clattered against my dish while my hands shook, as I forced myself to overpower their laughter. "I wasn't aware I was going to be a teenage bride."

Surprisingly, it was Arden who answered, one of the rare times he'd spoken to me. "It would be in everyone's best interest if you were wed sooner than later."

"Why?" I demanded. This was a ridiculously cruel joke.

"Why not?" Mother's smile gleamed as brightly as the chandelier dangling above us. "Last I checked, you had no plans. Surely, you two have discussed this by now."

"No." *I can hardly manage to kiss him—much less love him.* It wasn't clear why he remained with me, given he tried a hell of a lot harder than I did. How could I possibly be ready for marriage when I still had so much to work through? "I'm sorry, but isn't this between

Reed and me?" I shook my head, wishing I'd wake up from this nightmare delivered by the devil himself.

I held her piercing eyes, demanding an explanation. But it was Reed who gave me one, betraying me in a matter of a few words. "They're right. What are we waiting for?"

I contemplated shoving his cowardly words back down his throat while Father added from across the table, "It's vital we do this before the election comes up. We can't raise any red flags. Reed can begin his political career, while you begin your lessons on how society works."

"Oh, screw your election!" I shoved my plate across the table as I stood, needing to shatter it like they'd done to me. *How can I possibly get married before I've had the chance to live?* Did they truly see no other path for me than as a wife, throwing fundraisers and attending pointless luncheons with women more than twice my age? "I am not doing this."

"Collins," Mother warned, silently reminding me of her promise. "Sit down."

I chucked my cup across the room, shards of glass scattering across the tile. "I can't go on a trip, but I can get married! This is the most ridiculous thing I've ever heard," I yelled to no one in particular, as everyone in the room managed to piss me off, even Miriam, whose mouth pathetically hung open.

I gripped Reed's glass next, chasing the addictive high coursing through me. I'd barely lifted it to throw before Arden said, "That's enough." He towered over me, beady eyes looking down through his crooked nose. His next words were fouler than him. "I will not be insulted for a moment longer. You should consider yourself blessed to marry my son. I'm willing to oblige your mother's wishes, as I can see what your family has to offer, despite how flawed you may be. I can look past you for the bigger picture." I flinched, stumbling against my chair. "Sit down and learn your place."

I wasted a glance toward Father, hoping he'd come to my aid. He wouldn't allow anyone to speak in such a way to his daughter, especially in his own home. But he pulled out a pocketbook, refusing to acknowledge my plea. It was a small action, but it spoke volumes. Confirming how little he cared for me and how much he valued power.

Arden must've believed he hadn't inflicted enough harm, given I was still standing. "Did you actually believe my son would choose to be with someone like you, if there wasn't something for him to gain?" He ran a hand over his bald head and laughed. "Perhaps if he could find a wife on his own, he wouldn't have to settle for you. But what else can be done now? A deal's a deal."

What I'd failed to see before was now clear. Why he stayed with me when I gave nothing in return. Why he insisted I give in to my parents' will and stop resisting the inevitable. He wanted me to be a useless trophy, rather than a capable woman who thought for herself.

And I knew by Mother's smile Arden wasn't lying. This was her wish. This was the life she desired for me. She'd likely demanded a grand wedding in exchange.

"Are we agreed?" Arden sneered. It wasn't truly a question, but a reminder of what little power I had. What freedom would never be mine.

Something shriveled up and died inside me when I sat down like the coward I was. "Yes."

"Wonderful!" Mother's claps were pounding slaps of true joy, each one summoning emotion in my eyes. But I wouldn't let them see. I couldn't reveal they'd broken the remnants of my spirit. That they possessed so much power over me, even if it was obvious.

The remainder of the night was an unbearable blur. Reed placed a ghastly ring on my finger, without any sort of proposal. I contemplated slicing his face with the bitter, unwelcomed diamond as more plans were made—without my permission, of course. There'd be a wedding this winter, just in time for next fall's election.

Three months.

Wonderful.

When I believed it couldn't get worse, Reed pulled me aside while the others drank another round of champagne, too engrossed in their slurred laughter to notice him leading me to the stairs.

"Yes, husband?" I yanked my arm from his hold, wishing I possessed the strength to snap his bones. Better yet, I wished the tropical storm would arrive and destroy the house, along with everyone in it.

"I'm sorry." His eyes were a pitiful wreck as he stopped at the edge of the stairs. This time I wouldn't fall for his facade. He'd played me all along.

I dodged his slimy hands when he reached for me. "What for? For letting them bombard me? For going along with this disgusting scheme and forcing me to marry you? For refusing to recognize I'm my own person?" I didn't wait for a reply and stomped up the stairs, slamming the automatic lock into place.

Who would have known my prison could serve as my refuge?

I might have been mistaken, but most young girls didn't grow up believing their pillowcase would become an overgrown tissue after they got engaged, soiled with their pitiful tears. Most likely didn't have the imagination to dream up an arranged marriage. I knew I certainly hadn't. Not that I had any dreams of getting married—at least so young. A bride at eighteen? No.

It wasn't marriage itself I was opposed to, but rather the unequal partnership. With Reed, I'd be nothing more than a pretty object on his right side, awaiting his beckoning call. It wasn't a surprise he'd done this, not only because power lured him deeply, but because of his irrational desire to please our parents. He might carry a vein of care for me in his feeble heart, but not enough for us to be married. This wasn't a cherished love between the noble heroines and heroes I found in stories—one I was certain didn't exist.

And as angry as I was at everyone, I was more so at myself. This was my fault. I'd let them control every aspect of my world, so much so that I didn't know who I was supposed to be when I looked in the mirror. It was wrong to believe it would improve as time passed, because now their grasp had sealed to my soul and I was bound to a loveless marriage. Even if I dared to stand up, I'd have nowhere to go. Having memory loss doesn't leave a swell of loved ones in your corner. My parents were quick to remind me that without them, I'd have nothing and no one.

Wrong.

Now I'd have a husband.

I stumbled to the bathroom and emptied my stomach, gasping and choking on the sharp fragments of my reality. I dug my fingers into the cool edge of the toilet as I breathed through each twisting truth. This was my life.

More than ever, I wished I'd died in that accident.

But I hadn't. And I refused to believe my life had been spared only so the very essence of my being could be drained out of me. And I sure as hell wouldn't waste one more moment wallowing in self-pity as I hurled my guts up.

If my parents deemed me ready for marriage, then I was certainly capable of leaving the house.

Chapter Four

My heart and blood pulsed to the beat beckoning me through the dim alley. I'd walked most of the distance to a local club—one where a friendly bartender not only snuck me in but was the mastermind behind my escaping the house.

Sage was the closest person I had to a friend. I'd stumbled upon her on a rare outing with Reed, and the rest was history. There wasn't any hiding from her. She knew every detail of my mundane existence. She was everything I was not.

Wild, free, and utterly full of joy.

Her devious mind was responsible for the magnet beneath my window seal to catch the lock, which was how I snuck out without triggering the alarm, and hopefully how I'd sneak back in. The most difficult part would be scaling up the tree in the tightest jeans I owned—ones Sage insisted I wore for nights out. Which were rare and far between, saved for moments when I was on the brink of shattering. It was reckless to leave tonight, but I had nothing else to lose.

I smiled at the bouncer as I approached the entrance, his stoic face breaking into a grin. He only winked and moved aside, recognizing me for my hair as it billowed with the wind. Wild and untamed, exactly how I liked it. The exact opposite of myself.

I sucked in a breath of sweaty air as I forced my way through, feeling more strangers' bodies than I cared to, until I spotted the pint-sized blonde behind the counter. I smiled in awe, watching her somehow make a plethora of drinks, all while bellowing for the live band. It'd been months since I'd last seen her, but she was with the lead singer, last I knew. Much to our advantage, as his day job was working for the power company. I'd begged Sage *not* to divulge the details of how she convinced him to cut the power long enough to set the window trap.

I snagged the last stool at the end of the bar and rested my hands beneath my chin, waiting for her to notice me. My stomach squirmed while she made two green drinks, containing who knew what. I grinned as she released an ear-pinching squeal—so unnaturally loud for someone so small—when she at last saw me.

She smiled mischievously before extending into a dramatic bow, her ash locks curtaining her face. "And to what do we owe the honor of being graced with your presence tonight?"

I cut to the chase and threw out my left hand—the only reason I'd left the damn thing on.

"The hell?" I collided with the bar as she yanked my arm forward, examining the ring beneath the dim lighting. "Is this real? When did it happen?"

"Tonight. At dinner."

She raised her pierced brow and placed the ring on her own finger. "And I'm guessing since you're wearing it . . . you said yes to the stiff?"

I scoffed as I scanned the club, retreating when I caught the eye of a man across the room. "Please. It wasn't a question. Do you really believe I'd have a say in the matter?" I put the shackle—ring—back on, only so I wouldn't lose it.

"Collins." She crinkled her brows and frowned. "Don't marry him. You can't allow them to treat you this way."

"I didn't come here to be lectured," I snapped, regret knotting through me. I rubbed my temples and released a deep breath. "I'm sorry. I know you're only trying to prevent what happened to you . . ." I trailed off, unable to voice what Sage once confided to me. But our situations were different; hers had been controlling, abusive parents.

She was brave to leave, to start a life on her own. But I wasn't abused and my parents loved me. Even if I left, I didn't know how to live on my own. I was useless.

It was that fact that kept me from venturing beyond my window-pane and never looking back.

I wiped the sweat from my hands down my pants. "I really needed to get out. So could you please be my lunatic friend and pour me a drink? Maybe you can get me drunk enough to convince me I'm not scared, and I'll finally leave."

She smiled sadly at me but didn't protest. "Fine." She poured me half a shot and smirked, exposing the dimple in her left cheek. "But if you're going through with this, I'm getting raging drunk at your wedding."

I laughed, certain Miriam and Mother's friends would pass out—worth the effort of sneaking her in. "Deal." I winced as I downed my shot, swallowing the burn, and ventured into the crowd alone while she tended to other customers.

Even if I was free to roam as I desired, I wouldn't come here often. The club was a reminder of how out of my element I was. It didn't matter how much I drank or how I dressed, my off-the-shoulder top wouldn't make me any less awkward and lost.

Imposter. Imposter. Imposter.

The thought trailed me with each beat of the drum while I pushed through a wave of sweaty, grinding bodies, each leaving a bitter glow on me. I covered my ears, blocking out the crowd's rally when the band started a new set. I scrambled to claw my way out, unable to ease into their abrupt jumping.

I needed another drink.

"Could I get another?" I yelled over the noise. My cheeks burned when I glanced back to find a couple glaring at me, apparently bothered I'd interrupted their fondling in my haste to get out. "Please."

"They're great, huh?" Sage danced behind the counter, moving her hips in a way that made mine ache. "Felix is the singer." She pointed to the man behind the microphone as he flung his tangled bronzed hair up and down. "You have to stay and meet him. He'll be thrilled to know he helped you escape."

I rolled my eyes and waved a hand, resisting the urge to flinch when his voice scraped against my nerves. "Yes, yes. He's amazing." I tapped my fingers as I stared at the empty glass in her hands.

"This is your last one," she warned, pouring me another clear drink. "Any more and you'll be too drunk to climb up your tree."

"Booo. I'm hardly feeling it," I whined, as I still remembered every awful detail of what occurred at dinner. It wouldn't be a surprise if this wasn't actually alcohol she'd given me. Something she'd done before.

Her sweet breath filled my nose when she leaned forward, her icy blue eyes darting to the side. "Don't look. But that guy has been watching you since you showed up."

I rolled my eyes and peeked under my arm, hoping to inconspicuously catch a glimpse. Just past the bar was the same man who'd caught my eye before. His midnight hair was slicked back as he leaned against a wall, his arms crossed over a well-built chest. His shoulders were tight while he examined the room, almost as out of place as I was. But that was because he was entirely too beautiful to be real.

Greedily, I lingered over his muscled frame, regretting it once I slid over a smirk and found his eyes piercing into mine. "I told you not to look." Sage laughed as I dipped my head into the bar, banging my forehead in my panic. "You should talk to him."

"What? I'm engaged," I choked on the word, the thought more foul and bitter than the sticky alcohol on the counter.

"Please. You're hardly engaged." She grinned wickedly, dodging my hand when I reached for her. She adjusted the deep slit in her crimson halter top, flipping her hair back. "I'm going on a break. Have fun."

She slipped my grasp again, even daring to smile at the handsome stranger before she darted into the crowd.

I gripped the glass with my flushed hands, resisting the urge to look. Of course Sage would abandon me while a drunk eyed me. I silently cursed her when the stool beside me screeched, burning my cheeks even more. I nearly fell off my own as I whirled toward him, intent on shooting him down. But the words snagged in my throat as I fully took him in.

Oh, come on.

It truly wasn't fair he looked like that. It especially wasn't fair how the club seemed to fade away as I stared, somehow losing and finding myself in his smoky eyes. They were dark and deep, containing more than I'd ever seen. They held secrets and stories, pieces of him. Pieces I wanted to know.

And that was scary as hell.

"You do know it's rude to stare, right?" I hissed, though my annoyance was directed at myself rather than him.

My hands shook beneath the bar while he turned on his stool, relieving me of his gaze. "Sorry. You look like someone I used to know." His voice matched him perfectly, alluring and enticing in every way, and definitely not from Texas.

There was no way I wasn't drunk.

"Sorry to disappoint you." I gagged down the rest of my drink, its bitter contents doing little to ease my twisting gut.

My insides tangled together irrevocably when he smiled. "I'm not disappointed."

My heart whisked straight out of my chest, leaving me without a clue how to bring it back. "Okay."

His eyes flickered with amusement when he leaned onto the counter and propped his strong chin on a sturdy hand. "Now, what are you doing here?"

I was so consumed with the scar etched through his right brow that I said the first thing that came to mind. "For the band, obviously. I can't get enough of them."

He lifted that scarred brow, the fissure rough and raised. "If you're such a fan, why aren't you out there dancing with your friend?"

I easily found Sage when I trailed his gaze, the crowd avoiding her like a leper. I didn't envy her dance moves, but more how she easily let loose, not caring in the slightest what others thought. Horror and amusement raced through me when she climbed onto the stage, dragging Felix into a kiss.

I huffed a laugh when she leaped off and I turned back toward the wall of bottled liquid courage. Not even a monsoon of it would be enough for me. I searched my empty glass for a response, finding nothing. I didn't look up when the stool shifted, assuming he'd found someone else to bother.

I flinched, slamming my knees into the counter when his breath caressed my ear. "Dance with me."

He extended his hand, where a thick slate ring sat on his middle finger. "What?" I waited for him to laugh, but his sly grin never faltered. What was happening? I hadn't spoken more than twenty words to him, and he expected me to jump at the chance to dance with him?

"Uh." I cleared my throat. "No, this is hardly dancing music." I internally winced. If this was a Jane Austen novel, I'd be an unmarried burden on my parents. My stomach rolled at the thought, as my parents had already ensured that wouldn't be the case.

His full lips curved into a smirk before he called me out. "That doesn't sound like a true fan." His eyes flickered toward my hand. "Are you expecting your fiancé?"

"No," I snapped and covered the specifically-made-for-me-shackle. I waited for him to retract his hand, but he only smiled, not bothered in the slightest. What did that say about him? Better yet, what did it say about me if I considered it? I did come here with the intention of escaping . . . and what was a better distraction than dancing in the arms of a rugged stranger?

I slid my fingers into his rough palm, catching a glimpse of a tattoo beneath his leather sleeve. His warm hand tightened on my fingertips, leading us through the crowd, which had grown twice in size. But it parted like a body of water at the sight of him, allowing him to lead us to a dimmed corner. Though the poor lighting didn't deter the women who looked his way, no doubt wondering why he was wasting his time with me. Let's face it, I was wondering the same thing.

My voice wobbled while I stared at the peanuts discarded beneath my ebony laced boots. "I really can't dance." I'd never done it before. Any previous experiences here were spent at the bar with Sage and not in the arms of men.

"Neither can I." His smile was as kind as his touch when he grabbed my hands, moving us to the beat. Several inches lay between our bodies, but every pore was on fire while his eyes branded me. I wished he'd look away, if only so I'd be brave enough to unlock my knees. I focused on his leather jacket, avoiding the horror surely warping his face when I attempted to move and stepped on his boots.

"Don't think about it," he murmured and placed his hands on my waist, guiding me into a rhythm. I stumbled back a step when he pressed against me, not from discomfort, but shock from his near-scorching embrace. I never knew I craved to be touched until I noticed the lack of his.

I reached out when he stepped back, letting my hand fall between us. I bit my lip, cursing my burning cheeks when he shoved his hands into his jean pockets. His eyes widened as he stumbled over his words. "I'm sorry. We shouldn't—I need to go." Before I could fully process his rejection, he pushed back through the crowd.

My judgment was surely clouded, but I didn't want him to leave. "Wait," I called out, projecting my voice over the noise. As luck would have it, the music lowered to a quieter tune. Allowing not only him, but everyone else to hear my plea.

But their low laughs didn't reach me as I extended a flushed hand out, biting my lip as he strolled back to me, anxiously awaiting his touch. Reed had touched me countless times, but none had ever brought me to life. For a moment, it was as if the fog parted, and I could truly breathe.

This time he left plenty of distance between us when he towered over me, his hands lightly on my waist. "Is this okay?" he whispered. I nodded as I slipped my hands over his shoulders and wrapped them around his neck. We swayed steadily to the music, though I couldn't hear a word of it with his fingers occasionally brushing my skin.

"Why are you really here?" He scanned my face, as if the answer was woven between my freckles.

"I needed to escape." It was as much of the truth as I would reveal.

His hold tightened on my waist as his jaw clicked. "From what?"

"Where are you from?" I asked instead. It was subtle, but there was something distinctly different in his voice.

He broke our gaze, apparently as hesitant as I was. "You've never heard of it."

"And when do you return to this place I've never heard of?"

"Tomorrow."

I was already aware this would end tonight, but that didn't stop the weight pressing in on me. On the rare occasion he looked away, I'd foolishly steal glances at him, as if the melody was dependent on it. I memorized the cut of his jaw, the ivory tone to his skin, only intensifying his slate eyes. There was nothing monumental about our experience, yet I didn't want to forget a thing.

I savored the last of our dance when the music sped up, the assortment of couples breaking apart to move to a new set, fully expecting our time together to end. But he only pulled me closer, not seeming to care if we were the only ones slow dancing.

"You're dancing." His voice stroked my nerves when he leaned down, resting his forehead against mine.

"If that's what you call it." My voice was bubbly and light, inviting an easy smile to join mine.

My happiness faltered when he released my waist, but before it could fully settle, he grabbed my hand and spun me. My foot slipped on the tile—or possibly a peanut—not anticipating being jerked in the opposite direction. My useless legs cheated me and before I could catch myself, I gracelessly tumbled into him, grateful my back was against his chest, as I'd rather an array of strangers view my blazed complexion, and not the man responsible for it.

"I told you I can't dance." I squealed while I dug my fingers into his arms, refusing to fall in the crowd.

A deep laugh rumbled into my back as he steadied me. "No, you just have a poor instructor."

"No more spins." I tried to turn in his hold, stopping when he pulled me deeper against him.

"Is this okay?" His voice was soft as his chest rose against my back. His calloused hands slowly traveled down my arms, scraping in the most soothing way before he wrapped his fingers with mine. I closed my eyes and deeply breathed in the musky pine aroma and leaned back against his shoulder. This type of affection should send me running—especially with a stranger—but I welcomed it. His lips grazed my ear as he murmured, "Who are you?"

"Collins," I breathed, the only sure answer I knew. I turned in his hold, not caring as I boldly searched him for any familiarity. He was like an old song on the tip of my tongue, one I couldn't place the lyrics to. "Are you sure we don't know one another?" Perhaps he could fill in the missing gaps, explain how he stirred these feelings up in me. Ones I didn't know I was capable of.

An unreadable emotion washed over his face—he likely thought me mental. It vanished when he clenched his sharp jaw. "Wouldn't you remember me if you did?"

"You're right . . ." I shook my head, unwilling to reveal what was lacking with me. He certainly had his memories and would know if he knew me. My arms fell slack to my side as I caught a glimpse of Reed's ring, a painful reminder I didn't belong here.

This was my life. I'd leave here tonight, and nothing would change. My parents would stay the same, I'd become Reed's wife, and the empty pit inside me would forever remain. A partially drunken night with a stranger wouldn't change that. It was foolish to believe I felt anything with someone I'd barely met.

"It's late. I should go." Each word dropped ten pounds onto my chest, threatening to collapse it altogether.

He reached for me but stopped, as if a wall now kept us apart. His voice lowered, as did his eyes. "I'll walk you to your car."

"I walked here."

A sense of longing pulsed through me when his fingers swept over mine. "Let me escort you home. It's late."

I didn't bother to compose my face into anything but the truth when I looked up at him. Out here . . . I didn't need to hide the truth that I was drowning. That I was certain I wouldn't truly breathe again the moment I crawled back through that window. But by his wavering smile, I believed he was just as pained with the goodbye. I wanted to accept his offer, I needed to hold his hand the entire night. But this illusion was sure to end, and I couldn't bear to drag it out.

My fingers rubbed his palm, savoring his touch one last time. Hoping my nerves would somehow remember what it felt like to be touched, to be seen. "Thank you for tonight. You were exactly what I needed." Before he could reply, I forced myself through the crowd. I didn't slow even as drinks splashed onto me, nor did I search for Sage.

I knew if I gave him another moment to persist, I wouldn't be able to leave.

But yet, I wasn't sure I could go back home either.

I didn't run home. Usually, I would seize any opportunity to experience the burn in my chest, the ache in my legs. It was a privilege to feel such a thing, to be reminded I was alive. But I certainly didn't feel alive any longer.

Instead, I sipped the humid, warm night and peered up at the stars.

Usually, I could rely on an internal high from a successful night out, but this was different. Tonight, I looked up and didn't marvel at the beads of glimmer and hope speckled throughout the sky. I couldn't see past the void threatening to swallow up my dreams, to turn everything I desired into dust. Even a layer of smoke had trickled into the sky, as if the universe had set fire to those who dared to hope.

My boots padded against the asphalt, dipping into the occasional puddle from the earlier downpour. My heart ached while I looked down the sleeping street. But it was always like this, quiet and stagnant. Some people praised the strong foundations of stone, the alluring beauty of evergreen grass and vibrant flowers. The spitting image of luxurious, peaceful homes.

But behind their fogged glass-pane doors, were they drowning inside as I was? Were they suffocating in control and despair? Did they pay the same cost for stability as I did?

I stopped in the middle of the street, unable to take another step. The club was far beyond my sight when I looked back. What if I was brave enough to return? Would he be waiting for me? Was it possible he'd felt the same ache I had?

I rolled my eyes. It was an absurd notion he could feel that way for me. There was no doubt he was older, and therefore more experienced than I was. He could do this nightly, bouncing to different bars and dancing with an assortment of girls. The thought of him holding anyone else sent my innards rolling to my feet.

Pathetic.

This was why I was incapable of making my own choices. Here I was, foolishly falling over someone I met at a club. Someone who wouldn't waste another thought on me. I didn't know his name and he'd likely forgotten mine.

But I couldn't force myself to take another step, as if a once-silent piece of my soul had woken up, whispering to run. I'd unwisely consumed too much freedom and joy in one sip and now it was impossible to pretend this life was enough. There was a world waiting for me and I only had to be brave enough to chase it.

I sucked in one last breath before I spun and started back toward the club. It was foolish and reckless, but I didn't slow. I raced against my mind, avoiding the logic screaming at me to stop. No, not logic. Traces of my parents' voices, reminding me this world was too much for me.

Perhaps I should have heeded their warnings. My surety faltered when a shadow emerged from behind a car, heading straight toward me. My muscles seized as a voice laced the air.

"It's a beautiful night for a walk."

Chapter Five

I glanced around the shadowed street, dimly lit with few scattered light posts. Instincts screamed in tune with my beating heart, blurting warnings to run. *Move.* Do something. Don't stand there uselessly while the shadow closes the distance.

Despite this, I couldn't move. Not while the shadow began to form, slowly taking shape as it approached me. The blur seemed to forge into a familiar shape, one that made me believe I wasn't a fool after all.

But the truth stared me in the face when I learned it wasn't the man I'd danced with, but rather a shaggy-haired stranger. My legs shook, pleading with me to run from the man approaching me, alone in the middle of the night. But they wouldn't move. As if they were as shocked as I was to find a chip hanging out of his half-open mouth, gawking at me.

Tonight was weird.

He seemed to remember himself and shoved the chip into his thin mouth. I cringed when he openly chomped on it, extending the bag out to me. "Want one?"

"Um—" There was nothing I could do but stare at him when he flung his messy tawny hair from his eyes. Logic screamed to run home, but I feared he'd follow and break into the window I'd so foolishly used. And returning to the club safely was just as unlikely, as I was already halfway home.

I stumbled back a step when his hand flew in the air. "Sorry, I wasn't thinking. You definitely shouldn't accept food from a stranger." He extended a crumb-coated hand with a smile that likely led to many women falling at his feet but tonight only earned him an eye roll. "My name's Aramis, and you are?"

He made a show of thoroughly looking me up and down while I stepped back. "Collins." I gained another step away as I jerked my thumb behind me. "I should go. My parents are expecting me."

"I'm sorry if I scared you." He wiped his hand down his tan shirt and stepped forward. "I just moved in down the street. I was checking out the neighborhood."

My brows furrowed—he had to be lying. He was hardly older than I was, so unless he lived with his parents, or was recently retired, I doubted he lived here. But I realized when I looked back at the affluent houses lining the street I didn't know who truly occupied these homes. My existence might be as unknown to them as theirs was to me.

And I so desperately wanted to be seen. Seen as I had been earlier tonight.

I raised a brow, summoning a face of bravado. "Do you tend to stake out neighborhoods in the middle of the night?"

He grinned mischievously, as crooked as he might be. "Is that what you're doing, Collins?"

I bit my lip, unsure if I wanted to play along. But when he raised his brows in invitation, I couldn't resist. "Definitely. It's my greatest duty to protect this neighborhood from strange men roaming the streets in the middle of the night."

He reared his head up and laughed, a beautiful, lively sound that lifted my own lips. "Okay, I lied. I intended on speaking to you at the club, but you left before I had the chance."

"So you followed me home?" My breath hitched when I stepped back. This was a horrible idea.

"No." He fumbled with his words as he dropped his chips to the asphalt, splattering into a puddle. "I followed you to ensure you made it home safely." He pointed back in the direction I came. "My car's just back there. I only got out because I saw you staring up and I wanted to see what the fuss was about."

It wasn't surprising I hadn't seen him there. I was too wrapped up in the stranger to notice anyone else. Even now, I drifted back to him, back to the warmth and comfort in his arms. But I doubted he was still there, and well, I was here.

Maybe it wasn't the man from tonight who'd brought me to life, but the act of doing what I desired. Something unexpected, something new. Could I experience the same exhilaration of faux freedom with Aramis—yet another stranger?

Perhaps this was an offering from the universe. Letting me experience a night full of two gorgeous strangers. It would be rude to deny such a gift.

I deserted all reasoning and the flutter in my stomach when I pointed up and meekly whispered, "I was looking at the stars."

He hid his eyes from me and looked at his tan boots, stepping forward again. "Do you do that often, Collins?"

"Sometimes."

There was something soft, almost reverent in his tone when he asked, "Would you like to right now?"

I swallowed the uncertainty clogging my throat. If he intended to harm me, he would've done so already. He was as harmless as the crumbs lining his lips. He smiled when I nodded and simply sat down, apparently oblivious or unconcerned with a car coming.

I followed his lead and lay down, leaving a puddle between us. The asphalt held a hint of warmth as it met my exposed shoulders and arms, doing little to ease the chill coating me, when I looked over and caught him staring at me.

The lights flickered off his vibrant amber eyes. A matching pair to his warm golden skin. Those different, almost unearthly eyes bore into mine as he whispered, "You're supposed to be staring at the sky. Not me."

I rolled my eyes at his soft roll of laughter. "If a car comes, I'm shoving you down." My chest vibrated, resisting the urge to join his contagious laugh. Until now, I'd never desired to ask someone to laugh again. If only so I could taste the joy that appeared to radiate throughout him.

He folded his hands beneath his head, flexing a *very* sturdy arm while he looked up. Where the heck had this guy come from? I reprimanded myself for ogling him as he asked, "So what are we looking for?"

"Nothing." I bit my lip, breathing through the tightness in my chest before I admitted, "There's a tree in front of my window. It blocks most of my view, so most of the time, I close my eyes and attempt to imagine how it looks." The sky seemed to darken, losing its glimmer. "I was trying to memorize it so I wouldn't have to guess."

Aramis's chest stopped moving when my confession filled the air. I hadn't revealed much, but I was sure he was drawing his own conclusion. Instead of asking why I didn't simply go outside instead of peering through a window, he asked, "What do you see when you look up?"

"Hope." My eyes burned and I was surprised how easily the words slipped free. "It would be easy to look up and focus on how heavy and dark the night is. But instead, I choose to search for the light. It doesn't matter if there's only one star or a thousand, the night never fully wins. They're a reminder to hang on. A promise that the sun will rise again."

My breath hitched when Aramis propped himself up on an arm and looked down at me. He studied me for a moment before he grinned. "Did you steal that from a fortune cookie?"

Before I knew what I was doing, I flicked him on the nose. "Are you always this obnoxious?"

Despite that, I breathed easier when I joined his laughter. It was both freeing and exhilarating, something I wished to do again and again. But when his fingers grazed my temple, his elbow dipping into the puddle, our laughter halted. "Who did this to you?"

My mouth was beyond dry as he traced my scar, shocked by his boldness and how he saw it in the first place. "Who did it?" he persisted, this time with a hint of impatience.

"No one." I sat up, pulling my knees to my chest. "It was a car accident."

His jaw tightened as his gaze roamed my face, almost like he was searching for more scars. "How?"

"I don't know." His brows furrowed as he waited for an explanation. I huffed a shaky breath—there couldn't be any harm in revealing the truth to a stranger. "I suffered a brain injury from the accident. Which in turn took all my memories." My gut sunk and twisted, even though this had been my reality for a long while.

The warmth in his eyes flickered out. "So, you can't remember anything? Nothing at all from before your accident?"

"Nothing," I whispered, surprised to find his eyes brightening. A moment too late I learned they hadn't and had only consumed the light of an oncoming car. My soul must've accepted its fate, because my body refused to move, even when the brakes shrieked their final warning.

My back scraped against the pavement, searing as Aramis rolled over me and dragged me along with him. My chest heaved against a solid surface while I struggled to process what just happened, unable to hear anything among my ragged breaths, mixed with a dwindling yell.

I slipped back into reality when Aramis's hand rubbed my back, realizing the hard surface beneath me was indeed him. My cheeks burned as he said, "Tell me if I'm wrong, but I believe you owe me the chance to buy you dinner." Wet strands of hair clung to his sharp face when he grinned. "I did save your life, after all."

I scrambled to roll off him, wiping gravel free from my skin. "It's the middle of the night."

My throat clammed up, not only at the sight of his fully crooked grin, but how his damp shirt clung to his chest. "I'm sure it's supper-time somewhere in the universe."

I smiled while I rose, facing back in the direction of home. It would be wise to return and wrap myself in its safety. I knew there was little else my parents could take if I was caught, but I wasn't ready to face their disappointment. I swallowed past my own, readying myself to say goodbye. Not only to Aramis—and the man I'd danced with—but the short taste of freedom.

But when I turned, my goodbye was overpowered with a bittersweet aroma as Aramis stuffed a rag over my mouth. Tears welled in my eyes while I struggle to break free from his relentless hold, ignoring my muffled pleas for him to stop. He dragged me further from my home, until I was submerged into a darkness where light wasn't invited to follow.

Chapter Six

I willed my eyes to open. To push past the paralyzing throbbing in my mind and seize the light. But there was no lapse in the darkness when my eyes strained free, no warmth to be found. Slowly the darkness grayed while I blinked away the fog blurring my senses.

Where was I?

I wasn't granted a moment of peace to understand what had occurred, but rather I was shoved off a cliff of deep, unending horror when a shaky voice said, "You're awake." I froze, turning my head slowly to find Aramis running a hand through his hair. "Thank Aita. I was afraid I used too much."

I opened my mouth to scream, but nothing came out. As if my very soul crumpled and hid beneath the discarded white rag on the floorboard, deserting my body to face the man beside me in the back seat of a car alone. I looked out the window, finding more confirmation of what had happened to me. No longer was I at the feet of the homes in my neighborhood but hidden deep in an alley I didn't know.

I sucked down rapid breaths of truth as I registered the zip ties digging into my wrists, threatening to keep the starry night beyond the tinted glass from me forever. There was no light, no signs of life circulating the night. Beyond the faint smoke aroma lingering and teasing my nose, I was entirely alone. Alone with Aramis. The man who'd drugged me.

Fear's restraints detached and I wrenched on the handle, only for the door to remain locked. I slammed my shoulder into it as if I could plow through the hinges and winced, fully aware that Aramis only watched me struggle.

His voice was calm, confident as he said, "Collins. I'm not going to hurt you."

Had he forgotten he'd drugged and hauled me to an empty alleyway?

At last, my throat cleared, allowing me to release a heart-wrenching scream. "Help me! Help—" I thrashed against Aramis when he intervened, pleading for anyone to hear me. To free me from this hell and throw me back in my lonely house.

His hand smothered my trembling lips, trapping my screams. "Collins." His voice was soft and sweet, a twin to the drug used to subdue me. "I'm not going to harm you. I vow to you I won't. If you'd calm down and allow me the chance to explain, you'd realize that."

How could he possibly explain his reasoning behind luring and drugging me? I looked away from his treacherous eyes and scanned the car—or rather, my new prison. Discarded shirts lay among empty boxes of snacks, thrown in with the occasional plastic bottle. A thread of hope wove through the trash as I realized perhaps Aramis didn't intend to kill me. If anything, he was pressed for money, explaining why he was roaming my neighborhood.

This was nothing more than a simple ransom, one I supplied myself for when I walked into his trap. I was such a fool. A fool who'd proved her parents correct. I wasn't ready for this world. One night on my own and I managed to get kidnapped.

Aramis whispered, "Please don't scream." His hand hovered after he removed it from my lips, readying himself for more screaming. But I didn't. I obeyed.

He had the audacity to thank me.

Words fell out of my mouth as I pressed further into the door, fog glazing the glass from my heated breath. "Please let me go. My parents will give you anything you need. Just take me back."

He leaned against the opposite door, like this was a casual conversation between friends. "You don't need to be afraid." He clenched his eyes shut as he ran his thumbs over his temples. "It's complicated. I don't know how to explain this in a way where you don't find me insane. Give me a moment to sort myself, please."

I curled my lip and scowled. He was beyond the term insane. My lungs burned to scream how bonkers I truly found him. But I also wanted to stay alive. So instead, I listened to the small instinct in the back of my mind, warning me to go along.

One I should've heeded before.

My voice was quiet and weak, bound much like my trembling hands. "If you're in trouble, Aramis . . . my father's a lawyer. If there's something you need help with, maybe he could offer you some advice. Or if you need money. Anything at all." My hands shook when I extended them out to him. "Take this ring and pawn it off. I'm certain it's worth a decent amount."

His straight nose wrinkled in disgust while he stared at the ring, studying the overbearing pear diamond on my finger. "I'd like nothing more than to eradicate that ring from this planet." I was inclined to agree, but I didn't voice that when he spat, "Your father along with it."

I blinked. This was much worse than any simple ransom.

"Why?" My breath deepened the fog coating the window while I stared at the freedom beyond my reach. "Why are you doing any of this?"

I gasped and my shoulder thudded into the door again, shocked when he pulled out a gleaming blade. His free hand lifted as he whispered, "Relax. I'm only going to cut you free." He wrapped a hand around my wrist while the waved blade taunted my skin, its handle wrapped in a deep crimson leather. “I’m sorry I did this to you. Maybe I’m no better than the people who sold you and trapped you on this world. But I vow my intentions were sincere.”

A wise captive would’ve smashed their abductor’s nose the moment the blade sliced them free, but I made no move to flee. I could hardly breathe as his words sank in, slowing building into a tidal wave.

Sold.

The word haunted me while I rubbed blood back into my aching wrist, willing his claim to leave me. It was ridiculous to waste time on such ludicrous thoughts when I doubted my blood would flow much longer. I knew I should look up and face Aramis, but I was too ashamed to acknowledge how naive I’d been to be fooled by a friendly face.

The layer of fog thickened when he released a breath. “The reason I took you is because I’ve been searching for you for a very long time. I know you can’t remember me. But you and I know each other.”

My brows furrowed. “What? How? Are you from New York?” I didn’t remember living there; I only knew we'd moved to Texas right before my accident.

He rasped a dry laugh and shook his head. “No, I’m certainly not from New York—wherever that is.” He wiped a bead of sweat from his forehead. “I know this will sound unbelievable, but I assure you, it’s the truth.”

Silence filled the tight space while I waited for him to reveal how we knew one another. Despite the events that had brought me here, I couldn’t slow my racing heart at the possibility of meeting someone who knew me. But that possibility sputtered out with his smile. “Aideen, it’s me.”

My chest constricted as the name plowed through me. He didn’t know me. I was serving as a fill-in for whoever Aideen was. I was going to die. It was only confirmed when he leaned forward and held my cheeks, wiping my tears. His vibrant, wild eyes searched mine. "Aideen . . . None of it's real. The accident. Your life here. It's all a lie."

I yanked out of his hold, mistakenly slamming into the glass. I winced, grabbing the back of my head. Lingering jolts of pain pulsed through my skull while I wasted a moment to explain otherwise. "Considering I lived it and reap the repercussions of it daily, I'll have to disagree with you."

"It's a lie, Aideen. Your parents here stole you, and your mind with it."

I didn't let the surety in his voice blur my common sense. Instead, I shook my head and looked to the front seat—surely one of those doors would open. *Can I be quick enough to escape?*

I screamed when Aramis snatched my hand, anticipating my next move. "Don't leave. Please." Golden strands fell into his eyes as he shook his head, releasing his hold. I retreated to the false security of my corner as he said, "Hear me out first, before you decide to leave."

I sucked in quiet rasps as moisture filled his eyes, the strain and emotion in his voice repeating in my mind. I pressed closer into the door, needing to relieve myself of his performance. "What you're saying isn't possible."

"It's not possible here, but you and I originate from a different planet. One where it's possible to commit such a crime."

Yeah, I was going to die.

This was beyond the scope of my imagination. More unbelievable than anything I'd find in my books. It was maddening enough he believed my memories had been erased. But he thought we belonged to a different planet?

"I can see you don't believe me." I curled my legs tightly to my chest while Aramis leaned back and spread his legs out. "It's called Realm Trafficking. In our world, disgusting criminals who have no regard for life stole you. They wiped your mind and then sold you." He paused, allowing each word to writhe into my empty mind. "You were sold.

This isn't where you're from, who you are. You were hijacked and forced into a world that was never yours." My stomach sank when he smiled. "You're Aideen."

The conviction in his voice was almost believable—that is, if I were as deranged as he was. "Stop calling me that. My name is Collins. I'm sorry but you have me confused with someo—"

"But you are her!" Aramis's voice filled the space as he did, reminding me how much larger he was—how overpowered I was. His nostrils flared with his heaving chest. "You're Aideen."

I didn't attempt an escape, even when his head sank between his knees. I could hardly breathe, much less run for my life.

"I'm sorry. I know you're afraid." He leaned his head back against the glass. "I didn't anticipate this being easy. But, despite the horrific things they've done to you, there are things they can't change." I flinched as he waved a hand toward me, his thin lips rising into a frail smile. "The same red hair. Although it appears you actually brush it now." His smile faltered, aging his youthful face. "The freckle in your right eye. The way you look at your feet when you're nervous. Even though it appears they've smothered every bit of life out of you, I can see you. I can see you beneath their lies."

My throat burned with the desire to scream. To prove how wrong he was. That the things he pointed out were purely physical, not containing any true value.

But I needed to stay alive.

"This isn't real." My voice was as kind as I could muster. "I'm so sorry. I can see you're hurting and longing for Aideen. I don't know who she is, but I'm not her."

His throat bobbed while he pressed his lips together. "I wish there was a way I could prove it. Some way I could make you remember me." I stared at my boots, refusing to play into his delusion. "Aide—Collins. I have to know . . . do you wish to stay in this world?"

Out of all his actions tonight, somehow that was the most shocking: his genuine concern for my well-being. Was he offering me a chance to stay here? Even if it went against his desires?

My throat squeezed, lodged with what I longed to say. I wouldn't reveal how I'd wake up each day, hopelessly waiting for it to end. How I was wandering through this life, wishing I hadn't survived. That I wanted to vanish into oblivion and feel nothing at all, as anything would be better than this gaping hole in my chest, my soul.

But I wouldn't share this. Not only because it wasn't the answer to my escape, but because no one truly wants the truth. They want you to lie, to say you're okay. He didn't care for my thoughts.

So I settled somewhere in between. "I–I lost a piece of myself two years ago. A loss I'm still healing from. But dreaming of a different life has only reminded me of what I could never have." I paused, allowing it to plant in my mind so that I might at last stop dreaming of more. "So yes, I would stay."

His voice tightened while he nodded. "You deserve so much more than what this life has given you."

"Aramis, please let me go. I listened to your story and answered your questions." I didn't allow myself to fully register his ragged breaths or sunken shoulders. I didn't care. He needed help, but not from me. "Please. I won't tell anyone about this. I promise."

He rubbed his temples, whispering, "If I let you go, can you make me one vow?"

"Anything," I blurted, unable to ignore how he'd strangely used that word all night.

"Find out as much as you can about the accident, the memory loss. Everything." He huffed a bitter laugh. "Do they let you talk about it? Or do Peter and Jane leave you to drown, alone in your questions, as much as they do in that damn house? I can assure you, they are hardly innocent."

The chance of escaping blurred at the mention of their names. What else did he know? How long had he been watching me? I shook the questions away and lied through my teeth. “Okay. I will.”

“I’ll drive you home.”

I didn’t trust his words even when he climbed to the front, abandoning me in the back seat. The click of the handle filled the silence as I pulled on it, revealing I was still at his mercy. His golden eyes were dull, lifeless when he turned to me. “I don’t want to say goodbye. I know I’m not real to you . . . but you are everything to me.”

Once, I’d found him handsome, but now I couldn’t see anything but the harsh truth veiling his face. A surprising sense of pity consumed me as I realized this life had been beyond unkind to him. So much so he felt the need to create a delusion—one he could safely hide in. How many times had I wanted to do the same thing?

I forced a wall up to block his words out, refusing to allow the pity to fully settle. I couldn’t trust myself. “Goodbye, Aramis.”

Chapter Seven

This night had surely been crafted by the sandman himself. But rather than a warm, soothing dream, he had woven a nightmare straight from hell. I stomped across the asphalt, putting as much distance between Aramis and me as I could. I blocked out every word of his despicable goodbye after I convinced him to let me free, declaring I was capable of getting home by myself. I didn't dare look up and search for the stars watching me—I was content to view them from the safety behind my window for the rest of my existence. I'd find a way to escape the marriage to Reed, but it would be idiotic to run off alone in a world where Aramis dwelled.

I shook away the awakening rippling through my bones, demanding to be acknowledged. My first task once I climbed to safety would be to scrub my useless mind clean in the shower. Wash away the remnants of his delusion, which had already webbed itself into my every thought.

That plan evaporated once I nearly collided with a hidden figure beneath my tree.

A guttural rasp slipped through my lips while my knees skidded through the damp grass before I tumbled onto my back. A smile encompassed by glowing ash hair—courtesy of the moon—looked down on me. "What the hell are you doing here, Sage?" I clutched my rampant heart, certain a heart attack awaited me.

She grinned and offered me a hand up. "I know your social skills are taxed, but it's considered rude to leave without saying goodbye. Plus, there was a fire in one of the abandoned cotton fields by the club, and I wanted to make sure you made it home safe."

"What?" I gasped, forgetting the danger I just barely escaped. "Did they get it out? Was anyone hurt?"

"They're letting it clear out the field, but thankfully no one was hanging around there." She nudged an elbow into my ribs, moving on from the random fire. "But considering it's been over two hours since you left and you're barely returning home, I'm guessing you enjoyed your evening." She covered my mouth when I tried to protest and wiggled her eyebrows. "Please tell me you're ditching this disturbing engagement and running off with the brooding hottie."

I scowled up at the house, as meaningless as I left it. I pushed off her hand, hissing, "No, I'm not." I lowered my voice in case the sturdy branches above us could carry the message to my parents. "You would not believe the hell I just survived."

She raised her pierced brow in invitation.

I didn't waste another breath—those could still be numbered—on anything but the details of tonight. From lying in the street with Aramis to his disturbing revelation. Sage treated me like a broken record, forcing me to replay the moments repeatedly while she struggled to grasp how I'd escaped. Each time I did, it only deepened the confirmation of how bizarre it was. How it didn't make sense for a stranger to kidnap me, only to release me with a request to search for answers. Exactly how it had never made sense that I woke up with no recollection of myself, with a family who despised every bit of me.

I looked up at the window again—the breach of my confinement zone. I felt as uncomfortable and unsafe at home as I did bound in Aramis's car. But this wasn't a new feeling. It was one I'd lived with every breath of this new life. A nightmare that existed long before I'd snuck out tonight.

One I might not escape again, if I were to re-enter that house.

I looked at my friend, whose eyes were wide with disbelief but who remained beside me despite the outlandish story I shared, and I felt something I never had. A warmth as sure as the blood pumping through me, as solid as the earth beneath my feet—I wasn't alone. "I need your help, Sage."

Chapter Eight

"Are you certain you didn't land on your head when you snuck out tonight?" Sage grunted while she pulled herself through the attic hatch. I pinched my burning nose, holding in a sneeze from the disrupted dust. "You know, I'm aware you've never lived a day in the real world, but this isn't typically how friends hang out."

"Quiet." I stared down the hatch to where darkness drenched the room. I held my breath while I raised the attic ladder, carefully folding it up. I slowly closed the hatch, pleading it was enough to block out Sage's incessant whining. "You're going to wake them up and get us caught."

The darkness lapsed enough to reveal her grin, her dimple as deep as a crevice in the moon. "Oooo. Do you think they'll wipe my mind like they did yours?"

I clenched my jaw, ignoring her as I searched for the light. I didn't blame her for finding me insane—I was inclined to agree with her—but for too long I'd sat idle and accepted this as my life. How many times had I stared up at the latch above my desk, never once considering the possibility of searching for answers? I couldn't rely on my parents any longer. And if I found nothing, at least I'd have done something.

My hand shook as I gave the light cord a gentle tug, revealing towering boxes filling every inch of the tight space, all smothered in dust.

I'd never seen my parents come up here, but there had to be some form of proof hidden. Proof that Aramis was delusional and this was where I belonged.

"What exactly are we looking for?" Sage tapped her nails against a box, frowning at the grime. "We already tore apart your room. I don't understand how there could be anything of importance up here."

I swallowed past the weight in my chest. "Just entertain me and search those boxes." I raised my hand, stopping her before she could protest. "Sage, I know Aramis's story is far-fetched. But something feels wrong about my life. Please—just look for anything that ties me to my parents."

Her eyes softened while she looked me over, lingering on the fading red marks on my wrists. Mercifully, she didn't waste another precious moment. I wiped my sweaty nape before I began on my own set of boxes below a small window, revealing the empty street below.

My fingers hesitated on the musty box. Where would I go if my world imploded?

But it already had. And it was up to me to restore the pieces.

"Your dad was kind of hot." Sage shoved another photo in my face, one of the many useless things we'd found. Each pile of junk was proof of what a waste of time this was. As useless as the discarded baseball cards and retired baseball gear from when Father played. If anything, I learned my parents were serious hoarders, holding on to rusted bottle caps and withering newspapers. The most valuable item I'd stumbled upon were their wedding photos—something I'd never seen, as there were no photos of our family in the house. I searched for myself in their youthful faces, failing to find any resemblance. Sage insisted it was only because my eyes didn't see how I truly looked and that anyone else could point out the similarities. I didn't fail to notice when she didn't prove her words true and only started shifting through another box.

I peeled back a lid to a plastic container, different from the cardboard boxes damaged from this year's monsoon season. The contents inside wouldn't be any different from the last, but that didn't stop my heart rate from thumping when I tore into it. I smiled softly as I found a baby photo, one where I was wrapped tightly in Mother's arms. At least I could say my parents cared enough to carefully store my items away.

There was nothing else of significance beyond a birth certificate and a stuffed toy rabbit I'd seen in family videos. Per Sena's request, they'd allowed me once to watch a few home videos of my life before—though it was never anything beyond my childhood. I suppose it wasn't an entirely useless box, as I could now put Aramis's theory to rest.

I sifted through endless grade-school papers, birthday cards, and even a few stained infant clothes. I smiled uncontrollably when I found a packet of pictures, at last finding more than just baby photos.

This was it.

No. This was garbage.

My brows furrowed, my hope shriveling up into a pit of confusion. I couldn't find myself in any of the photos. Granted, most were group pictures—looking to be outside a school or church—but I failed to find myself.

I sucked in ragged breaths as I studied a photo of my parents with a young girl placed between them. She wore a gold graduation gown with a hat placed neatly on top of her straight crimson hair. I didn't know who she was—perhaps a niece of some sort. I hadn't met any family members, but maybe I had a younger cousin back in New York.

I stopped breathing in the dusty air when I read *Collins's Eighth Grade Promotion* scrawled on the back. I willed the burning in my eyes to ease, reminding myself this was over four years ago. It was normal not to recognize yourself before puberty. Except the longer I stared, the more my stomach sank.

Her eyes were brown. A deep chestnut—nearly a matching set to Mother's.

"Collins?" Sage's whisper joined the roaring in my mind. "Are you okay?"

I wiped the sweat from my hands and dug deeper. The picture quality was poor, it meant nothing. I devoured the pile in search of relief, but it only became a growing mound of proof.

"This isn't me," I rasped as I shoved the photo into her hands. Her usually lively blue eyes seemed to dim as she glanced between me and the picture. The girl in the latter was nearly a clone of Mother, down to the tight-lipped smile. "Sage." My voice shook with my hands when I found a driver's license, one sharing my birth date and name, but not my face. Even her height was different, shorter than me.

"Collins. There has to be an expla—"

I dumped out the heavy box of denial. There was an explanation for this. Something that didn't involve my parents having a different daughter. I steadied myself as I swayed, reading the words to truly erupt my already-crumbling world.

CORONER'S REPORT–COLLINS J. AVERY.

DECEASED MAY 2ND 2020.

CAUSE: ACCIDENTAL OVERDOSE

The world ceased to exist, transforming into a whirlwind of only those words. Collins. Deceased. Overdosed. The ink blurred while the room spun, and before I could stop it, I tumbled to the ground, taking several boxes down with me.

Sage grasped my shaking shoulders. "Collins. What's going on?" I let her tug the paper free as I rolled onto my knees and gasped for air, intruding thoughts suffocating me.

Stolen. Sold. Aideen.

This life wasn't real.

I wasn't real.

"Someone's coming." Sage gripped under my arms and yanked me to my feet. "Collins. I don't know what any of this means, but we're leaving. You're not staying here."

Before I could even manage a step, the attic door lowered. The room darkened as the ladder creaked, each step louder than the last. The last rung groaned as Mother's head popped through the hatch, her dull eyes finding mine.

"Collins, what is going on? Your father and I heard a noise." She fell silent as she settled on Sage and the discarded, smashed boxes at our feet.

I clutched Sage's hand while we both stumbled back into the wall, only a few feet separating us from Mother. No, not my mother.

My abductor.

As if I'd voiced my thoughts, her voice shook when she called out, "Peter, you need to get in here. We have a problem."

"I won't let them hurt you." Sage's whispered promise did little to ease my trembling soul when Mother consumed the space, Father trailing behind her.

The ladder creaked beneath his weight as he climbed through the opening. "Why is she in the attic? And who is this girl?"

Something snapped in me when he met Sage's gaze but refused to meet mine. It was all the confirmation necessary. He wouldn't dare look in the eyes of the girl whose life he'd stolen. Even now, Mother was incapable of anything but scowling while she stared at me. Looked at the girl who failed to replace her daughter.

My voice was broken, gutted, as I breathed, "What did you do to me?" I yanked the paper from Sage's hand, shaking the perilous proof. "What is this? *Who* is this?"

"Jane." Father's head dipped lower in the hatch, blocking our way out. "I'm going to notify Cyrbus. There's a possibility they're still near and can rectify this."

Mother stepped forward as Father disappeared down the steps.

"Don't come near me!" I shoved over a box and the wooden floor shook. "Call for help," I hissed to Sage as her nails dug into my arm.

"I left my phone in the car."

I failed to find a way out as Mother gained another step. Her frail hands extended out as she soothed, "Sweetie, why don't we go downstairs and talk about this? You're very confused."

"You've ignored me for two years, but now you want to talk?" I choked on a laugh while I scanned the room, uncertain if we could reach the hatch in time. I nudged Sage in the direction of the window. "How many mornings did you ignore me? When I'd wake up screaming that I didn't know who I was." My eyes burned as I desperately bought us time. "You abandoned me. You deserted me in my grief and ushered me around like some doll."

I trailed Sage when she took another step to the window, with only a layer of boxes protecting us. I prayed the window was functional, allowing us to escape unscathed.

But Mother's calm demeanor worried me, as if she knew we were trapped. "Collins, please. Let us explain." She glanced back at the hatch. "There is a perfectly reasonable explanation for what you've found."

"You'll only spew more lies."

"No." She staggered a step to the right, her eyes locked on where Sage stood below the window. "Everything we've ever done or said was to protect you. Let us protect you now."

But that was the biggest lie of all.

The entirety of the past two years was shielding me from a world I wasn't ready to face. They swore I was too fragile, too weak. Yet I'd never tasted this world and I was broken regardless. Not from this life, but from them.

I'd allowed their lies and control to snare me. I was reliant and complacent—too afraid to push back and demand answers. I thought controlling and protecting were one and the same, but I was wrong. No longer would I remain in their bounds. They wouldn't claim me again.

I stood taller and spoke stronger than I ever had, summoning every bit of drive and heart I had left. "You won't control me any longer. You kidnapped me and stole any remembrance of my life. I am not your daughter."

The truth rippled into the air as Sage yanked up on the window. It wouldn't open. Fresh, sweet freedom was unattainable to us. She grunted as she shoved her shoulder into it. I stumbled into her as Mother barreled through the boxes, desperate to keep her illusion alive.

Sage shoved me behind her, protecting me, and hissed, "Break it."

Sage's cries pulsed through me, giving me purpose, as she strained to hold Mother back. The room spun as I frantically searched for anything to shatter the glass. I'd almost settled on using my fist before I caught sight of Father's bat.

I swung at the glass, sending another crack into their fracturing delusion. The two collided to the ground and Mother's hand wrapped around my ankle. I swung again, kicking off her hand as glass shattered among their screams.

I swung the bat into Mother's back before I yanked Sage up, shoving her to the window. "Go." I didn't give her a chance to protest and turned around, raising the bat in warning. Mother gasped on the floor as Sage pulled herself through and onto the roof, extending a hand back to me. I spared one last look back to where Mother choked for air before I grabbed on, pushing off the boxes. Glass carved into my skin, remnants of my prison attempting to trap me again. I cried out as I was yanked back, tasting blood as my face smacked against the roof.

"Sage!" My nails tore at the shingles as Mother pulled on my legs, begging me to return. I writhed in her hold while Sage braced her legs on the side of the window, tugging on my arms. Her face strained with tears as she fought to hold on, refusing to abandon me. My boot collided with Mother's jaw, and a small *oof* slipped past Sage's lips as she fell back onto the roof.

Shards of glass sliced into my stomach, in time with my gasping breaths when Sage pulled me out. I whirled around, anticipating the fight to follow us, only to stumble back, shocked as I met a pair of stern, paralyzing eyes. It was the first time I'd ever fully looked him in the eye, yet I was grateful he'd never taken the time to look at me until now.

I shivered, a bitter chill slithering through me when he looked down at his trembling wife in his arms. "Cyrbus is coming to fix this. We needn't worry. We'll have our Collins back."

I fled his arrogance and ran after Sage, who had already dashed across the roof and was at my tree. My stomach wrenched when I climbed down the level to my window, praying I wouldn't slip. I winced as I jumped from the tree, collided with the ground, and raced toward freedom. My body pumped of its own accord, forbidding the sickening truth to paralyze me. At least not yet.

"Holy hell." Sage's laugh trailed behind me as we darted down the street toward her parked car. "Was that real? Tell me that didn't actually happen!"

I forced a laugh to build in my chest, but it never touched the air. I halted, no longer breathing, as I saw the familiar black car parked along the street. But I didn't run when the door opened—I could now see the truth with clear, fresh eyes.

"You're still here," I rasped through my raging throat.

His crooked smile consumed me. "You didn't believe I'd go through all that trouble just to give up so easily, did you?" His focus was entirely on me, even when Sage wrapped an arm around my waist. "You're coming home with me."

Chapter Nine

"Like hell she is." Sage blocked me, earning a grin from Aramis. "You get the hell out of here, you weird space boy."

His mouth fell open and he lifted a hand to his solid chest. "Space boy?" I watched over Sage's head as he raised his brows at me. "I understand our meeting was less than ideal, but you could have at least informed her I was a man."

Words wouldn't form past the swelling truth in my throat, refusing to play along. This was real. I had been sold and discarded on another planet. I didn't have a home.

I slipped back into Sage and Aramis's incessant bickering, interrupting them as I choked, "I'm going with Aramis."

"What?" Sage whirled, clutching my hands. "Collins, you're in shock and not thinking clearly. We need to go to the police. They can't deny the report." She glared back at Aramis—who was as wide-eyed and shocked as she was. "You don't have to go anywhere with this goon."

"No one will believe me." I hardly believed it myself. My voice was dull, without hope. "I have nowhere left to go."

"That's not true." Tears filled Sage's eyes as if they were the sea. "You and I can pick up and start somewhere new. I've been wanting to leave this state anyway. I only stayed for you."

My throat swelled while I looked at my loyal friend. One who'd saved me in more ways than she knew. Who taught me courage and showed me joy when none was to be found. One who fled her own prison and started a new, authentic, and treasured life.

And if this was my first choice in what I hoped would be a life of freedom, I wouldn't—couldn't—be selfish.

I steeled my spine, bracing myself as I said, "Then you should leave, Sage. You should go anywhere your heart desires. You should chase it around the world." My eyes burned while tears streamed free. "And as much as I'd love to run with you, I have to go. It's not safe here."

Her nails dug into my palm, as if she feared I'd dissipate into nothing. "Then let me come with you. You're not alone in this."

"I can't have you near me. I won't risk something happening to you."

She opened her mouth to persist but stopped when tears overpowered her. There was nothing more she could say. I didn't know what we were dealing with here, but I wouldn't put her in harm's way. Whether by Aramis's or my parents' hands.

Sage reached into her back pocket and shoved a wad of cash in my palm. She firmly closed my hand. "It's my tip money from tonight. Use it to get away from here."

Aramis cleared his throat, interrupting her heart-wrenching generosity. "That won't be necessary. It's too much of a hassle to exchange Earth's currency with our planet's."

I blocked out his words and pulled her into an embrace. "Use it yourself, Sage." Salt lined my lips as tears fell. "Thank you for saving my life. For everything."

She released a shaky breath. "No matter how hard it gets, don't you dare come back. You are strong enough to survive without them. You deserve to thrive." She slipped out of my arms and pointed at Aramis. "You have a phone, space boy?"

His crooked grin twitched at his lips. "No. Those don't exist where we're from."

Where *we're* from—not solely him, but both of us.

Sage's voice lifted me from a pool of panic. "Fine. But don't believe for a second that'll impede my ability to hunt you down if something happens to her." Her glare didn't waver. "I'm serious."

Aramis's eyes flicked to mine. "I'll protect her." He held my gaze, letting me see the strange integrity mixed within his golden flecks. "And in order to fulfill that promise, you and I need to leave. I can only assume more trouble is on its way."

My eyes burned when Sage only gave me a short hug before running toward her red car parked further down the street. I wasn't fully in my body as I sat in Aramis's passenger seat, even as the car whirred to a start. I held my breath while Sage blurred out of my vision—out of my life.

A whisper pulled me back into reality. "Aideen."

I twisted in the leather seat as my gut did, facing the consequences of what I'd chosen. How could I possibly believe this was a good idea? Running off with a man who had the sliced zip ties he'd used on me in the back seat.

I curled my fingers into a fist, hiding the way they shook, while fear begged to break through. My body's response to my poor, thoughtless choice. I was going to get myself killed. The proof I'd found didn't change the fact other worlds didn't exist—and I certainly wasn't from one.

Warmth rushed over me when Aramis adjusted the temperature, soothing what nerves still contained life. His voice was soft, tentative. "Are you okay, Aideen?"

I closed my eyes, blocking out his faux concern. "No, I'm not okay. I just found out my entire life is a lie." I wrapped my arms around my stomach, igniting the cuts from my escape, and winced. "Apparently, my entire existence here was being a fill-in for someone who's dead. And not only that, but I'm from a different planet." An empty laugh drained me, snagging any fight I had left. "Though I couldn't tell you anything about it because my memories were wiped clean. So, no. I'm not okay."

"Do you want to talk about what happened?"

"What do you think happened?" I scoffed. "You exploded my life." A faint whisper in a dusty corner of my mind reminded me he only unleashed the truth, but I didn't care. Anything was better than acknowledging the swelling black hole in my chest.

I ran a hand across my chest, easing my voice. "They didn't even bother to deny it. Even after I found all the proof I needed—the previous life of their deceased daughter—I hoped they'd deny it. But they were only concerned with hiding in their delusion." I looked up to find Aramis's hands clenching the wheel. "How could they do this? How do they not care that they stole me from another family?"

I didn't have the chance to fully examine what that possibly entailed for me before Aramis said, "I'm guessing they couldn't bear to endure the pain of losing a child." His fingers barely grazed mine before my hands darted to safety beneath my thighs. "Sorry—it's hard to break old habits." He shook his head, brushing off my rejection. "But I imagine the traffickers work throughout all the universes. Meaning anyone can buy from them, but it comes with a steep price. The potential is endless because once the memories are gone, they can influence anyone to be anything they want. So instead of grieving—her parents found a replacement."

I believe I might've freaked out about the reality of multiple universes had I not been stuck on the truth that they were her parents. Not mine.

"So because their daughter died, they're justified in stealing another child? That's the sickest thing I've ever heard." I buried my face in my hands, smothering the emotion I'd yet to face.

I didn't know what would become of me once I truly accepted the fact I'd been sold.

"Hey." Aramis gently placed a hand on my knee, tracing the grass stains. "I would never try to justify what they've done. Trust me, I hate the disgusting act they've committed. I was only saying desperate people are capable of dangerous things, Aideen."

They weren't desperate. They were despicable and foolish—the vilest scum of Earth. Now I understood why they'd controlled and altered me. Because every day I failed to become her, it was a reminder she was dead. I didn't care if their grief had been manipulated, they were as evil as those who did this.

I sucked in a ragged breath, unable to acknowledge it any longer, and shoved his hand off me. "I swear, if you call me Aideen one more time, I'll lose my mind. My name is Collins."

A light chuckle eased the tension as he pulled onto the nearly empty freeway, leaving us accompanied with only truckers. Streetlights caressed Aramis's sharp features when he smiled. "You have no idea how relieved I am to see some of that fieriness remain."

I pulled my knees to my chest, protecting my core from his words. One night. That was all it had taken for my entire world to wither away. What would I give to return to earlier this evening when I was forced into a loveless marriage? I'd sell my soul to return to the club—to run away and dance forever with that man. Truly anything would be better than living with the knowledge of having no place—no purpose in this world.

I wasn't born of this world, yet I was no longer the person from the last. The gods were playing a cruel game of life, laughing while they failed to fit me anywhere. I clenched my eyes shut, failing to resist as my mind dragged me back to this morning, when my father's words rang true.

You can try to alter the pieces all you'd like. But it doesn't change the fact they're useless.

They had tried to alter me, and I had proven useless.

Would my fate be the same in this new world?

Chapter Ten

Flutters of light peeked through my lids as a draft tickled me awake, followed by an abrupt slam. The fading night was cast with green as I blinked in time with the neon light above me. The wind swept through again as Aramis opened his door, carrying a black bag over his shoulder. I struggled to understand the heaviness in his eyes, his lips parted as though he might've said something, just as I failed to understand how I'd gotten here. And while I may have slept, my mind was anything but rested, nor was the ache in my being eased.

"What are we doing?" I shivered as another gust invaded my torn ebony shirt, covered in grime and flecks of blood. Dark billowing clouds lingered in the rising dawn, where sunlight grazed the parked cars beside us, all placed in front of a two-story stuco building. My throat fell dry as I rasped, "Why are we at a motel?"

Aramis adjusted the strap on his shoulder. "Unlike you, I wasn't given the liberty to sleep. Besides, we have to wait a few more hours before I can take you home."

That was something I'd yet to ask—though I barely had the courage or interest to speak to him at all—but how the hell were we traveling to a different planet? I was not quite ready to board his crazy train.

I bit back my remark as I climbed out of the car, though it had little to do with disinterest in speaking to him. A shiver of warmth crawled up me as I listened to what I could only assume was the faint crash of waves. I closed my eyes and inhaled the thickly coated salt air, inviting the taste to summon me to life. The world seemed a little less gray—a little more hopeful—when I opened my eyes.

The truth awakened again as Aramis's warm, radiant eyes filled my vision. Beautiful things are deceitful and harmful. He had harmed me. And this cruel, beautiful world had too.

I kept my distance as I trailed Aramis up the rickety iron staircase to the second floor, stopping at a dented red door. But once the door opened—with a slide of a key and a shove from his shoulder—I didn't pass the threshold.

Tears blurred Aramis as he tossed his bag on the quilted bed, going straight for the bathroom. My knees shook as I grasped on to the handrail, the iron digging into my palms as I fought to remain steady. Perhaps the adrenaline from fleeing for my life had blurred my mind, but no longer could I do this. I'd run away with a complete stranger and was willingly entering a motel room with him. The bleach remnants seeping out of the room and burning my nose should serve as enough warning to run.

Maybe I'd overreacted. I was so desperate to believe I was destined for more, I'd taken the first opportunity to leave. Which was far-fetched and likely to kill me.

I leaned back onto the railing and looked up at the last bits of sunlight submitting to the continuously darkening clouds, swallowing up any color they touched. If I hurried, maybe I could return home before the disturbance I'd caused fully settled.

I could be who they needed.

My knees were still jammed, unable to flee, when Aramis stepped out of the bathroom. The cool railing slipped beneath my shirt and dug into my back, the off shoulders doing little to protect me from the howling wind. He tentatively approached me with a hand out, letting me truly see him for the first time.

He was molded entirely from the sun. From his golden, tanned skin to his eyes—even his messy tawny hair was interlaced with loose, bronze waves. His solid chest filled my line of sight as he stopped before me, standing steady against the barreling winds.

"Collins," he breathed in a soft rumble. "I know you have little reason to trust me, or anyone for that matter. But you are safe. You are safe with me."

My hands ached in thanks as I released them and forced my knees to cross the threshold, accepting there was nowhere else to go. I couldn't forget what I learned. The reason behind why my mother resented me, why my father disregarded me.

But maybe . . . there was a better life ahead of me. One I could claim as my own again.

That frail tendril of hope escorted me to the stiff bed while Aramis closed the door and leaned against it. "There's blood on you." My cheeks flushed as he openly surveyed me, lingering on the scratches the branches had clawed into my arms. "Did they harm you?"

I stared at my boots as I pulled at a loose string from my shirt, scraping off flecks of dried blood. "Um—" My fingers snagged in my hair as I pushed it out of my face. "No. I had to break the window and climb through it. It must have cut me . . ." I trailed off, blocking out how I'd scarcely escaped.

"While we have time, I should take a look. Make sure there's no glass in there. You can take a shower if you'd like."

I pulled down the hem of my shirt. "It's fine." I shifted off the bed and moved toward the farthest corner in the musty room. "You should sleep. I assume we have a long journey . . . home."

He moved toward the bed and shifted through his bag. He unfolded a tan shirt, matching to the one he wore, and placed it on the bed, alongside what appeared to be a brown wool blanket. "If you'd like to be somewhat decent when you return home, you can wear this. It won't be much longer until we're there."

My remaining pride dissipated as I asked, "How are we doing that exactly? Since you're from a different planet and all."

He chuckled under his breath as he closed the distance between us. I rasped in a shaky breath of acrid, pungent air when he grabbed my hand and placed a ring in it. "You and I will Drift through a Gateway using this ring."

I was wrong, he wasn't riding the crazy train. He was driving it.

I glanced around his large frame, calculating if I'd be swift enough to escape through the door. Aramis laughed and blocked me with his arm against the wall, revealing he wore a charcoal ring I'd failed to notice before. "Believe it or not. But this is how you and I are returning to Aita."

And now I knew the name of his delusional home.

I cocked my brow. "Then why aren't we using it right now? Rather than wasting time in this lovely establishment."

His lively laugh rumbled into me as he grabbed the ring I refused to look at. "Because I need magic to power it."

"You what?" I choked on a laugh. "Then how are we traveling to Aita? Clearly there isn't magic here."

He sighed as he plopped down on the mattress, his sturdy legs hanging off the edge. "Back home, magic flourishes across the entire land. There's a tower that sources the magic, allowing us to travel without restraint." He lifted his hand, rolling the ring between his fingers.

"To pass through a Gateway, you need some sort of common denominator between the world you're in, and the world you're trying to travel to. A natural occurrence that ties you to others, one that generates natural energy."

I blinked. Not understanding a word of that. "Which is?"

He rolled over and propped his head on his fist. "You'll find out soon enough."

I drew in a deep breath for patience. I pulled my knees to my chest as I sat on the stained burgundy carpet. "Aramis . . ."

"Yes?"

My words squirmed through my tightening chest. "The people who did this to me . . . who sold me. Are they going to be on Aita?"

"Yes." He rolled off the bed and knelt in front of me. "But you don't need to worry. I won't let them harm you again."

Even with the absence of alcohol fogging my mind, I believed him. He'd proved his loyalty when he stayed after letting me go. "My father—" I shook my head. "Peter mentioned something called Cyrbus and the possibility of them being close. Do you think they did this?"

His jaw sharpened as he looked down. "I don't know. They're well hidden on Aita, so I've never heard of a name." The copper in his eyes flared as he looked up. "But it's likely to be them. You and I are going to be out of here soon, and you won't have to worry any more."

I flinched as a gust of wind rattled the window, the torn curtains veiling any remaining light. Aramis frowned in what I could only assume was pity before he laid back down, this time with his back to me.

I waited until his back rose steadily before I deemed it safe to expose a piece of my deepest desires. "Aramis, do I have a family on Aita?"

A part of me hoped he was asleep, if only so that hope could remain with me a moment longer. The silence parted, burning my heart as he whispered, "Yes, Aideen. You have family back home."

My chest eased as I slouched against the wall and let the words wash over me, filling me with enough strength to continue. I could do this. There was a family back home waiting for me. A reason to hang on a little longer.

Chapter Eleven

I'VE READ BEFORE YOU die, you see your life in flashes. Perhaps a few cherished memories or ones you'd prefer remained buried. But given that my mind was mostly blank, all I wished for was a moment of rest. I'd give anything to swap out those moments where I'd stayed on guard, waiting for Aramis to wake up and attack me, for a nap instead.

Because the howling winds rattling the car windows, stirring up waves of sand on the once-serene beach, were just a prelude to my fate.

"There is no way in hell I'm getting out of this car." I gripped the door handle. "Go ahead and run out there on your own, space boy."

He wiped a wet wave out of his eyes. "You and your friend aren't nearly as funny as you believe you are." He yanked my hand free and shoved the slick ring onto my middle finger. "Do you remember what you're supposed to do?"

No. I'd stopped listening the moment we left the motel and I learned he intended for us to run out into a hurricane.

I bit my grin. "Repeat 'I can fly' three times fast."

He scowled and rolled his eyes. "I wonder if Cyrbus is aware they failed in erasing your attitude." Just as I tasted my snide retort, he said, "You're going to slide the ring three times to the right for us to Drift to Aita."

I stared at the bluish-gray ring on my left hand—the only one, as I'd ditched Reed's proposal ring in the motel—and spun the thin disk topped with a single moonstone to the right three times. A boisterous roll of thunder boomed—the universe laughing at me for playing along with Aramis's fantasy.

His knees slammed into the steering wheel when a branch collided with his door, one of the many hazardous items dancing with the downpour. He shook his head and lifted his charcoal ring. "Aita is separated into realms. We're going to the sixth one, so now do it six times to the left."

At least his faux traveling system appeared simple.

I rolled my eyes and pressed my thumb against the iridescent stone, containing ribbons of violet and blue, clicking my ring in time with his. My stomach sank as I looked out and faced the raging storm—mild compared to the one in my mind. If I'd known Aramis planned to run into a hurricane, I would've reconsidered my actions.

The lights flickered out with the heat as Aramis turned off the car. He smiled amid the storm promising to swallow us whole. "Alright, let's go." He reached into the back and grabbed two russet cloaks—what I previously believed to be a wool blanket—and placed one on my lap. "Put that on."

I cringed as I raised my hands, refusing to touch the stiff material. "Uh—no. I'm not wearing something that smells like moths have lived in it for the past decade."

His shoulders lifted as he laughed, sliding on his own cloak. He fastened a silver clasp together and covered the dagger he tucked behind his back. "Don't be dramatic. It smelled perfectly fine when I wore it."

I feigned being appalled and raised a hand to my chest. "I don't know how things work in your world, but it's rather scandalous for a man to wear a woman's cloak here."

Aramis didn't allow me a moment to bask in my joke and reached across, brushing my hair behind my back. I didn't breathe as he absorbed my space and lifted the cloak from my lap. Warmth settled against my back as he clasped it around me, fastening a tie around a silver brooch.

His eyes flicked up to mine as he pulled the cloak fully around my shoulders, covering the borrowed shirt I now wore. "Scandalous—" He huffed a laugh, retreating back to the safety of his side. "I've not even been with you a full day and you're already driving me mad."

My thumb roamed over the ridges in the metal clasp at my throat, focusing on that and not the way his fingers had felt against my skin as he said, "We need to go. When I tell you, hold down the disk. The coordinates are already set, so that's all you'll need to do."

Not a soul was in sight among the swirling sand on the beach. I clenched the door handle again, certain I could snap the plastic. "Can't we do it in your car? You've heard of time-traveling cars, right?"

His laugh overpowered the wind. "One, we're not time traveling. Two, we can only travel with what's on us. Hence why I ditched my bag in the room and wore, no sorry, *scandalized* your cloak by wearing it here." He grunted as he shoved open the door. "Besides, I assume the owner I stole this from wants their car back."

The vigorous wind swallowed my shock as Aramis stepped out and braced himself. His eyes widened as he yelled, "Get out now! We don't have a lot of time until the coordinates fade!"

"Hell no!"

His eyes flared as the wind slammed the door shut. My hands shook worthlessly as I fumbled with the door latch, a second too late before Aramis ripped it open. I screamed as he wrapped an arm around my waist, the other reaching for the buckle. "You are absolutely ridiculous," he snapped and yanked me out, throwing me over his shoulder. "This is nothing compared to what you and I have done."

I thrashed against his hold, elbowing him in the head. My screams bowed to the wind, just as the Sabal palms did. The beach blurred as rain spat in my eyes, drenching my cloak already. "You're going to get us killed," I cried out as Aramis crossed the sand. "You are a lunat—" I choked mid-scream as flecks of sand slapped my skin, coating my tongue.

Aramis's arm wove tightly around my waist, holding me as he placed me down. Despite the shaking earth, his voice remained steady. "We need to do it now. The energy from the storm is the only way we can Drift through a Gateway." The flame of my hair swelled around us as I lifted my head from his chest. "I don't want to steal another choice from you, but if you don't press the ring, I will. Please don't make me do that."

The storm seemed to fade with his broken plea. His hands braced me, supporting me in more than simply this storm. His eyes—the only light breaking the shadowed sky—eased the fear grasping me, the same fear I'd existed in for too long. My hand didn't shake, refusing to falter to the wind as I reached for my ring.

Aramis's voice smoothed over my cheek as he leaned down. "Press mine for me. We'll do it together." He straightened his back and tugged me deeper into his chest, wrapping me in his salt-coated skin and worn cloak. "I'm with you." His eyes peered into mine as he wrapped my hand with his, raising them between us. Our hearts hammered together while I pressed down on both rings and held down.

No longer did I feel the gusts of wind or slaps of rain as a glowing orb encompassed us. Aramis's smile consumed me while the world seemed to evaporate and silently Drifted into an endless—yet not—sort of darkness and absorbed the turmoil beyond us.

Chapter Twelve

At some point during our hallucination, I buried my head into his chest. I didn't loosen my hold, gripping tighter even after the winds ceased and the storm dissipated. It wasn't until his lips grazed my ear that I yanked out of his sturdy frame and joined reality again.

My boot caught on a root as I stumbled out of his hold and collided with the ground. "What the hell was that?"

His cheeks burned amid the night enclosing us. "It was nothing. I was going to tell you to let go, but you freaked out before I could."

I dug my nails into the dewy ground, sand replaced with tangled weeds and dirt. "Not that. How about the fact you dragged me into an actual hurricane." It hardly classified as one—considering we'd stood in it—but I was still pissed.

He shrugged and leaned against a thin tree, whose ivory roots clawed their way out to me. "Unbelievable."

Red consumed my vision and mind as I shot up. I shoved his chest, not caring about the dagger he concealed behind his back. "You could have killed me, you arrogant jerk!"

He gripped my wrists and yanked me closer. His callouses scraped my skin, tightening his hold while I strained to get free. He narrowed his eyes as he breathed, "If you'd open your damn eyes and relax, you wouldn't care. You'd thank me for setting you free." His hand caught my waist, steadying me as I at last escaped his hold.

I didn't bother to shove his hands from my waist, as I was too wrapped up in what he said.

Free.

I was free.

Aramis smiled and dropped his hands, truly setting me free. The night spun as I did, into a whirlwind of change. My eyes adjusted, letting me peel the night's veil back and view the beauty around me. His laughter encompassed me, his hand catching me again when my boot snagged in the intertwined shrubbery, mingling vines and roots. I reached beside him and ran a hand over the smooth trunk no wider than my hand, a stark contrast to its broad-trunked neighbor reaching the sky.

I slipped out of his hold and stepped back, searching for the stars. There were none to be found—the tree crowns consumed the sky. My gaze leaped from tree to tree, swinging with the maze of vines. I reached up and rattled leaves, inviting drips of water to kiss my skin in time with the rushing creeks and the soft melody of life above.

Aramis's grin was as full as our surroundings when I faced him. My voice was breathless as I asked, "Why didn't you tell me I lived in a jungle before?"

He chuckled as he closed the distance between us, rustling the foliage beneath his boots. "Because you didn't. This is Mazoe." I sucked in the humid air as his hand grazed mine. "You and I descend from Kaira."

I almost begged him to repeat it—if only so he'd roll his tongue again. "Why wouldn't—" I paused, searching for the term he'd used. "Why wouldn't we directly Drift to Kaira if that's our home?" I smiled as the word fluttered through me.

I had a home.

Aramis smiled, as if the word brought him joy too. "Aideen, I—" He stopped as a snarl filled the night, wrapping down my spine. He grabbed my hand and pulled me alongside his lengthy steps. "Let's get to the village. I don't need you to accuse me of trying to kill you again because I allowed a Panthera to get too close."

I gripped his hand as another snarl sounded. I didn't dare look back, refusing to put a face to the growls and squeals taunting us. Only when I could see a faint glow of lights past the dense trees did I whisper, "Why aren't we Drifting to the village?"

I stumbled as Aramis bumped into me, dropping his hand. "Do you actually listen when I talk?" His laughter rolled in time with my eyes. "Even on Aita, we can't simply Drift wherever we please. The Council placed one beacon in each realm, so when you travel to a different one, you'll go exactly where that beacon is placed. And before you ask, no, there are no vehicles here. So unless you have a stallion, you'll walk the remaining distance."

I shook my head, struggling to grasp these unearthly concepts. "If this is the only beacon in Mazoe, why aren't there other people around us?"

Aramis winked. "Because most are wise enough to not walk through the jungle in the middle of the night."

I slipped on a fallen branch as a howl coaxed my ever-growing fear. "Maybe Mazoe should consider moving their beacon into the village and not in the middle of the jungle."

"Ah—but Mazoe is almost entirely a jungle, so that'd be hard to accomplish. But I'll present you to the Council first thing in the morning so you can make a formal request."

"The Council?"

He shrugged as we wove through dangling vines, their coarse leaves caressing my cheeks. "It's Aita's government. There are six leaders to represent each realm. They're a bunch of lifeless prudes who mostly keep to themselves. As long as you follow the laws, I doubt you'll ever have a run-in with them."

My stomach wrenched, afraid of tainting this world with the truth. "Is the Council aware of the trafficking?"

"No." Aramis grabbed my hand, pulling me to a stop. "If they were, I would have found you sooner. I would have ensured they searched relentlessly to bring you home."

I stared at my hand, his finger tracing over my ring. "You can take that back now."

He pressed my fingers into my palm, stopping me. "It's yours, Collins. I held on to it in hope of returning it to you."

I lifted my hand, examining the ring in a new world. Not even the dim light concealed the hues of gray and violet in the nearly translucent stone. It hadn't occurred to me it was mine, despite how well it fit.

Aramis smiled as I wiped a tear. "Sorry," I muttered while I wiped another one. "I've never had something of my own. Not truly." I cleared my throat, starting back toward the lights. "You made it sound like this was something you and I did frequently."

The jungle fell quiet, reverently listening. "Yes, there was a time when you loved it. I could hardly keep up with you. But you and I were synced and it would never take me long to find you." His voice drifted off with the dwindling calls of life before he said, "But then I couldn't find you again."

Perhaps Aita air was purer, but for the first time when I looked at Aramis, I didn't see the man who'd drugged me. I only saw the man who'd searched fervently to bring me home.

"You and I were synced? What is that?"

He rolled his thumb over his ring. "A trace of magic exists within these rings, the same sort that was used to forge the tower that allows us to Drift. The Council only allows there to be one beacon in each realm, but if someone wishes, they can sync their ring with another. It's not a practice commonly done, as it makes you vulnerable. But—" He paused, staring at me with undeniable vulnerability. "You and I had done it, we bonded our rings together with a spell. If there comes a time when you and I are apart, and you wish to find me, all you have to do is hold down your ring and say *Eunoia*. Your Drifting experience will be different—a red orb will surround you—but it'll bring you to me regardless."

I stared at him with all the disbelief and wonder in the world, unsure how this had been my reality. "How is that even possible? What does that word even mean?"

His fingers skimmed over mine, as soft as the cricket's melody. "It's a binding word."

I stepped back, aware of the intimacy that act seemed to insinuate. I ran a hand through my hair, grasping the first thought I could think of. "Have you been to Mazoe before?"

"A few times." He cleared his throat of any lingering emotion. "Everyone tends to roam in the realm they were raised in, but after you were taken, I searched all of them. It was only after I couldn't find you on Aita that I started searching other planets."

I didn't know how he'd done it. How he found me among billions, but I was thankful he had. "Thank you," I whispered, grateful the night concealed my blazing cheeks. "I should've properly thanked you before for finding me."

He grinned. "Does that mean you forgive me for drugging you?"

My soft roll of laughter was lost in the thrum of the jungle. I pulled the cloak tighter, its thin wool material nearly dry as it pooled at my feet. "Would you have brought me back even if I hadn't searched for answers and fled on my own?"

"Yes." His hand wrapped around my arm, my cloak preventing him from truly touching me as he pulled me to a stop. He didn't balk from my burning gaze. "Initially I told myself if you were happy and well, I would leave. I thought I could be selfless and accept it was enough to know you were alive. But once I heard your voice, I knew I couldn't leave you." His hand found mine, grazing my thumb. "I'm sorry."

I shrugged and left his hold. My voice wobbled as I climbed over a fallen tree. "Don't be. I wasn't happy."

"I expected to be relieved to learn you weren't happy. Because then I could justify taking you away. But I never felt sicker than when I saw how empty your eyes were."

I poked him in the ribs, failing to slow the effect his words had on me. "We can't all be blessed enough to carry the sun in our eyes like you."

His arm gently nudged mine, as if he couldn't resist even the faintest of touches. My stomach didn't squirm like it had with Reed—there was something endearing in Aramis's hands. As if his brushes were only to ensure I was truly here. "That explains why you can't resist staring at me."

"Actually, I was trying to find out where you store all that arrogance."

His chuckle caressed my neck as he leaned over. "Tell me, did you win your fiancé's heart with such flattery?"

I ignored his waiting gaze, pushing through my tightening chest as I kept walking. Unable to forget the reminder of my parents seeing no other potential for me. Nothing more than a voiceless wife—not even an equal.

Only when I could fully breathe in the thick, moist air did I admit, "He wasn't truly mine. He was just another thing my parents forced me into." I forced a dry laugh. "Moments before you found me, I was considering running away. I didn't want to get married, I wanted to live." My heart lightened as I remembered the reason behind that. The man who danced with me and reminded me I deserved more than simply surviving.

The stranger's shadowed eyes faded from my mind as Aramis said, "It's a miracle soul-bonding doesn't exist on Earth, otherwise you might find it more painful leaving him. But you're allowed to live now, Aideen." Before I could ask about soul-bonding or even retort about the name, he whispered, "Tell me about your life."

"There isn't anything worth sharing." I dismissed him and continued onward, even as he stayed behind.

"Please." My legs stopped as his voice broke. "If only so I can assure, from here on out, that every moment of your existence is better than the last."

I strained to swallow through my tight throat. He wanted to know me. He wanted my thoughts and desires, pieces I hadn't ever shared. I faced him and the trailing shrieks of the jungle. "You talk like you plan to stay around for a while."

The vines shifted in the wind, tickling my shoulders as if they were trying to soothe my pounding heart. But it only worsened when Aramis towered over me. "I didn't solely search for you out of kindness or even out of moral obligation. I had my own selfish intentions." I bit my lip as he lifted my chin. "Reasons which will prohibit me from leaving your side again."

I froze as his thumb rubbed my lower lip, pulling it free from my teeth. The light in his searching eyes radiated into me, washing anew the once-tainted pieces of my soul. Leaving in its wake only hope and possibilities.

Maybe Aramis could be one of them.

I held his gaze, forgetting the world and the vines tickling my back as he smiled, even when I teased, "Seeing as you're the only one I know on Aita, I'll let you hang around."

Aramis was surely blindsided by the vault he'd unlatched when he asked me to share details of myself. But given he wore a smile every step through the mulch, I didn't believe he minded. He never complained—not even when I went into vivid detail about *Little Women* and how I preferred the novel over the movie. To say I was disappointed I couldn't share my love for Laurie with him was an understatement, given neither television nor the novel existed here.

I stepped heavily through the vegetation, exhausted from our trek—I had done my best to stay active during my solitude, but rarely leaving the house was proving to have its effects on my body. I slowed my breaths, drawing silent as the ground shifted and slowly changed into stone. Peace settled over me once I left behind the hidden dangers of the jungle, unable to look away from the bursts of flame lining the stone aisle.

"What is that?" I whispered, fearing the uncontained fire that existed without wood could somehow seep through the grooves in the rough stone and reach me.

Aramis smiled as warmly as the flames providing light for any lingering citizens this time of night. "Those are everflames." Shadows cast over his face as he tugged up his hood before reaching over and pulling up my own. "Just in case. Keep close." He gave no other explanation of the everflames and tugged me deeper into the village.

Various stone buildings stood alongside the aisle, some concealing quiet laughs and whispers, others carrying no sign of activity. I traced a hand over the structures as I followed the trail of flames, the coarse grit scraping against my palm. No stone was the same, each deviating in shape and color in a way that could only be carved from nature, not created by man.

I left Aramis's side, unable to help myself from rubbing a hand over a wooden door, its surface as rough as sand, softly nipping at my fingertips. But that wasn't why I stopped. It was because of the image engraved within it. I ran a finger over the roots that veined through the door, tracing up the carved tree's core and through its bare, clawed branches.

Aramis's breath tickled my ear, startling me. "I assure you, there are far more captivating things awaiting you in the square. Although it could be exciting when whoever lives here catches you fondling their door."

I rolled my eyes before he placed a hand on the small of my back, ushering me to the square. Smoke grazed my nose as merchants blew out lanterns, while others cleaned their wagons from a day of work. My stomach rumbled as Aramis led us to a cart and bought the few golden rolls remaining—after passing on dried slabs of meat already claimed by a swarm of flies. Mercifully, the rolls were fresh and welcoming, much like the merchant's evergreen eyes, so bright not even the night concealed them.

I paused, looking back between Aramis and the merchant, seeing what I hadn't truly realized until now. I ignored Aramis's questioning look and lifted his hand against mine. His hand remained still while I curled my fingers up and down his, feeling the surety of his warmth, the rough callouses on his palm. "When I think of life on other planets and universes, I imagine the people to be little green men." I shook my head, laughing quietly as I realized I'd spent years as an alien on a foreign planet. "But you look exactly like the men on Earth."

His crooked grin toyed on his lips. "I'd argue that I'm far better looking than the typical human. But maybe I would've had an easier time convincing you we were from a different planet if I was a little green man." I lowered my hand back to my side while Aramis chewed on his lip, deep in thought before he said, "I can't imagine any of this is easy for you, but thank you for coming home with me. For trusting me."

I nodded, unwilling to dive into how heavy this was becoming. It would be over soon, I only needed to get home to Kaira. To the family waiting for me.

"Is that. . ." I paused, watching as a merchant cranked a handle on a wooden bucket, stopping to pour what appeared to be salt into it. "Please tell me that's ice cream."

He grinned and grabbed my hand, pulling me towards the cart. We watched quietly after Aramis ordered, listening to the grinding of ice and salt while the merchant continually pushed the iron handle, the flickering lantern leaving his features shadowed. I looked around the square, realizing it was without lampposts—or any electricity. And they didn't have cars . . . using wagons or horses to travel.

This was a different world—one of magic, no less—but it was as though I'd stepped back in time.

A thick lump grew in my throat when I settled on what I assumed was a bar, the only activity in the square beyond the merchants cleaning up. Tears brimmed in my eyes, dripping free as I watched the bartender filling steins to the brim. I closed my eyes, sending a silent prayer across the universe that Sage was safe.

"Thank you." I smiled when Aramis handed me a bowl of whipped, full ice cream. I bit back my moan as I ate a mouthful, only ever having had a taste from a bite Sage once gave me. I swallowed, unable to enjoy its rich flavor, willing my burning tears to remain hidden.

Aramis smiled warily, likely believing I was emotional over ice cream before he jerked his thumb over his back. "There's a few more things I need to get for us. Are you okay here?"

I nodded, eating another spoonful so my voice wouldn't betray me. I ate only a few more bites, until I couldn't manage another and tossed the bowl into a bin. Not because I was full, but because I was too enticed with the fountain in the center of the square, somehow only noticing it now.

It wasn't the slate sphere itself that caused the air to flee my lungs. Nor was it the vast pool of water. Even the stars reflecting onto the glistening stones beneath weren't responsible for my awe.

The water was dancing.

There was no symphony—no beat to be found. But jewels of water moved as if they contained one of their own. Rods of water shot up from every angle, crossing through the air. But where they should have fallen, they only rose. Glistening beads twirled together as they absorbed the night sky.

"How?" I rasped as Aramis stepped behind me, his chest rising against my back.

He stepped out from behind me, dropping a bag beside my feet. His soft smile blocked my view of the show as he slipped in front of me. "Magic." He winked, and before I could protest, his hands threaded around my waist, lifting me into the fountain.

I squealed, anticipating being drenched head to toe, but a warmth swept through me instead. It was as if my soul beckoned the resting water below to life. Warm water formed a sleeve, cocooning and roaming over me, until I lost sight of Aramis's grin as a cyclone absorbed me. What should've left me cold and wet invited comfort instead. I laughed in disbelief, wide-eyed as the remaining water trailed up my arm and floated into the sky.

Not a single speck of water dwelled among my freckles when I reached a hand out to Aramis as he said, "You'll find our world to be far different than Earth. Magic truly pulses through every vein—supplying life to us all." I failed to hold in a gasp as his thumb brushed over my cheekbone before dropping back to his side. "Even the air has its effects. It's why you seem to believe my eyes carry the sun," he teased, reminding me of what I hastily revealed before.

Magic or not, I believed Aramis would radiate light regardless, based on the blooming in my heart. I couldn't help but wonder if Aita's magic could weave through me, somehow ignite my own eyes.

I traced the edge of the marble fountain, where an unreadable text was inscribed within the basin. "What does this say?"

"It's the old language of our ancestors. Most of Aita is fluent in English—or other languages from foreign worlds. Only some still speak in that tongue." His hand touched mine for a fleeting second. "It reads, '*May the weary and afflicted souls seeking refuge find peace. Need they know, they only ought to be brave enough and take a drink.*'"

The dancing water completed its performance, slowly dipping back into the pool. I doubted there was enough water in all of Aita to replenish my soul.

"And what is this?" I ran my hand over another engraving, only this one was covered in ash. Smudges of black coated my fingers as I cleared the image, revealing what appeared to be an engraved knot within a sun.

"The loops signify each realm. Symbolizing that we are united and equal as one."

I raised a brow as I traced a nail through the knot. "There are seven loops here though. Before you said there were only six Council members to represent each realm."

"Look who's starting to listen to me." Aramis glanced over his shoulder, lowering his voice as he said, "There was a realm formerly known as Blythe. When you and I were young, Blythe became cursed. The magic there was drained dry, rendering it unlivable. Not a soul has roamed there since."

Before I could ask more about the curse, Aramis lifted his brown bag and ushered us out of the square. "Come on. We should get inside." We wove through endless buildings and fire-lit trails before he stopped at a quaint round structure. I hardly had a chance to read the fading sign dangling above the door before Aramis dragged me in.

"Why are we here?" The inn's door creaked as I shut it.

Aramis's head grazed the domed ceiling, too close for comfort to a jagged edge. "As intriguing as sleeping in the jungle may appear, I'd rather have a room."

"Why are we staying in Mazoe?" Before Aramis could explain, a man slipped out of a room behind the ivory wooden desk, slamming a door behind him.

"I'm all booked." His voice was rich and deep, much like his chestnut skin. He didn't look up from his desk as he pointed a sturdy, scarred arm at the door. "Lock that on your way out, would ya?"

Despite his dismissal, I couldn't move through my shock when he pulled back his dreads, revealing a set of pointed ears. Points as sharp as the dagger strapped to his waist. Something Aramis appeared unfazed by when he approached the man shuffling through papers. "You're certain you don't have an empty room?"

"Can't you hear?"

Aramis leaned onto the counter, removing his hood. I removed my own as he said, "Listen, you'd be doing me a great favor if you found us a room or at least pointed in the direction of another inn." He winked over his shoulder at me. "My lovely friend behind me has vowed she'll unleash a Liedra on me if she doesn't get a good night's rest."

Loose dreads slipped free while he shook his head and snorted. "I couldn't care less if I'm hurting your chances of showing your lady a good time. Now get—" He fell silent as he looked up, catching me in my act of gawking. The wrinkles beside his burnt-copper eyes deepened. I stared down at my boots, cheeks roasting, aware of the thorns and weeds I'd trekked in here. I fussed with the snags in my unruly hair, aware I likely looked like hell.

The man tightened his bearded jaw, clearing his throat. "Uh—I might have one room." His arms strained beneath his cream shirt as he leaned onto the counter, meeting Aramis's gaze as he straightened to his full height. "I'm not sure you can afford it, kid."

My stomach wrenched. I had nothing to my name other than what I was wearing. And even that was borrowed. But Aramis only shrugged. "We'll take it."

"Alright." He reached behind him and opened a drawer, pulling out a bronze key. "Thirty gold coins."

Aramis chucked a pouch onto the counter, something he must have stored within his cloak. "There's enough for the whole week and some for your discretion."

"I'll pay you back," I whispered as I stepped behind Aramis. But even when he reached back and pinched my side, I swore I would. I didn't want to start out already dependent on someone.

The man pulled out a scroll, dipping a crimson feather into an inkpot. "Names."

"Aramis Enver."

I pinched Aramis's hand, stopping him before he could wrongly introduce me. "Collins."

I bit my lip as the man looked me over, his eyes glistening off the everflames within an iron chandelier above us. "What's your surname, Collins?"

I doubt he understood the power his question held. He only needed it for identification, he didn't care where I came from or who I belonged to. He didn't know those very questions clung to my mind. And while I knew Aramis could reveal it, I wanted to hear it from them.

I wanted my family to claim me.

"It's just Collins."

Mercifully, he didn't protest. He stepped out from behind the counter, dominating the already tight space. Were all men on Aita this large? I wasn't short—falling somewhere around average—but Aramis and he stood at least a foot taller.

He revealed a full smile, extending an lightly aged hand to me, and I was certain he was the most attractive man I'd ever seen. "Name's Vidaar." He dropped my hand and looked at Aramis. "You're in the last room in the building to the right. There are two simple rules. Don't break my shit. And don't stir any up."

Chapter Thirteen

Vidaar didn't bother with pleasantries and kicked us out the moment the key touched my hand. We laughed the entire walk through the cramped alley between two towering buildings—one of which was leaning.

Our laughter vanished once the door opened and we saw the poor excuse of a room. I practically dug my nails into Aramis's arm, begging him not to bother Vidaar for a different room. I quickly reminded him the wilting leaves and smell of rotting wood were far better than sleeping in the jungle, leaving us vulnerable to what lurked within. I only hoped a creature wouldn't crawl through the gaping hole in the corner of the kitchen. Just to be sure, I tossed a linen blanket over it.

"That sneaky Elf ripped me off." A wooden chair creaked beneath Aramis, one of the four legs shorter than the others. "By a lot."

"Elf?" I wiped the kitchen counter with my hand, brushing off a layer of rubble. Flecks of stones and twigs were scattered through the room. Not even the torn cloth sofa and worn cot in the corner were unblemished. "Is that why—" I sucked in the musty air and waved a hand by my head, unsure what would appear rude. "Vidaar's an Elf?"

"That he is. Other than overcharging us, he seems rather mild compared to other Elves I've met over the years. The women are even more alluring and sharp than the men. Years ago, I was walking home at night, and I saw this creep threatening this woman. Before I even managed a step to aid her, she had already disarmed him and used his own dagger against him. I even asked her to teach me to fight like that, but all she did was wink and walk away." He leaned back in his chair, stretching his legs out. "They descend from Elysia. You'll find migrants from other worlds here. Sometimes our people bring others back with them on their journeys, as long as they agree to not practice magic."

"Oh," I whispered. It wasn't even a fragment of the chaos in my mind. This was . . . a lot. The entire experience was frightening and overwhelming, but also exhilarating.

This was living.

"I'll find us somewhere else to stay tomorrow." Aramis stood and shuffled through his market bag, pulling out a threaded sack of colorful fruit and a loaf of bread.

"Why? Why aren't we returning to Kaira now?"

The silence lingered while Aramis removed further items, and my chest tightened. I stepped in front of what I assumed was a wooden ice box—acting as what would be a fridge on Earth—stopping him before he could open it. "Tell me, Aramis."

He turned around, grabbing a pile of clothes off the table. "I got these for you. We can get you more pieces tomorrow."

"Aramis," I spat, finding his name wrong and sour. "I want to return to Kaira now."

"You can't." His eyes glistened off the lanterns dangling from the ceiling as he unclasped his cloak, tossing it onto the sofa. He unsheathed his blade from his belt and cut into the loaf of bread. "You can't possibly expect me to immediately take you back to Kaira. That's the first place Cyrbus will think to check."

"I don't care." I grabbed his wrist, forcing him to give me his attention. "Please don't keep me from my family." I gasped for air when he shrugged off my hold, turning away. "Aramis, please."

"I can't!" His blade thudded to the stone floor, along with my hope, slowing seeping out. "I can't take you back to them because they are dead."

"What?" A roaring wind of silence consumed me, thick enough to smother the everflame placed in the corner. My hollow voice was unrecognizable as I rasped, "But—but you said—"

"I know what I said." His golden locks covered his face as he leaned against the table, lowering his head. "I was afraid if you knew the truth, you wouldn't come home. I knew it was wrong, but I needed to give you that hope."

Home. They wouldn't be there. There wouldn't be the reunion I'd let myself imagine. I wouldn't hear stories of my childhood or learn how my parents met. I wouldn't see their faces for the first time and find our similarities. I wouldn't experience their love or love them myself.

"Aideen." Aramis stood and gently rubbed my arms before grasping my hands. "I'm sorry, Aideen."

I faintly registered the delicate strokes of his fingertips, but nothing beyond that. Nothing but the usual void devouring my soul. One that was worsening with every breath, sucking me further into oblivion.

"How?" I whispered.

A smooth wooden edge pressed deeper into my back as Aramis braced his arms beside me, forcing me to remain with him. "It was about a year or so before you disappeared. Our capital, Irenec, has a tower that helps convert the magic for us. The one that allows us to travel. But a storm hit it—" He closed his eyes, clearing his throat of emotion. "I don't know why your parents were on it, but they were. And after the storm was over, they didn't come home." He dropped his arms and pulled me into his chest, bracing for grief to overcome me.

I braced myself too. I waited for the agony and despair—anything at all. But there was nothing. No pain. No hope. Nothing.

But I didn't know how to force emotion for mere strangers. How could I dig into my heart for pain, when I held no remnants of love for them? I didn't know their faces or even their names.

Shame burned me thoroughly, as the only sorrow I experienced was one of selfishness. Full of self-pity for what I'd miss out on. I didn't miss them, but the idea of them. And it was because of that truth I knew it was better my parents weren't alive to greet me. If only so I wouldn't disappoint another set of parents when they learned someone so selfish and unacceptable was their daughter.

"How could you lie to me about that?" I slipped out of his hold and fled across the room, putting the sofa between us. I took in his exhausted, red-rimmed eyes and my voice softened. "What was your plan here? Would you have kept me from Kaira forever?"

"No." The cedar icebox creaked as he leaned into it. "Losing them nearly killed you. I didn't want to immediately throw you back into it, Aideen."

"Collins." I didn't deserve it, did not want to be called the name given to me in this world. Not when I couldn't respectfully grieve those who gave it to me. "My name is Collins."

"Collins." I didn't move as he closed the distance between us and grabbed my hands. He stared at where they dangled between us. "I'm sorry. I should've been honest with you. You deserve better than that."

I wanted to scream. I wanted to break him and scatter the pieces of his soul, forcing him to be as lost as his lie had made me. But the truth was, I was broken and lost before this. And besides Aramis—I had no one left.

I couldn't bear to drown alone again.

"It's fine." I shook my head. "I should've suspected it when it was you who found me and not my family."

"I'm sorry about your parents. If you need to talk about it, I'm here. I'm always going to be here for you."

My chest burned with the truth begging to be released. But I couldn't share it. I wouldn't reveal who I truly was. Someone who didn't mourn her true parents, but wished for love from the ones who stole her.

So instead, I focused on his fingers delicately rubbing my palms. I looked at his chest as I asked, "Why did you search for me?"

"Because what happened to you was wrong."

"No." I released a breath and looked up to his eyes, burning as bright as the everflame. "Why did you search for me, Aramis?"

His soothing traces ceased. "Because my world was stolen from me and I wanted it back." His fingers tightened, as if he feared I'd be taken again. "I wanted you back."

Any bravado I'd mustered collapsed—not solely because of his words, but when he glanced at my lips. "Oh—" I stumbled out of his hold, internally cursing myself as I tripped on nothing but air. "Thank you." I glanced at the pile of clothes discarded on the table. "Those are for me?"

He smiled, crossing his arms over his chest. "Yes. As satisfying as it is seeing you in my shirt, I'm afraid it's not doing you justice."

"Thanks." I yanked them into my arms and walked around the table, putting as much distance between us as I could. I planned to flee to the bathroom—the only place for privacy—but when I met his eyes, I couldn't help but stay put.

For two years, I'd been alone. Each day, I had felt myself withering away as I suffocated in my thoughts. The only hope that truly kept me afloat was the possibility of someday living.

And now that hope had blossomed into something real—something within reach.

I didn't need to hide any longer.

I put the clothes back on the table. "If you can't take me to Kaira, then fine." I closed the distance between us, bracing my spine as I looked up at him. “Then show me another realm, even if it’s only for a moment. I could use a little magic right now.”

His eyes flickered with mischief, as his crooked grin grew, accepting the challenge. He lifted my hand, dipping his chin towards my ring. “Two clicks to the left, Collins."

Aramis was the only constant as our surroundings shifted. His grin remained, steadily bracing me as the world evaporated, morphing into something new. Until the orb absorbed us and I was nothing more than a fleeting atom, migrating through realms. The comforting absence of light peeled back as the world became concrete again, revealing a bitter, unending winter.

“What did you do?” I shivered as I yanked my hood over my head, certain my frigid ears would shatter if I spoke too loudly.

The color from Aramis’s lips faded as a glacial gale swept through us, leaving a trail of frost beneath his nose. “You wished to see another realm. Eirlys was the only one I was certain Cyrbus wouldn’t be in.”

I stepped back from his fading heat once the wind scattered, sinking deeper in the plush, snow-coated ground. “Because no one in their right mind would deliberately Drift into a blizzard!” My voice ricocheted off the bare, broad tree trunks gathered among us, the only lapse in the consuming, whitewashed land. “You’re telling me people actually live here? That we’re still on Aita?”

He gritted his teeth and ran his hands briskly up his arms, having abandoned his cloak back at the inn. “Yes. Now get back over here.” I didn’t protest when he yanked me back into his hold, as the raw temperature was making a mockery of the thin wool material draped over me. He buried his head into the crook of my neck, mumbling, “There’s a ward around Eirlys’s village. It protects them from this brutal weather.”

His heart beat rampantly against my ear as I nuzzled deeper into his chest. "Are we going to stand here and freeze to death? Or can we go to the village now?"

His chuckle grazed my neck, warming my insides. "Well—"

"You're not welcome here, wanderers."

Before I could fully register the gruff new voice, Aramis shifted, tucking me beside him. I gripped his hand tighter as the burly man stepped closer, his beard as thick as the animal coats draped across him. He lifted his spear, pointing the glistening jagged edge our way.

His cobalt eyes dominated the night as he said, "You might approve of Aita's magic being defiled, but you will find no such believer here." Waves of slate hair scattered across his pearly skin as the breeze quickened again. "Leave now."

Aramis huffed a laugh, as if the man across from us couldn't tear us apart with his overwhelming hands. "I always forget how welcoming it is here. It might do you well to Drift to another realm occasionally. Perhaps it would unfreeze the stick in your—"

"Aramis," I hissed as the man's eyes flared, finding no humor in Aramis's arrogance. "We'll be leaving now." I didn't give Aramis a chance to argue as I stepped in front of him, lifting his hand between us. He stared over my head, warily watching the man behind us as a faint growl laced the air. "How many clicks?"

"Six."

I internally groaned, remembering we'd have to trek through the jungle again. Never again would I ask Aramis to show me another realm. Especially not after hearing a thundering growl that rattled my soul as I finished the final click and pressed down. Aramis's arm wrapped around my waist as if he could somehow protect me from the stocky heap of fur racing toward us, its sleek coat blending in with the deep snow. The bitter, unwelcoming air shifted just as the creature's ivory teeth bared, threatening to gobble us whole if the darkness didn't first. The endless void claimed us, Drifting us from one realm to the other, but not before a boisterous roar shook the universe.

"Your hair's bound to burst into flames if you keep glowering like that." Aramis's chiseled chest tightened as he ruffled a towel through his freshly washed hair, oblivious that my glare had indeed shifted to gawking instead. It was wrong to ever refer to him as a boy—every bit of him was tightly corded muscles. I failed to find any flaw among the cuts and deep grooves of his stomach as he said, "I let you shower first—might I add, you used all the warm water—isn't that apology enough?"

"No." I rustled deeper into the sunken couch, tugging the linen blanket tighter around my sides. "You almost got us eaten by a bear—or a cat. Whatever that thing was."

He chuckled, releasing me from his trance as he slipped on a loose olive shirt. "That was a Belta. And I'll have you know, if I had to pick between that and the man who summoned the creature, I'd choose the Belta every time." He reached up, brightening the room as he adjusted one of the lanterns above us. "The bite from a Belta is lethal, but our death would have been quick. His master would've dragged us back and let the villagers deliver a brutal fate." He huffed a laugh as he sat on the sofa, draping my legs across his lap. "It's a mercy from Aita they choose to remain in Eirlys."

My voice was dull, flat as I said, "And yet, you chose for us to Drift there." He only shrugged before he dipped his head back and closed his eyes. I closed my own, failing to understand what had occurred. I wasn't truly angry at Aramis—after all, he'd only granted what I asked him to do. I thought experiencing more of Aita's magic would ease my soul, but it had only awakened questions I didn't understand.

"Is Aita a . . . god?" I asked, noting how he referred to it as if it was more than a planet.

He didn't lift his head, nor open his eyes as he said, "As with all things, I would say Aita's people are heavily divided on what they believe. Some worship several gods, while others only believe in one grand being. But most can agree, Aita isn't a physical presence, but rather a force. A gift granted from whoever roams above."

I bit my lip, unsure what I believed. Days ago I was trapped within narrow-minded walls, limiting my beliefs. But now . . . now there were universes. Ones with gods, or even other beings like me. Maybe ones who weren't like me at all. Perhaps the cold from Eirlys still seized my mind, but I didn't hesitate before I blurted, "Do you have magical powers?"

"Do I what?" Aramis's eyes widened as he flung strands of hair from his face. "Do I look like I possess magical powers?"

"No." I bit my cheek as his grin grew. "You said magic flourished through every vein in the planet." I waved a hand at him. "I didn't know if some of that magic shimmied its way into people."

I scowled as he erupted into laughter, jabbing my heel into his thighs. A whiff of something pungent filled the air as I smacked him with a pillow. "It's not a stupid question! We literally appeared out of thin air using a ring! And you even said anyone who lived here had to agree not to practice magic."

His face was a deep red as he wiped tears lining his eyes. "No, Collins. I don't have magical powers." He wrapped a hand around my foot, stopping me as I tried to kick him again. "There was a time when magic was wielded by our people. But now it's only harnessed through the planet."

While it was a relief to not live among magical beings—as living in a world where magic existed was overwhelming enough—I didn't understand the change. "Why can't we wield magic anymore?"

"Why the sudden interest? Do you have an urge to seek retribution against Cyrbus? Perhaps destroy them in a hurricane?" I narrowed my eyes. The thought hadn't occurred to me. Nothing would bring me more peace than remaining out of Cyrbus's reach for the rest of my days. Sensing my annoyance, Aramis flatly said, "Sorry. If it's any consolation, I don't believe you found me amusing before either."

I crossed my arms over the smooth emerald shirt covering my chest. "It's good to know some things never change."

Aramis stretched his legs out and rested an arm across the back of the sofa, unintentionally brushing my neck. I didn't move, even as his finger dared to touch it again. "There was a time Aita granted magical gifts. Those who received them were called Caelitis." I tucked my legs against my ribs, intently holding on to every word. "There's conflicting history regarding the Caelitis. Some believed they were created through genes, as several emerged through specific lineages. But others believed Aita granted it to those who were noble in heart.

"But not everyone received a gift, creating rifts in society. There were two extremes—ones who believed the Caelitis to be gifts delivered from Aita to help the planet flourish and grow. While others believed they were out of control, draining Aita of its magic. Which is exactly why the tower in Irenec was built, in hopes of severing the connection from planet to man. As you witnessed tonight, the citizens of Eirlys don't exactly agree with that decision."

"But what happened to the Caelitis?"

Aramis's golden waves skimmed his shoulders as he shrugged. "They disappeared. There hasn't been a sighting of one in at least a century. They've likely gone extinct along with the other magical beings who dwelled here. That's why the Council forbids the use of magic—they don't want to disrupt the peace we've finally established."

I ran a hand over my tightening chest. Elves. Caelitis. What else? "What do you mean? What's gone extinct?"

"Relax." I squirmed as he tickled my foot, bunching the gray silk sweats swallowing my legs. "I won't let anything harm you. Unless a Gale Dragon snatches you up. Then I'm afraid you're on your own."

I snatched my foot from his ruthless fingers. "A what?"

Aramis laughed, enjoying every bit of my discomfort. "You know—a fire-breathing dragon who moves as fast as light. A wonderfully extinct creature who roamed among the Noetics and Dwarves."

"You're annoying." I rolled off the sofa and moved to the bare cot—we'd agreed I'd use it while he slept on the crusty couch. "I've had my fill of ridiculousness for the night."

He grinned, tossing the tan linen blanket at me. "Oh, come back. We're just getting to the interesting stuff."

The cot groaned as I lay down and draped the blanket over me, despite the everflame providing plenty of heat. "Goodnight, Aramis."

Darkness absorbed the room as Aramis blew out the hanging lanterns, leaving only the orange glaze from the everflame. I waited for him to smother it out, but he only lay down, apparently unbothered with the possibility of burning Vidaar's inn down. I shoved away my concern, certain I couldn't handle another detail about magic.

I could face it tomorrow.

And the next day.

Because I was free.

After several grunts and shuffling of pillows, Aramis whispered, "I don't know if I can sleep. What if I wake up and you're gone in the morning?"

Something warmed in my heart, easing out an effortless smile. "I trust that you'd bring me home again."

"Always." Aramis's promise thickened the air in the room, strengthening something between us that I wasn't sure how to acknowledge. He released a tight breath. "We should sleep. We have a busy day tomorrow."

"Doing what?"

I could've sworn Aramis's grin brightened the room before I closed my eyes. "I meant it when I vowed to ensure every day of this life is better than the last. Tomorrow, Aideen, we're going to live."

Chapter Fourteen

It prompted little surprise when Aramis awoke before daylight fully vanquished the night, claiming we couldn't spare a moment. I groaned with my eyes closed while I stuffed my feet into boots and snagged a slice of bread from the counter. I might have grumbled more when Aramis revealed we were walking.

But once the fresh air caressed me, inviting me to open my eyes, I stopped complaining.

I lost myself somehow as I absorbed the world—truly seeing it for the first time. The lavender sky welcomed the rising sun over the canopy of greenery, reaching beyond my sight. Warmth radiated through me as a wet breeze billowed through the stone alley, awakening all within reach. A fine melody swirled through the rebirth of a new day, dancing through the aromas of roasting bread and sweet flowers.

We walked in silence, but Aramis's hand in mine spoke louder than any words. I didn't know what this was between us. I didn't have experience in how a typical relationship worked—of any sort—but a fluttering heart had never accompanied me with Reed like it did Aramis. Peter and Jane had insisted my solitude was to protect me, but I'd never felt more safe than now. Exposed and vulnerable in a world of not only magic and traffickers, but dragons and more I'd yet to learn about. But still, I was alive. So I welcomed Aramis's touch, willing to learn what this was between us, what seemed to motivate him into diligently searching for me.

"Where is everyone?" I asked as we crossed the square, emptier than last night. Only a few spare wagons were set out, along with silent merchants preparing for a day of work. Beyond that, the quiet everflames were the liveliest thing among the closed shops and resting homes.

Aramis's muscles shifted beneath his wine shirt as he adjusted the leather bag on his back. His boots quietly padded across the pavers as he said, "It'll likely be quiet this morning. Most of the village will rest in preparation for the Kefi festival tonight."

We eased into the edge of the jungle, even the outer corners drenched with vegetation. His hand tightened, the other landing on the small of my back, catching me as I slipped through the damp soil. "What is that?" I asked as I adjusted my cloak and removed the hood, deeming it safe out here.

He dropped my hand and wiped his slick forehead. "It's a celebration of balance—when night and day coexist at the same time. Some spend the festival thanking Aita for harmony, but most use it as a chance to drink and be merry. I've only celebrated it in Kaira, but I imagine Mazoe won't be a disappointment."

I focused my attention on the vine maze at my feet, unsure how I'd successfully crossed it twice last night. If I was lucky—or clever—I'd twist my ankle and have a viable reason for not attending the festival.

A coarse lime-colored vine scraped against my palm as I walked, trailing it until it led me to a moss-ridden tree. I closed my eyes and deeply inhaled, rubbing a hand along the felt-coated bark. My heart smiled at the familiar yet different musky freshness swimming in the air. As if my soul recognized this as something of home.

Heat flourished through my cheeks as I opened my eyes and found Aramis watching. I wiped my hands against my charcoal pants—whose leather laces I'd spent an embarrassing amount of time trying to learn. Aramis had laughed the entire time I cursed, stating if Aita contained magic, then its people should be capable of wearing pants with buttons.

"I love that smell." I stared down at the mud coating my black boots—new ones Aramis had acquired for me from the village, pausing as I swore a vine slithered through the mulch. But when I blinked, it was still. "Back on Earth, I jerry-rigged my window so I could sneak out occasionally. If my parents weren't home, I'd sit on the roof after a rainstorm and marvel at how the planet's essence grew. I loved it. Everything was brighter and better after a storm, washed clean of whatever tainted it. I love when it rains, because every piece seems to come together, melting into something heavenly, musty, and warm." I looked up when Aramis's boots nudged against mine. "That was the only time I ever felt at home."

"I think—" Aramis cleared his throat, doing little to remove the emotion glistening in his eyes. "I think you're going to love Kaira very much."

I bit my lip, eyes burning, as if the water steaming down the leaves had filled both of ours. "Would you tell me about it? Our home?"

His smile radiated as brightly as the loose golden tendrils framing his face. His fingers twined with mine again as we resumed our adventure. "As I've said, Earth doesn't even compare to Aita. Magic flourishes in every piece of our land. It flows through our trees, allowing them to grow without restraint. Through the rolling hills, cascading for ages, to forests containing more life than you'd ever believe. Everything is grander—full of spirit and color. Aita grows freely and we are merely its guests. Never conquering or taking what wasn't offered.

"Kaira is all of that—and more. I can't wait to share it with you again." Aramis squeezed my hand, but it may as well have been my heart. "Kaira is in the northern region, at the edge of the coast. The realm is filled with endless forests and rushing rivers, both of which are a lively force. If you desired, you could climb to the top of the forest and graze the stars."

"It sounds like a dream," I whispered, as it truly did. It reminded me so much of the dream that had lingered with me for years. Had I been dreaming of Aita? Or even Kaira itself? "Should I expect to live within a tree when we return?" I teased, unable to hide my smile.

Aramis's laugh awoke a chatter of hoots and howls beyond us, carrying their calls to the sky. "You'll have to find a dormant one. Unless you wish for your home to be destroyed when the forest wakes up at night." Aramis winked when I came to a stop, incapable of anything beyond staring. "But yes, some homes are implanted within the trees." His hand softened with his voice—even the calls soaring through the endless greenery fell quiet. "Your home was atop the highest hill, within a grand tree. The sea and forest were at your disposal . . ." His words drifted off, overpowered by the steady hum of the jungle.

I wiped my slick braid from my neck and removed my sodden cloak, unable to bear the humidity and sun boiling me a moment longer. "Aramis . . ." I whispered as I tugged on the hem of my ebony shirt. "When was the last time you were home?"

"A while."

My gut plopped into the thick soil as the ground shifted upward. Never once had I realized what Aramis had lost when he devoted his time to finding me. "I'm sorry I kept you away from your home."

"No." Sweat raced down the sharp edge of his jaw. "It wasn't you. I'll admit it was difficult to live there after you . . . disappeared. But it was unbearable after my mom passed."

"I'm sorry," I whispered as I ran a finger across a swell of yellow flowers, wishing I could pocket the joy contained in such a dainty petal. "I hadn't realized."

"Don't be. It was a while ago." His arm wrapped around my waist, as if I was all the support he needed. "She was the one who pushed me to find you. I like to believe she was somewhere up in the universe guiding me to you."

I smiled, incapable of forming words beyond the lump of gratitude filling my chest. I could never repay Aramis for saving me. Our steps slowed as I rested my head against his shoulder, savoring the harmony between us. "I hate that you've been alone this whole time."

"I told you, you're my whole world. I would never abandon you. If the roles were reversed, you would do the same." I felt the surety in his words, as solid as the ground hardening into uneven stone. My heart raced with the faint rushing of water, speeding up as Aramis's lips grazed my forehead. "We're almost there."

The surge of greenery and flora slowly weaned, revealing trickles of the beaming sun within the iridescent sky. All chirps and howls vanished the farther we trekked up the slick bedrock, overpowered by the rapid crash of water. All it took was one final corner before the jungled erupted anew below us.

My pulse followed suit with the lively waterfalls, glistening and cascading down jagged cliffs. I stumbled away from the edge, certain I wouldn't survive a free fall into the olive water, its muggy nature concealing whatever roamed beneath. Flocks of vivid, glorious birds soared through the evergreen vegetation, swerving through dangling leaves and branches as they challenged one another to a race. I watched in awe as they dipped their wings through the graceful water, unable to look away until Aramis tugged me down onto the damp slate stone and sorted through his bag.

Beads of sweat trickled down my face and onto my smile as I accepted a jar of water, silently consuming the world around me, stopping only when I met Aramis's gleaming amber eyes. His grey linen pants strained as he stretched his legs out, encompassing me in them from where I sat, facing him. "Tell me about your family," I said over the roaring water, if only so I could better understand the man who'd sacrificed everything for me.

He grinned at the soft pockets of clouds watching over us. "I suppose now would be a great time to discuss my wife waiting back home for me."

"Liar." I pinched his calf, welcoming the smile on my lips. "Are you even old enough to be married?"

"I'm twenty, which is only a year older than you. So considering you were engaged—"

I cut him off. "Two years. I'm only eighteen." Aramis's eyes seemed to dull as they met mine, sharing a look where words weren't necessary. Despite the moist air, I struggled to swallow. "Did they change my age too?"

I didn't understand why my gut twisted when he nodded. It was only a year and didn't truly change anything. It only confirmed everything about me was a lie. *Was anything real?*

Aramis's hand gripped mine, pulling me from the suffocating thoughts that lingered too often, waiting for the chance to swallow me whole. "My mom and dad loved you. Probably more than they did me." He laughed softly. "Don't get me started on my sisters, Naira and Piya. They worship the ground you walk on. They're thirteen and eleven now, but I could hardly have you to myself before. But I don't think you minded—you seemed to dive right into their grimy hands."

I smiled, savoring the idea of him with a family—fussing and fighting with his sisters. "I hope you have a brother to help take them on."

"No." Aramis's eyes flickered, containing an edge I didn't understand. "It's just me." He released my hand and ran it through his damp hair. "I'm most excited for you to see my sisters again. Even if I have to fend them off the moment they see you."

My smile strained against the overwhelming pressure beneath my ribs, unable to be fully present. I knew I would return to Kaira eventually, but I hadn't anticipated returning to those who knew me—or at least the version who no longer existed. What if I was just a disappointment? Before I knew the truth about my real parents, it was worth facing that reality. But they weren't there . . . so why bother returning? Aita was home enough.

"What is that?" I nodded at the distant high peaks, where lush land shifted into steep slopes, colorless and bleak with daunting clouds. But rather than a gradual change, it was sharp and sudden. As though an imaginary line was drawn between the domains. "Is that a part of Mazoe?"

"That's Vadon." Aramis squinted at a faraway mountain range, its summit reaching what could have been the top of the world. "Vadon and Irenec are the neighboring realms to Mazoe. The other realms are further spread across Aita."

I stared at the tallest summit, wondering who would willingly live at such a height, certain I would slip off the jagged edge. "Are all the realms distinctly different?" I asked, as I was currently sweating in the jungle, while last night I'd quickly Drifted to an unwelcoming, icy climate—Eirlys.

"Yeah, they're all nature based, of a sort." He paused, smirking. "Except for Irenec. No better place for the Council to dwell than in a city of stone." He stood, but rather than explaining more of the realms, he lifted off his shirt. "Are you ready to live, Collins?"

I focused on the freckles stippled across his cheeks—rather than his shimmering stomach—as I warily asked, "What are we doing?"

The newly fascinating rock seized my attention when he kicked off his boots and tossed aside his pants. "We're going to jump off the waterfall. Why else would we come here?"

"What?" I stumbled back as I stood. The roaring panic in my mind drowned out the rushing water. "No, we're not."

Aramis laughed, oblivious to my shaking hands. "Come on, you'll love it. You and I used to do it all the time."

I dodged him as he reached for me, tripping over a deep notch in the stone. "I don't care. That doesn't mean I wish to do it now." I swatted at his incessant, playful hands. "Aramis, stop!" He tossed me over his shoulder, wincing as it dug into my cuts. It only worsened as he neared the edge, ignoring me as I thrashed against his hold. "Put me down now!"

My panicked plea must've settled into his dense skull because he finally released me along the edge, revealing a free fall of at least seventy feet. "What is wrong with you?" My chest heaved as I backed away, dodging him as he tried to grab my hand. "What part of *no* don't you understand?"

Aramis shoved his sturdy legs back into his pants, fumbling with the laces. "I am only trying to help you. You would've leaped right off that cliff before."

I ground my teeth. "I've been locked inside nearly every day for two years. I've never even swum! So you'll forgive me if I'm not keen on using my first day of freedom to plummet to my death." My blood heated as he said nothing and only forced items back into his bag. "You can't try to force me to become who I was before, Aramis."

"You're right," he seethed, closing the distance between us. His chest heaved as he narrowed his eyes. "I can't force you to become the beautiful, lively girl you were before. I can't demand you remember you were a force to be reckoned with, someone who chased the sun. And I can't ask you to recreate that contagious laugh you only shared with me." His words delivered me to the crumbling edge, but it was the next ones that caused me to plunge. "You used to be so full of life, Aideen."

I didn't know how much Aramis meant to me until his words thrashed me apart, leaving my body hollow, my spirit in threads. Not even Peter and Jane's disdain for my existence had gutted me to this extent. Aramis had searched for me—his world—because he cared for me. But even he hated what he'd found. He'd searched for bold and beautiful and stumbled upon damaged and lost—irrevocably unfixable.

I wouldn't be Aideen again. Someone who ignited life in others. Not when I felt like death myself. And if his words weren't enough, it was the fact his stolen touches and affectionate words weren't for me. They were for a ghost. I was undeserving of such love and devotion.

The lively waterfall, joyful calls, and squeals ceased to exist, leaving nothing but my aching chest. Even Aramis's eyes failed to glow as I said, "You wasted two years of your life." My voice was flat, dull. "There is nothing to me. I am not reckless or bold—I am ruined." I breathed through my heaving chest, needing him to grasp the bitter, hard truth. "No amount of magic will fix me. I have been torn apart and I will never be whole again. I do not remember you and I never will. The girl you loved is gone. The sooner you accept that, the sooner you can move on."

Chapter Fifteen

Had I known not even a different universe could divert the same misery and hollowness from trailing me to Aita, I would've remained on Earth. It didn't matter if I dwelled in an intoxicating, alluring world—it didn't change the core problem. Me.

I had no purpose, no home.

I wasn't enough.

The unsettling, tainted silence between Aramis and me worsened each step in the scorching sun back to the village, serving as enough confirmation I was alone. However, it was when the ground solidified into stone that the truth was sealed. Aramis only accompanied me back to our barren inn before fabricating an excuse to visit the local treasury to attend to some funds.

All it took was a few ragged breaths of the stale, musty air before I fled out the door, abandoning my cloak behind me. There was more awaiting me, I knew it.

Squeals wove through lively chatter as children ran through the fountain, cooling their flushed skin in the dancing water. I threw my sodden hair into a bun, unsure how to navigate this weather. Texas was anything but cool, but Mazoe must be at the gates of hell itself. I wove through the hustling street, dodging ladders and rolling carts. Beaded lights and streamers were laced across the buildings, twining them together for the Kefi. Despite the heat, my mouth watered as whiffs of yeast and roasting golden fish filled the air, an introduction to what would be served at tonight's festivities.

I slowed at the sight of a whistling man, lost in his melody as he unslung a large pillowy sack from his back. His smile met his wrinkled sea-glass eyes, even as a swarm of villagers encircled him, each careless hand dropping letters into it without uttering a word. His tune drifted off as I did, stopping at the first merchant at the edge of the market. Light beat through the torn cloth tarp above, glistening off gemstones scattered across the wagon. Before I could truly admire the vibrant stones—I'd never seen such alluring colors—a slender bronze hand snatched my wrist.

"Let us see if one speaks to you, my dear." The woman's rich voice captivated my attention, as did her onyx eyes, hidden behind a crimson birdcage veil. A thick, ash-colored braided hive remained steady atop her head when she tilted it, staring at my pale hand. "How peculiar." Unexpectedly she dropped my hand, and it thudded against the table, the stones jumping. She motioned toward her jewels as wine beads clanked around her wrist. "What is your knowledge of fate stones?"

My brows furrowed as I threaded my hands behind my back, uncertain if I'd heard her words correctly through her thick accent. "Fate stones?"

Her thin smile grew. "They say they were molded when Aita was. Crafted by the gods themselves." My stomach twisted as she lifted an amber stone—a matching pair to Aramis's—into the beaming light. "If you listen closely, you can hear the whispers of the gods who sealed our fates long ago." She stretched a bony finger out. "Let us see your fate, my dear."

I wiped a sweaty hand on my pants before I extended it out, certain this day couldn't worsen. Her eyes closed the moment her clammy fingers clutched my wrist. I wavered, failing to break her grip, her lips mumbling words laced in a foreign tongue.

A surge of raw, bitter air claimed the edge of my nerves, worsening the panic in my gut, until her eyes snapped open and she released her hold. I stepped back, shocked to find a layer of mist lingering through her eyes, fading while she ran a clawed nail through the stones before snatching one up. Her lips tightened as she placed a smoky—almost opaque—black crystal into my palm, her fingers latching onto my wrist.

I ran a finger along the jagged ridges, relieved the warmth had fully returned to my hand as she said, "Your fate wavers. Your spirit is torn—stuck between fates." Her voice lowered with her head. "Either the gods have extended a gift of choice, or they have laid upon you a great curse. Eternal drifting." A chill withered my spine as she closed my hand into hers. "For a small fee, your fate can be changed."

She hissed as I yanked my hand free, letting the gem clunk against the wooden panels. I planned to retort something to her, but all discomfort and fear pivoted to the booming voice behind me. "How many times do I have to throw you out, witch? You know the law."

The supposed witch rolled her eyes as the man rounded her wagon, clad head to toe in white, along with a fine ivory bow sheathed across his sturdy back. She clicked her tongue, as if the dagger suddenly in her fist kept her knees from quaking like mine. "Oh mighty Keeper of Aita, you spew such flattering words. I'm honored you believe my silly charms are within the same realm as witchcraft. I can't say I'm not offended though . . ." She cocked a brow and even dared a wink. "Honestly, how many times have you and I done this dance? Certainly you know my name is Hekate by now."

I stepped back when the Keeper bared his gleaming teeth, ready to dismiss myself. "Wait." I stopped at his command, uncertain if he'd nock an arrow and fire it at me if I fled. He glared at Hekate as he asked me, "What was she trying to seduce you into buying?"

I sucked in a breath, grasping for an answer I didn't know. I didn't know whether she was capable of changing fates, but I certainly knew the discomfort I'd felt in her presence. The strange fog within her eyes, the deathly bitter grip of her hands. If she was indeed a witch, I wasn't willing to face her wrath. I forced a laugh and shrugged. "She only said she was a fortune-teller and predicted a wonderful life was ahead of me."

I deemed Hekate's satisfied grin as permission to walk away from the Keeper. Her unsettling words latched onto me, trailing me as I shoved my way through the market. I struggled to focus with the fog occupying my mind as I searched the crowd, looking for the leaning inn. I wove through bobbing heads, stopping only when I met a strangely familiar glare. Her icy blue eyes stuck me dumb as her knowing smile grew.

Iveh.

I hadn't fully comprehended what Peter meant when he said Cyrbus was near. Hadn't heard the truth in his promise that they'd bring me home. But when I stared her down, I learned it wasn't a psychologist who'd interviewed me for my well-being. It was Cyrbus. Iveh was with Cyrbus.

Cyrbus was here.

I bolted back in the direction I came, escaping fear's paralyzing bite. Bellows of frustration filled the air while I forced my way through the crowd, searching for the Keeper. I shoved through vases, glass shattering and foul curses following me as I trampled flowers beneath my urgent boots. My soul strained to keep up with my legs as I stole a glimpse back and found that icy glare.

"Watch it!" a man roared as I tumbled into him, spilling his roasted grain drink. I blinked through the unsettling liquid seeping down my face, unable to find the Keeper or Hekate at her cart. My lungs burned as brightly as the everflames as I ran among them, pleading they'd lead me to the inn.

I glanced back as I rounded a corner, yelping as I found Iveh closing in. "Help me!" I ran toward a woman stringing up her dripping laundry. Her straw basket collapsed to the ground, snapping as she fled to the safety of her home. "Please." I pounded on the bare wooden door. "Please help me."

I savored my last breaths and started back down the empty street. My ankles protested as I sharply turned down a dim alley, not daring to look back at the stomps trailing my heels. I turned down another alley and another, biting back a groan as I scraped against the wall, racing through the stone maze.

I nearly collapsed with relief once I spotted the leaning building. But if Aramis wasn't there, I was just racing against the inevitable. I didn't wish to know the fate awaiting me in Iveh's merciless eyes if I was trapped there alone. If I couldn't return to the inn, I had only one option.

My legs ached as I pushed them to their breaking point, raging with my lungs as I raced back to the square instead. I winced once I broke through the shadows, exposing myself fully to the blinding sun. I shoved through the unwavering crowd, chasing the soothing laughter of the children I'd seen earlier. Laughter that erupted into blind joy as I leaped atop the stone edge of the fountain.

Water sprang to existence, concealing me as I ran through the pool, leaving a shimmering wall behind me. Not one drop of moisture licked my skin as I beckoned it awake, protecting me from outside eyes. I rounded the slate orb and vaulted out of the fountain, praying Iveh was deterred.

My knees wobbled as I stumbled into the dim alley across from the inn, concealed by the only non-stone structure here. I hissed as I leaned against the steel building, too hot to touch even in the midst of shadows. I managed one shaky step before the world was dragged out from beneath me. I thrashed against the scarred hand smothering my screams as it pulled me through a cracked door.

I collapsed onto the floor, gasping for air atop the cool surface as a deep, rich voice spoke. "You broke rule number two."

Chapter Sixteen

I clutched a muggy blanket around my shoulders, willing the shakes coursing through me to drift away with the steam rising from my cup of tea. The crate beneath me creaked as I shifted, careful not to send the mattress stacked beside me toppling. My slowing breaths filled the stiff air as I listened to the oblivious, merry cheers beyond the steel walls.

An unwelcome ray of light intruded into the dim room as the steel door groaned open. I settled first on Vidaar. My gratitude at his coming to my aid wavered once I saw Aramis—whom Vidaar had rounded up despite my insistence that it was unnecessary.

But if I was Vidaar and a hysterical girl was claiming to be chased by traffickers, I'd pawn her off as well.

A frown dressed Vidaar's sharp face as he looked me up and down, deepening as he settled on my shaking knees. "The herbs won't help you if you don't drink it."

I wrinkled my nose at the steaming cup of dirt. "I am."

Vidaar grinned, as if he knew I'd taken half a sip and spat it out. His grin faded as Aramis said, "Vidaar told me what happened. Are you alright?"

"Yes." The knot in my throat swelled when Aramis only stared at the floor, remaining several steps from Vidaar and me. "It was nothing."

Vidaar snorted and crossed his arms across his bulky chest. "It sounds like you were a few steps short of having your brain obliterated.

I'd hardly call that nothing." His copper eyes hardened on Aramis. "What part of your witless mind believed it was a good idea to abandon her unarmed?"

Aramis's jaw tightened. "I didn't abandon her." He glowered, slicing through me as he said, "A weapon wouldn't have made any difference if Cyrbus caught her again."

The air thinned, stretching unbearably taut as Vidaar glared at Aramis. Vidaar was handsome—in a sort of overwhelming way—making Aramis look more boy than man. His voice edged closer to lethal as he said, "Then I suppose it's a good thing Collins ensured that didn't happen." He unsheathed a blade, different from the dagger he'd worn last night, and placed it within my shaking hand. His gaze burned into mine. "Don't count someone out because they've never been given the chance to win. I've watched the gentlest of spirits overcome the bleakest pits of darkness."

I traced my thumb over the coarse white handle, as if the tree it was carved from could offer comfort. But there was none to be found among the curved edge or daunting point. "I'll only hurt myself."

The crate groaned as Vidaar sat beside me, not protesting when I handed the blade back. He grasped it between scarred fingers, dangling it over the concrete floor. "If you plan on sticking around, I can show you how to maneuver it. It'll have to wait until after the festival, but you'll find the lessons from my kind . . . more beneficial."

"That won't be necessary. We're leaving tonight since Cyrbus is aware we're here." Aramis deemed me worthy of a look and jabbed his thumb toward the door. "Let's go." His eyes flared when I remained where I was and sipped from my tea.

Golden beads attached to Vidaar's dreads swayed as he shook his head, stifling a laugh. "Where do you intend on taking her? Surely you can't be arrogant enough to believe Cyrbus won't track her down in another realm?" He cocked his head. "Or do you intend on persuading the Gatekeeper to send you both to another planet?"

I side-eyed Vidaar, not missing the way Aramis's posture tightened even more. "Gatekeeper? What is that?"

Vidaar raised his brow. "The Gatekeeper?" He paused, warily watching me before he looked to Aramis, clutching the dagger. "Don't tell me you brought her here illegally."

"I did what I had to do," Aramis hissed, not giving me a moment to catch up. "I couldn't risk bringing her through the Gatekeeper. I didn't know if there was a possibility of Cyrbus being there as well." He waved his hand, dismissing Vidaar's displeasure. "If the Council wants everyone to Drift to the Gatekeeper, then maybe they should do a better job at restricting us from directly Drifting to each realm."

"They don't restrict it because they expect us to follow the law," Vidaar clenched out, red creeping up his neck. "And then you had the audacity to come here. I could lose my livelihood if the Council found out I was aware you both didn't check in—"

"Can someone please explain what's going on?" I interrupted, gripping the cup in my hands. "What did I do wrong?"

Vidaar huffed a laugh. "Nothing, Little Flame." He rubbed a hand down his face, his shoulders loosening. "I'm sorry—I'm sure it'll be fine. It's not like you're the only ones to do it. I just . . . have a habit of abiding strictly to the Council's laws." He paused, giving Aramis a pointed look. "Typically, when someone Drifts in from another planet, they are required to check in at the Gatekeeper. It's the same if they wish to Drift out to a different planet. It helps the Council keep track of who's coming and going."

"Oh," I whispered, choosing not to focus on the fact Aramis hadn't divulged that to me—at least not yet. "Are you going to get in trouble? If you need to report us—"

"No." Vidaar patted my knee. "Don't worry about it. Like I said, people do it all the time." He shifted to his feet, sheathing his dagger. "I should go. I have guests coming in for the festival. You better hope this Cyrbus shit doesn't interfere with my livelihood." He placed a sturdy, comforting hand on my shoulder. "Regardless if you choose to stay or not, the room is yours for the week."

I smiled, surprised by his kindness. "Thank you." Any peace I felt vanished the moment the door creaked shut, sealing in the thoughts I was stewing in.

"Collins—"

"Don't," I cut him off, seething. Later, I'd ask more about the Gatekeeper. But right now—I was too angry to focus on anything else. "How did you find me, Aramis?"

"What?"

Tea spattered onto my pants as I slammed the cup against the crate. "Were you aware Cyrbus was near me on Earth? That I sat in my room with the woman who chased me today?"

Aramis's silence confirmed what I already knew, the dots I'd failed to previously connect. It never fully made sense how Aramis found me among billions of people. But he showed up only hours after my visit with Iveh. After she told me my damage was irrevocable. When I demanded she leave and she only laughed—laughed because she knew the truth.

Aramis sat beside me, resting his head on his hands. "I didn't believe it mattered whether or not I told you. I didn't want to give you any more reason to panic."

I didn't know why that made my blood boil. Maybe because I was tired of choices being stolen from me. Sweaty curls cascaded down my face as I shook my head. "I might have fled sooner if you'd revealed the truth about Iveh. Or at least I would've been aware of who to look out for."

His question was no more than a whisper. "Did you see anyone else?"

"No." Our soft breaths mingled with the faint melody beyond us, growing louder as the light continued to dim. I released a steady breath, bracing myself. "Look, I get it if you don't like what you found.

But you have no right to wreck my entire world, only to desert me." A silent tear rolled down my cheek. "If you need to leave, I understand. But at least tell me first."

"You truly believe that?"

"Yes. I heard every word you said, Aramis." I couldn't stop hearing them, despite the threat of Cyrbus so near.

You used to be so full of life, Aideen.

"I'm sorry." His hand grazed mine as he stood, shifting in front of me. "I was wrong to leave, I'm sorry. But you did nothing wrong. I just needed to clear my head." His chest shuddered as he ran a hand through his hair. "I'm not waiting for you to become someone you're not. I know you see yourself as two separate people, but when I look at you, all I see is Aideen. I knew going into this that you'd never remember me, or what we were. So don't push me away."

I shook his words from my mind. There was nothing to say. He wouldn't understand how hollow I was inside. How it felt to be nothing more than a body—completely lacking a soul. I was nothing.

"Talk to me."

The tension between us strained when I slipped between him and the crate, putting necessary distance between us. "I don't know what you want from me." My voice shook with my hands. "I see how you look at me, but I know it's not truly for me. You're waiting for me to become her, and you're only going to be disappointed."

I couldn't bear to fill another impossible role.

"Disappointed?" His voice rose as he closed the distance between us. "You think I'm disappointed with you? Maybe I haven't made my feelings clear to avoid overwhelming you, but allow me to spell it out for you, Aideen."

"Stop calling me that," I snapped. "My name is Collins."

"Fine. Aideen, Collins. I don't care what you go by." He reached for my hand and placed it atop his hammering heart, strengthening mine. "I'm sorry. I'm sorry for what I said and didn't say." His freckles became like constellations I'd never seen so close as he pulled me in tighter. "I refuse to believe you're gone. I didn't give up hope searching for you, and I won't now. No matter what Cyrbus has done, you'll always be the same fierce, strong—and now free—girl from before. If I have to remind you of that for the rest of my days, I will. Because what I feel for you right now is stronger than anything I've ever felt. I didn't go searching for Aideen or even Collins. I went looking for the girl I loved. And I found her. And I love you the same."

His starry copper eyes absorbed any words I could've possibly uttered. He bared his heart to ease my fears, confirming he was staying. He was vulnerable, despite the real chance I'd never return his feelings. It was a gesture that summoned enough bravery to push through my own constricting fears.

"I can't remember you . . . but I want to. I don't know how I felt before, or really what I feel now. But I feel something." It was the most I could offer. I wished I could say it was love, but I hardly believed I was capable of such an emotion when I struggled to love myself. But for now, it was enough.

He traced a thumb across my cheek. "I can't believe you're here. Every moment I'm reminding myself this isn't a dream. That this is real."

"It's real."

My breath caught as the back of my knees met the wooden crate. His eyes vigilantly held mine while he leaned down, but he made no effort to close the remaining frail distance. But I heard the silent invitation in our shared breath. He was allowing me to choose.

This was my life. I had the freedom to make choices now—no matter how reckless they may be. I was in charge of how broken I remained, of whether I allowed Peter and Jane's control to overpower me.

So perhaps an ounce of lingering adrenaline remained, or maybe I was desperate to understand how it was before—to be the brave and confident girl he loved. But with as much courage as I could muster, I reached up and pressed my lips to his.

His soft, warm lips kissed me with a fierceness he must have held in for years. Even when his boldness caused me to stumble back, I clung to him. I didn't know what feelings a true kiss would summon—having only shared a few with Reed—but I'd never felt a flutter of excitement in my stomach before now.

I awakened fully as he deepened the kiss, allowing a seed of hope to plant in my heart. Hope that I wasn't entirely lost. Perhaps Aideen was still within me, buried beneath the ash of a ruined spirit. Maybe I could be her again.

A girl with a home.

His lips and hands turned hungry as he firmly lifted me onto the crate, stepping between my legs. I tangled my fingers into his hair, gasping as his lips trailed down my neck. I closed my eyes, losing myself in the sensation until I gasped, "Cae—" My mouth snapped shut as his kisses ceased.

His ragged breaths caressed my throat. "What did you say?"

My stomach wrenched, appalled and startled. *Why did I say that?* I shook my head. "I was about to ask you to stop."

"I'm sorry." He fisted his hands as he stepped back, like he was resisting the urge to reach for me. "I'm sorry if I came on too strong. I was out of line."

"Please don't apologize. You did nothing wrong." I grabbed his hand and pulled him back, allowing our ragged breaths to mingle as I sorted my thoughts. I might not have experience with relationships, but I knew trying to explain why I nearly said a strange word—or possibly a name—while kissing him wouldn't end well. I shook my head. Maybe Cyrbus had inflicted more damage than I initially believed.

His heart thundered beneath my hands as I braced them on his chest, silently promising to never acknowledge the word coursing through my mind before I gave a tidbit of truth. "I don't know how intimate we were before, but this is new to me. You're new."

"You don't need to be embarrassed with me." He smiled, even as he avoided my watchful gaze.

"What is it?" I put a hand on my knee, willing it to stop shaking.

It did as Aramis placed his hand over mine and whispered, "It thrills me to know my feelings are being reciprocated. But I'm afraid I'm forcing this on you while you're too impressionable. I'd planned on letting you settle for a few months before I broached the possibility of there being something between us still. But I look at you and I see that same fire in your heart . . ." He blew out a short laugh, shaking his head. "I want your feelings to be real—not because I told you how you once felt."

But it was his honesty right there that proved this was real.

"Aramis." I wrapped my hands around his neck. "While I may not understand my feelings, I know they're real. I've lived a life of constantly having my choices laid out for me, and I'm relearning how to live again. This is overwhelming and I need to move slowly, because I can't promise you something if I don't fully understand it. But I can promise you this is entirely of my own free will." I paused, letting my words fully register before I tenderly sealed them to his lips.

Chapter Seventeen

The world was painted with fire. The familiar dense fog lingered, muting my view while I traveled the forest. Something was new, off from the usual rocks beneath my bare feet as I wandered the same path. I stopped, sensing a foreign presence within my lungs, as if I was now sharing breath with this unexpected guest. The air thickened as I remained steady and still, the sound of the shifting gravel growing closer. Perhaps I should have been frightened of someone joining my journey. But their presence was warm, inviting only confidence and wonder. Peace radiated through me as I turned toward the source, smiling as a dark figure emerged through the slowly thinning fog. My racing heart was a beating drum, beckoning the guest forward as I heard a faint call.

Aideen.

The fog dissipated all at once as I settled on the familiar, welcoming eyes. "You're okay." I blinked through tears as Aramis rubbed my cheek, kneeling beside the cot. "You were only dreaming, Collins."

"What happened?" I rasped as I scanned the room, finding his pillow and blanket discarded beside the cot, as the couch was shoved in front of the door. We'd both decided it was safe enough to remain in Mazoe tonight—assuming Cyrbus believed we fled. But still, I'd demanded we take extra precautions.

"I couldn't understand what you were saying, but you were so distraught." The bronzed light of the everflame radiated off his steady chest. He pressed a kiss to my palm as he mumbled, "What were you dreaming about?"

"I don't know." I flinched as shouts chased the remnants of the dream away. "You weren't kidding about the villagers going all night long." Aramis smiled before he fell back onto his pillow, stretching his arms up. I bit my lip, remembering his initial excitement to attend the Kefi festival. "I'm sorry you're missing it."

The cot groaned as I peeked over the edge at Aramis. "Me too. It's such a bore being trapped in here with you." His crooked grin distracted me enough I failed to dodge him when he tugged me off the cot. "Now it's a little more bearable." He wrapped me in his laughter and arms, tucking me against him.

I hid my smile beneath my palm while his thumb traced my back and tucked my legs closer to my chest, as the everflame licked too close for comfort. I narrowed my eyes at the dancing, uncontained fire in the corner of the room. "At the risk of being your amusement for the night, are you ever going to explain what exactly the everflame is and why it always burns? Am I wrong to assume it's magic as well?"

His laugh vibrated through my smooth emerald shirt, the soothing sound slowly becoming familiar. "I was shocked when you didn't demand I smother it out last night." He twined our fingers together and rested them on my hip, his chest rising against my back. "There's an annual burning ceremony, Vimniran. The everflame is crafted from the leftover ashes. You only need to light it once and it'll burn forever. They provide light for all of Aita, while also serving as a remembrance of the generosity Aita bestows upon us all."

Warmth swam through me as I watched the dancing flame, requiring not even a stick of wood or a pit to conceal its daunting strength. "So," I started, remembering there was yet another detail of Aita I didn't understand. "Are you going to explain to me what the Gatekeeper is? Or do I need to go find Vidaar and ask him?"

His throat bobbed atop my head before he said, "I hope you know, it wasn't my intention to keep that from you. It just never came up. But we're not going to be in any trouble, okay?" He paused and I squeezed his hand in acceptance, urging him to continue. "The Gatekeeper is exactly how it sounds. They have a Keeper posted at the Gateway in Irenec—it serves as the portal to other worlds. Unless you or I have some sort of beacon connecting us to a different planet, the Gateway is the only way we can Drift to one."

I scrunched my nose, unsure if I entirely understood. "So, if I wanted to Drift back to Earth, I would have to go to the Gatekeeper? For permission?"

"Yes."

I lifted our joined hands, staring at our rings. "Do I have to go to the Gatekeeper if I want to Drift to Mazoe? Or another realm on Aita?"

"No," Aramis explained. "The Council placed the beacons in each realm, so we're free to use them as we wish. The Gatekeeper is only for Drifting in and out of Aita. Think of it like a check-in point—like Vidaar said, the Council just likes to keep track of who's coming and going. The tower in Irenec and the Gateway are connected—it sources enough energy to let us Drift. If you and I had come in correctly, we would've only needed to slide our ring three times to the right for Aita—it would've delivered us straight to the Gateway." He lowered our hands and pulled me in closer to his chest, his breathing slow and comfortable. "It's really not a big deal that we Drifted directly to Mazoe from Earth. Just think of it as finding a loophole around the Council's laws."

"Oh," I murmured as I strained to wrap my head around it, assuming the longer I dwelt in Aita, I would learn more on how Drifting worked. But if I understood one thing, it was that I hadn't anticipated how . . . strict the Council appeared to be. Of course it made sense for Aita to have laws and some form of government, but I guess I imagined it differently in a world of magic.

But it wasn't one of magic, not truly, it seemed. Just today I'd watched Hekate—who might or might not be a witch—get kicked out of the market. Even Aramis had told me of magical beings who had gone extinct, the tower in Irenec severing the connection from planet to man. And then there was the unwelcoming man in Eirlys who said the magic was defiled.

I hadn't lived here long, nor could I remember my former life—so it would be unfair to form a judgment just yet. But all I knew was that I'd been trafficked to another planet, and yet no one was aware of it. Wouldn't I have to go through the Gatekeeper to be sold to Earth? Or had Cyrbus found another way to Drift to other planets? Used a different beacon?

I looked to the everflame, its heat no longer soothing me. Not as Aramis and I lay in silence, listening to the celebration beyond the door. The incessant hollering and ever-growing music was so full, the beat could surely lift the leaning inn. But their oblivious joy didn't bring a smile to my lips. No, it made me sick.

I'd run for my life today, and not one person—other than Vidaar—had offered to help. It wasn't their duty, of course, but if I'd seen someone urgently fleeing, I liked to believe I'd intervene. Yet there were villagers outside absorbed in song and dance while others were being sold. As I locked myself in a stuffy inn, praying Cyrbus wouldn't hunt me in my sleep.

How many had stood by while I was sold?

Nothing would deprave my conscience more than abandoning those who had yet to escape bondage as I had. I wouldn't allow my gift of a new life to begin in selfishness. I couldn't remain idle while Cyrbus demolished the minds of others.

If I survived tonight, I wouldn't hide any longer.

I released a shaky breath, steadying myself for what I'd yet to face. "Aramis . . . what happened before? How did Cyrbus take me?"

His finger ceased its trail up my side. "I-I don't know. I wasn't there." His callouses scratched my hip as he clutched the thin silk material. "I initially believed you ran away while I was gone."

I slipped out of his hold and sat up. "Ran away? If you were gone, how did you figure out what Cyrbus had done?"

"Collins." He sat up, looses waves bouncing as he shook his head. "There's more to your disappearance than I initially let on. I planned to tell you, but I didn't know if you were ready."

My building frustration didn't spew, as my stomach was twisting beyond the point of caring. How do you listen to the tale of your kidnapping? Or how you ceased to exist?

You jump into the fiery abyss and escape logic's grasp, pleading the blazing flame will paralyze your nerves before the pain can fully manifest. Or in layman terms—you rip the band-aid off.

I nodded in permission, if only to prevent this from occurring again. His hand squeezed mine when he glanced at the door, as if he feared this truth would cause me to flee. "After your parents died, you stopped existing. I'd never seen your eyes so hollow. Your body was present, but you weren't." His eyes gleamed off the flame before he looked down, clenching his jaw. "I couldn't bring you back and it was taking a toll on us. So for a while I left. I thought the space would do us good, but I was wrong." He released a shuddering breath of warm air. "Every day I've regretted leaving you when you needed me the most. Maybe things would've been different if I'd stayed."

"Aramis." I brushed strands of hair from his sorrowful eyes. Perhaps if I felt an ounce of the grief I'd felt when my parents died, I'd be angry at him for leaving. But I didn't even know their names. It wouldn't be fair to hold on to that. "There's no sense in playing with what-ifs. We both know if you'd been with me, Cyrbus could've taken you as well."

He nodded, pressing a kiss to my palm. "I left for a while. I was drowning myself in liquor with a group of friends as we Drifted through the universes. Occasionally, I'd return to check on my mom—she was in the infirmary then." He closed his eyes and released a shaky breath and my heart fractured. "Eventually, I shoved my pride away and was determined to be there for you. Only when I went to you, something had changed." I tightened my hold on his hand, even as he released his grip. "You didn't appear lifeless anymore . . . but you were different. You were softer, reserved, but you said you were okay." He shook his head and huffed a laugh. "You also said you had no interest in being with me anymore. That the only way you could heal was to leave me behind. So I let you go because I believed you had stopped loving me."

"I'm sorry I hurt you." The apology felt inadequate and foreign on my tongue, but I had nothing else to offer. "I don't understand. If I told you that, why bother looking for me?"

"Because I loved you enough for both of us." His voice was as mellow as the kiss he delivered to my lips. He kissed me gently once more before he continued, "One of the last times I visited my mom, you were officially gone. You left most of your things behind, including your ring and this letter, stating you didn't want to be found. That you couldn't live in a world you'd outgrown." His tone sharpened with his jaw, edged in a way that kept my hands from reaching for his. "There were whisperings you'd left for good, but you know how everyone adds in their own tidbits. It was a bunch of bogus."

A lonely tear streamed down his freckled cheek. "But my mother—well, being my mother—wasn't convinced you had run off. One day while in the infirmary, she heard whispers of a trafficking ring. How individuals from all over Aita were disappearing without any explanation. I tried to reason with her, but she was inconsolable. She made me vow on her deathbed to bring you home. If she hadn't been so ill, I'm certain she would've torn through all the realms to find you herself."

I didn't know why, but that was what broke me. There was a woman—who didn't share even a drop of blood with me—who'd loved me so fiercely. If she hadn't begged her son to find me, where would I be?

And now her son—who cared for me just as fiercely—held me as I cried in his arms, wishing I could remember my own parents, who I hoped had loved me that strongly. There was so much I wished to understand. Why I had pushed Aramis away, or left that letter. But most importantly, why had Cyrbus chosen me?

Aramis smiled as I wiped the emotion coating my cheeks. "What made you keep looking? I know eventually you found Cyrbus, but after not finding me for so long, how did you not lose hope?"

The pit in my stomach swelled with each breath that Aramis said nothing. The silence grew insufferable, pushing me toward a cliff I'd surely fall from. I clung to the jagged edge, accepting a painful fate as he cracked his neck and stood. What wasn't he telling me? Didn't I deserve the truth behind my kidnapping?

Before I could demand an explanation, a screeching noise clawed my nerves as he shoved the couch from the door. I remained where I sat, even when he smiled—the gesture no longer singing to me. "Come with me. I want to show you something."

I scoffed, brows furrowing. "In case you forgot, I barely escaped Cyrbus hours ago. It doesn't seem wise to push my luck."

Aramis shrugged on a wine shirt before retrieving our cloaks from atop the table. "I think they would've found you by now. I truly doubt the couch would have deterred them. Besides, everyone's out tonight. Cyrbus won't find you. Do you think I'd really put you at risk if I wasn't confident that you would be safe? Have a little faith in me." He groaned as I made no effort to unwind myself from the pile of blankets. "Please," he whispered. "Please live a little with me, Collins."

My fear dissipated at his plea—as I remembered his disappointment and cruel words when I refused to jump off the waterfall with him. And after learning how he'd searched for me against all odds, I couldn't bear to disappoint him.

At least, more than I already had.

Chapter Eighteen

"Wasn't this worth the risk?" Aramis's voice slipped into my enamored trance with the moon—though I suppose it was with the sun as well.

When I'd initially thrown on my crusty cloak, I doubted anything would be worth risking my safety. Especially after I shoved my way through the drunken, slothful bodies who filled the square, carelessly dancing through their spilled drinks. I almost retreated back to the inn after a wandering hand slipped beneath my cloak and wrapped around my waist.

But if I hadn't trudged through the reeking crowd and the terrifyingly rambunctious jungle, I would've missed a chance to live.

"Thank you," I whispered, so as to not disturb the balance painted above me, allowing light and dark to coexist as one. My remaining fear and hesitation withered into nothing, absorbed by the orange radiant hue filling the night sky where the sun dwelled behind the moon. But despite the eclipse's prominent beauty, I continuously looked toward the quiet, subtle beads of light.

It's not always grand, obvious lights that lead us out of darkness and despair. Sometimes, it's gentle, soft reminders of hope that give us enough courage to push forward. To remind us there is joy to be found, even in the loneliest of times.

"I've dreamed of this for so long." Fine flecks of sand coated Aramis's hair as he rolled toward me. He smiled as freely as the flowing river swaying at our feet. "When I found you on Earth, I was afraid you'd be too far gone. But when I followed you home and watched you walk the entire time with your head in the sky, I knew you were in there."

I propped a hand beneath my head, allowing my unruly curls to scatter along the riverbank. We shared breath as I whispered, "What do you mean?"

His hand found mine in the sand, containing endless grains of possibilities. "You cherished the stars before. Each night, you'd lay on your roof and intensely watch them, as if they were watching you back. One time I asked why you were so enticed with them—especially with an entire world of magic at your disposal." He turned his head and glanced up. "You said they deserved to be marveled at. You believed whoever forged the universe deemed them so vital and sacred, they ensured every world was given their own set of stars. A gift to unite each planet, despite how different they may be."

I doubted Aramis knew the power laced between his words. How, for the first time, I truly felt hope. I'd never understood why I sat beneath the window and stared up at the night sky, even when smog and city lights overcast them. I thought I'd watched out of longing, searching for something deeper.

But a muffled piece of my soul had remembered the gift they were, a gift that had brought me home.

"Collins." Aramis's eyes gleamed with mischief in the light of the blood moon as he glanced at my lips. "I'm truly trying to hold myself back and not overwhelm you." My pulse raced, throbbing beneath my skin. "But my self-control is withering away and I'd like nothing more than to kiss you until you remember me."

I bit back a smile, his words doing something to me, my body feverish from the inside out. But before his lips could graze mine, a taunting voice shattered the peace. "As entertaining as that experiment might be, I'm afraid I'll have to disrupt it."

The once-perfect balance shifted into jagged chaos as Aramis tore me up and shoved me behind him. My hands shook while I clutched his cloak and stared into the shadowed, tangled trees. "You know, I was enjoying myself at the festival. So much, I almost failed to notice you leaving." The voice was cruel and rough, a duplicate to the man who carried it. Moonlight beamed off his flowing white hair and ghostly pale skin, a wicked tattoo trailing down his arm. I only studied its intricate whorls for a moment before he grinned. "Iveh won't be pleased that I'm the one to deliver you back, but unfortunately she had other duties to attend to." My core froze, solidifying with panic when he found my gaze and reached behind his back. "But I do love that history's repeating itself."

Aramis clutched my wrist, catching me as I stumbled against the loose river rocks. He wrapped an arm around my waist, pinning me to him as he scanned for an escape. "Your ring," he mumbled as he released me and reached for his. "Just go anywhere and I'll follow you."

Before I could spin it once, another taunt filled the air. "Go ahead. Let's see if you're quick enough." I dropped my hand, frozen as I took in his smirk, half of it covered by his hand drawing back a bow. My mouth dried as his gleaming, arrogant eyes focused on Aramis, pointing the arrow at his chest. "Now, Collins . . ." he drawled. "We can do this the simple way or the exciting way." A shiver wove through my tightening chest—his idea of excitement was beyond what I could imagine. "If you come with us, you'll leave unharmed." He extended a long finger off his bow, beckoning me forward. "I vow you won't remember a thing."

Aramis backed up and water licked my boots, threatening to swallow me whole. "She's not going anywhere." His voice held strong, not displaying an ounce of the fear I knew we shared—fear we would be torn from one another again.

The man laughed, a disgusting sound carving into my ears. "Oh, she's coming. It's up to you if she's leaving alive or not. It doesn't matter to me, but I'd hate to be wasteful." He clicked his tongue and looked back into the shadowed trees. "Wouldn't you?"

I dug my nails into Aramis's arm, learning of nightfall's betrayal as a figure emerged from the trees. Aramis shifted and blocked my view as the shadows veiled back, so I could only hear a gruff voice. "I'm not here to play, Conon."

Head pounding, I forced myself to return the gaze of the ghostly man—Conon—who cocked his head as he adjusted his bow. His piercing, deathly eyes lost my attention as I heard a new voice. The same one from moments before, yet different. Softer. A voice that haunted and sang to me, triggering some sort of inkling between my bones. "It's over, Aramis. Do the right thing for Collins, let her stay alive."

No.

I tripped as I shoved my way out from behind Aramis, unable to breathe beyond that voice. The world stumbled as my heart did, as I took in the broad shoulders and the ink peeking out from beneath his leather jacket, leading to the hand that once held me. Only this time, his gray eyes weren't locked intently on me, but on Aramis.

"No," I gasped quietly, the rushing river gobbling up my shock, my fingers shaking against my lips. His eyes met mine, stripping me bare, containing nothing of the man who'd danced with me days before.

Before I could shudder a sob, Aramis jerked me back into his protection. "Go to hell." His voice was rough as he staggered us back another step, water filling my boots. "Don't come any closer."

"Collins." The man's voice deceitfully caressed me as he slowly stepped forward, revealing a dagger draped to his side. "You can trust me." He extended a hand and gained another step. My fingers loosened on where I gripped Aramis's cloak, aching to take his hand. So badly, I was filled with deep shame as I stared at the man who at times weaved his way into my thoughts, unable to control the way he danced through my mind. "Come with me, Collins."

Aramis unsheathed his knife, moonlight gleaming off the curved blade, stopping me before I made a grave mistake. "I will slice off your filthy tongue if you dare speak to her again."

Conon's ghostly laugh slithered down my bones, reminding us he was present. "Now we're getting to the interesting part." He dropped the bow string from his cheek, taunting Aramis. "As a courtesy for your success in tracking us, I'll let you decide your fate. Either I kill you, or your brother does."

A heavy, consuming weight dragged me under, the word ringing through me.

Brother.

Aramis's brother was with Cyrbus.

The same man who'd danced with me, who'd awoke my weary soul.

Aramis left my side, not faltering at Conon's threat, and I slipped deeper in the shifting rocks, water climbing to my calves. With the ever-shrinking distance, I couldn't shake Aramis and his brother's undeniable similarities. Their towering height. The sharp cheekbones. Even the same straight nose.

Despite this, Aramis still seethed, "I don't see my brother."

"Now that the family reunion is over with. Let's get on with this." Conon dropped his threat at the same time as his bow and raced toward me. My body betrayed me, acting as if it was lodged in the rocks, failing to move before Aramis mercifully barreled toward him. I screamed, sinking deeper in the ominous water as Aramis and Conon collided to the ground.

I rushed through the stones, ankles groaning, to aid Aramis. Water slopped out of my boots on the edge of the river before I was tackled back into it. Grains of sand joined the screams in my mouth while I writhed beneath the force restraining me.

"Aramis!" I uselessly screamed as I caught a glimpse of him tumbling farther from my reach. I swallowed another mouthful of sand before I was flipped onto my back. I clamped my eyes shut, unwilling to meet his brother's deceitful eyes while I clawed at him.

Aramis's faint commands to Drift wove into my screams, offering a strand of hope. Before I could wrap a trembling finger around my ring, my captor shifted his weight. His legs pinned my arms to my side as he claimed my last hope and yanked the ring from my hand. "Stop fighting. I don't want to harm you, Collins." Sand tickled my skin, filling my ears as he pushed me down further.

My name on his lips broke me. He swore as I bit down on his wrist, his vile blood coating my tongue. I flinched as he tore himself free, bracing myself for his punishment. But he only hooked an arm around my waist and threw me over his shoulder, towing me toward the jungle.

"Aramis," I screamed, not in fear for myself, but for him. "Stop it," I cried as Conon knelt over him, choking him with his bow. My heart shattered completely once his eyes found mine, wide with the truth.

We were losing one another again.

Just as Aramis flipped Conon over on his back, my elbow collided with my captor's jaw, a shock firing through it. I flailed against his hold, regretting not accepting Vidaar's blade. By some form of luck—or perhaps Aita—his boot caught on a root, forcing him off-balance. I tumbled to the ground, the mulch and brush failing to soften my fall, and my lungs choked for air. Aita's mercy didn't extend far because hardly a ragged breath later, Aramis's brother was on me again.

"You're making things worse."

My head was ringing, my mind blurred, deceiving me into believing his hands were a gentle breeze as he grazed my aching head. Had I fallen unconscious? Or was I hallucinating? Because just as a sturdy arm wrapped around my waist, the other cradling my head, I was dropped again. Only this time a root wasn't responsible for stopping him, but a vine.

I lay heavily on the ground, a stark contrast to the veering vine clasped around my captor's waist, lifting him into the air. A flicker of awe—and a bit of horror—coursed through me as another wrapped around his boots, inviting countless more tendrils seeking to enjoy this new game. I rolled to my knees, somehow forgetting myself as I watched the man dangling above me, the vines weaving together to create a web. Strangely, he made no effort to unsheathe the dagger from his back and slash at the vines holding him hostage, but instead held up his hands and mumbled inaudible words, as if he was attempting to soothe the jungle's fury. Wide-eyed, I watched with dread as the vines appeared to slacken, as if my captor had somehow explained that Aita's magic had unnecessarily come to my aid.

"Collins!" Aramis's bellow tore through my invisible snares. I didn't waste another moment to see if the jungle released Aramis's brother and raced toward the riverbank, allowing the eclipse to beckon me forward.

Just as my boots sunk into the sand, I collided with a solid force. A hand seized my wrist before I fell, half dragging me forward even as I fought, stopping after I learned it was Aramis. Gleaming blood dripped down his face while he urgently took me in, ensuring I was unharmed. "We need to go. Just click your ring seven times. We'll go to the Council for help."

"I–" A groan filled the night as I clutched my hand, as barren as our dwindling options. "It's gone."

Your brother took it.

Aramis yanked his ring off and grabbed my hand. "Then use mine. I'll find another way to get to you."

"No." I clenched my hand shut, refusing to release his fingers. "We'll figure a way out of this together."

His hands shook as he held my cheeks, pressing his lips to my forehead. "It's going to be okay." He scanned behind me, searching for an escape in the erratic jungle. He looked over his shoulder then, and my stomach churned, already anticipating his next move.

Aramis clutched my hand and dragged me through the river, adrenaline overflowing my urge to protest. The rushing water crashed against my ribs as Aramis led us forward, his ragged breaths drowning out mine. I clung to his hand, straining to hold on as the water gripped my cloak, tightening on my throat until I was gasping for air. I blindly fumbled with the clasp, failing to unlatch it before Aramis heard my silent plea and yanked me into his arms, carrying me the remaining distance through the river.

Our boots scuffed against dry land just as thunderous yelling erupted across the river. But rest wasn't an option. This wasn't over. It would never be over.

I'd never be able to stop running.

Chapter Nineteen

How long can you outrun death?

My burning chest longed to find out, pushing my legs until they no longer felt like mine. Fear propelled me forward over plunging, overgrown roots. I grasped onto slithering vines as my legs threatened to give out, refusing to bow at the jungle's feet. I clung to reality as fervently as my drenched clothes did to my aching bones. But the farther we fled down this endless trail, the more I lost myself to the black hole that had been looming by, promising to swallow me since the day I'd woken up two years ago. My breaths turned ragged, edged with sobs despite my best effort to slow them, to force away what I'd been holding in.

Cyrbus was hunting me.

Aramis gripped my hand tighter and a war erupted within me, reminding me of the hands that had tainted me. The same hands that had brought me to life.

Aramis's brother.

Except he hadn't brought me to life. He'd sold me.

I'd been sold.

I yanked my hand free and scratched at my skin, feeling his touch everywhere. A touch I'd eagerly welcomed. I choked on a sob as I remembered how afraid I'd been to never feel as alive as I had with him.

But he may as well have killed me.

I was a fool. A ridiculously naive fool. So pathetically desperate for love and attention, I'd thrown myself at the first man who treated me like I was something. Except I was nothing to him.

Are you sure we don't know each other?

Wouldn't you remember me if you did?

He'd known who I was and mocked me. He'd taken advantage of my situation and made it into a game, getting off on the thrill of whether or not I'd remember he'd done this to me.

And Aramis knew.

I slipped out of the depressing carousel as Aramis shook my shoulders, his voice sharp. "What the hell is going on? We don't have time for you to lose it right now."

I shoved his hands off, resisting the urge to snap, as now wasn't the time to be angry. Not when blood smeared his tangled hair, as bright as the thick line around his neck. Proof of how tonight nearly ended, a reminder of a sadistic fate lurking closer with each breath.

A faint growl snapped our lingering tension. Aramis shook his head and turned away. "We need to hide. It's not smart to keep wandering—it's easy to get turned around out here. We'll find a way out once it's safe."

I didn't protest when Aramis grabbed my hand, leading us onward. But something was off, strange. I didn't know if it was because he'd lied again, or because I knew it was pointless to enjoy his touch. Was the effort of running—of this life—worth it, if it was only a matter of time until Cyrbus inevitably won?

My hands shook as I dug myself into moist leaves and twigs, praying that the thick, overgrown roots plunging out of the ground around me didn't wake up as the vines had, if only so they wouldn't nab the burrow we cowered in. I clutched the surface, holding myself there—grounding myself in the fact Cyrbus hadn't found me yet.

I was alive.

My name is Collins and I'm alive. I repeated the mantra over and over, begging that it would hide within a spot of my mind Cyrbus couldn't reach. I wouldn't—couldn't—forget again. I wouldn't lose myself.

Aramis's still shadow offered little comfort, his silence only confirming the high possibility of not making it out of this burrow together.

I inhaled the rich smell of wood, using the unwavering trunks to solidify my courage. "How did you escape?" It was such a blur, I had yet to fathom how—or why—the jungle had come to my aid, snaring my captor in a vine.

"I don't know." His filthy shirt clung to his chest as he shuddered a breath. "Once I saw you being taken, I managed to get him off long enough to use one of his arrows against him."

I didn't let myself imagine the frightful deed he'd committed on my behalf.

I ran my fingers through his hairline, smearing dirt along the crusting blood. "Are you hurt?"

"No." His fingers wrapped around my wrist, pulling it down to his lap where his cloak rested. He ran a finger over my palm, whispering, "Did he hurt you?"

My wet curls shook around my face, jostling debris free. "No, I'm not hurt." My pain wasn't visible; there was no quick fix for the wound inflicted upon my soul. My voice wobbled with my knees as I asked, "Why did you lie about having a brother?"

His finger halted in my palm. "Because I don't have one."

"But I heard that man, he sa—"

"I know what you heard," he spat, consuming all our air. He made no effort to stop me when I pulled my hand free and wrapped it around my quivering stomach. "We may share a mother, but he stopped being my brother years ago. He's nothing but scum now."

You still lied.

"Did you know he was with Cyrbus?" My voice strained, holding myself back on a fine, thinning string.

"Of course I knew. How do you think I found you? I followed him to Earth." Aramis's laugh slithered down my bones, the sound foreign and wrong. "I'll admit it was a shock to see him tonight. But I shouldn't be surprised he'd involve himself in anything that concerns you."

He followed his brother to find me. He'd been lying all along.

I wondered if Aita was somehow aware of the animosity building in me, if it would indeed send a vine to capture me this time.

I spoke softly, crumbling dirt in my hands while I sorted my thoughts. "You followed me home from the bar. So you saw him there. You saw him and me."

There wasn't a fleck of Aramis within his cold, bleak eyes. This wasn't the joyful, lively Aramis who radiated hope. He was careless and cruel, much like his words. "Yes, I got to experience firsthand that even without a single memory, you still would make the same reckless choice." He shook his head, huffing a laugh. "He attacked you tonight and yet here you are, wanting to learn all you can about him."

"Aramis." I reached for him, desperately pulling his hands closer. "I'm only trying to understand what's going on."

He pulled his hands back, further fracturing our bond. "What aren't you understanding?" His voice rose, too absorbed in his rage to care if we were caught. "Yes, he was my brother. But he stopped being family the day he took you from me. It's not a coincidence he works with Cyrbus—the very company who sold and brainwashed you."

I pressed myself further into the tree's roots, distancing myself from the disdain in his voice. He'd been gruff before, but this was different. He was . . . he was angry at me.

"You're saying he directly did this to me. But if he's your brother, that would mean he knew me. Why would he have any reason to do this?" I whispered slowly, so as to not set him off.

"Because he's sick, probably something he inherited from his twisted absentee father. I gave up long ago trying to understand how his mind works."

"Do you think he worked with them before I was taken?"

"No, I don't think so." His voice deflated, softening as he said, "I didn't connect the pieces until a few months after you both disappeared and then he miraculously reappeared. Alone."

"Why would he and I disappear together?"

"Who do you think you left me for? Who you ran away with?" His face was empty and cold.

I clenched my eyes, blocking out his unreasonable accusation. There had to be a different explanation. "I don't believe you."

He accepted defeat, lowering his head between his legs. "I made a mistake leaving you after your parents' death. If I'd known my brother would use that time to drive us further apart—use your vulnerability to coerce you into feeling something for him—I wouldn't have left." He clutched a clod of dirt, tossing it at a root. "When I came back, it was too late. He already had his claws in you. When I tried to do something about it, you were both gone, leaving whispers that you'd run off together. But then Mom mentioned the trafficking and begged me to look for both of you. So I did—only I found him, alive and well. He refused to talk about you, to acknowledge what he'd done. But then I learned who he was involved with and what they were doing, and I knew he was to blame for your disappearance." His eyes found me, slicing at my withering restraint. "It's not a surprise you don't believe me. You made every excuse for him in the world before."

"Stop," I hissed. "Don't you dare use my past choices against me. Not when you are constantly making a choice to lie to me."

"I couldn't tell you about him. I couldn't risk losing you again."

I blinked, unable to see past the pooling rage flowing vibrantly through my veins. I was so tired. Tired of everyone deciding what was best for me—what details I deserved to know.

"You lied to me." The words were edged and brutal, but true. "You know my entire existence is already a lie, yet you do it anyway. You make a big show about me having choices now, but you decided I didn't deserve to make that one. You didn't trust me to pick you, so you lied. You lied about my disappearance. You withheld the fact that my parents are dead, that you abandoned me in my grief. All to spare yourself, and only yourself, from heartache and disappointment. How are you any different from Peter and Jane—or even Cyrbus? How am I supposed to trust that you aren't molding me into someone you deem worthy?"

"Collins." He clutched my hand, stopping me as I tried to crawl out from the burrow. "Don't leave. Be angry and fight with me. Tell me every awful thought you're having. And even after you have, I'll take you home." His lips shook against my hand. "I'll take you home to Kaira and we can leave this behind. Please, Aideen."

I didn't believe him. He didn't want to take me home—he wanted Aideen.

"My name is Collins." I yanked my hands free, digging my nails into the ground as I pulled myself to safety. There was no more safety within those crumbling walls, where all I could smell now was rot and musk. The fresh, wet air outside no longer tasted of home. Home didn't exist for me anymore.

I was nothing more than a wanderer of realms.

Chapter Twenty

My sense of direction had clearly not been invited to my trek through the jungle. I wove through an endless array of broad trees and ferns—steering clear of any rowdy vines. I apologized endlessly for trampling over hidden shrooms and orchids, hastily trying to get distance from the shrieks and clicks of the jungle's watchful protectors. But mostly I fled from Aramis's voice, his pleas for me to come back.

All I heard was lies.

I didn't know how to discern which of his words were real or fabricated. Anything could've been a lie, even who he was—what we were. I barely knew myself, so why did I believe I knew him?

I'd trusted him. I let him in, shared myself in a way I never had before. I'd been entirely honest, yet he couldn't offer the same gift. I didn't know how to move past this—if we'd even survive Cyrbus and have the chance to try. But truly, my gravest mistake wasn't trusting Aramis.

It was coming to Aita. I'd traded one void for another. I had no family or friends, no clue who I was.

I couldn't see past the uncertainty lingering in the air, the tangles and twists of knotted roots and vines. I lay back onto the tilted ground, my sodden cloak beneath me, finding not even a flicker of light beyond the thick, lush canopy. It was my exhausted legs and mind that kept me from running from the predators' warnings filling the night, certain it would be unwise to travel deeper into the jungle. I didn't know how long I lay there—somehow unscathed by both Aramis and Cyrbus. I knew the sun would soon conquer the night, but I didn't believe its light would break through. Its gracious, comforting rays wouldn't embrace me again.

A sudden snap interrupted the usual melody of howls, buzzing, and rushing creeks. I sank lower, hoping the brush would conceal me as I watched a figure wind through the trees. He moved slow and steady with the breeze, his hands grasping each thin trunk. Besides the one intrusive snap, he managed to avoid any debris as he scanned the land.

I rolled to my stomach, biting back a groan when a hidden stone irritated my healing wounds. I held my breath while I peeked through the leaves and overgrown grass, fearing he'd feel my thumping heart through the ground as he knelt, washing his face in the creek. The shadow's build was large, powerful, much like Aramis, but I knew by the lack of sloppy, golden hair it was his brother.

Yet I didn't run.

Instead I watched him stiffen into stone as a small, round creature emerged from the bushes beside him. I covered my mouth, holding in my cry as he flicked out his dagger and the gleaming blade drew near the rodent, which somehow failed to gain an inch of escape, bucking and whining. I soon learned why as the blade traveled past the animal and sliced through the lacings of a net snaring it in place. My shoulders slacked with my mouth—not only did he free it, but he spared a moment to brush a hand through its plush coat. The creature pushed back against his palm in thanks, wrapping its lanky tail around his forearm before it barreled up the nearest tree and ascended into thin air.

Perhaps the sight should've warmed my heart, a relief to learn he valued life. But it only bludgeoned against my chest, worsening tonight's countless blows. He might value a wild animal's life, but he didn't value mine.

He'd sold me.

I didn't know if it was the thrum of the jungle or watching the squirrel-like creature soar away above us, but all logic and reasoning abandoned me. I stood and descended to his level. "What did you do to me?" I demanded, heaving in the heavy, wet air. "What did you do?"

His eyes widened as he pivoted on a knee, taking me in. My bravado faltered when I truly saw him. I'd forgotten how intimidating he was until he stood, towering over me. I staggered back with regret while his brows furrowed, likely confused as to why I'd given myself away.

He cocked his head, a predator assessing his prey. Only I refused to cower as he openly examined me, making my blood boil. "What are you waiting for?"

His dark brows furrowed again, deepening his scar. "What?"

"You found me. Isn't this the part where you steal my freedom? Or will you simply kill me this time?" If I had half a brain, I'd stop taunting him. But I was incapable of doing so when each moment I looked at him intensified the pain of what he'd done.

He spoke slowly, as if he also believed I lacked a full brain. "I'm not going to kill you. I-I suppose I was taking the moment in."

His eyes had a kind of hollowness to them, a mirror of my own. I wasn't overwhelmed with hatred as I met his gray starlight gaze. Instead I was welcomed with familiar feelings of the night we danced—followed by my own disgust. I breathed through the sour taste filling my mouth, waiting for him to become triumphant at my capture. But my heartache only worsened as he watched me, as we remained transfixed on one another.

Any heartache vanished when he reached for my hand and asked, "Are you okay?"

I yanked my hand away and his face hardened. "Don't touch me," I breathed. "Did you enjoy the thrill of not knowing if I'd remember you?"

His cheekbones sharpened, unlike the dagger at his side he'd yet to unsheathe. "You don't know anything."

"Clearly. You and your friends made sure of that."

His eyes left mine and instead scanned the land behind me. "That's fair."

I rasped a laugh and he flinched. "At least you're honest. That appears to be a rare trait on Aita."

He left my side, as if I hadn't spoken at all, and stiffly stepped closer to where I'd hidden, examining the bushes. "Why isn't Aramis with you? I saw you both get away."

I didn't know why I didn't flee as he ventured further away. I checked my boots, ensuring no vines held me there. But it was as if there was something inviting me to stay, despite common sense begging me to run. I didn't dare let myself wonder if I remained because I wasn't ready to face Aramis—or because I was desperate to remember his brother. To learn why he'd done this, why it felt like utter betrayal when I didn't even know his name.

"Who are you?" I whispered, almost hoping he wouldn't hear me over the flutter of wings and ominous calls.

Our soaring guests fell silent as I anxiously awaited his answer. He didn't deliver it until I could see the truth in his eyes, having brought my cloak back with him. "Caelum."

Their wings erupted, furiously flapping away as if they witnessed what dwelled within my mind.

Caelum.

The damp, suffocating air drew cold, nipping at me as I fought to keep myself rightly planted. It wasn't a word I'd nearly gasped when Aramis kissed me, that had played through my mind ever since. It was a name. His name. One that had somehow etched its way into my mind before I knew what it was.

But how could I know his name and not remember him? Perhaps he—or Cyrbus—used some sort of magic and planted it as a further taunt. Or my subconscious had stored it, a fleeting effort to remember his actions. How he'd sold me.

Unwilling to give him the satisfaction, I didn't demand to know how his vile name had slipped through. I wouldn't reveal his power over me. Though it was likely obvious when I didn't move, as if his presence was another maze of roots, holding me in place.

And when Caelum leaned against a tree, rubbing his jaw as he intently watched me, I couldn't help but wonder if he felt inclined to stay too. His face wasn't hardened into a glare, nor did he watch me curiously. It was as though he was savoring this moment, watching me as he had before he asked me to dance.

I had allowed myself to be swept up in brilliant smiles and warm hands—blind to his manipulation. But now I was aware Caelum was from my past, someone who might reveal details of it, if only to prolong this dance.

Only this time, I would lead.

"Um—" I cleared my throat, willing my rattling soul to solidify. "I'm clearly lacking better judgment and you seem to be in a state of undecided, so why don't you answer some questions for me?" My cheeks heated and I winced internally as a gale of wind rushed through, carrying my pitiful attempt for all to hear.

He crossed his arms over his chest and laughed under his breath, a sound unfit for such a monster. "Ask me." Nor should he have such an alluring voice, causing my traitorous heart to race.

"Did you know who I was at the bar?"

"Not exactly." The leather from his jacket scraped against the bark as he shrugged.

I sucked in a breath of fresh air, relieved to learn Aramis was wrong. I didn't leave Aramis for him—Caelum hardly knew or cared who I was. "Did you follow me there?"

"No. I wasn't aware you'd be there." His voice grew distant while he scanned our surroundings again, searching to see if the obscured animals howling were near.

My hand shook as I ran it down my face, wiping the humidity's kisses from my forehead. "So you knew me from before. But how?"

"Correction: I said I didn't exactly know you." He pushed off the tree, dropping my cloak at his feet. "Before we continue this, answer something for me."

I slipped on a slick rock, stumbling as his stare branded me from only a step away. "Okay."

"How much do you know?" A strand of ebony hair fell forward as he cocked his head, veering his gaze to my scar.

I brushed my curls over it and stared at my boots. "I've been filled in on the basics, but besides the other night, I didn't know you existed."

He muttered something beneath his breath, clearing his throat before he said, "I meant if you had any memories from before. Or has it all been retold to you?"

Was he doing damage control? Like Iveh had—taking notes on what they could improve? It would explain why he was here and not dragging me away. Did this mean other victims were having some sort of flashbacks of their previous life? Besides a few blurry dreams that appeared to resemble some realm on Aita, I didn't remember anything of my past. Even so, divulging my theory to him didn't seem like a good idea.

"No, I don't have any memories of my own." I didn't allow myself to be swept away in that vulnerability before I asked, "How did you know me?"

He ran a hand through his slicked-back hair, still neat despite our earlier tumble. "I suppose the same way you knew Aramis. We grew up together, but I was a few years older." He paused, scanning the blackened canvas surrounding us. "Where is Aramis? He shouldn't have left you out here alone."

I rolled my eyes. "Who says I'm alone? Maybe he's up in a tree watching you. Giving himself the perfect view when a vine decides to snatch you up again. Maybe this time it'll throw you in the river."

A faint smile traced his lips while he tugged on a vine, daring it. "And if it decides to get you too?"

I shook my head, clearing away this distraction. "Were you and I close?" I needed to know if what Aramis had said was true, even if the evidence was so clearly laid out before me. I needed him to admit it.

"Is that what Aramis told you?"

I bit my lip, anticipating I'd have to reveal some truth if I wanted any. "No. But I assumed so after I learned he hid the fact he had a brother and was less than enthused to reveal more about you."

He dug his hands into his pockets, and I couldn't help but wonder if my stolen ring was within one. He stared at the resting flora beneath his boots as he said, "He was right not to tell you about me."

This was a waste of time. He wouldn't share any vital information with me; he only stole it for himself. "See, that's the problem I'm having." My voice rose while I trampled the ground, retrieving my cloak. "I'm sick of being lied to. I'm tired of everyone deciding what I need to know so they can create their own version of my past."

"Don't go." His plea laced the air, stopping me in the few tracks I'd taken. "I don't remember you well, but I believe we were close."

It was interesting. The different effect I had on a set of brothers. One loved me and devoted his life to me—while the other destroyed and sold me.

Yet, here I was, willingly with the latter.

My fingers fumbled mindlessly with the lacings of my pants—grateful I'd changed out of my nightclothes before we left—while I leaned against a tree, careful to leave distance between us. "We couldn't have been close if you can't remember me." I should probably be insulted with how forgettable I was. Common sense whispered to leave again, but when he leaned against the tree beside mine, I asked, "Why are you involved with Cyrbus?"

His eyes widened into ash pearls. "Not all of us get the liberty of starting over like you."

Thorns bit into my palm as I tightly grasped a low-hanging branch beside me. "Liberty? You do realize I'm on the run for my life from people like you."

He raised his scarred brow. "But you're not running right now. Unless you forgot it was you who revealed yourself." He stared at me, daring me to admit why I was here. Why I wasn't running from the man who might as well have killed me.

But to answer his silent question, I'd have to know the answer.

"Did you do this to me?" The leaves trembled with my voice, as if they knew the severity of what I asked. What would change once he admitted it?

"I don't believe so," he whispered softly, as if it wasn't safe to utter aloud.

I scrunched my nose at his words, not expecting that. How did he not know if he did or didn't? I wanted to scream—to demand the reason why he cared so little for my life.

But then it hit me.

I narrowed my eyes, scrutinizing every deceitful, flawless feature. "Why are you answering like that?"

"What?"

"You haven't given me a single definite answer. You're answering as though you're not sure."

He looked down at the ground. "Are you so sure of everything?"

Dried clay shook free as I ran a hand through my curls, releasing a shaky breath. "I need you to say it."

Because what was running rampant in my mind wasn't possible.

He leaned back and looked up, wearing the same expression I did when I watched the stars. Their light didn't reach his face as he whispered, "You and I are not so different. In terms of memory loss."

I clamped my eyes shut, grasping on to the tree, needing it to come alive and sustain me. "I don't understand. You—you are a part of Cyrbus."

His voice was gentle, yet gutting. "Did you get to choose what life you woke up in? Did you know instantly you didn't belong?"

No. I would've spent the rest of my days—and even in death, believing I was a failure.

"How do you know?"

He huffed a laugh, grabbing a prickly vine dangling between us, seeming to care little about the thorns. "Aside from the obvious—not having any recollection of my life—it didn't take much to put it together when you're involved with the organization that does it." He dropped the vine, placing a hand on the pommel of his dagger as a growl traveled through the night.

I held my breath when he left his tree and leaned against the back of mine, leaving only a trunk between us. His voice carried from the other side as he said, "I assume you received an explanation for why you couldn't remember, correct? Well, mine was that I volunteered as a test subject. I believed them, too. At least, until I started having flashbacks."

"You have flashbacks?" I gasped, grateful he couldn't see my failing composure.

"They're vague. But they're enough to make me question everything."

I paused . . . This was the most he'd spoken all night. What could he possibly have to gain from revealing all this to me?

I bit my lip, unsure how long it would take him to notice if I fled. I scanned my surroundings, looking for gaps between the gnarly roots. "Were they about your brother?"

He appeared in front of me and I jolted, scraping my back against the tree. "No, they weren't about my half brother," he bitterly pointed out, the only fracture I'd seen in his rigid composure. "He was a part of the story they gave me. I assume they left him in since there was a possibility of interacting with him. And considering how much he hates me, I don't believe their narrative was far off. I'm sure you can attest to that." He laughed quietly. "I can't say I blame him. He believes I did this to you."

"If you didn't, why haven't you told him? Why haven't you shared with him what happened to you?"

A soothing cry of thunder vibrated through the trees, silencing the jungle as he admitted, "Because I don't know what the truth is. While I didn't play a role in your kidnapping, I have contributed to countless others."

That was the signal to run. I'd received my answers, there was no reason to stay. If anything, him divulging this information was worrisome. There's no harm in being honest with someone when they won't live to tell your secrets.

But I couldn't stop the slowing of my pulse, the concern as I saw the pain riddled through him, hidden beneath his callous surface. Pain I wanted to ease, if only because I shared the same loss and emptiness. Before I could stop myself, I reached for his hand, a small attempt to soothe him. His eyes widened when he noted the movement and he not-so-subtly jerked over to another tree, slipping out of my reach.

I clutched my filthy, worn cloak between my hands and blinked through my burning eyes, disgusted with how badly I wanted to feel him again. What was wrong with me?

The burning in my eyes leaked free when he whispered, "I'm only trying to do what's best for you."

Perhaps it was because I was lost, or I believed the mild, sputtering rain dripping down the canopy would conceal my secrets. Regardless,

I didn't hide the shaking in my voice. "Then why the other night? Why would you risk exposing yourself to me?"

Beads of rain caught on his thick lashes, sliding down his cheeks. "I don't know. Before I could realize what I'd done, you had already taken my hand. But I saw you and I had to know. Nothing else mattered."

I needed to leave. A harsh reality existed outside of this engrossing jungle of magic, one where Caelum worked with Cyrbus and I was their victim. But I was here, and I couldn't bring myself to leave—to abandon what it felt like to have someone truly see me. "You had to know what?"

"You." Every fiber in my lonely, foolish soul quivered with anticipation when he lifted his hand, anxious for his touch, only to rapidly perish when he only stuffed it in his pocket instead. "I didn't anticipate seeing one of their projects there." He paused, noting how I winced at the word—a reminder of how little they valued life. "But I especially didn't expect to see the person who consumes my memories." His fierce gaze held mine, full of a different, new vulnerability.

I looked down at my boots, mushing the ground beneath them. I sucked in a shaky breath, finding the air thicker than before I'd learned I dwelled in his mind. Not only my present self, but a version I didn't know, one who shared memories with him. Aramis wasn't lying about my relationship with his brother, and I was so foolish to doubt him.

The desire to beg for details of my life was almost unbearable. But I couldn't encourage him, nor could I trust him. Even if I felt the surety in each word, as real as the rain washing away the mud on my skin.

"Are you staying with Cyrbus?" I boldly stared into his cloudlike eyes, willing them to part so I might see his true self.

I already knew his answer, but my airway tightened regardless as he said, "I don't have any other options."

"How can you say that?" My voice rose as I forgot who I spoke to. "How can you know all that they do—what they did to you—and still stay?"

"This is who I am," he pressed, his tone sharp and desperate. He paused and blew out a breath, his voice no longer harsh. "I have nowhere else to go. It's different for you. Your life was mourned. But everyone believed I chose this path—and even if they believed differently, they're strangers to me now. It's easier to stay like this." He retreated from my gaze. "There comes a point when you must accept your fate and live with it. This is me accepting mine."

I didn't care if it was my own tears or rain streaming down my cheeks. "Well, I don't accept this fate. I refuse to believe I was meant for nothing more than to be discarded like trash. There has to be more than feeling like this. Feeling like my soul was stolen from me, leaving me hollow and broken. Or that my entire existence is sitting on a teetering edge, waiting to plummet into a black hole." I stepped forward, inhaling a somehow familiar whiff of pine. "I am more than Cyrbus's property. I deserve the chance to live."

Raindrops pestered my vision, blurring it as his face eased and he tentatively lifted his hand, gauging my reaction. I stopped breathing, unable to move as he brushed a curl behind my ear and whispered, "Don't you think I know that? That I believe you deserve the chance to live?"

His words frightened me in the strangest way, so much so I stumbled back into the tree, unable to focus on what it possibly meant for me while his hand stroked mine. Caelum slowly closed the step between us, watching me for any discomfort. But that was the last thing I felt. I could hardly breathe—much less feel anything beyond his rough hand in mine. There was nothing but what I felt for him, what I shouldn't.

"Collins," he murmured. "Collins, you are everywhere in my head. I've tried to fight, but I can't." His eyes glistened like the stars, at last bringing light to the void within me. "You know what I think?"

"What?" I breathed.

"I think somewhere deep inside, you know me." His voice vibrated off my skin as he leaned down, blocking out the world until he became the only being. "It's why you danced with me. Why you ran to me and not away. Why you're still here."

I swallowed, admitting the truth with a nod when my ability to form words evaded me.

"I believe you feel something for me, and it terrifies you, probably as much as it does me." There was nothing I could do to stop how I shivered as his hot breath kindled my ear, surely setting my hair on fire. "I should've run the moment you revealed yourself. Because now I don't think I can fight this." His voice turned guttural. "I don't want to fight it."

Mistake.

Each gasping breath I drew confirmed that notion. I'd traveled too far down this dangerous path, inviting trouble along the way. Caelum was awful, unacceptable in every sense, destroying lives despite bearing the same wounds he inflicted. And I was the fool who was drawn to him. Or at least that was the lie I kept telling myself, not trusting my broken mind that believed he was something more than what Cyrbus had created.

Heat radiated between us, inviting one of us to close the space. I stared at the rain trailing down his chest, not trusting myself to look up at him. I should've fought and shoved him away, but I wasn't his captive. I knew I should leave, but every despicable piece of me begged to stay.

Kind, tender eyes greeted me as his fingers gently lifted my chin, so at odds with the man he was. He was beautiful, so much so it was wrong, just like the way he was looking at me. Our hearts pulsed together into the silence while we watched one another, searching for any explanation as to what this was.

I leaned into his feverish touch as he cupped my cheek. My pounding heart drowned out anything but us while his calloused fingers traced my scar, then made their way to my collarbone. His touch radiated a fire into me, as if my nerves were feeling for the first time.

"Caelum," I murmured, at last tasting his name. "Caelum." I hated and relished the sound of it while I traced a finger down his neck, studying every inch of him. He flinched beneath my touch, like he felt the same intensity I did, before he tangled his hands into my hair, persuading a small gasp to slip my lips.

Logic screamed at me to stop, beating against the walls I put up in my mind, but my body ignored it. I deeply breathed him in, finding it so intoxicating I could've consumed all the air between us. If I survived this, I'd roll in pine, so as to live with that smell forever.

My hands meandered down his neck and broad shoulders, feeling the planes under his leather jacket. He joined in my exploration and brushed his fingers over my lips, then traced the freckles on my cheeks, as if he could draw constellations between them.

"Collins," he breathed, leaving a ghost of a touch down my sides, surely to haunt me forever. "Collins." A smile formed on his lips, and I realized my name felt so right sliding off his tongue I could listen to him call for me the rest of my life. "This is . . ." He trailed off, but there was no need for words.

Each innocent and simple touch left me wanting more. For a moment, I easily forgot who he and I were and listened only to the desire in my barren soul, selfishly wanting to feel more alive. I slid my hands up his chest, marveling at the sharpness of his jaw. I couldn't help but grin, triumphant as I tangled my fingers into his no-longer-neat, silky hair. I gasped when his hands locked on my waist, pressing against me as he pinned me to the tree. His soft breaths caressed my face, tickling the edge of my hairline while we locked eyes. But neither of us moved, both of us begging the other to bravely close the distance. Neither willing to take that first shaky step. Perhaps because we knew, in the end, this wouldn't change anything.

But I refused to accept that fate.

I smiled and pushed past the flutter in my stomach and reached up on my toes. My trembling lips had almost brushed his when a woman's voice clawed through my bravery, slicing the bubble consuming us.

"Caelum, I must say—when I said to keep her occupied, this was hardly what I had in mind." Iveh stomped through the creek, each step fracturing this absurd fantasy until only the devastating reality remained. And if her words weren't enough proof of how foolish I'd been, the sharp blade of truth Caelum held to my ribs confirmed it.

Conon followed Iveh, shoving a bound Aramis to the ground. His disgusted, agonized eyes told me all I needed to know. Perhaps Aideen did still live within me, as I had yet again made the same stupid mistake.

Maybe I didn't deserve the chance to live after all.

Iveh's growing grin seemed to agree with me.

Chapter Twenty-One

I was beginning to believe thoughts had a way of manifesting themselves—as now I was certain that Aita's sun would never embrace me again. But I couldn't find it in myself to truly care. Not when my own hands had led me here. And now I'd lost the right to do anything when I was forced into suffocating darkness, the only proof this was real the manacles digging into my wrists, holding me against frigid stones.

That and Aramis's sullen shadow served as company.

The darkness wouldn't let me cower, forcing me to relive the betrayal in Aramis's eyes when he saw Caelum and me. Watching as I familiarized myself with his brother, allowing him to mark me in a way that I still felt his deceitful touch. And even if our heads hadn't been shoved into sacks before they forced us to Drift with them, I knew Aramis would never look at me the same.

He couldn't unsee me as the girl who wasted his sacrifice and devotion with my own selfish desires—desires that would likely lead us to our deaths.

I sucked in a shallow breath, rot and dirt filling my lungs. A small cry slipped through my chapped lips when I strained to adjust my throbbing shoulders. "Aramis," I whispered into the dreary cell. "I'm sorry."

No answer was carried back. If I hadn't heard his chains snap into place after they shoved us in here, I wouldn't have known he was with me. Maybe his presence should've offered comfort, but I would have rather been alone.

Salt coated my lips while I blinked through tears, a sour aftertaste after being graced with Aita's rain. A last simple gift I hadn't taken the time to cherish, as I was too captivated with Caelum to notice the heavenly, pure scents filling the air. Too blind to see the deception in Caelum's beautiful, shadowed eyes.

I'd forgotten that beautiful things still held the power to harm.

I didn't know how long we knelt there, my throbbing knees offering no measure of time, when Aramis's voice sliced through the shadows. "I'm trying to find every excuse for what I saw. I keep lying to myself that he was forcing you, that you were fighting back." He paused, releasing a tight breath. "But I saw you. I watched you welcome his hands and smile at him, like you hadn't just fought to escape him while he tried to drag you from me again." Chains clanked while he rasped a laugh. "This is why I didn't tell you about him. Because I knew what would happen when you learned the truth. Only I didn't anticipate you dragging me down with you."

"You're right," I whispered, allowing his truthful words to writhe into my mind. "And I know there's nothing I can do to fix this, but you have to know how truly sorry I am. I will—"

Aramis cut through my apology. "You're sorry for what, Aideen? That I'm not enough for you regardless of what I do?"

"That's not what this is."

"Then what is it?"

"I am—" I cleared my throat, forcing myself not to break. "I'm lost, Aramis. I know I screwed up badly and you're right to be angry, but it wasn't a matter of whether or not you're good enough. You don't understand what it's like to not know who you are or understand your purpose in this world. I'm only trying to find myself."

My core chilled when Aramis laughed, worse than the bleak, stiff air trapped between us. "Well, I have a feeling I'm about to find out. It's a real shame I won't be around to see if you make the same mistake a third time."

I choked back emotion, unable to voice it, when a blinding light filled the room. I winced and blinked as a figure emerged, his ghostly hair absorbing the sun's glare. Conon's grin reached his crimson-colored eyes when he taunted, "Ready to play, Little Doll?"

I lay atop an altar, the cool concrete branding my skin, eternal bellows drifting in with the bitter draft. My ebony shirt was ragged, as torn as Aramis's pleas when I was dragged from the cell. My raw wrists were useless, despite not wearing a single restraint. My body lay heavily, unable to move past an unknown weight. A weight that increased as an herb of some sort—smelling of acidic lavender—was rubbed over me by a frail woman who bore a similar tattoo to Conon and Caelum, winding down her tender, lethal hands.

But nothing froze my rattling bones more than the bright red eyes surveying me. Moonlight carried through his skin, somehow not offering even a crevice of peace. Especially when Conon's bony finger scraped my cheek. "There's something exhilarating about being in the presence of your past successes." He cocked a silver brow. "You can't remember at all, can you?"

Perhaps it was because I knew my fate was unchangeable, but I didn't hesitate before I said, "Obviously." I smirked, making good use of my only working body part. "I would have a hard time forgetting a rat on my own."

His cackle slithered through my exhausted, lifeless nerves. "If my memory serves correctly, you spoke with such flattery before." Silver strands pooled over me as he leaned lower and gripped my jaw, blocking my view of the everflame above me. "This time I'll be thorough, ensuring no bit of you remains." His grip hardened as his finger slipped between my lips. "Maybe I'll even slice off your tongue for good measure."

He hissed as I bit his finger, gagging on his filthy taste. I braced myself for his retribution when rage immersed his beady eyes and he raised a solid fist. He lowered it just as the steel door grinded open, leaving his other hand on my jaw. I wasn't sure if I would've preferred Conon's fist or Iveh's triumphant smile.

The pit in my stomach swelled as Iveh filled the room, leaving the door open. Her striking gaze landed on his hand wrapped around me. "Alderick told you no games, Conon."

"Everyone tells me that." His fingers firmly squeezed my jaw once more, earning a whimper from my lips before he released his hold. "You of all people should understand I have a particular process in these things. Collins and I were only reacquainting ourselves."

Iveh shrugged off her russet cloak, revealing her slender, soft frame, deceptively lethal. Conon also seemed to sense her hidden strength, stepping back when she approached the altar. "There's a perfectly good toy you can play with down the hall. Alderick won't want her brain scrambled until after he sees her."

Even if I wasn't ridden with drugs, I wouldn't have moved while she ran her eyes over me, scrutinizing every flaw. She clicked her tongue. "You've given me quite the headache."

I summoned my last ounce of bravado. "Likewise."

Her raven curls bounced as she shrugged. "Frankly, I don't understand why you're here. If it was up to me, I would've ensured you didn't see the sun rise again the moment you touched foot on Aita." She crossed her arms over her chest, revealing the coiling tattoo on her right arm, one she'd successfully hidden on Earth. "I'm afraid your escape has wounded Alderick's confidence in our system, and now he's compelled us to see if we missed something."

I didn't have a chance to interpret her words or try to understand who Alderick was before a new voice drew air from the room. "I already told you, she doesn't remember a thing."

I didn't follow Iveh's gaze to him, unable to face my mistake. I focused on Iveh's hand gripping the altar, trying to make out the ink covering her arm, one they all seemed to share. "Last I checked, Caelum, I don't answer to you. And seeing as how you and Conon almost allowed her to escape again, you're hardly in a position to question me or Alderick."

Caelum's voice tightened, as sharp as the dagger he'd threatened me with. "If you and Weylin hadn't vanished, we would be rid of this problem already. Where did Alderick summon you to go?"

Problem. My useless body allowed his words to plant within my heart, forcing me to acknowledge how much of a fool I was.

"Don't worry about things that don't pertain to you, Caelum." Iveh's laugh drained the everflame's comfort and warmth. "If anything, tonight has proved how incapable you are. Both of you get distracted too easily."

My cheek rested against the bleak concrete slab as I followed her steps. She crossed her arms across her beige shirt while she leaned against the wall, looking from me to Conon. While Conon and Iveh were vastly different in appearance, I realized there was a disturbing balance between them.

Which could only mean carnage after Iveh winked at Conon and said, "Regardless of Alderick's wishes, I believe you and I deserve to have our own fun after the thorn Collins has been." She trailed Conon out of the room, pausing where Caelum stood at the door. "For research purposes, of course."

I never confirmed whether or not she left, unwilling to look away from the crevices and grooves of the stone ceiling. Even when a new warmth swelled in the air around me, rekindling my nerves, despite the absence of his touch. But there was nothing I could do to drown out his low, deceitful voice. "I meant what I said. I do believe you deserve the chance to live. This is me giving you that chance."

His words barely kissed the air, burning into me, before the door slid shut, leaving me utterly alone.

"Stop," I gasped. "Please, stop." My tears burned with the everflame in the iron brazier above, a silent witness. "No more." My head pounded as Iveh's figure slipped back into my vision, morphing into Conon's ghostly frame. But a blink later, his bloodied eyes had vanished, leaving only her.

My fingertips shook against the rough granite of the concrete altar. I stepped off the carousel of hallucinations, struggling to unravel one from the next. The only surety I had that this was real was when Iveh and Conon returned—there was never a lapse in pain. If it wasn't the pounding ache within my skull, it was the eruption of panic and agony from within.

This was the longest breath of reality I'd had—a break from the drug or something laced in the air that was making me dwell in a perpetual free fall. I didn't know truly what was sending me under. I knew nothing but the cruel delusions now marking my soul, making me live moments I pleaded weren't real. Aramis's screams filled my mind as Caelum stabbed him. Forcing me to watch while he slowly drained the life from Aramis, as I did absolutely nothing to stop him, unable to even wash away the blood.

It's not real.

I must've said those words aloud, because Iveh's eyes suddenly blocked the everflame's comfort. "It's unfair that I'm unable to view what's happening inside your head. I'm being cheated—I can only see what your body does while you're immersed." I shivered as she ran a finger down my cheek, taunting me with the ring around her finger. "I can draw my own conclusions, of course. But I am curious." Her burgundy lips hovered around my ear after she slipped out of my vision. "Why do you scream for Caelum and not Aramis?" Her nail wiped a betraying tear slipping down my cheek.

Another fell free when Conon blocked the everflame next, his own eyes ablaze. I clenched my jaw shut, huffing through my nose as the sharp, invisible blow from within claimed my mind again. "That's enough of a break," he whispered, settling me within the dark.

I groaned at the overpowering light slipping through my closed eyes, enticing me out of unconsciousness. I strained to rub them but my arms wouldn't move, courtesy of Conon and Iveh's drug.

My pounding head worsened when I pried open my eyelids, opening and closing them repeatedly until the light dimmed. I tilted my head, neck aching, perplexed as to why the everflame had transformed into little suns. I silently stared at them until at last my mind grasped they were only fluorescent lights.

But . . .

Those didn't exist on Aita.

Heart racing, I tried to roll over but failed. At least this time there was a source. My wrists ached in agony as I yanked against the straps binding me atop a metal table. The white-tiled room blurred as I examined it, finding a tray of medical instruments beside me. I caught sight of the blue plastic operating gown draped over my body and my stomach rolled.

Where had Cyrbus taken me? An infirmary?

Hearing approaching voices, I stopped a scream before it could depart my lungs. I willed my breathing to slow and fluttered my eyes shut.

"She's right in here." An unknown man spoke as the door creaked open, inviting a blasting chill in with him. "You can examine the package to guarantee it meets your standards. Of course, you must understand it's impossible to find an exact match." My eyes pulsed under their lids, begging to see who was leering over me. "If you're unsatisfied, I'll need to know so I can make further arrangements."

"You're certain this will work?" It was another man, deeper and faintly familiar, but I couldn't place the voice.

"She won't know any different, allowing her to become anyone you need her to be."

My muscles sagged in my binds, heavy with panic and dread while I contained the scream within my burning chest. I wasn't in an infirmary. I was being sold again.

"How long?" the second man asked, his clammy fingers touching my arm, and I fought the urge to flinch.

"It'll be a few weeks." I teetered on an edge when he paused. "We'll need to take her back to complete the process. After that, we'll need time to ensure her mind is fully subdued."

I willed my heartbeat to slow, fearing they would hear it. *I'm going to forget again.*

"She has her red hair, Peter." It was a woman's voice that triggered me, though I'd never heard it with such gentleness.

Peter?

My eyes opened, confirming my worst fear. Standing above me were my parents, with no emotion or recognition on their faces. "No!" I fought against my binds, metal digging into my wrists. "I won't go back. No." Their faces didn't falter, unfazed by my pleas—if anything, they were younger and hopeful while they watched me struggle, hardly seeing me at all.

"Kill me! Kill me!" I screamed, until an unknown source of liquid was poured onto me, choking my cries. I couldn't see what gripped my arms and shoved me against the cool metal. I gasped as the water filled my lungs and blindly thrashed against their hold until a sharp prick shot a blazing fire into my arm.

My muscles turned to stone, weighing me against the table. No longer was I drowning, but my vision continually blurred, until their faces disappeared into nothing. I grasped on to consciousness, willing myself to stay alive. But it was too much—too hard. I wanted to give in.

So I did.

Chapter Twenty-Two

The darkness didn't depart with my slow, broken blinks. My wrists hung heavily from chains above me, but I didn't know if this was real. If the bitter liquid dripping from my hair and pooling at my knees was really there. If the hollow screams rattling off the stone walls and into my mind were authentic.

Nor did I know if the concerned voice splintering the shadows was truly Aramis. "Aideen, talk to me." His voice broke. "Talk to me, please. Tell me you're okay."

"I'm okay," I lied, needing to soothe him, protect him—prove this wasn't one of my nightmares. Those had been before and after the hallucination of Peter and Jane. *I think.*

Wet curls clung to my face as I sagged, adding to the pressure on my knees. The darkness thickened, nearly pulling me under again before Aramis said, "I vow I will get you out of here." Chains rattled somewhere beyond my sight and I flinched. "I'll do whatever it takes to get us out of here. And then you and I will go home, okay? We'll go home and start over, Aideen."

But I didn't know where home was.

I didn't know who I was.

"Collins," I whispered to myself, pleading that Aita's magic would pity me and hide it within my mind. "Your name is Collins and you're from Kaira. You live atop the highest hill, in a home within a grand tree, where the forest comes to life at night. Your parents—" I closed my eyes, unable to say it—to face it.

"Your parents are Alois and Selene Stallard," Aramis whispered.

Something in me reacted at the sound of their names—my family name—inviting my wayward soul to come back.

"Your parents are Alois and Selene Stallard," I whispered again, this time fervently. Tears slid through my closed eyes, washing away the grime. "Cyrbus may have stolen your memories and sold you. But they didn't steal your soul. Regardless of what happens, there is a purposeful life ahead of you. You will not hide and continue to allow Cyrbus to erase the minds of those they deem insignificant and unloved."

The darkness seemed to lapse when I opened my eyes, as if the golden ring within them truly glowed. "You're going to find the light."

Chapter Twenty-Three

The swaying everflames within the brazier burned bright as I watched them, as if they sensed the change in the air. Igniting a new sense of focus and purpose. Even my limbs didn't hang quite as uselessly against the altar. My mind was clear, aware this was real, as Iveh and Conon had yet to arrive with their concoction of drugs. Which meant I was finally awake enough to get the hell out of this place.

I sucked in a deep breath and looked at my last chance leaning against the door. Lifeless, heavy circles rested beneath his bored eyes. He hadn't said a word to me since I'd last seen him—not that I knew how many days or hours had passed.

"How do you know your flashbacks are real?"

He flinched at my bold question and tightened his jaw, sealing my answer in before he faced the opposite wall. But if he thought turning his back would deter me, he was wrong.

"I dreamed I was being sold again." I bit my cheek, grounding myself with the pain. "I'm not sure if it was real or something they created. It wasn't like a typical dream—I *experienced* everything. Almost like I was two people at once. I was aware of this life, but not enough to fully understand what was happening. But even then, once I saw Peter and Jane, I was absolutely terrified."

Heat rushed through my cheeks when it was clear silence was the only answer I'd receive. I didn't know why I believed he'd care. Why

I suddenly hoped he would be my chance at freedom—to perhaps finally see Kaira. Find out if the forest of flame was nothing more than a figment of my imagination or perhaps a treasured space from home.

Just when I was about to depart into the flaming forest, desperate for escape, Caelum whispered, “I knew it wasn’t a dream because it was unlike anything I’d experienced in this life. Such happiness doesn’t exist here.” He kept his back to me, unable to face me after admitting something so intimate.

I didn’t know what to make of it, unsure if he was referring to the memories he shared with me. But I didn’t have time to care, not when I needed to sway him.

“Is there a reason you stay?” My voice was mellow, genuinely curious. “If you’re so unhappy, why haven’t you left?”

Caelum finally turned, his eyes glazed while he thought it over. “Were you happy with the life you were given?”

“No, I wasn’t.”

“Then why didn’t you leave?”

I bit my lip, gnawing over my answer. “Because I was scared. I didn’t have anywhere else to go. I didn’t know how to survive on my own.” My own words sank in.

We really weren’t different at all.

He crossed his arms over his chest, kicking a boot up against the door. “It’s not so easy then, is it? To abandon the only thing you know? They were your family, and this is the only one I’ve somewhat had.”

“But I left,” I pointed out with a shaky voice, desperate for him to understand. Maybe it was foolish to believe a word he’d shared before he deceived me, but I couldn’t shake how real it felt. “I couldn’t stay with them after learning what they’d done.”

I flinched as he snapped, “Your entire family died and you were sent worlds away.” He paused, softening his tone, as if he regretted the pain his words inflicted, the tears in my eyes. “My own brother spent years searching for you. I was still here, on Aita, yet no one came for me.

I forgot everyone and they may as well have forgotten me." He hid his hands in his pockets, but not before I saw their trembling. "They already think I chose this, so why should I be any different? No one cares what I do."

"I do." I turned my burning eyes toward the ceiling. "I care."

Beyond my capacity of understanding, it was true. Maybe because his decision directly affected me. But in some strange way, he and I were connected.

Really, more than anything, I wished for him to be free.

I could share with him how his mother had Aramis search for him, but it wouldn't fix anything. Caelum was right. My family was dead, leaving me little reason to be found, while he had been here the whole time and they hadn't helped him. Aramis had abandoned him solely because he believed Caelum harmed me, never allowing him to explain. I wouldn't condone his cowardice, but I could see his reluctance to leave.

He had no home.

"I'll help you, Caelum." I looked at him, letting him see the truth there.

He stared, long and hard. "And where will I go? Do you believe anyone will accept me after what I've done? That Aramis would allow me anywhere near you?"

I rolled my eyes, resisting the urge to clarify that Aramis didn't decide anything for me. This wasn't the time. "We can explain. It's not your fault this happened to you."

He shook his head, running a firm hand down his face. "I know what you're trying to do, and it won't work." He lifted the hand wearing his ring, pleading with me, eyes wide and sincere. "I can't help you. There's nothing more I can do for you than what I already am. You'll go back to Peter and Jane, and it'll be like none of this happened."

My voice broke, betraying me. "Do you truly think that's offering me a chance to live? I will die if I go back there!"

"Collins, this is not a life worth remembering."

I clenched my fists, wishing I had the strength to shake him. "Then why?" I seethed. "Why bother sharing your flashbacks with me? Why would you let me believe for even a moment that you were with me?"

"Because this will be the last time you remember who I am." His chest rose faster. "You will forget me, but I will remember you. And I couldn't bear to have my last moments with you be anything but the truth."

Tears slid down my temples, falling to the altar in defeat. "I don't want to forget." I turned my face to see him, letting him see my hurt. "I don't want to forget anything, Caelum."

The air thickened with the truth while he stared at me, holding himself in place as he gripped the handle of the door. He opened his mouth to say something, but then stopped and turned away, ready to rid himself of me.

But not before I could utter one last attempt. "Do you think I'll remember your name again?"

The quiet click of the steel door sliding into place was my only answer.

Iveh sat at the foot of the altar, swinging her legs over the edge like this was nothing more than a pleasant day with a friend, paying little attention to the flecks of dried mud falling onto her leather pants from my boots. Somehow forgetting that moments ago she and Conon had drunk themselves silly on my pleas while they submerged me into a montage of hallucinations.

But this time, only Iveh remained.

She patted my useless knees before she leaped off onto the concrete floor, stretching her arms up as she yawned. "Well, as fun as it has been to acquaint myself with you, I'm afraid our time has come to an end."

"Pity." My hand strained, failing to extend her a final farewell. "You should wash me clean of these herbs so I can give you a proper hug goodbye."

Her smile didn't thaw the ice in her eyes, somehow colder than those brief moments in Eirlys's wintery climate. "As fun as that might be, I'll have to pass. I have one last task before I can be rid of you." She leaned down to her boot, revealing a dagger she'd stuffed away. She pressed the point against the tip of her finger, its bronze blade no larger than my hand. "Alderick is anything but wasteful and I did vow to be thorough."

A swell of hot air washed over me as she stepped closer, slowly soaking in my discomfort as I fumbled, "This seems like a lot of wasted time if you're only going to erase my mind and send me back to Earth."

She cocked her head, ponytail swaying, and halted at the edge of the concrete. "Oh dear, you really are as dull as you look." She flicked her wrist, taunting me with the blade. "Is that what Caelum's led you to believe? That you'd walk out of this alive?" Her cold laugh vanquished any remnants of hope. "I'm impressed. That man plays more games than I thought."

I bit my lip, refusing to reveal the hurt forming in my eyes. Iveh clicked her tongue and traced a finger down my forearm, hard enough I experienced every point where her nail pressed in. "As I've said, Alderick isn't wasteful. And since you've proven you're incapable of being quiet and happy in the life you were sold into, that leaves you with only one option."

Pounding blood filled my ears as I croaked, "Which is?"

She hovered her dagger over my rapid chest, the jewels within the dagger's hilt a mirror to her eyes. "After we prove you'd be useless to Alderick, we'll dispose of you." Before I could ask another question—a lame excuse to bargain for more time—she gripped the edge of my wrist and pressed the dagger's sharp edge into my arm. "Let us see if you're worthy of carrying Cyrbus's mark."

The herbs once carefully slathered onto me yielded the moment the fine point was met with blood. I couldn't manage to even wiggle my toes, but I felt every agonizing slice. I gasped for air, as if the blood coating my arm was filling my lungs instead, while she intricately carved between my freckles, marking me in a similar manner to the ink across her own arm. Warm liquid caressed my side as she wiped my blood free, as if it was nothing more than paint covering her work. Iveh smiled, satisfied with my tattered and torn skin, where crimson continued to seep free.

My chest heaved as I blinked through tears, unable to control my sobs even after Iveh stepped back and declared, "As I said, useless."

I didn't know how this test possibly proved anything—as my body reacted how any normal one would—but perhaps I'd find the answer in death.

Fog trailed me while I slipped in and out of a delusion, unsure why Iveh and Conon were dragging this out after having completed their task. Nor did I understand why Caelum blocked the door, shouting at the kind woman who patched up my arm—though I suppose she wasn't that kind since she was the one repeatedly drugging me. But this time, her hands didn't lather me with the acidic herbs, at least not before Caelum stormed in.

I scowled, earning a sharp jolt of pain as I willed him to vanish from my mind. If I was about to greet death, I didn't want him with me. Not after learning he'd beguiled me all along.

Go away.

Be gone.

Shoo.

Caelum's muffled shouts stopped when he looked at me, with what I swear was a flicker of a grin. But when I blinked, it was gone.

I lifted my throbbing arm, the movement spreading red across the white bandages. I closed my eyes, running a heavy hand over my temple while I focused on the noise I'd blocked out.

"—you're going to get us both killed. Leave now or I will report you." It was the woman, her voice thick with urgency.

"Don't make threats you don't mean, Akira. Or I will follow through on my own." His voice was harsh, so much so I opened my eyes, shocked to find him looming over the woman with a dagger in his hand.

Akira didn't back away but clenched her small olive hands into fists. "You know as much as I do there's nothing more anyone could inflict upon me."

Caelum's face softened and he stepped back, returning his dagger to his hip. "I'm sorry." His hand grabbed her wrist, stopping her as she tried to move around him. "Please, Akira."

Her aged, elegant face looked back at me, wearing something that appeared to be sorrow. A long black braid swayed at her frail hips as she shook her head, muttering in a language I couldn't decipher.

Caelum stepped out of her way when she slid her wrist free, allowing her to walk to the door. She paused and looked back, just as Caelum slid to the ground, hiding his head between his knees. "I have to gather more herbs to clear her system. They want her mind and body fully awake before they put her down." Her friendly golden eyes slid to mine when she firmly said, "You will be gone, Caelum."

My hallucination seemed to falter, shifting when she passed through the doorway. I closed my eyes, ready to flee to another delusion. But before I could, sturdy hands slid beneath my knees and back. My head spun when I was lifted up and pressed into a solid surface that smelled of pine.

My heavy eyes only allowed me a glimpse of Caelum grabbing my hand and replacing the ring he'd stolen. "What are you doing?" I rasped.

His eyes slid to mine, safe and grounding. "I'm taking you home, Collins."

Chapter Twenty-Four

No longer was there a sharp altar resting against my back. Nor did the comforting everflame hang above me, a beacon to hold on to. I wasn't wrapped in acid and pain, once as consistent as the faint screams embedded in my mind.

Instead, I stared at musty drapes and strands of light breaking in, the first I'd seen in days. Broken pleas had been replaced with soft flutters of wings and shifting trees, proof happiness still existed. The only consistent variable from this hallucination and the last—was Caelum.

I watched him from beneath my lashes where he sat at a cramped wooden table, his own eyes fluttering shut while he leaned on a sturdy arm. Any time they lingered closed for too long, he jerked himself awake, the chair beneath him groaning. A strand of pity slipped into my delusion at the shadows beneath his eyes, deeper than before. When was the last time he'd truly rested? If he was forced to dwell in my mind, the least I could offer him was rest.

"You should sleep," I breathed through my dry mouth, the edge of my tongue foreign and wrong. Before I could say more, Caelum was up and overwhelming my vision, stopping after I retreated deeper into the plush mattress, unsure of his urgency.

He knelt beside the bed, looking down at me. "I didn't mean to startle you. That's just the most coherent thing you've said in hours."

My brows furrowed, the absoluteness of his voice confusing me. His lovely, hard features were as clear as day, so much so I could remember how they felt beneath my hands. I blinked repeatedly, watching as the crease between his eyes softened. He raised a scarred brow.

"Why are you here?" I asked, growing tired of waiting for him to disappear.

He reached for a glass bowl atop the nightstand beside the bed, wringing a rag out above it. "I need to change this." He motioned toward the rag I hadn't noticed resting across my forehead. His fingertips brushed my hair back and replaced the damp rag, casting a fresh mint aroma over me. "This will help your head."

I settled deeper into the mattress, savoring the peace before this delusion faded, knowing the singing calls and welcoming breeze would vanish. But they remained, ever after the intensity of the mint fled.

Tears lined my eyes while I watched Caelum, his steady breaths mixing with mine. I shook my head and picked at the maroon patchwork quilt covering me. "Is this real? Did you truly bring me home?"

"Yes." He quietly glided to the kitchen, filling the humble space. "It's real."

My breaths were steady, savoring how it felt to have Kaira's air filling my lungs, igniting the vitality within me. I was home. It didn't matter what I had endured, I had done it—I survived. But before my relief could truly burn, it was smothered out.

My blinks were quick, excessive while I glanced around the room, nothing more than four logged walls with a modest kitchen, wood stove, and discarded bathroom to the side. Leaving me in the center of the refreshing pine cabin. On the bed.

Alone with Caelum.

"Where is Aramis?" I whispered sharply. "Where is he?"

"What?" His voice filled the kitchen while he searched the cupboards. "Collins—" He shook his head, facing me. "We're not on Aita. Why would Aramis be here?"

"But—" I sat up, wincing at the intrusion of brisk air from where the blankets fell from me. My voice grew cold as I understood what he'd done. "Tell me you didn't bring me back to Earth." He ignored me, his attention back on the nearly empty set of cabinets, and heat crept up my cheeks. "Tell me you didn't!"

He crossed his arms, leaning against the wall. "I don't understand the confusion. I told you I was taking you home."

The quiet, charming noises of this world shifted into deafening silence. A world I'd be damned if I spent another moment in. I ignored the rampant warnings firing through my body as I stood, clenching an iron headboard in hopes the room would steady.

"You—you are—" I flung my arms out, exasperated at his relaxed composure. "You are an absurd, arrogant ass! How dare you bring me back here." Sweat dripped down my brows, burning my eyes. "And you're nothing more than a coward! How could you leave Aramis behind? What is wrong with you?"

He sucked in a deep breath, stuffing his hands into his pockets. "Aramis is not my concern."

"I am not your concern!" I cried, ignoring the lapse in his stoic expression. "Do you have any idea what they'll do to him? Killing him would be the kindest option!"

I groaned, pushing through my rolling stomach while I searched the room for my things, tossing the pillows and quilts on the floor. "Where are my clothes?" I knelt to look beneath the bed, not letting myself dwell on the fact he'd dressed me in a fresh, oversized sweatshirt and leggings which weren't mine. I hadn't fully stuffed my feet into my surprisingly clean boots before I clenched my bare hands. "Where is my ring?"

Caelum remained against the wall, unfazed when I closed the distance and seethed up at him, "Give me my ring. Now." He shook his head, holding my gaze while he reached into his pocket and dropped the ring into my shaking hand. His voice was quiet, faint when he said, "There's nothing for you to use to connect with a Gateway. You're better off accepting Earth as your home."

I sucked in deep breaths, letting his words stir over in my mind. I knew little of Drifting, only knowing magic powered the beacons on Aita, allowing us to travel through the realms. But there wasn't magic here. And when I'd last left Earth, Aramis had us use a hurricane. Something about needing natural energy to connect to the Gateway. But unless rage was capable of stirring up a storm, I knew by the mild sky outside this room, I was stuck here.

"Is this it?" I motioned to the room I covered in a matter of furious steps, a tornado destroying its tidy nature. "Is this the home you've intended for me? With you?"

"No," he whispered, looking down at where my navy sweatshirt pressed against his leather-covered chest. "I brought you here solely so you could rest and heal." He slipped out from against the wall, leaving an absence of heat. "Once you've recovered, I'll return to Aita and you'll remain on Earth. You may live any life you desire."

I leaned against the wall, watching while he cleaned up the mess I'd created. He was quiet but swift while he folded the quilts and fluffed the pillows, straightening the burgundy linen curtains. He said nothing when he brought the glass bowl to the sink and washed it clean of the oils, taking my anger with it.

He wasn't cruel to bring me here. He genuinely believed he was helping me, giving me a chance to live.

But I didn't want it.

I hissed when I shoved the sleeves of my shirt up, failing to remember the bandage around my forearm. I pushed back the imagery of what Iveh had done, bleeding the life out of me as she scrawled . . . I shook my head and shoved off the wall. "Thank you for saving me. And for all you did afterwards. But I'm leaving. I need to free Aramis and find a way to stop Cyrbus."

"You what?" He gripped the bowl, slowly setting it down. "Don't tell me you've decided to crown yourself as Aita's liberator." His eyes hardened into cruel pits. "Anything you do for Aramis will be entirely useless by now." He waved a hand at the door. "If you want to waste your life, then go. I won't stop you."

I shivered, despite the uncomfortable warmth building around my neck. "Have you always been this much of an ass?"

His shoulders dropped and he released an exhausted breath. "As long as I can remember."

I watched the floor while I walked to the door, flustered at the tears lining my eyes. "I've been told I'm useless for as long as I can remember. I don't care if it kills me—just once I'd like to prove those voices wrong."

I yanked open the door and walked across the rickety porch, the steps creaking beneath my wobbly steps. A fading sky greeted me, remnants of rosy light behind towering trees. Dry leaves and needles crunched beneath my boots when I quickened my steps, panicking when the door creaked open behind me and closed again.

I bit my cheek, ignoring the silent warnings within my throbbing head as I climbed uphill, each heavy step welcoming another broad trunk. I didn't care that I was mindlessly traveling—anywhere was better than here.

The fading light retreated, translating into darkness and fog. I slipped on the incline, struggling to get myself upright, and sharp points pressed into my palms where I dug into the ground, searching for leverage.

A pleasant pressure found the small of my back, settling me against the forest floor. "I told you, you need to rest. Your system isn't clear."

I ran a sweaty hand through my hair while I rested my head against my knees, breathing through my twisting gut. "I need to get to Aramis."

His shoulder briefly touched mine as he sat down, crunching needles. "How does running off into the woods accomplish that?"

"You told me to leave."

A low laugh caressed the air. "I can't argue with you on that." I fought the desire to lean back into his hand as he brushed my hair off my back, leaving a trail of soothing circles. "I will disagree with you on one thing. I don't believe you're useless." I opened my eyes when his fingers halted, waiting to see if his words would shove me down the hill. "I do think you're underestimating how powerful Cyrbus is—but that has nothing to do with your ability. If I believed you to be useless, I wouldn't have thought you deserved another chance at life."

His words barely had a chance to warm my insides before he rolled to his knees and slipped off his jacket, resting it on my shoulders. I was too enthralled in the familiar, comforting scent to stop him before he hooked his arms beneath my knees and back.

"Let go of me." My eyes were heavy, struggling to remain open while I grappled against his hold. "I can't leave him."

"And you also can't walk."

My rebuttal lodged in my throat as he glided down the incline, entering the gray glaze veiling the forest. I couldn't help but lean into his chest, welcoming his steady heart against my cheek. "Why does it feel like I've been tossed off a cliff?"

His hands tightened while he wound through an aisle of trees. "They had you on an assortment of potent herbs for too long—you're in withdrawal. I don't have the proper ones to fully clear your system. They're helping, but your body is having to make up the rest of the work."

I pressed my forehead deeper into his chest, willing my heart to slow. "There won't be any more nightmares, right?"

"No." His voice softened while he held me tighter. "They can't harm you here."

The cabin came into view as the ground leveled out. In my haste, I hadn't taken the time to look at it. Cabin was too generous of a word—as it better resembled a large shack. Surely the murky light didn't do it justice, but it was hard to miss the sunken roof or leaning stone chimney. Most would probably believe it to be abandoned, never knowing the inside was quite charming.

"Where are we?" I asked as Caelum climbed the steps, catching a glimpse of the night sky through broken gaps in the awning.

"We're in some place called Idaho." He shoved open the groaning door, carrying me over the threshold. "I come here every so often. I remembered it from before."

Idaho? What—are there magical potatoes here or something?

I didn't dare ask about his time on Earth and why he chose here, fearing those visits were truly crimes on behalf of Cyrbus. "And you don't believe Cyrbus is aware of it?"

He eased me onto the bed, holding a firm hand beneath my neck while he lowered it onto the full pillow. "There's plenty Cyrbus doesn't know about me." He left my side and knelt at the end of the bed, grabbing my boot. His hands held firm while I failed to yank it away, earning me a grin across his full lips. "Seeing as you can't walk, I don't see the purpose of you keeping these on."

I slipped it out of his hold, curling my legs to my chest. "I'm more than capable of doing it myself. Besides." I paused, retying my laces. "I'm going to leave here shortly. I might as well save the energy and leave them on."

He groaned, plopping his head into the mattress. His voice was muffled as he said, "This again? Did you forget I had to carry you back from your last attempt?"

I fought the urge to touch his hair, wanting to disrupt its usual neatness. I wrapped my arms around my legs. "What part of *I'm not abandoning him* do you not understand? Just because you hate him—"

"I don't hate him," he whispered into the safety of the mattress. "I have no connection to Aramis. He's a stranger." He looked up, rubbing his scarred brow. "I was focused on getting you out. That was it."

I didn't know why I believed him, especially with his betrayal fresh in my mind. How he'd allowed me to share a piece of myself so he could trap me. I should be angry, fighting against him, because it was his actions that had led to my capture—to Aramis being left behind.

But I was too exhausted to walk, much less be angry. Especially when it was my own selfish desires that had blinded me. But maybe Caelum was blind too, doing what he needed to survive in Cyrbus's world. It seemed wrong to hold it against him when I'd also made an overwhelming amount of mistakes.

"Thank you for saving me." My voice was clear, genuine. "I'm sure you had your own reasons for fleeing Cyrbus, but I'm grateful you freed me."

His cloudlike eyes retreated from mine. "I shouldn't have led you there in the first place."

"It's fine."

"It's not fine." He tightened his jaw, pinching the bridge of his nose. "Collins, about the other night. I need you to und—"

"It's fine," I cut him off, shocked by how deep the wound I carried from that night was, not yet healed from his betrayal. How I'd eagerly welcomed his touch, let him see me. "It doesn't matter anymore." I lifted a hand, stopping him when he opened his mouth. "I need to get to Aramis. Are you going to help me or not?"

"I won't help you."

"Oh." I wasn't shocked by his words, but I was at the pain they inflicted. I cleared my throat, rapidly blinking my eyes. "Then I don't see the need for me to stay here any longer. If you could please tell me how I could Drift from here, I would be grateful," I pressed, assuming we'd Drifted here illegally and not through the Gateway—meaning there had to be a beacon nearby. I knew I couldn't use the magic within the beacon to return to Aita, but I gathered since Caelum had brought us here—with the intention of him returning to Aita—there had to be some sort of energy I could use here to Drift back.

"Collins." He stood as I did, his chest filling my line of sight. I stumbled back into the nightstand, knocking off a lantern. "You may not believe me, but there is still time for Aramis. You don't need to limp off alone and get yourself killed." He gripped my wrist, stopping me when I tried to shove around him. "I will help you find him, but I need you to wait."

I stared at his rough hand, a reminder of how gentle they'd been when they studied my body. I closed my eyes, blocking it out. "You just said you wouldn't help me."

"I won't." My hand fell limply to my side when he dropped it, though he still offered no amount of space. "I will help you find where he is, but that's it. Don't expect any more from me."

"Okay." It left me with complications, but I wouldn't refuse his help. "Why the change of heart?" I asked, unable to shake his betrayal. *This could just be an attempt to force me to stay here.*

"It wasn't fair for me to decide for you." His eyes were glazed but sincere when he looked down at me. "I know that's something no one's let you have the privilege of doing, and I don't want to take that from you. But Collins." He paused, closing the final step between us. I was certain he could feel my pounding heart. "I need you to give me the same gift. Don't ask me to take on Cyrbus with you. I won't survive them again."

His voice broke, his honesty revealing a secret painful journey I knew nothing of. My hand shook when I reached for his. "Thank you, Caelum."

It didn't surprise me when his eyes bore into mine, saying more than our lips could ever share. Maybe I should have been uncomfortable with how intensely he watched me, but I wasn't. I would have let myself look longer if I wasn't aware of how easy it was to get lost in him, to willingly drift into a black hole.

But there wasn't time to get lost with Aramis on the line.

"How long until we can leave?" The tension between us withered away as I backed up against the bed.

He cleared his throat, putting more distance between us while he shrugged on his jacket, covering the tattoo I'd yet to fully study. "In normal situations, there's roughly two to three days of a resting period. They need the mind completely muddled before they can begin. It takes time to fully complete the process. And even if they intend to sell him, they'd have to find a buyer."

I hid my face into my hands and sank back onto the bed, sick at how easily Caelum spoke of what Cyrbus did—what he'd done. I hadn't let myself fully understand the gravity of the situation. I'd sealed Aramis's fate, putting him in the hands of those who sold me. I'd harmed the one who protected me.

The mattress sank and heat radiated against my side. "Collins," Caelum whispered. "While you were being held, they didn't lay a hand on Aramis. I don't believe they have any intentions of selling him, especially now that you and I have escaped. They'll likely hold on to him for bait."

I rubbed my temples, fighting back tears. "How is that supposed to comfort me?"

"I wasn't aware you wanted comfort. I thought you'd want honesty."

I couldn't stop myself from looking up at him, staring at his beautiful, stark face. Wasn't that what I'd wanted all along? To not only hear the brutal, ugly truth, but to decide what I would do with it.

"What is it?" Caelum raised his scarred brow.

I shook my head, laughing quietly to myself. "I'm struggling to understand how you could live among people as vile as Iveh or Conon, yet not be like them."

His eyes darkened, not hearing it for the compliment it was. He stood, his words stripping me bare as he said, "You don't know me. Not truly."

But I wanted to.

But I couldn't be selfish again. "How long until we can leave?"

"Could you settle for two days, starting tomorrow? You need to ensure you're fully recovered before you consider taking them on. In that time frame, his mind won't be shredded yet, and you and I can also be protected."

"Okay."

I hated to wait, especially when Aramis had wasted two years of his life on me. I didn't want to be responsible for more time. But I knew by the tightness in Caelum's face he wouldn't be swayed. And I couldn't push his generosity—it was a miracle he was willing to help at all, considering Aramis never bothered to save him.

I froze when Caelum invaded my space and knelt in front of me. I tried to slow my breathing but failed when he rested his arm on my thighs and grabbed my wrist, gently pushing up my sleeve. He paused at my elbow, noticing how I trembled.

"Sorry." He shook his head, misinterpreting my nerves for discomfort, and shifted, kneeling beside me instead. "Living in Cyrbus's world has left me with few manners. I'm working on it."

I smiled before I knew I had, unsure why. "We'll have to disagree on that. I think you're plenty decent." My smile remained at the proof—his fingers hardly touched me while he lifted my sleeve, exposing the bandages carefully wrapped around my wound.

I caught a peek of the ink beneath his sleeve—a shared mark with those who'd harmed me, who'd relished in my suffering. But Caelum never had; even on the night of the Kefi, he'd maneuvered himself in a way to contain me, but never to harm.

He slowly unwound the wrapping, revealing jagged, raw slices snaking around my right arm. My stomach wrenched at the thick, raised, angry coils and curves knotted between my freckles.

Caelum ran a thumb across it, soothing the irate flesh. "It'll scar. I've been applying Catalean to help with the pain, but its healing properties are slower. I should've been more thoughtful with what I grabbed when Akira was gone, but I could only fit so much in my pockets. I'm sorry."

I covered his hand, stopping his trailing thumb where heat rose off my healing wound. "I'd carry a thousand scars if it meant I could hold on to who I was."

His eyes were heavy, solemn. "This isn't a mark you should be forced to bear."

I didn't know the truth in his words, the meaning behind Cyrbus's tattoo. But the genuine emotion in his eyes was enough that I didn't hesitate to touch his own.

I pressed against the leather sleeve, rubbing my hand over the tattoo beneath, one he hadn't let me see. "You don't deserve to bear it either."

Chapter Twenty-Five

Was there an appropriate amount of time you were allowed to freak out in the bathroom? If there was, I'd certainly surpassed it. I'd held my breath the entire time Caelum layered on Catalean—derived from some of Aita's herbs—and redressed my bandage. Its delightful vanilla hues had deceived me into believing it wouldn't ignite my nerves.

But nothing set me on fire as much as when I took off my shirt in the safety of the bathroom, catching the familiar scent of Catalean, and learned the cuts on my stomach were almost gone. It was impossible not to picture Caelum's hands there, carrying the same devout tenderness he'd used only moments ago. I didn't feel a hint of intrusion—I was certain without a doubt he wouldn't violate me. No, I felt flustered, almost envious I'd missed out on a moment where he'd shown his true self.

I shoved away the thought and instead focused on the swollen eyes watching me in the mirror, the glowing light from the lantern offering little clarity. My snagged curls were flat, my pale skin covered in bruises I didn't remember obtaining. All proof of what I'd endured.

But I didn't cower from what I saw.

Each cut and bruise was a reminder of what I'd survived—what I hadn't before. This time, I could proudly bear the memories of what had happened within Cyrbus's prison. The girl in the mirror—one who was frighteningly different from who I was only days ago—didn't scare me, because I knew how hard she'd fought. I wasn't angry at the change Cyrbus's hands had caused yet again, because this time it was on my own terms.

I'd changed. For the better.

Facing the Belta in Eirlys again was more appealing than leaving this cubby-sized bathroom.

I took my time, carefully tearing through the snags in my hair and washing away the marks on my skin in the sink—there was no shower. My body ached when I tediously slipped into a matching pair of ebony leggings and sweater, my nerves worsening at wearing another woman's clothes. I wasn't brave enough to ask Caelum if this was his cabin or if he was a squatter.

I wasn't hiding because I was staying in a secluded place with my former captor.

There was only one bed.

I gathered my courage—and quickly learned I'd wasted my time cowering. He was already passed out atop it. Something warmed within my chest as I leaned against the doorway and watched his back slowly rise with burdenless ease. His sweatshirt matched mine, covering his arm as it hung over the edge, the rest of his large frame consuming the remainder of the bed. I set the lantern on the nightstand and couldn't resist gently brushing his hair back, savoring the way his cheek squished against the quilt.

Cold air crawled through the cracks in the walls, forcing me to reconsider lying beside him, but my guilt was too heavy to slide beneath those warm quilts. I wasn't against sharing a bed with a man—though I never had—but it felt wrong to enjoy simple comforts when Aramis was chained in the dark. Or lying on an altar, enduring punishment on my behalf.

Caelum hardly stirred when I slipped a pillow and blanket free, forming a makeshift bed on the kitchen floor. I stared at the columned roof, hoping sleep would overwhelm me quickly. But the flickering light from the lantern didn't ease my nerves, worsening every crack or scruff outside. Wondering if Cyrbus would find us.

Exhaustion settled in and I'd just closed my eyes when a thump sounded across the room. I put a hand to my chest, trying to slow my breaths when I found Caelum lying back on the pillow he'd tossed on the floor. Blocking the door.

"Is something wrong with the bed?" I rolled to my knees, tugging the blanket around me.

He sat up, his sweater clinging generously to his frame, one I didn't have to imagine after memorizing it with my hands. I forced myself to meet his gaze when he said, "I don't know. You tell me."

Caelum turned the lantern beside him off, and I narrowed my eyes and lay down as darkness claimed the room. "Could we light a fire on the stove?" I mumbled through clenched teeth, cold drifting beneath the quilt and burrowing in my bones.

"Can't risk the smoke. The bed's warm."

I rolled my eyes, imagining the smirk he wore. I clamped my jaw shut tighter, refusing to give him the satisfaction of hearing my teeth chatter. I closed my eyes, and as suspected, exhaustion overpowered my shivering and swept me into unconsciousness.

Chapter Twenty-Six

Not a single dream had been woven before a piercing howl of anguish tore me awake.

They found us.

"Caelum." I stumbled blindly, tripping over my feet when a scream shattered the room again.

How had they found us?

My arms shook as I crawled, searching for the lantern, fearing the worst. I found it and light erupted, revealing the bitter truth as another cry pieced the room.

It wasn't Cyrbus. It was Caelum.

"Caelum. Wake up," I hissed, relieved and annoyed in the same beat. Relief vanished when he arched his back, releasing another bloodcurdling yell. I flinched, knocking over the light beside us, and covered my ears when he did it again.

"Caelum." I clutched his damp shirt, crawling onto him and shaking his sweltering shoulders. "Wake up." I softly smacked his face, willing to do anything to end his nightmare. Before I could do it again, he rolled over, dumping me to the ground. "You've got to be kidding me." I clenched the lantern in my hands, stalking toward the kitchen to retrieve water.

My annoyance dissipated when he quietly cried for help, his plea rattling my soul. A deep, hidden sort of instinct seemed to take over as he began struggling through the covers, searching for help. I'd never seen anyone so torn—so lost.

I lay beside him, placing myself within his nightmare as much as I could. I wrapped an arm around his heaving chest, the other above his head, while I soothed and coaxed him along, offering assistance in finding his way out.

"Come back to me." The invitation rolled naturally off my tongue, tasting familiar and real.

I applied as much pressure as I could—short of climbing on top of him—holding him while he trembled. My sweater clung to my skin, absorbing his heat and sweat as I whispered, "You're safe. Come back to me, Caelum." I ran a hand through his silky hair, willing the dream to follow my hand out.

The screams slowly left us, and I rested my head against his, leaving only our quiet breaths. He sat up suddenly, hauling me up with him. "You're safe," I said quickly.

"What's wrong?" His chest heaved against my side while he gripped my waist.

"You were screaming," I whispered.

Strands of ebony fell into his face, doing little to hide the shame coating him. "I'm sorry." His arms left me as he scanned the room, looking everywhere but me.

I pushed against his shoulders, easing him back to the floor, and knelt beside him. "Don't apologize." My voice was firm, needing him to know there was no room for shame between us. "Are you okay?"

His eyes were lost on the ceiling. "I'm fine."

"Look at me, Caelum."

Several breaths later he did, more weary than I'd ever seen him. It hurt. His trembling chin and watery eyes hurt more than anything Iveh had carved into my skin. More painful than when I struggled to escape my own nightmares.

His arms quivered against mine when I lay down, pulling the blanket over our legs as he rolled over to meet me. Only our eyes spoke while I let myself stare into his, not solely because he needed it, but because I did as well. I needed the assurance he was okay, he was safe. Something I didn't know I truly cared about.

"Is it always like that?" I asked, unable to shake the image of him writhing.

My gut sank when he only shrugged, and I realized Caelum suffered alone, so he wouldn't know. How long would it have gone on had I not been here? I didn't dare ask for details, not wanting him to relive it. I hated that he couldn't escape the life he was dealt, one that was more of a nightmare than what he dreamed. *What did they do to him?* Why was he so afraid, he wouldn't dare rise up against them?

"I'm sorry." His thumb brushed my cheek, wiping a tear I hadn't notice. "I'm sorry for scaring you."

"No." I grabbed his wrist, halting his hand on my cheek. "I was scared for you, not of you. I only wished I could've helped more."

"You did." He rolled onto his back, releasing a tight breath. "Collins, I need to tell you something."

I bit my lip, fearing where this would lead. "What is it?"

Only my pounding heart filled the room before he said, "You should reconsider staying here. I know you want to stop Cyrbus, but you're going to get yourself killed. And even if you somehow survive, you're not meant for Aita. You'll be happier here."

I sat up, confused as to what had prompted this, and as his words settled, any remainder of sorrow turned into hurt. Why was he so intent on me staying? Did he hate what he'd found as well?

I gripped the blanket. "How could you possibly know if I'd be happier? Do you have any idea what my life was like? That I was isolated inside their house? Only allowed out when they had a use for me?" My chest tightened as his words embedded within. "How dare you suggest I go back to my prison. I would never tell you to return to yours. Maybe you should've left me to die since you believe I have no place in your world."

"That's not what I meant—" He tore the blanket off and stumbled to his feet. The wooden door scraped against my back when he pulled it open, slipping into the night.

Good.

I pulled my knees up and rocked, refusing to let his words in. But it was too late. I swiped roughly at my cheeks, wiping away my absurd tears. It didn't matter what Caelum believed, Aita was my home.

Before I could unravel countless curses at Caelum in my mind, the door hit my back again. "You—" My snide comment snagged at my lips when Caelum knelt down, cupping my jaw.

His breath replaced mine, filling my lungs. "I don't know what the hell I'm doing. I'm trying to say and do the right thing and I'm failing miserably." His eyes roamed my face, ensuring I was at ease. "I'm selfish. For years, I thought only of myself and did what was necessary to survive. And then you—" He looked away, staring at the blankets beneath us, and cleared his throat. "You come into my world and obliterate it. And now I am terrified beyond belief." He tentatively looked up and stroked my cheek—my heart. "The thought of you returning to Aita makes me sick. There are things you don't know about our world, things that could kill you. Because you are gentle and pure, Collins. And that gets destroyed by people in our world."

Caelum's warmth lingered on my cheek, his rough hand reminding me I'd yet to speak. I was at a loss, unable to understand his deep concern for my safety—or what dangers he spoke of.

In my selfishness, I'd failed to see the disturbance I created in Caelum's life. He'd given up everything, accepted a life on the run. Yet he feared for *me*. And while I wanted to be angry that he suggested I stay, I wasn't.

There was no need to be angry or afraid, as Caelum had never hidden himself from me—even revealing his cold and emotionless pieces.

With Caelum, there was no pretending. He didn't remember who I was, nor I him. His unwavering honesty unlaced my deep-rooted hesitation, setting me free.

I placed my hand over his. "Would you go outside with me?"

Caelum opened the creaking door and I shivered as the breeze intruded beneath my blanket. I wrapped the quilt tighter around my shoulders, as thick as the layer of night beyond the porch.

"I want to start over." I knew I could have easily said these words within the comfort of the cabin, but beginnings are usually anything but comfortable. Beginnings are uncertain and difficult, requiring us to take the first shaky step. I braced myself—and my heart—as I whispered, "I promise if you'll stop viewing me as one of your escapees, I'll stop seeing you as one of my captors."

His voice steadily caressed me from behind. "I'd like that."

I bit my smirk and whirled around. "Hi."

His brows furrowed as he glanced around the porch. "Hi." It was emotionless and dry, but it brought an easy smile to my face. He raised a brow. "What did I do?"

"Nothing. It's just—" I shook my head, hiding my smile. "It sounded so strange—you saying hi. I don't think you and I have ever properly greeted one another."

His shoulders loosened beneath his sweatshirt. "I don't know. I particularly enjoyed when you popped out of the bushes in the jungle. I was surprised you didn't attack me."

I laughed, startled at how effortless and full it was. "Let's not forget the time you arrogantly asked me to dance, even after you saw my engagement ring." I laughed harder when he did, relishing in the sound. "Or the time you welcomed me by tackling me on a riverbank."

He grinned, so brightly I was sure I would feel its essence my even if I saw it from as far as Aita. "You can't deny we add a certain zest when it comes to saying hello."

"Should we come up with a greeting of our own? I don't particularly want you to tackle me every time I see you, but a simple hi will never do."

He drifted off into silence and furrowed his brows, apparently taking this task to heart. I didn't mind. I liked him like this—being silly. Maybe this was a piece of the Caelum who existed before, another piece Cyrbus had tried to crush.

He stared at his bare feet as he timidly said, "Our names. That'll be our greeting." Even in the dark, I swore his cheeks burned as bright as mine.

"Caelum," I said by way of acceptance, cherishing it. I loved his name, the way it rolled off my tongue. How my mind held on to it.

"Collins." A faint smile tugged at his lips. "Unless you prefer I call you Aideen?" He laughed deeply when I shook my head, going so far as to stick out my tongue.

"I know it's strange to willingly bear the name of the girl I was supposed to replace. But I'm afraid if I start going by Aideen, I'll be accepting another role I can't fulfill."

"I think Collins suits you." His fingers brushed a curly strand of hair behind my ear, holding it in place as a brisk breeze drifted through. "Let's go in. You're freezing."

I wanted to object. I wanted to mess up my hair, if only so he would do it again. But I could hardly feel the wood splintering beneath my toes and I doubted he was better off.

I didn't protest when Caelum tossed our pillows and blankets on the bed, declaring I wasn't sleeping on the floor. Nor did I object when he lay beside me. And while I certainly was warm and comfortable, I could hardly breathe with Caelum's shoulder pressed against mine.

By the way Caelum's chest hardly rose, I assumed he felt similarly.

"How long have you been like this?" I asked, if only because I was afraid the roof would collapse if we stared at it a moment longer.

He rolled onto his side, resting his head on a fist. "I stopped knowing who I was two years go. The same as you."

I nodded. It confirmed my suspicion that our lives had been ruined in the same moment, that we were stolen and torn apart together. Needing further answers, I pushed past my fear and asked what I hadn't let myself think about. "Do you think it's possible we chose this? Aramis said I was acting differently before you and I disappeared together . . ."

Maybe the story Cyrbus had formed for Caelum wasn't a lie.

Caelum was silent for a long moment before he quietly said, "Cyrbus always said they offer a choice. Offer a new life for those who want it. Even after I suspected that wasn't true for me, I thought maybe it was for others. So I ignored it and continued to assist them in destroying minds. I wanted to believe I was helping people, not manipulating them. But then—" He sat up, baring his face to me fully. "But then I met you and all I could think was how I'd never choose to forget you. So no, I didn't choose this."

My eyes burned with uninvited emotion. "I wouldn't have chosen it either."

The mattress sunk between us when he leaned closer, his own eyes nearly overflowing. I held my breath, waiting for his lips to meet mine, frantically debating what I wanted. His gaze flickered down to my parting lips, but rather than meeting me halfway, he only frowned and shook his head, ending the moment.

I didn't know if it was disappointment or relief I felt when he lay back down, the tight space forcing our arms to touch as we stared at the ceiling once more. I didn't know what to do with Caelum and the pieces he'd shared. I only knew my eyes were heavy and I desperately needed sleep, but I wasn't sure if Caelum and I were ready to face another one of his nightmares.

"They didn't give you a different name when you woke up?" I asked, only now realizing he retained the same one.

"No." He laughed under his breath, lifting his arm up from beside mine and rolled his sleeve up. "They only gave me this."

I watched him while I ran my fingers up his arm, silently seeking permission. I didn't know why a tear slipped free when he rolled toward me, extending his arm out. But I knew by the way Caelum wiped my tear, this moment was more than simply showing me his tattoo. This was him allowing me the chance to see parts of himself he despised.

His right arm hovered above my head while I traced a finger along the intricate pattern I'd initially believed to be whorls and vines. But up close, there were delicate but sharp branches and thorns clawing up his arm, connected to a smooth base of a tree with twisting, thick roots that dissipated into ash at the edge of his wrist.

"What does it mean?" I asked, recognizing it to be similar to the mark I'd seen carved in the door in Mazoe.

"It's just a brand." He rolled away, retrieving his arm, unknowingly taking a piece of me with him.

"I'm sorry." I shook my head in disbelief, hating how they'd marked him as their property. If I found a way to stop them, they'd pay.

Caelum rolled over with a mischievous look in his eye, turning my scheming to ash. I bit my lip, suddenly aware of how tight the space was. "What?"

"I want to ask you something."

"You can ask whatever you'd like. I can't guarantee an answer."

He smiled, briefly running a finger over my hand. "Even if it's nagged me every moment since you said it?"

I sat up against the headboard, steadying the waves in my head as my body worked through the remaining herbs. "What is it?"

He lay on his stomach, looking at me so intensely my toes curled. "You knew my name."

It was an effort to not bury my face in the quilts and release a scream that would surely rattle the realms. Instead, I feigned indifference while I fiddled with a copper curl. "I don't know what you're talking about."

He sputtered a laugh, rolling onto his knees. "Is that so? Then why did it look like you'd been punched in the gut after I told you my name in Mazoe? Or how you tried to seduce me into helping you by revealing you remembered it?"

"I'm not telling you," I murmured into my sweaty hands, certain death awaited me in this conversation.

He tugged my hands free. "Tell me."

"No."

"Why?"

"Because it's embarrassing."

He dropped my hands, surprising me when he didn't push it. He lay back on the foot of the mattress. "There are moments when I forget I'm not as familiar to you as you are to me. Because, well, you know . . ." He trailed off, motioning to his head, where memories lay that I hadn't dared imagine. "You're the freshest breath of air I've had in so long, it's difficult not to overindulge myself. I'm sorry, I will do better at respecting your privacy."

Neither of us moved, leaving more than just his words between us. It wasn't guilt weighing on me but something else. Perhaps kindred longing. A shared desire for more. Trusting the other easily—but yet not—after being alone for so long.

"Please, don't believe this means anything. Or laugh." I wasn't sharing this to ease his conscience, but because I too needed to be vulnerable with someone—to feel safe. "I remembered your name while Aramis was kissing me. I didn't know what it was, but I almost said it, and then I couldn't stop thinking about it."

I was awful. No wonder Aramis appeared set off after I'd nearly said it.

"I don't see how that's embarrassing for you." Caelum's shoulders shook as he sat up, biting back a laugh I knew he was dying to release, his cheeks red. "I would say it's embarrassing for him. Please say you didn't tell him."

"Of course not!" I tossed a pillow at him, releasing a laugh. "I thought I was mental and imagining new words."

He laughed wonderfully, filling the room and my smile with it. But my smile faltered when he grinned wickedly. "If it'll help, I can kiss you and we'll see if his name pops into your head."

I glowered at him and leaned forward on my knees, smiling when he fell still. His eyes widened at our distance—close enough we'd share breath if he wasn't holding his. Before he dared to close the distance, I flicked him on the nose. "I'm going to bed." I smirked as I backed away, delighted with this game and his smile.

"Goodnight, Collins." He crawled beneath the quilt, lingering closer to the middle this time, his laughter and heat encompassing me. His fingers pressed against mine, and I didn't hesitate to take his hand, too exhausted to fight this.

Neither of us reached to turn off the lantern, a silent agreement to avoid nightfall's absoluteness. Even with the weight against my eyes, I tossed and turned, unable to dispel my unease. Not because I shared a bed with Caelum, but because of what lingered outside. What awaited me the next day, and the next—and the rest of my life.

"Caelum?"

"Hmm?" It was gruff, laced with sleepiness.

"I'm scared."

His hand tightened, fully awake again when he said, "I have felt frightened almost every day. I'm afraid of far too many things. But I'm learning you can choose to let fear work with you or against you. It's always going to exist, but it doesn't have to be bad. If anything, it means you're alive—you have something worth fighting for. The moment I stop being afraid will be when I stop living."

Before I could express my gratitude, he rolled over and hovered an arm over my waist. "Is this okay?"

I rolled over and settled perfectly against him, lowering his arm down. An unfamiliar peace washed over me while his chest rose against my back, his breath warming my ear. As if he felt the same, he tightened his hold.

"If it's any consolation . . . I have never felt more afraid yet more alive than with you, Collins."

An inkling in my mind warned me to slip out of his embrace and retreat from this dangerous path. But it was exhilarating for his heart to beat into mine, summoning feelings I couldn't master. They were easy and familiar, but wrong. Wrong because Aramis loved me, had freed me from my prison on Earth. But each shared breath with Caelum only strengthened my lungs, reminding me how it felt to breathe.

I closed my eyes and promised myself this was nothing but offering comfort and body heat. I waited until his chest slowed with his steady breaths until I whispered, "If this is being afraid, I never want to stop."

Chapter Twenty-Seven

I believed myself to be a light seeker. I have counted through endless parades of stars, waiting for the night to end. I thought light was the source of comfort in darkness. But now I wondered if the veil of night was perhaps a comfort in itself. A time when our own darkness and faults sought to live, to experience the quiet hum of life. There's a sense of freedom and bravery that only occurs in the darkest hours. But as with most things that prowl in the shadows, that bravery vanishes once a tendril of light brushes it.

Unfortunately, I didn't have the luxury of hiding with Caelum pressed against me, his arm secured tightly around my waist. My hammering pulse must've beat into Caelum's hand because he quickly shifted awake. I didn't know why my cheeks stung when he stumbled out of bed—fleeing what we'd done. I buried my face into the covers, praying he believed I was asleep so I wouldn't have to face his regret. I lay motionless, listening to his dull groans and shuffling clothes.

Only when his boots paced against the wood floor did I turn around, catching him walk with a slight limp. "Are you okay, Caelum?"

His back tightened beneath his denim shirt before he murmured, "I'm fine." His next step was slower but steady, as if I'd imagined the limp.

Perhaps I imagined last night too. Maybe it was nothing more than a beautiful, uplifting dream. One where your soul is crushed when you learn it wasn't real.

He slipped into the kitchen, quietly opening the cupboard. "There isn't much to eat, but I can make you some porridge."

"Okay." I eased myself onto the floor, pleased to find the room remained steady. "Thank you," I whispered, aware of the empty ache in my stomach, unsure the last time I'd eaten.

A pot clattered onto the stove as he said, "There are more clothes in the dresser if you'd like to change."

Silence wove through us while I sorted through an assortment of clothes within the chest, refusing to overthink it when I slipped on a pair of faded jeans and a flannel shirt. I pulled my hair free from the collar and rolled the loose gray sleeves up, exposing my bandage beneath.

I ran my thumb over the shimmering moonstone on my ring, my only true belonging. Someday. Someday I would have something to call my own—a stable foundation I forged myself.

"Is a bear going to bust in here and demand to know who's slept in the bed and eaten their porridge?" I leaned against the door, blocking the cold air supplying the thickening tension.

But it only worsened when Caelum turned, slowly taking in the surprisingly well-fitting clothes. His smooth raven hair slipped down to his brow when he shook his head, at last meeting my gaze. "A bear?"

I shrugged, jostling my bouncy curls—courtesy of last night's quick rinse in the sink. "Nothing. It's a silly story I've read."

He turned back to the stove, his voice no more than a fine caress. "You like to read?"

"Yes." It was a tender mercy Peter and Jane had allowed me to do so, not truly caring what I did within my isolation—as long as I stayed within it. "Do you?"

He shrugged beneath his shirt, one that he might've worn before he fully settled into adulthood, snug to his frame. "I don't know. I never had the chance."

He served me silence and a bowl, the steaming aroma of cinnamon doing little to ease my aching chest, knowing there was nothing pleasant or comforting in Caelum's life. "Do you think you'll go back to Kaira once we return to Aita?"

His jaw tightened before he swallowed a spoonful. "No."

I was grateful he didn't look up from his bowl, missing the way my face dropped. I wasn't entirely surprised to learn he wanted nothing to do with the home that had abandoned him. "Why even return to Aita at all?"

He shrugged, discarding his bowl in the sink. "It'll only be for a time. Besides assisting you in finding Aramis, I need to check on a . . . friend."

I bit the inside of my cheek, swallowing my tasteless porridge. I didn't know the nature of his relationship with this person, but that didn't stop my stomach from splattering to my bare feet. He was handsome and alluring—it wasn't at all surprising he cared for someone. It didn't matter what he'd said of me being his air. I'd uttered nonsense last night too.

I forced a few more spoonfuls before I set it aside. "Thank you."

He nodded and retrieved my bowl, quietly reassembling the kitchen, leaving me to be nothing more than a dwindling cobweb in the corner while Caelum cleaned the dishes. I lessened to the state of forgotten dust under the bed while he remade it, folding my discarded clothes and straightening the room, stopping only when it was neat and orderly.

Something in my chest squeezed when he eased onto the bed, releasing a deep breath as if he couldn't rest unless there was peace. Peace I knew he didn't have the courtesy of existing in.

"Where can I find Aramis?" I clenched my palms, seeking retribution against myself for not allowing him to rest.

He lay back, rubbing his temples. "I'm not certain. There are many things I'm unaware of with Cyrbus. They were careful never to disclose more information than necessary, especially to lessers like myself." He huffed an abrupt laugh. "Cyrbus has two holding grounds. One in Blythe and the other in Thalas. My guess is he'll be in one of those."

I straightened at his words, remembering details Aramis had shared with me. "Blythe? But isn't it cursed?"

"Yes."

I narrowed my eyes, uncertain if I could trust this information. After all, he made it clear he had no intentions of standing up against Cyrbus. He could be wasting my time. "Why would he be in Blythe? Isn't it unlivable?"

He tilted his head towards me, raising his brow. "It might be barren, but it's not necessarily unlivable. People just tend to avoid it, given it's cursed."

I nodded, accepting his explanation. It made sense that Cyrbus would use a land heavily avoided, but it didn't ease my nerves knowing Aramis was likely being held there. I waited for more information, any sort of clue as to how I could do this. But he only closed his eyes, smothering my hope. I was beginning to doubt the likelihood of freeing Aramis alone.

"What about the Council? Do you think if I went to them, they'd help?"

Caelum snorted. "You'd have to convince them to see you first. But I doubt it. They're far too busy containing Aita, not aiding it."

"What does that mean?"

"Nothing," he breathed, running a hand through his hair. "Aita's not what it used to be."

What could possibly be missing in a world of magic? One where water danced and trees shifted, following their own path while they supplied life to all. But I supposed magic's existence didn't defeat suffering or corruption. Caelum and I were living proof of that.

I lay at the foot of the bed, careful to leave distance. "Aramis told me about the Caelitis. How they grew out of control and drained Aita dry before they fell into extinction. Do you think they harmed the magic?"

"I don't know what I believe. It was far before our time, and I'm afraid the truth is blurry. But at one point, there were far more exquisite and powerful creatures who dwelled on Aita, and they slowly disappeared. There are those who say Aita demanded a balance. But I don't understand why Aita would rid itself of the grand, magical essences, but allow Cyrbus to exist." He rolled off the bed, hardly letting his words settle. "Sorry, I know you don't fully understand our world yet. And I'm likely wrong."

I sat up and caught his hand, stopping him. "Caelum . . . Just because you view the world differently doesn't make you wrong." I couldn't help but think of those in Eirlys, who questioned the abrupt change in magic.

He stared at our intertwined hands as he whispered, "Some days, I think I might not be truly alive. That one day, I'll wake up and just have disappeared. And no one will notice or ask questions. Just like when the Caelitis disappeared, when Aita shifted." He smiled, not with joy but sorrow. "But I suppose Cyrbus already ensured that happened."

My heart burned, kindling at the brief glimpse into his soul. It was odd, the desire I felt to comfort him. How I wanted to promise to whisper his name to every tree in each realm, ensuring it was planted within the soil, so that he would be remembered for as long as Aita prospered. That even when I passed away, I would share with every soul in the eternities about the man who'd freed me. Who'd gifted me another chance to live.

But when I squeezed his hand, I was reminded of how he'd deceived me. And while he had a change of heart and freed me after all, I couldn't risk being vulnerable again. I was broken and healing, and I needed to protect those pieces as best as I could.

"I'll remember you, Caelum." I whispered, only because I knew he was as lost as I was. "I'll make sure all of Aita does."

He shook his head, looking at me with stormy eyes. "It would be enough to be remembered by you at all."

I smiled and braced myself while I eased myself back down on the bed, tugging his hand along. He watched me cautiously as he slowly lay beside me. I closed my eyes and breathed, "Show me the world through your eyes."

I was aware as I listened to Caelum divulge the wonders of Aita that I should be using my time wisely—forming a plan to free Aramis. Because in two days, I wouldn't be hiding in this cabin, but facing those who sold me. And while I may have seemed determined to stop Cyrbus, there was a piece of me that hoped I'd never get the chance. It made no difference whether I was locked in Peter and Jane's house, I was still the same frightened girl, hiding in a fantasy.

So when I heard the quiet joy in his voice, I didn't stop him. Not while I listened to him share the unique qualities of each realm. How Vadon was placed within the highest mountain range—the people nicknamed cloud drinkers. A civilization not solely existing but flourishing in the land of ruthless rocks and hills of evergreen trees—different from Kaira's dense forest. But Thalas was unlike them all, being a dry climate with red sand and lofty boulders beneath the sweltering sun. One would have thought such an environment would be too harsh to live, but its plants, creatures, and people thrived—thanks to Aita's sustaining magic.

Caelum about lost his mind when I divulged I'd briefly visited Eirlys, forcing me to promise I'd never visit that place again. I wisely kept my mouth shut about the Belta.

Despite his interest in the Caelitis, he knew little—only stories of those who were once gifted with Aita's magic. Beings who contained the power to wield water, and harness the wind, even some who could change their form. After much harassment and promising to wash the dishes after the beans Caelum had heated up, I persuaded him to reveal what gift he'd like to harness.

His voice was quiet, hesitant when he shared his fascination with the annual burning ceremony, Vimniran, revealing he'd enjoy making fire dance. I couldn't resist the urge to call him a pyro, earning a flick on the nose.

I forgot the world, losing myself in his voice and our shared whispers, remembering it only after the sun rested. I sat on the bed while Caelum switched on the lanterns and cast a warm hue over the room. He placed it on the table, retrieving a glass vial in return.

"May I?" He nodded at my arm from where he knelt at the edge of the bed.

I smiled as I teased, "I thought you said you lacked manners, Caelum Enver."

He didn't smile in return while he unwound my bandage, the flesh more at ease than before. He dabbed the vial against my skin, tenderly rubbing his calloused hands over the glistening oil. "I don't carry Enver as my name."

My gut sank as I realized my mistake. I remembered Aramis sourly mentioning Caelum's birth father being absent, but I'd assumed Aramis's had filled the role . . . But even he hadn't come for Caelum. "Is there one you do carry?"

His fingers slowed. "No, I never learned who my father is. I'm not sure he exists." He shook his head, running a finger down the center of my arm. "There's no need for the bandage any longer. We can retrieve some Bueterleaf when we return home. If we're lucky, it might not be too late to help with the scarring."

"Butter leaf?"

He laughed, gifting me a faint smile. "Bueterleaf. It's like Catalean, only the herbs it's derived from have stronger healing properties. Unfortunately, Conon had some on hand after Aramis stabbed him. Aita would've been a better place if he'd bled out."

I flinched, pushing away those cruel bloody eyes, and instead focused on Caelum's addictive stormy gaze. He leaned into my touch while I ran a hand up his cheek and traced his brow, soothing its rough edge as I whispered, "I've never minded scars."

His hand encompassed my wrist, removing my hand from his face. My breathing hitched when he brought it to his full lips, slowly skimming his way up my injured arm. It was an intimacy I'd never shared, but I didn't pull away, savoring the way he kissed each slice as if he could heal them himself.

But nothing was as healing as the words he whispered into my skin, "I'm sorry I failed you before. But I vow, I will never do so again." His lips met my skin again, sealing his promise.

I released a shaky breath and glanced at the sheer oil coating his lips, resisting the desire to taste those words. "Is it for dramatic effect, or is there a reason behind why everyone on Aita says *vow* and not *promise*?"

Caelum laughed, brushing his thumb over the pulse in my wrist. "I suppose it's something that's stuck around by habit, but there was a time when vows meant something. They were sacred and binding—not in the same way as binding souls with Aita's magic, but they were valued. You didn't dare vow anything unless you were certain you could keep your word. Some used to believe the gods would release turmoil on those who dared break it. But as I'm sure you've learned, it's a phrase used casually now."

I bit my lip, unable to help but wonder if the vow he'd just extended was sacred. "And what about you?" I asked, focusing on his hands touching me—not willing to see the truth conveyed on his face. "Do you believe vows mean something?"

Caelum's hands left mine, as though the question had taken him by surprise. But that didn't stop him from admitting, "I've never extended one until now. So, you tell me."

Chapter Twenty-Eight

Caelum's nightmare proved to be as terrifying as the last, embedding its way into my senses forever while his cry echoed off the flimsy walls. A comforting hand was the most I could offer, wishing I could instead take his place. No nightmare or pain Conon and Iveh inflicted was as agonizing as watching Caelum suffer alone. So I ensured he wasn't alone when he lay awake. We clung to one another, exchanging insignificant whispers beneath the heavy, comforting quilts until we drifted asleep.

His arms warmed my waist while I lay against him, unable to sleep with the birds crooning, singing deep in the woods. Carefully, I peeled my body from his to clear my mind of this complication. I hadn't intended this, but I held little control over how drawn I was to him. How effortless it was to share intimate thoughts and touches.

And while these moments brought me genuine happiness, I didn't know if I could trust them. Was my time here with Caelum as authentic and delightful as I believed it to be? Or was I so inexperienced with relationships—of any sort—that I was embellishing this to be something it wasn't?

I believed taking charge of my life was the key to finding myself. But all I knew for certain was how frightened I was.

I was sharing myself with the man who at one point hunted me down. Who had been dealt the same fate, whose path was intertwined with my own. But it wasn't that which had me leaving the bed more lost than when I entered it, but fear that I was slipping onto the same path again.

I couldn't afford to lose myself.

I didn't dare look back when I crept out the door, leaving my boot laces undone. I'd planned to tie them outside, but when I took in the forest for the first time in daylight, I was incapable of moving.

Besides the flashes in my dreams, I'd never been surrounded with such infinite spiritedness and beauty, not even in Mazoe. Now I knew why the birds were eager and boastful each morning, as I would be too if this was my home. I hated that I'd already wasted a day inside, denying myself this view. I ran off the cabin steps, realizing it belonged after all, as it didn't deter from the forest's beauty, quietly existing while adding its own essence.

Color erupted from every angle as I followed a rugged animal path, blooms of red and yellow meshing with the evergreen, dancing in harmony with the wind. Everything was alluring in its own exceptional way, from the trickling of a nearby stream, to the groaning branches stretching awake.

My breaths were easy and quiet while I steadily ventured farther. I stepped meticulously slow, ensuring I didn't miss a single detail, whether it was the earthy aroma swirling with the rising leaves or the rustling loose rocks beneath my feet. The cabin slipped from my view, but I couldn't stop once I saw the astonishing sight spread before me.

An endless meadow with leaves designed from the color of sunshine and flame, where orange flowed in the sky, clinging to the lean, yet strong ivory trunks. They were steady and true against the wind that fueled the leaves, carrying the fireless flame for miles. Autumn was in full season, embracing the high, full mountains encompassing the meadow. It was so exquisite, I wouldn't have believed it to be real, if I hadn't dreamed it.

Not a dream, but a memory.

Not of this life, but the one before.

Not of Aita, or even Kaira. But here.

My body moved of its own accord, as if the ground thrust my legs into a run, pushing me toward the meadow. My heart surged at the sight, welcoming me home. I dropped to my knees, not from exhaustion, but reverence.

It was how I dreamed it to be.

I lost all semblance of time while I knelt, only remembering when I looked up to find the sun watching high above the trees' canopy as Caelum emerged from the forest.

His steps were quiet, thoughtful, as if he was aware this was a sacred place. I didn't need to ask how he'd found me—it was why he remembered this cabin. He too had been here.

We'd been here.

The straw grass swayed when he sat beside me, its fading green ends stroking his arms as he laid his jacket over my shoulders. "Are you okay?"

"Yes," I whispered truthfully, even if it did little justice to explain how I felt more myself than I ever had.

His voice was thick, catching in his throat. "I thought you left." My stomach knotted, and I regretted not waking him. But before I could apologize, he smiled. "And then I thought to check here."

"Because I've been here before."

"Yes."

"With you?" I asked, already knowing the truth. I only needed him to confirm it.

He fidgeted with the slide on his chrome ring before he whispered, "I believe so."

"Tell me everything, please."

His eyes may as well have been colorless amid the enthralling sight, but even in this astounding grove, he was where I'd rather be. "I don't remember much about my life before. But here is where I remember you. I've dreamed it so often and vividly that I was able to piece it together until it led me here. It was the strangest thing—to visit a place I couldn't remember, yet I knew with every fiber in my being my dreams had led me here. To this forest, this grove and cabin." His silver-lined eyes swam to the view, soaking in the intensity laid out for us. "It's my most treasured dream."

"Tell me, Caelum."

He smiled softly, holding my world. "They vary, but it's always here. Always in this place." His hand trembled into mine. "Most of my flashbacks are foggy and distant, but with you it's always clear. Strong enough I can experience every emotion." His eyes cleared of any shadows as he said, "You would be bundled up in the cabin reading, demanding I stop staring, and I could feel the laughter building in my chest. I'd feel rocks pressing into my feet when I'd find you lying in this meadow, doing nothing but watching the sky. I would chase you through the trees and your squeals would wake me up. Your touch was clear as it is right now. At times, the dreams of us here were my only refuge, much like I believe this place was ours."

"It sounds lovely." I swallowed past the lump in my throat, at a loss for words. I didn't understand how we were here—why we came here before. "Did you and I Drift directly here?" I asked, uncertain how long I'd been unconscious. Nor how he could have traveled through Idaho, much less trek this entire forest with me in his arms.

He furrowed his brows, likely confused as to why I was skipping over his declaration. "Yes, we Drifted here."

"Why is a beacon on Earth? I thought the Council placed those."

He said nothing for a moment, only the leaves crunching in his hand breaking the silence. "The Council decides where beacons go on Aita. They use the same magic that is sourced to the tower, and place it within each realm. It's planted like a seed." He paused again, rubbing his jaw. "When I first visited the cabin, I stumbled upon a beacon. I assume we must've found a way to plant one before . . . but that's how we were able to Drift here the other day."

"How is that possible? Magic doesn't exist on Earth," I pressed, not understanding how we'd planted a beacon in a magicless world.

He stared at me long and hard, before releasing a heavy breath. "I don't know, Collins. I only remember what I told you." He looked away, staring back towards the cabin. "I'm sorry it wasn't enough for you."

I swallowed through my aching throat, guilty for dismissing Caelum's bravery in sharing such an intimacy. But I didn't know what to make of his dreams—of any of this. He loved them, cherishing each breath he experienced here. But why hadn't he shared this before? Did it not matter if I knew because he no longer felt the same? I supposed while the dreams offered peace, it didn't mean they brought back the emotions he felt during them. Perhaps he knew as I did, that he and I no longer fit. Too broken and ruined.

But what of our time here? When we'd shared a bed and pieces of our souls? I loved and retained each moment—did he not? What if he didn't think I could make him as happy as those dreams?

Misery slowly amplified through me, realization decaying what I thought this could be. I wasn't the girl in his dreams. I was incapable of being anyone's sanctuary in their pit of despair when I was drowning in my own. You can't cast out darkness by adding more. No, you accomplish that by seeking goodness and light—not me.

But I was so tired of dwelling in the dark alone. Was it ridiculous to wish for someone to part the shadows and not run when they learned I might be in shreds, but I was healing? To embrace the unlikable and raw pieces of myself?

But all anyone saw was the remnants of a ghost. Even Caelum.

"I should go back inside. I didn't sleep well," I whispered and dropped his hand, not only because I felt unworthy to breathe in this sacred place, but because I couldn't help but wonder if he was being fully honest about our previous time here. I knew Caelum was missing memories just as I was . . . but after Aramis had withheld so much history and truth regarding my previous life, I feared Caelum was doing the same.

"Collins . . ." I stayed where I sat, hoping he would further explain and ease my fears. But then he only said, "I'm going to stay here out here for a bit."

I nodded, crunching the ground with my unlaced boots as I stood, returning his jacket. I didn't let myself look back as I walked away, each step heavier than the next as I realized I was walking away from more than this moment. I knew my time with Caelum was limited, but I hadn't realized how quickly it would pass. There weren't enough hours to learn him, to relearn myself. There was more separating us than just forgotten memories. There were years of trauma, loneliness, and even secrets. There was a foolish piece of me that hoped we could work through those together, but I knew we couldn't. Not if we didn't trust one another.

I wanted to trust him. To believe the way he looked at me was genuine, that there wasn't an ulterior motive behind his kindness.

But I didn't know if I had the courage to fully trust again—if I would survive another heartbreaking deception.

Chapter Twenty-Nine

When I returned to the cabin, I'd barely slipped off my shoes before I was back in bed, not caring when I woke up that he was still gone. I must have dozed off again, because I was certain I was trapped in a nightmare when Caelum shook me awake, informing me I needed to learn how to defend myself. I promptly rolled away, telling him I was still considering Vidaar's offer. But instead of asking who Vidaar was—like any normal person would—he practically dragged me out of the cabin, claiming he couldn't in good conscience send me into Cyrbus incapable of defending myself.

Which was clearly evident after I fell on my ass for the twelfth time.

"Again," Caelum instructed. "You're not doing it right."

"Forgive me," I groaned, rolling to my feet atop the rough ground, crunching brittle pine needles. "It hadn't occurred to me there was a proper way to be tackled." I wasn't entirely certain if Caelum was punishing me for leaving the meadow without acknowledging what he'd shared. But he hadn't uttered a word of it, as if he didn't care. So I decided not to either, grateful he was willing to help me at all.

And I wouldn't protest to feeling the hard planes of his muscles through his thin white T-shirt.

"We'll go slower this time." Caelum's voice was steady, a contrast to my heaving gasps. Something he ignored when he dove for me again, my finger pointing at him to stop having no effect. His arms wrapped around my quivering legs, then halted mid-tackle. "Come on, Collins. What are you supposed to do?"

I rolled my eyes and wrapped a flushed arm around his neck, the other resting on his bowed back. "Shouldn't you be teaching me how to avoid being tackled?"

The world shifted as he hefted me up, then briskly dropped us to the ground. He hovered over me with a faint grin. "You're supposed to keep your arm around my neck, Collins."

I lowered my arms to the ground and crinkled leaves in my hands, pretending his body wasn't on top of mine. "Again, why am I learning how to be tackled?"

He shifted his weight onto one arm, lingering above me while he grabbed my hand, stopping my incessant crunching. "Do you remember how quickly I took you down in Mazoe? You need to be prepared for it to happen again."

I grabbed a handful of leaves and dusted them over his head. "Maybe a magical vine will come to my aid again. Which reminds me, are you going to explain how you convinced them to release you?"

He raised his brows, shocked I'd noticed the way he whispered to the jungle. "I explained it was a misunderstanding." He wrapped a hand around my wrist, pressing it back against the firm ground as he breathed, "Some things, Collins, you'll learn can be solved with a little bit of communication and honesty." He rolled away from me and extended his hand out. "You can't rely on magic or anyone else to help you. You need to learn to take care of yourself."

My knees wobbled when I stood, grateful my face was already burning and wouldn't reveal how sharply his words stung. He didn't seem to notice—or care—when he waved a hand at me. "Turn around. We'll try something different."

I faced the shack, its outside a mirage, concealing the warm, appealing home inside, one which had once been *ours*. My heart ached at the thought just as Caelum's arms wrapped around my heaving chest, encompassing me as his deep voice caressed my ear. "Lean forward and push your body back into mine."

I didn't let myself focus on how I pressed my hips back into him, following his instructions. "Good," he murmured. "Now when you do it, force your arms up into mine in the same motion. Once you have me off-balance, reach between your legs and pull one of mine up."

"You've got to be kidding me. This is pointless—"

He tightened his hold, trapping my complaint in my chest. "Collins," he whispered, his body heating mine. "I want you to think of your most treasured dream. Something you cherish more than anything, even if you can't explain why. You only know you can't stop." His lips lingered beside my ear as he loosened his hold. "Wouldn't you want to protect it? Do everything within your power to keep it safe?"

"Yes," I breathed, unable to think clearly once his hands settled on my waist, understanding the deeper meaning within his words.

"Then protect it." He shifted, bringing his arms back around my chest.

I remained still in his arms, letting his beating heart pulse into mine and bracing myself to face what he said. Not only moments ago, but in the meadow, where he'd admitted I was his treasured dream and I hid from it. No, I ran. How could I possibly be brave enough to face Cyrbus if I couldn't face the truth?

And even after I'd dismissed Caelum's dreams, he hadn't run from me. He might have taken a moment to gain composure after being vulnerable, but he'd sought me out. Even ensuring I was capable of protecting myself. Beside Vidaar, this was a gift no one had offered. Peter and Jane had trapped me in that house, assuring I was reliant on them. And while Aramis meant well, even he hadn't, promising he could protect me.

But Caelum . . . he was protecting my freedom. And that changed everything.

Be brave, I whispered to myself. *You deserve to thrive, not just survive.*

I leaned against him, heeding his instructions, and brought my arms up. But instead, I wrapped my hands around his forearms, feeling the strained muscle beneath. His chest didn't rise, nor did his arms resist when I unwound his hands and brought one to my lips. The other found my hip, bracing himself when I tenderly kissed the hand that had always been gentle with me.

His chest shuddered against my back. "Collins."

"Caelum." His eyes widened when I turned and steadied a hand against his chest, as if he didn't believe I was openly touching him, only having done so in the dark. I traced the hard lines of his face, savoring how he felt beneath the sun before he interrupted my curiosity and kissed my palm. He pulled me into his heat and lowered his head, carefully watching me for hesitation. His lips halted when I broke our gaze and I feared he assumed the worst, despite it only being my fluttering stomach getting the best of me.

I planned to pull his lips down to mine. But if I hadn't looked away, I wouldn't have seen the blood seeping through his shirt. "You're bleeding." I reached to lift his shirt, but when he followed my line of sight, he slipped away, leaving me for the cabin.

"Are you hurt?" I ran after him, barely getting through the door before it closed.

His jaw flexed while he searched the dresser for another shirt. "No."

"You're bleeding. Let me see."

"It's nothing," he snapped, even as trails of blood wept through his white shirt.

"Let me see." I reached for him, nearly ripping his shirt up.

He grabbed my wrist. "It doesn't concern you, Collins."

I shoved away his dismissal and grabbed his hand, stopping him at the edge of the bathroom. "Don't push me away." I tightened my hold, bearing my feet down when he tried to move again. "I've let you take care of me, Caelum. Let me offer you the same." He didn't persist, remaining still as I placed a hand on his jaw. "How is this any different than sharing your dreams with me?"

He closed his eyes and wrapped a hand around my wrist. "There are some thoughts I'm not scared to share with you. Because I'm not ashamed of those dreams, who I was in them. But this—" He shuddered a breath and opened his eyes, waving a hand at his bloody shirt. "This is who I really am, Collins. I don't want you to see how weak I am and how I can't protect myself. How I can't protect you."

I lightly traced the seam of his shirt, not fully understanding the meaning in his words. I only knew with certainty that Caelum had been hanging on an edge for far too long alone. "Then maybe it's time I protect you, Caelum," I whispered, my eyes bearing into his, slipping my fingers beneath the edge of his shirt. Only when his eyes and jaw softened did I lift it up, easing it over his head.

"It's fine," Caelum murmured.

It was anything but fine.

I couldn't breathe—couldn't move as I studied his torso, finding not even an inch that was unscathed, covered in red slashes running sporadically across his chest, even wrapping around his back.

He didn't resist when I eased him to sit on the bed, twitching beneath my touch when I lifted his head and ran a hand through his locks. I gasped while I tentatively traced the lines, varying in size and color, some brighter and smoother than others. Two, however, stood out with jagged edges, blood seeping through the cracks.

They were fresh.

"Did Cyrbus do this to you?" My voice wavered, not in fear but rage at the thought of someone harming him.

"A few." His hands trembled against my thighs. "Most I had when I woke up."

"What?"

His voice was detached, robotic. "It was a part of their control tactic—to inflict a similar pain to one you received before. Apparently, you're more inclined to submit to a pain your mind can remember. I resisted more at first, but then eventually I stopped fighting back."

The weight of his words crushed me. If he'd endured such pain in this life—and the last—it meant someone who was supposed to protect him had hurt him enough Cyrbus used it to control him further.

I flexed my jaw. "Who did it?"

He swallowed hard. "My stepfather."

I was certain I had never hated someone more. Was this why he was reluctant to return to Kaira? Partly why he was hesitant for me to do the same? Did Aramis know about this?

My hand shook against the angriest fissure. "This one looks recent."

"It's from the other day. After we brought you in."

I stopped hearing anything but the agonizing bellows that had sounded within those stone walls, sounds I thought were an illusion, or another prisoner. But it was Caelum. Caelum being whipped. He'd stopped fighting back.

Until me.

I thought he'd played me, believing him to be cruel when he demanded I return to Peter and Jane, but it was the best he could offer. A gift to save me while keeping himself alive. He didn't have to help me at all, but he had—and suffered greatly for it.

"I'm sorry." I threw my arms around his neck, a feeble attempt to protect him.

I didn't let go as he fell rigid at my touch, afraid he'd crumble if I did. Slowly his muscles relaxed and he let me in, wrapping his arms around me as I climbed onto his lap and rested my head on his chest. I focused on his beating heart, reminding myself he was safe as I allowed silence to weave within our unyielding hold, aware there was nothing I could properly say.

I'd judged him unfairly, called him a coward when he didn't instantly leave Cyrbus, never once thinking of the repercussions he'd face. And didn't that mark me the biggest hypocrite of all.

How many times had I bent to Peter and Jane's will? Allowing them to suck the life from me—just as Caelum's life was beaten out of him. Of course he didn't want to return to his family.

I pulled back and cupped his strained face, aware this was a privilege many didn't experience—to lie in the midst of another's despair and shame. "I will never allow anyone to harm you again. I will protect you, always." My words were firm, a promise—a vow. It was evident he was stronger and more capable than I was, but I would protect him from all that I could.

Even Aramis.

He pushed a wild hair behind my ear. "I know."

I rested my forehead against his, cherishing how natural it was. He understood me and I him. We were entwined within the same tree, our roots stretching beyond realms. It was why it was effortless, easy to be in his presence, as if we'd shared the same air always. No longer could I deny myself the replenishment I needed.

I pressed a breath of a kiss against his lips and whispered, "Caelum."

His lips trembled against mine. "Collins."

Neither of us dared move as we allowed the truth to settle. We wanted this. We were no longer running from this connection. Even if only for this moment.

A breath shuddered against my lips before I was greeted with a heartfelt, full kiss. I twined my fingers into his hair, trapping him while his lips moved strongly against mine, his tongue teasing for more. Our kiss was different than anything I'd ever experienced, desperate and raw, but it wasn't draining. Each shared moment and urgent caress drew out my emotions until I was welcoming the anger, the despair, and even the emptiness. I traced my fingers across his chest, as if I could somehow weave together his marred skin, swept away in darker emotions until they slowly disappeared, leaving me warm and full.

Caelum rolled me over, smiling, and gently pressed me into the bed. His lips brushed mine. "What of tomorrow, Collins?"

For a fleeting heartbeat, a glimmer of reality disenchanted this breathless moment. But I couldn't bear for this to end, to face the fate that awaited us tomorrow.

I wrapped my arms around his back, feeling the surety of him against me, and brought his lips back to mine as I said, "I'm not ready to wake up from this dream." He kissed me soundly while our hands explored confidently, familiarizing ourselves yet again. I trembled beneath his delicate fingers, aching for more—body and soul. I'd been so desperate to connect with myself, not knowing he held answers all along. He was a part of me in every way, and I him. I kissed him harder, losing and finding myself in the sensation.

Chapter Thirty

If such a thing as being intoxicated by a kiss existed, I certainly was. But not in the unstable, staggering-through-the-room sort of way. Warmth kindled within me, pulsating bliss and euphoria through my veins and lifting me from captivity. I was on top of the roof—no, the stars.

I didn't worry about the awaiting hangover and drank myself silly.

Our day was lost in bed, doing nothing more than sharing kisses and pieces of ourselves. A gift I stored deep inside me, so I might never forget him again. Even when nightfall lay heavily over the cabin, neither of us acknowledged sleep. We didn't speak of tomorrow, agreeing that, for now, it was only us. Him and me in a world where Cyrbus didn't exist, nor all the ambient pain, and we could be together.

But beneath this blissful surface was a crippling wave of guilt for betraying Aramis in every way. What would he think if he learned of my actions while he was captured? I'd done the very thing he'd tried to protect me from, but he could only be disappointed if I hadn't miraculously wasted too much time. The joy I felt right now wouldn't allow me to outrun tomorrow, but I wouldn't regret my time with Caelum or the clarity I'd found.

I rolled over, shoving Aramis aside for his brother again. "Distract me."

His grin was nothing short of wicked. "If you insist."

A gasp slipped my lips when he rolled onto me, softly kissing my neck. His lips traveled upward and trailed over my jaw, tasting every bit of me before seizing my lips. But when his hands hungrily gripped my hips, I couldn't ease the flush of my skin. No amount of intoxication could blur the truth of my inexperience. We hadn't done more than kiss—he hadn't even suggested more—but I was quickly learning how easily enchanted I was with his alluring lips.

"Not like that," I quickly breathed, despite my nerves being fully awake, begging for more. He rolled off without hesitation and I tossed the quilts over him, covering any further temptation. "As much as I enjoy this." I gestured toward his muscled frame that made me flush by simply thinking of the moments he'd held me. I ran a hand over my feverish neck. "I'd like to just be with you right now."

My stomach wrenched with insecurity once the words were out, and I wished I hadn't revealed that. I didn't know the nature of our relationship, if he had any expectations from our previous intimacy. And because I refused to ask if he had memories of *that*, I was left without a clue how to act. I'd only experienced dull, taxing kisses with Reed, and then the few I'd shared with Aramis.

But I knew Caelum understood the tenderness between us when he kissed my cheek, soothing my fears. "All I want is time with you. It doesn't matter how we spend it."

He smiled and slung an arm around my waist, pulling me close. I gently kissed his chest, soothing the pain above and within. "I love that," he whispered when I did it again.

I pulled back and looked at him while he stroked a hair behind my ear. "What?"

I leaned into his searing touch. "That you see me. You see every bit of me and yet you keep running toward me."

Run with me, Caelum.

If I were brave, or even the lively girl he dreamed of—the one Aramis remembered—I'd brace my spine and share those words. But instead, I smiled and kissed his brow. "How did you get this scar?"

He solemnly ran a finger over the scar on my temple. "It's another reminder of what Cyrbus did to us. Before, they would slice into the minds of their victims, believing the magic could help the memories slip out." His jaw tightened as he paused. "But now their method doesn't require any sort of physical interference. They can do it without even lifting a finger."

I shuddered beneath my chestnut sweater, not wanting to ponder what those methods looked like. It hadn't occurred to me Cyrbus was responsible for this scar, though I supposed it should have. Even if Iveh hadn't mangled my arm, they'd already marked me forever.

I buried myself beneath the blankets, content to remain in his hold forever while his warm breath caressed my ear. "Do you remember me at all?"

I frowned at the emotion in his words, his deep desire to be remembered. I knew I could share the meadow with him, but I couldn't give him false hope. "Besides your name, I have no memory of you."

"That's okay. I hadn't known if you were being honest before." But his arms slackened at his sides while he smiled weakly, as if it meant I cared any less for him.

I kicked the blankets down and rolled onto him, slipping my thumbs through the loops in his jeans. "I know you, Caelum. And it's not because you've dreamed of me or even that you're Aramis's brother." I traced his sharply lined jaw. "I don't understand it, but something in me recognizes you.

"Even when I believed you were against me, I wasn't afraid. Afraid of Cyrbus, but never you. I've never felt more comfortable than in my time with you—because you're the only one who has never asked me to be something I'm not. When I'm with you, it's the closest I've ever felt to myself." I exhaled, bracing myself against his bare chest. "I feel home."

It was the truth. But that didn't stop my stomach from squirming at such an intimacy, especially when our futures were undecided. I didn't know his feelings, if he was disappointed with this version of myself. Silence stole my breath while I ran my fingers through my hair, yanking at tangles to distract from the pain trailing my rash declaration. I always revealed too much with him.

"Collins." One hand surrounded mine, and blissful heat followed his fingers as they brushed my hair back, then traced down my cheek. "The first time I dreamed of you, I didn't know who you were or why I couldn't escape you. After Aramis found me and accused me of selling you, I connected the pieces." He frowned, drifting his attention to the ceiling. "For years, you were nothing more than my brother's girl. One I dreamed of, but could never have." His voice lowered, no more than a frail whisper. "My dreams weren't far off from reality."

I waited for him to say more, to confirm that I too was his *home.* I wanted—needed—him to say it so badly, I almost reassured him I wasn't Aramis's. That I hadn't spent the day in bed with his brother, but with *him.*

But as the silence continued, I realized something.

Caelum dreamed of me. He remembered pieces of me I'd long forgotten. Of who I used to be, how he and I ran away to this perfect little cabin. A cabin he remembered so well, he could easily envision it to find his way back.

But he'd only gone looking for one of them.

And it wasn't me.

My throat ached when I rolled off Caelum, noting how his hands fell to the side, not persisting at all. It worsened, constricting beyond belief when I looked down at his chest, the splintered skin still gleaming of oil I'd rubbed over him, chastising him for not doing so in the first place. Only for my annoyance to dissipate when he'd admitted he wanted to ensure there was plenty for me.

Further scars and pain he received on behalf of me.

He'd protected me. But he hadn't come for me.

Had he only freed me from Cyrbus out of moral obligation? Perhaps guilt for betraying me? Maybe he didn't care for me directly and was only desperate to save the girl he dreamed of.

He too, knew as I did. She didn't exist.

I crawled off the bed onto the floor, stumbling to my feet. I turned at the foot of the bed, finding Caelum wide-eyed, cautiously watching me. "Collins," he whispered, with all the care and tenderness in the world, so much I put up my hand, stopping him when he stood.

"Why didn't you come for me?" I breathed, no longer willing to exist in this fragile state of unknown. "You remembered this cabin and you looked for it. But you didn't look for me." Somewhere in my mind, I knew this wasn't fair to Caelum, seeing firsthand the control and fear Cybrus had etched into him. But the emotions I'd long kept pent up were beyond reasoning. "You left me."

My nails pressed into my palms, as I forced myself to be brave and face Caelum, only the mattress between us. He clenched his jaw, running a hand through his hair. "I should've looked for you. I wish I had. But when those dreams first started, I was a very different person than who I'm trying to be now. Those dreams were full of a beautiful and enchanting woman. I didn't search for you because I am completely undeserving of someone whole like you."

"I am not whole." My lips trembled as my voice did, conveying just how broken I was. "I am not this enchanting woman. I am broken and angry." I waved a hand towards him, his mouth tightly strained. "I hardly resisted you in staying here longer, despite knowing it could put Aramis at risk, because I am beyond selfish. But most of all, Caelum." I paused, releasing a shaky breath. "I'm tired. I'm so very tired of feeling this way. Of not being enough."

Silence lingered, the cabin filled only with my shallow rasps. I stared at my feet, unable to watch Caelum while my admittance set in. I closed my eyes when the floor creaked, not willing to see the pity warping his strong face.

I shuddered a breath, holding in tears when warm fingers lifted my chin, his voice a gentle soothe. "Look at me, Collins." His rough callouses traveled to my jaw, his hands cupping my face. "You don't need to hide."

I didn't want to hide, not after cowering for so long in the shadows of the expectations of others. I wanted to be confident in who I was now and believe I was worthy of acceptance. And maybe—maybe no one would accept me, until I accepted myself. Perhaps I would no longer seek the approval of others if I gave myself grace instead.

I didn't know how to do that. How to be brave enough to honor who I was now. But at one time, I'd been afraid to run, believing I would fail because that's what was crammed down my throat. But I hadn't failed, not truly. And maybe that girl who chose to keep going even when she was scared deserved to be loved.

Even if it was only by me.

I opened my eyes, finding nothing but worry and care in his while he intently searched mine. "Hear me when I say, I want this. I want you. I know you are entirely too accustomed to people needing you to change to fit their needs, but I want you like this."

He wiped a silent tear cascading down my cheek. "Yes, those dreams mean everything to me. But you." He smiled boldly, as if he crafted it solely for my eyes. "You mean so much more." He pressed a chaste kiss to my lips before he wrapped me into his hold. "I used to believe Cyrbus intentionally let you slip through. To serve as a daily reminder of the happiness I'd never have. I hated my dreams for taunting me. Hated you. But then I found myself clinging to them, because at times they were my only peace. And now that I've tasted the real you." He paused, sprawling my heart over the edge. "My dreams will never suffice again. You are more beautiful, stubborn, passionate, and courageous than I could've imagined. When I am with you, for once, I don't wish to dream. I have all I want right here."

His lips pressed a hint of a kiss to the top of my head, sealing his words. "But I cherish you more than anything. And with you, Collins. I won't be selfish. You deserve more than anything I could give you. The best thing I can offer you is to get you home and allow you to live a full life."

Caelum knew better than anyone how ruined I was, and he didn't care. He wanted me—not despite those things—but because of them. He believed himself to be unworthy, but when I looked at Caelum, all I saw was someone worthy of love. To be fought for and loved fiercely.

I looked up and held his smooth jaw in my hands. "The best thing you can offer me—is to let me make my own choices."

He rested his forehead against mine, one corner of his lips tilting up into a sorrowful smile. "You aren't the only one who is fighting an inner battle. There is much about me you don't know. Things that would cause you to see me in a different light. I won't risk harming you."

I shook my head, rubbing my thumb across his full lips. "You are not alone in this darkness, Caelum. I see you . . . and I will remain with you in it for as long as you need."

I grasped his jaw and claimed his lips. Claimed him. But when I made to deepen the kiss, needing him to understand I wasn't ready to give this up, his lips slipped out of my reach. He closed his eyes, his hand gently encircling my wrist. "I'm going to take you home now, Collins."

But I already was.

Chapter Thirty-One

"I thought we needed to wait one more day," I whispered, a breath of fog into the cool night, trailing Caelum closely while he lit the way with a lantern, winding through shadowed trees. "Why the sudden change?"

"It's been almost two full days. If we wait until tomorrow, we can't leave until nightfall."

His words didn't ease the war in my mind, confused at his abrupt decision to leave. I looked over my shoulder, yearning to be back in the cabin, wishing I'd taken the time to memorize every crook and cranny so I could remember it with ease. I would've run an admiring hand along the structure that held strong despite its fractured frame. I would've said thank you for being my refuge.

And now I'd have to prepare for an even more painful goodbye.

I bit my lip as I blindly followed Caelum, unable to imagine a world without him. I fought the urge to demand we remain here, as that would crown me the most selfish person alive, to willingly abandon Aramis. But it was also fear stopping me, unable to shake what Caelum had said—how he'd pulled away from our kiss. Despite wanting me, he knew it didn't change that our fates were no longer entwined.

I willed the harrowing reality from my mind, choosing to savor the moments I had left with Caelum. His hand tightened in mine before he dropped it and turned around, smiling while he ran his hands up the smooth leather material swallowing my arms, having insisted I wear his jacket.

"Close your eyes." I obeyed his words with a racing heart, embracing the spinning world when he lifted me up and held me against his chest. He pressed a tender kiss to each closed lid. "Don't open them until I say."

After what could've been only a few rapid heartbeats and an uphill climb, he returned me to the ground. He wove arm around my waist, pinning my back against his chest. "Open your eyes."

The joy in his voice carried into my smile, only to vanish when I opened my eyes. My mouth slipped open with a gasp as I beheld the sight before me, faintly registering his hands steadying my waist when I swayed.

Never before had I seen anything so astonishing, so unworldly as the color dancing in the sky. Ripples of emerald with violet hues shimmering beyond it flowed through night's blanket. Glimmering stars settled in awe around the show, watching from above and aiding the color's mirror onto the water below. My pulse thrummed faster, as if the iridescent waves rippled into my soul, awakening me. Even if I hadn't stepped foot on Aita, there was no doubting the existence of other worlds while I watched the vitality flowing around me.

"Caelum." I managed to peel my gaze away, just enough to find his eyes glowing, absorbing the color around him. No longer did I believe hoping was for fools while I watched it glimmer through his eyes into mine.

"Collins." Fresh tears lined his lips when he smiled, cupping my face and kissing me into what felt like eternity. The world continued to dance through us, threaded our very beings together so we might never forget one another again. If a kiss could ever be described as heaven, this was it—I felt hope and joy ebb through me into the sky.

"Drifting to different planets is different than how we Drift on Aita. On Aita, we count on the magic, but if the planet is without it, we have to rely on energy to connect us to a Gateway. The energy from the Northern lights will allow us to travel—only you and I are going to Drift directly to Mazoe. I don't want to risk going through the Gatekeeper." Caelum's chest heaved with mine as he slipped my ring off and placed it atop where it sat on his palm. He looked up at me from beneath his thick lashes. "Would you allow me the honor of having my ring synced with yours?"

I bit my smile back as I recalled the faint memory with Aramis, understanding the intimacy of such an act. "I would love that," I whispered before clearing my throat. "I don't remember when Aramis and I did it before. So I don't know how it works."

If Caelum was envious that I was synced with Aramis, it didn't show in his genuine smile. "Long before you and me, when magic was used freely, there were Noetics. They're branched from Witches, but most of their magic was in practicing spells. They no longer exist, but a trace of their magic flows through the rings. We'll only need to utter a binding spell one time, and our rings will be synced. Then we'll use one of the binding words the Noetics once created."

"Is it *Eunoia*?" I asked, remembering the word Aramis told me to use.

"No. I'm assuming that's the binding word you and Aramis share. But you and I will have a different one, one that's special just between you and I." He winked, still showing no sign of discomfort. "That way your ring doesn't accidentally send you to Aramis when you intended to Drift to me."

"Okay." I smiled, tears building in my eyes, unable to stop the hope that maybe our journey wasn't nearly over. "Go ahead."

He smiled once more before closing his eyes and pressing down on our rings, clicking their outer layer and uttering words in a foreign tongue, smooth and chilling me to my core. He held me firmly as he whispered, "*Saudade.*"

He looked up at me and nodded, and based off the way his throat bobbed, I realized he was waiting for me to repeat it back. I swallowed, my voice breathless as I accepted this bond. "*Saudade.*" And as if that very word contained magic, a veil of amethyst washed over each ring, brightening our smiles before Caelum replaced my ring on my finger.

The glowing lights reflected off the moonstone while my fingers shook, sliding the ring three times to the right, followed by six to the left. Exactly as I'd done with Aramis. Only this time, despite having just shared a wonderful moment with Caelum, I was more afraid than I'd ever been. Perhaps because I knew there was more at risk now.

I stared at his heart beneath his ebony shirt as I whispered, "I don't think I can do this, Caelum."

His hand slipped to the small of my back, bracing me against him. "Talk to me."

"What if I return and nothing changes? What if I can't free Aramis and I fall into their grasp again? They've stolen nearly every piece of me—I can't afford to lose myself again."

"Collins." He firmly held my jaw, pressing his forehead to mine. "They may have stolen your life and memories, but they haven't taken away who you are. This is you." He pressed his finger to my chest—my heart. "This is what you're fighting for. This is your chance to reclaim yourself. To take back the freedom they've stolen from you. Show them you do not go softly."

"I'm scared."

"Then you are alive," he murmured with a breath of a kiss, easing every violent wave in my tormented spirit. His lips captured mine while he pressed down on our rings, clinging to me as darkness curled around us. Claiming me in such a way I would surely be marked forever. Staining my soul so I would remember what it was like to be touched, to be seen for who I was. Taunting me with the cruel truth of what I'd never have again.

United as one, we translated through darkness, Drifting through effervescent cosmos while the magnificent, steady forest was transformed into rich and tangled foliage, where lively hoots and shrieks embraced the dusk hour. As we parted, I wondered if our harmony would slip away too, forgotten in the humid air as we traveled into the village.

We pushed through the busy streets, everyone parting at the sight of Caelum. His eyes were deep, focused on the path at hand, ignoring the endless merchant offers of wine and fine jewelry that trailed us to the inn. I snorted when Caelum's head smacked against the domed roof, swatting his hand as he tried to tickle me, unable to contain my squeal.

My cheeks burned, wishing I had when I was greeted with Vidaar's grunt. "I believed you to be long dead, Little Flame." His eyes flickered as I shrugged off Caelum's jacket, taking in my mangled skin. "But it appears you might have tangled with death."

I stepped up to the counter while Caelum leaned back against the door. "Is my room still available?"

He cocked his head, resting his bulky arms on the counter. "You paid for the week, didn't ya?" His copper eyes drifted behind me, darkening as he sized Caelum up. "He'll have to pay, of course."

I gripped the edge of the counter, narrowing my eyes. "You already overcharged Aramis for it."

"I did no such thing," he scoffed. "Speaking of, where is your friend? Did the brooding shadow behind you scare him off?"

"No." I warily paused, gnawing over if it was wise to disclose anything. But hesitation and doubt were the reason why Cyrbus had gone free for so long—because no one was doing anything about it. "Aramis was taken. I'm leaving in the morning to get him back, so I'll only need the room tonight."

Vidaar stared at me for a long moment before he quietly said, "It might be wise if you count your losses and get lost, Little Flame."

My blood boiled, as if the ridiculous nickname he'd abruptly thrown on me had taken root. "I will do no such thing. I'm going to free him, and then I'll burn Cyrbus to the ground." My body ignited as he huffed a laugh. "You're the one who said not to count someone out when they've never had the chance to win. This is my chance. I'm going to report to the Council everything Cyrbus is doing, and they'll put a stop to it."

"You're what?" he breathed, the sharpness in his voice making me drop my hands in shock. "Don't tell me you believe you can stop Cyrbus by ratting on them to the Council. Do you think there aren't whispers of what's happening? That you're the first to share this tale? The Council would rather stay blind to what's erupting than face the truth."

"I am the truth." I gripped my hands into fists, not backing down. "I will not hide and continue to let Cyrbus obliterate the minds of those they deem disposable."

He expelled a harsh laugh, the points of his ears deepening in color. "You have a lot to learn about Aita, Little Flame. You can't set fire to a planet that has long been burned to ash." He jerked his chin at Caelum. "You're going to let her do this?"

Caelum's voice firmly stroked my courage, reminding me of my strength. "I don't let her do anything. Collins is free to do as she wishes."

Vidaar released a tight breath. "Fine. It's none of my damn business, anyway. But what is my business is this inn." He pointed a firm finger at Caelum. "It'll be thirty gold coins."

Heat enveloped me from where Caelum stood behind me, pressing a hand to my back. His voice was low, hesitant. "I haven't any money. If you give me a few days, I can arrange something."

I closed my eyes, biting my wobbly lip as I discovered again how I'd uprooted Caelum's world. I focused on Vidaar, begging him to hear my silent plea.

He rested his hands on the counter and shook his head once. "Don't worry about it. I haven't rented that room in weeks. I still need to clear out the mold, and then there was this incident with some Chimchiras." The beads on his dreads rattled as he titled his head back and laughed. "No one's rented it in fear of those swinging demons showing back up."

I might've had the urge to demand Aramis's money back—or set whatever a Chimchira was on him—if Vidaar's strong hand hadn't snatched my wrist. "You don't go near the Council, you understand?"

Caelum's presence wrapped around my side, at my aid if I needed it. I grabbed his hand while yanking my other free from Vidaar. "Why?"

Vidaar didn't use cold, biting words to persuade me. Instead, he softly said, "I will ensure word of Cyrbus's doings is reported to the Council. Aramis needs you to focus your efforts on finding him."

I wavered, uncertain why Vidaar was helping me. But I never had the chance to voice it as then a wave of brisk air filled the room, just as I was shoved to the ground, large arms softening my fall.

Caelum held me down, his attention not on me, but Vidaar, who was holding a dagger by its blade as though he'd caught it with his bare hand. My mouth gaped, realizing he had when he caught another with his free hand, his eyes gleaming. But rather than delivering the blade back to the unknown assailant, Vidaar only laughed and said, "You've lost your touch, Sander."

Vidaar lowered the daggers to the table and turned to where Caelum protected me on the ground, cocking his head. "If I didn't know any better, I would've thought your brooding friend carried some Elf in his genes with how quickly he moved, Little Flame."

Despite Vidaar's ease, Caelum didn't immediately roll off me, at least not until a smooth voice said, "If that were the case, he would've known there was no danger."

"Thank you," I whispered to Caelum when he shifted to his feet, accepting his hand as he helped me up off the floor. I believed I would've thanked him further, not missing how quickly he'd protected me, but I was too focused on the new man standing in the inn to do anything else but stare.

Not a man, I realized—or at least not a human one—but an Elf.

The Elf crossed his sturdy pale arms across his chest. Dark wavy hair was pushed behind his pointed ears, falling at his shoulders. He leaned against the wall, slouching where he stood, taller than both Caelum and Vidaar, his frame impressively tight. He winked at me, likely knowing how handsome he was despite having thrown two daggers at Vidaar, presumably for fun. "Well . . . hello there."

"Hi," Caelum dryly answered for me, and I couldn't help but laugh under my breath, even with how rigid his posture was.

I slipped my hand through Caelum's, assuming there was no danger considering Vidaar had turned his attention to a stack of papers on his messy desk, the two daggers he'd caught beside it. And based on the absence of blood—I wondered if perhaps I should take Vidaar up on those lessons, seeing only a glimpse of how skilled he likely was.

Before I could tell Vidaar both Caelum and I would be taking him up on his offer, he said, "I assume you'll be needing a replacement key to your room?"

I nodded, rolling my eyes. "Yes. I wouldn't want the mold to get lonely."

Vidaar grinned and made to hand me the key, only to hold it just out of my reach. "I mean it—you and your friend steer clear of the Council. Focus on Aramis and I will deal with the rest." He dropped the key in my hand, jerking his chin at the stranger. "Sander has business with the Council, and I was going to be accompanying him to Irenec anyway."

Maybe it was because of the way Sander and Caelum were staring one another down, but I didn't press Vidaar on why he was helping me. I knew I couldn't do this on my own, so it would be wise to accept any help. "Thank you," I said, urging Caelum to the door, his body relaxing with each step.

"Wait—" Vidaar called, stopping us.

I spun on my heel, watching while Vidaar shifted through the messy piles on his desk. "This came for you the other day. I almost tossed it when I assumed you were river bait."

I clenched the folded parchment he handed me. "Who is this from?"

He shrugged, moving as Sander shifted by him, disappearing into the room behind the desk. "I don't know. Some woman." He winked. "She asked me to deliver it to Aideen Stallard."

I stared at him, certain I'd never divulged my real name. But when Caelum's arm wove around my waist, I shrugged my wariness away. Aramis had likely told him.

"Come here." Caelum pulled me into his chest when we left the inn and entered the alley, neither of us speaking of what had occurred with Vidaar or even Sander. I breathed in the remnant of pine, savoring him. "I'm proud of you."

My heart ached, not in pain but something else. "I haven't done anything."

I closed my eyes when his fingers tangled into my curls, rubbing my scalp in the most soothing way. "If only you could see the world through my eyes."

I lifted my hand, holding the withering parchment between us. "I'm afraid of what's inside this. Only Aramis would know I'm here." My throat tightened with the truth, unable to say who else was aware.

Caelum's thumb brushed over my wrist, soothing my scars. "Open it."

My fingers shook as I unfolded the stained parchment, cursing as I tore the edge while straining to read the messy, scrawled ink in the twilight.

Only light can be found in the land of the cursed.

"What is this?" My mind fumbled into mush, worsening each time I reread it.

Caelum scanned the parchment. "I suppose the light could be the sun?"

The sounds of the jungle and the merchants drifted away as I searched my mind, dredging through every memory, trailing the faintest inkling. "You're going to find the light," I murmured to myself, repeating what I'd shared in my last moments with Aramis. I flung up my head, making Caelum step back. "You said Aramis would either be in Blythe or Thalas, correct?" My pulse spiked when he warily nodded. "Aramis is in Blythe—*the land of the cursed.* He must have sent this to me as a clue."

"What?" Caelum clutched the note, snagging it out of my hands. "Collins, think logically here. There is no way Aramis managed to smuggle you a letter. It doesn't make sense."

"Why?" I gaped, refusing to allow his doubt to smother out my first glimpse of promise in finding Aramis. "You don't know how he is—he would have found a way. Akira could've helped him, just like she helped you." I looked up, searching for the small jewels of light I'd once shared with him, before we were torn apart. "Aramis never gave up on me. And he knew I wouldn't give up on him."

Something sorrowful swept over Caelum's beautiful features, washing away his voice until it was no more than a distant whisper. "So I take it you'll be going to Blythe in the morning to free Aramis?"

My eyes burned while I struggled to pace my uneven breaths, aware he hadn't included himself. "Yes," I rasped, unable to fathom how tomorrow was here—our inevitable goodbye. "I guess I will." I strained against my tears so I could clearly memorize the sharp cuts of his face, the gentle pressure of his hands. I only wished I could convince him to conjure his smile, giving me my most favorite sight as a parting gift.

But this wasn't a moment of joy.

He'd done what he promised to do.

He'd helped me find where Aramis was.

He was free.

And I was bound in an unbreakable cage, yet again.

I staggered back a step into the leaning, crumbling alley walls, wishing they would flatten me as I faced Caelum. Faced what we'd avoided all along. "Okay," I whispered while I toed a shuck of rubble, clenching his jacket between my hands. "Thank you for everything."

"Collins—"

I closed my eyes, unable to do anything while my chest clawed itself apart. "I hope you find the happiness you deserve, Caelum." I spun on my heel as my goodbye chafed the air, failing to outrun heartbreak's relentless claws.

I'd yet to face Cyrbus, and they'd already won—stealing the only life I wanted.

My back bowed from the darkness crushing against me while I made my way to my room. It refused to leave me as I fumbled with the lock, collapsing to my knees the moment it latched shut. I couldn't breathe—couldn't see beyond the agony consuming me.

I was alone.

If this was freedom, I didn't want it. I didn't want to follow through and make the hard, honorable choices—I wanted to hide. I might know where Aramis was, but I didn't know how to save him. Even with the swelling, stable everflame in the corner, I couldn't find the light.

At least not before light flashed before me, weaving violet over the slits in the cracked walls. My back crashed against the locked door and

I clutched a hand over my flushed chest while Caelum Drifted inside, my ring carrying a faint purple glow. "What are—" His turbulent eyes absorbed my words, containing a storm I was afraid to face. "What are you doing here?"

His chest heaved. "Why did you lock me out?"

I slid up the door, forcing my knees to cooperate and stand. "I didn't." I shook my head and stared at his jacket in my hands, unwilling to return it. "I didn't know you wanted inside. You could've knocked, you didn't have to Drift to me."

He raised his furrowed brows, like he didn't understand why tears streamed down my flushed cheeks. He stepped back as realization dawned on him. "You thought I was leaving," he whispered so quietly I wasn't sure I heard him correctly. "You truly believed I would desert you the moment you discovered Aramis's location?" His voice wavered, conveying the hurt. "Even if I intended to leave, I would have ensured you made it into the holding grounds. I wouldn't abandon you to search those damned lands yourself."

"I didn't think you were abandoning me." My quiet voice carried across the barren space separating us. "You fulfilled your promise."

I gripped the door handle as he tightened his jaw and finished the distance between us. His fingers soothingly lifted my chin to his burning gaze, carrying none of the same fierceness in his voice. "Is that how you would leave me then? To have me watch as you run away from me—from us, not even giving me a chance to say goodbye?"

"You ran away from us," I pointed out, my lips trembling with emotion. "You didn't even want to try because you believe yourself to be unworthy of me."

"Because I am." He ran a hand across my jaw, lacing his fingers into my hair. "I could be a god and I would be unworthy of you, Collins. But I'm here, aren't I?" He leaned down, his words a puff of fresh air. "I told you: I am fighting my own battles inside. Not sitting in it, and allowing it to win, but *fighting*. And it wasn't until you walked away that I realized I was letting go of the only reason I was fighting at all."

I pressed a hand to his chest, refusing to slip back into this fantasy. "Caelum, tomorrow is here. I can't pretend any longer." I clenched his shirt as my voice shook. "It hurts."

"Collins," he said with such compassion and care. "Tomorrow never came. This is a new world. A new life. One where we can choose a different tomorrow. One where we may craft our own dreams and desires." He brushed a curl behind my ear. "We don't have to forget."

"I can't be selfish with you, Caelum." My eyes burned with clarity and purpose—to protect my dream. "I won't ask you to face Cyrbus. I refuse to put you at risk. You've given all you should. Let me protect you."

"We can protect each other." His hand tightened around mine, clutching it to his chest. "You brought me back to life, Collins. You've given me something to live and fight for. If I let you walk away, then I will have allowed Cyrbus to win." His lips faintly skimmed between my brows. "Run to me, Collins. I'm running to you."

My lungs burned for release, reminding me I'd been running my whole life. Running to be the perfect daughter, to fit into this mold that everyone needed me to be. But I was exhausted from chasing the approval of others, seeking their love. But now with someone running to me—meeting me halfway—I could run a little longer.

I braced myself against the door and took the final step. "I've always had this recurring dream, a memory. When Aramis brought me to Aita, I assumed I was dreaming of Kaira. But when you took me to the cabin and I saw the grove, I realized I wasn't dreaming of Aita. I was dreaming of my time there with you. Even when I forgot you, I never truly did." I ran shaky hands up his chest, soothing the torn soul within. "It's you I've been running to."

I traced my thumb across his check, wiping the single tear there. His hand grabbed mine, pressing a kiss to my palm. "Dance with me, Collins."

I choked on a laugh, wiping tears while the memory swirled through me. "This is hardly dancing music." My hand quivered in his, letting him lift me from the remnants of sorrow and loneliness—out of oblivion.

He pulled me against him, engulfing me in his warmth while he swayed us to the inaudible music, moving to our own beat, much as we'd always done. Against all odds, we had found our way back to one another. In his arms, I no longer felt broken, but whole.

I leaned into his chest and listened to him utter the greatest gift he could ever offer. "I love you. I have loved you since I woke up in this hell, but even more as you have led me out of it." His hands tightened, stopping me as I tried to convey the same emotions. "My hesitation of being with you was never because of who you are. There is much about me you don't know, a darkness that I've failed to smother. I believed I was protecting you by running away, but I can't be without you." He cupped my face, wiping the evidence of his touching words. "If you'll have me, I want to share myself with you. If you'll grant me the honor of merely existing in your world, I vow you'll never question if you are loved. I only ask in return to never be parted from you again."

I didn't know whether to laugh or cry while I held on to him, his words. I didn't doubt he cared for me, but I was asking for much more than love—I was asking for him to risk his life with me, to grow and be better than the damage bestowed upon us.

I fought the desire to share how wholly enchanted I was, wanting to save it for when we were home, when we found a refuge of our own. So instead, I settled for the next best thing. "Caelum."

"Collins." He kissed me slowly and firmly, until I was confident there would no longer be a tomorrow we didn't face together.

Chapter Thirty-Two

My smile filled my core while I rested against Caelum's sturdy chest, mindlessly weaving through his scars. Our souls were one, as twined as our legs beneath the ragged blanket, offering little comfort against the hard, grimy floor. But I didn't care. I especially hadn't cared when Caelum carried me to the couch, kissing me so intensely, we'd rolled right off the edge and plunged into a free fall of laughter.

I'd never felt so right, so free as I did now. So much that as we planned for the future, I thoroughly believed we would have one, trusting tomorrow would be a success. Aramis would be free. Cyrbus would fall. And Caelum and I would begin again.

"Where will we go?" Joy trailed my fingertips as I ran soothing strokes down his waist, leaving trails of gooseflesh in their wake.

I rolled over to find Caelum's eyes closed above his sleepy smile. His voice was dreamy, deep. "Wherever you wish to go. I'll follow you to every corner of the universe. We may even go to Elysia. Perhaps Vidaar will escort us to his home planet."

His eyes opened into a playful glare when I pinched his side and teased, "Careful, Caelum. I might start to believe you're my captive and not my captor after all."

I squealed while he rolled onto me, placing teasing bites beneath my jaw. I smiled, closing my eyes when they turned to loving, careful kisses. He was mine. This beautiful, quiet, compassionate man was mine.

But even with the truth reverberating into my soul, a thorn of fear snagged its way through. "Is Kaira within the scope of your universe?" My words paused when his kisses halted, fearing I'd pushed him too far. "It wouldn't be forever. But there are things there I need to learn for myself. About you and me . . . and my parents. But then I will follow you forever. It doesn't matter where I live as long as you're with me." His kisses roamed across my collarbone and I smiled, tangling my hands into his hair. "We could go home to the cabin. Or we can build a new one. Create a new home."

He looked up and stroked my cheek, silently watching as I lost myself in his stormy eyes. "I will return to Kaira with you. But there are . . . things there I'm not ready to face."

I ran soothing hands down his back. "Okay," I whispered. "When you're ready, we'll face it. Together." He kissed my cheek before he rolled off me, revealing every marred piece of skin when he stood.

I sat up and slipped into his jacket, despite the sweat building beneath my shirt. Something reverent settled over me while I watched Caelum fill two glasses of water, unsure how someone so tender had emerged from such bleak shadows. "Do you remember your mother?"

His eyes were hidden from me as he handed me a glass. Only after he'd settled atop our makeshift bed did he say, "I only know she died."

"I'm sorry."

"I'm not." His voice was soft, dazed. "If anything, it means she was a wonderful mother. They wouldn't want me to remember the good, only the bad."

I set my glass down and wrapped my hand with his. "She loved you." His calloused fingers tightened, giving me the confidence to go on. "Before she passed, she begged Aramis to find you."

His scar deepened when he clenched his eyes shut, unable to do anything but simply breathe. My heart strained not only for him, but for my own mother. What would she make of me? If she were alive, would she tear apart the realms to bring me back?

I closed my eyes, willing myself to envision a night with a mother I couldn't picture. We would watch the stars, laughing and learning while she pointed them out, and have conversations I supposed normal mothers and daughters shared. I would be honest and share my loneliness, tell her about the void that once consumed me, one finally beginning to fill. I would confess my fears of never being enough, and she'd assure me I was. She would remind me to be brave while I cried in her arms, whispering how much I'd longed to know her, how much I'd missed her.

But no matter how much I willed it, the fantasy wouldn't take form outside my mind. And this was the closest I'd ever get—a dream with a faceless stranger.

"Collins," Caelum whispered gingerly, as if he knew where my thoughts lay. He waited until the moisture in my eyes cleared before he said, "When this is over, I want to build us a home."

"Okay." I smiled, surprised at how easily I accepted it. "I would like that."

"I'll have to find work, of course. Cyrbus's enlistment didn't come with a wage." He pinched the bridge of his nose, laughing coldly. "I don't know what I'll do. Maybe I can find a craftsman who needs a laborer. Or perhaps be an apprentice to a blacksmith." My eyes brimmed with tears again, overflowing with the possibilities within our reach if we survived tomorrow. I didn't dare let myself wonder what I would possibly do with myself.

Caelum eased me back to the ground, lying my head on the flat pillow. "For so long, my hands were used for corruption. For once, I'd like to create something of value." Those very hands wrapped around my waist as he settled himself against me for the night, and I knew he didn't see himself authentically.

I smiled softly and closed my eyes, breathing him in while I blocked out the worries and fears of tomorrow, rooting myself here. In his warmth, his arms, the world didn't exist. Nothing existed beyond this peaceful, delicate moment. I pressed a kiss to his chest. "Tell me about our home."

Chapter Thirty-Three

The sweltering sun intensified the pounding in my head from where I stood at the edge of the inn's alley, each drum punishment for our poor sleep habits, too lost in our plans for the future to rest. We'd shared more over a loaf of bread this morning—courtesy of Vidaar, who'd strangely dropped it off before his travel with Sander to Irenec to report to the Council. I didn't know who was more shocked, me or Vidaar, when I threw my arms around his neck, thanking him. And this time when he placed the ivory dagger in my hands, I accepted it and even asked if he could supply Caelum with some weapons as well.

Its sharp edge taunted my ankle within my boot, where Caelum had instructed me to conceal it. His own blades were sheathed to his back, a twin set tucked in the safety of his belt. Despite the distracting flecks of water trailing down his rigid stomach, I'd eagerly absorbed his instructions earlier on how to use it. I rubbed my aching shoulders, sore from the lessons Caelum had snuck in while we planned for the future, morbidly reminding me it was necessary if I wished to live past today. I'd never been more grateful for a warm shower than this morning, loosening my joints, so much so I added it to the short list of requirements of our home.

The highest on the list were vast, open windows, so that not even an inch of the world could be hidden from us again. Never again would lifeless, debilitating walls trap me.

"I'm not certain if she's here," I muttered from where I leaned against the alley wall, the shadows doing little to shield the incessant heat. "Maybe we should go."

I imagined Caelum rolling his eyes from behind me. "We've waited all of five minutes. We can spare a few more if it helps ensure we aren't falling into a trap."

I fidgeted with the lacings of my charcoal pants—no longer wearing clothes from Earth—while I scanned the market, searching through the hustle of the morning crowd, regretting having mentioned the woman who read fates last night to Caelum. We'd gone back and forth several times about the authenticity of Aramis's letter until I revealed I knew someone who could possibly help. I conveniently avoided revealing that I wasn't entirely certain of Hekate's abilities, only hoping she could read the fate entwined with this message.

"She might be gone. The Keepers were less than enthused with her presence when I last saw her."

"Why?" Caelum warily asked, just as I zeroed in on Hekate, her braided hive bulging above the crowd.

"Let's get this over with." I bit my lip and pushed my way toward her booth, certain her piercing, strange gaze was watching me. I froze, nearly shivering when I found it indeed was, accompanied by her knowing smile. Caelum's hand found mine as she looked him over, surveying his tattoo, fully visible in his tan tunic. "Hello, Hekate."

She stretched out a bony hand, each finger clad in bronze rings. "Have you at last decided to change the fate bestowed upon you?"

I pushed Caelum's jacket up my arms and thrummed a finger against her table, scanning the scattered stones. "How does it work? Are you a witch like the Keeper accused you of being?"

A low cackle rolled off her tongue. "It is a great insult to be placed on the inferior level of a witch." Her eyes darkened beneath her veil. "Any other Verda might be offended by such idiocy."

"What?" Caelum hissed in my ear, stopping when I squeezed his hand.

I rolled my eyes, hoping she couldn't sense the fear building in me. "And what exactly is a Verda?"

Caelum spoke softly beside me. "Some fear the Verda because they are believed to practice witchcraft. But anyone who is knowledgeable is aware they only share a connection with past spirits. As if their souls are tethered between the afterlife and now."

Her eyes danced, and she licked her crimson lips as she thoroughly looked Caelum over. "Such flattery to know someone of your kind is so well informed of mine." I started to turn when I felt his body stiffen, stopping when she clicked her tongue. "Alas, things are different now." She glanced to her stones on the table. "There was a time I could listen to the wandering spirits by simply closing my eyes. Hear the whispers trailing their tattered feet, revealing everything they witnessed from behind the veil of death. But I am left with only a drip of what I once possessed. Hardly enough to fully hear the whisperings of fates . . . as our magic is now summoned elsewhere."

I clenched the frail parchment of hope in my hand. "Can you only read fates through stones? Or can it be anything?"

"Perhaps." She thrust out her chestnut hand, admiring her fine jewelry. "However, I am only permitted to use my stones." Her smile turned purely feline, making me wonder if Verda weren't quite human. "But for a price, anything can be arranged."

I leaned closer, following the twisting intuition in my gut that this conversation was prohibited. "I don't have any money."

"I have no interest in gold." Her breath was painfully sweet. "There are far more desirable things of value."

"Fine." I didn't let my hand shiver when I extended it, offering her the note. It didn't matter what her fee was, I'd pay anything. "I don't know if it's within your capabilities, but I need to know if this is from my friend. He's in danger."

She clicked her tongue. "I would need something that is tied to him."

My arm fell to my side. I didn't have anything of his. But then Caelum admitted, "He's my brother."

"What a treat." Her tongue darted out, licking her lips while she looked Caelum over again. "A drop of your blood will do."

I fought the urge to snatch Caelum's hand back, unsettled by the devouring look in the dark eyes beneath her veil. I frowned—not when she pricked his finger and placed a drop of blood on the parchment—but when she licked it. When I looked over to share my discomfort, Caelum's face was distant, unreadable to me.

I focused back on Hekate, whose lips muttered something I couldn't hear. I staggered back into Caelum as her eyes shot open, a misty fog overlaying the ebony pools.

Her deathly cold skin bit at mine when she grabbed my wrist, as if her soul hadn't yet returned to her body. She looked through me as she said, "It reads true."

"Thank you." My healing slices burned as I strained to retrieve my hand.

She tightened her hold. "Payment."

"What is it you want?"

Her blinks were slow, meticulous, until the fog at last parted. "Let me see your fate."

"I-I thought you did. With the stone."

Her laugh slithered down my spine. "These are nothing more than feeble tricks, offering me a faint taste. A mockery of what I can do." She yanked my wrist forward, my stomach hitting the edge of the wagon. "I wish to dive deeper into your fate."

She closed her eyes, but before she could mutter a word, Caelum was at her side. Her nails dug deeper into my wrist, even as he pressed his dagger against her throat. "Let her go."

She clicked her tongue, eyes still closed, releasing a breath of icy air. "Careful with your threats. It is not only I who is forbidden."

I stopped breathing when he pointed the second dagger to her side. His voice was lethal, raw. "I will slit you so thoroughly you will never again feast on the souls of those who are foolish enough to make a deal to change their fates."

Her retort cut off into a hiss when Caelum edged the blade tighter against her throat. I was certain my soul fled when thick, black blood seeped through the faint line, pooling against the sharp edge. Never had I wished to return to Earth until now.

"Caelum," I whispered, aware the market had grown quiet, afraid the Keepers would arrive at any moment. "Let her go, please."

But even when the woman released my hand, Caelum's dagger remained steady, taunting her with death. His teeth flashed as he tilted her head farther back. "Release her fate."

"Caelum," I hissed, willing him to hear me. "Caelum, stop it now." I smacked my palm against the table, the burning gaze of the slowed market hot on my neck, hearing faint whispers of those leaving to retrieve the Keepers. "Please. She's let me go."

Only when inky blood crept out of her side as Caelum eased the blade in did Hekate's eyes open. They were dark, lost, as cold as her bitter, sensual laugh. But nothing frightened me more than when she breathed, "It appears Aita has plagued your fate, Tempest."

Caelum slipped out of whatever trance he'd fallen into quick enough that we escaped the Keepers unseen. It helped they were far too engrossed in the fact a Verda had snuck her way back into the market, caring little about the man responsible for the wound gouged in her side.

But I cared.

So much I hadn't fully taken a breath of the dry plains Caelum Drifted us to—with four clicks—before I whirled towards him. "Would you care to explain what that was?" Only his short rasps filled the barren land—not even a bird or breeze dared to present themselves, sensing trouble as they scented the blood smeared across his hands.

"Caelum." Dry, lanky stalks of grass crunched beneath my boots as I slowly approached him. "Caelum, what's going on?" I placed a hand on his rising back, the only confirmation he was within his body at all. I ran a hand down his arm and winced, finding him warmer than he'd ever been, and unraveled his fist, pretending the thick, inky liquid wasn't blood.

"Are you feeling okay?" I wiped my hand clean onto my pants before I ran it over his forehead, wiping beads of sweat. "Come back to me, please."

"I'm fine." But his eyes were torn, ashamed, when he opened them. He smeared Hekate's blood onto his pants before he grabbed my wrist. He placed a tender kiss on my palm. "I'm sorry." His voice was thick with emotion, a stark contrast to the empty, rising plains, not a single soul in sight. I turned away from the desolate land when he whispered, "This is exactly why I tried to stay away. I am not good for you."

"Don't." My voice was edged, as jagged as the crimson rocks closing in around us. "Only I can decide what is or isn't right for me." My voice softened while I cupped his jaw. "Don't hide from me, please. What happened back there?"

"That was me losing control." He looked down at the parched, cracked ground beneath us. "The moment I learned she was a Verda, I should've insisted we leave. But I knew we needed answers. Not all Verda are dangerous, but some have been known to purposely damage fates. They'll lie about what they find in order to snare a victim. I should've known her fee would be to dismantle yours." He released a deep breath, at last meeting my gaze. "In moments like that, it's difficult to not sink back into my instincts. How Cyrbus made me to be. It's not an excuse for my behavior, but I'm sorry for scaring you."

"I wasn't scared of you." I ran a hand through my curls, licking my parched lips. "The entire situation got out of hand. We should've run the moment she licked your blood." Caelum smiled, loosening the pain in my chest. "I will admit it was a shock to see you like that, but I'm not angry. How could I be when you were only protecting me?" I reassured him, no longer carrying the unease from before, knowing he deserved patience while outgrowing Cyrbus's influence.

"You deserve more than what I can give you."

"I don't believe that." I wrapped my hands around his neck. "You're not alone in this. I will help you every moment for the rest of our lives to keep you from falling back into that world. You are not what they made you to be." I stood on my toes, brushing my lips against his for a fleeting breath. "When you're ready to share yourself fully with me, I'll be here. I want to learn every piece of you, Caelum."

He gently encompassed my face, as if he held the world in his hands. "I don't know if fates are real and if the gods truly decide them. But I'm grateful to whoever mistakenly gifted me you."

"I certainly hope they aren't real." I paused our kiss with a teasing bite to his lower lip. "Unless you're the plague Aita cursed me with." I laughed when he squeezed my sides, gently nipping my ear. "Wherever we decide to build our home, we are putting it as far as we can from any Verda."

"We'll add it to the list, Tempest."

I swatted his sweaty chest, smiling as he tilted his head back in laughter, hoping these lands cherished it as I did. I yanked off my stolen jacket, cursing at the sun for frightening off even the clouds. "Add this to the list of realms we won't live in, please. Where did you Drift us anyway?"

Caelum didn't look at me but at the crimson rocks entrapping us. Somehow the land drew even more silent as he said, "Blythe."

Chapter Thirty-Four

If not for the lavender sky wavering over us, I wouldn't have believed we were within one of Aita's realms. Because in a world where life flowed, there wasn't a drip of it to be found here. There wasn't a drip of anything, no scurrying feet or soaring wings, nothing to replenish these lands. The only existence here beyond our cautious breaths was the faintest trickle of water in the distance, not yet aware it was forbidden to dwell here.

Land of the cursed, indeed.

"How is Cyrbus possibly here?" Coarse, dry grass scraped against my thighs while we traveled the open, endless plains. "There's absolutely nothing out here."

He pulled us to a stop and pointed east. I followed the sharp cuts and edges of the clay formation, painted as if the setting sun kissed it, with smooth waves imprinted from where water once embraced it. "Within those canyons, Cyrbus has a confinement zone. They have wards to keep them unseen, appearing as nothing more than crevice in the wall."

I nodded, remembering how the village in Eirlys existed within a ward, protecting them from the harsh weather. I arched my brow, staying where I was as he made to walk away. "Then shouldn't we be going that way?"

He rasped a laugh and grabbed my hand, stopping me mid-step. "We can't simply walk through the ward. Nor can we Drift through it. The only way through undetected is over it."

I waved my hand back towards the canyons. "And how is going in the opposite direction going to accomplish that? Aramis is that way."

He jerked his thumb over his shoulder to the canyons behind him. "Yes, but the path to freeing Aramis is this way."

He smiled, even when I dropped his hand and crossed my arms. "I'm going to need a little more information," I teased, biting back a grin. "It would be unwise to follow my captor carelessly through this cursed realm."

He raised his brow. "I thought we decided you were my captor?" He grabbed my hand again, rubbing his thumb over it. "Not only will this way get us through undetected, but we'll save time too. There's a ride waiting for us."

I scrunched my nose, allowing him to tug me forward with him. "Like a horse?" I asked, remembering Aramis said stallions were one of the only forms of transportation.

He rubbed his jaw, thinking it over for a few steps. "Something like that."

I nodded, accepting his answer as I had better things to worry about. I yanked my slick curls up in a bun, the relentless heat doing nothing to thaw the fear that had seized my hope the moment I learned we'd Drifted to Blythe. "If what the Verda said was real and Aramis is here, will he still have his memories?"

He nodded. "Knowing Iveh and Conon, they were ecstatic to use him as a pawn."

I sucked in a breath of parched air and looked at my arm, knowing all too well how much they enjoyed games. "You never told me . . ." I hesitated, unsure if I wanted the truth. But when I met his watchful, careful eyes, there wasn't a trace of fear. "What did you actually do for Cyrbus?"

I expected for him to pull away, for his voice to disappear into the notched cracks at our feet. But there wasn't a moment of hesitation. "I suppose I was a sort of overseer. A team and I would travel and assess cases. Make sure the subject was adjusted. If we sensed any resistance, or possibly an escape, it was our duty to ensure the crime remained hidden." He lifted my hand, pressing a kiss to my knuckles. "Other than you, we never had someone actually retaliate. I heard Alderick lost his mind."

I couldn't help but wince, remembering the cries I'd bellowed because of him, courtesy of Iveh and Conon's hand. "Who is Alderick?"

"I don't know. I only interacted with a small group of individuals, never anyone new. If anyone reported to Alderick, it was Iveh or Conon."

Perhaps the roasting sun had driven me mad, but I couldn't help but smile when Caelum's words filled my mind. No, not his words, but his honesty in sharing pieces he despised about himself.

My smile deepened, reaching my eyes when I found Caelum warily watching me, likely believing I'd developed heat stroke. I pinched his arm, feeling the muscle beneath. "Were you working when we met at the club?"

His shoulders eased. "Yes and no. Yes, because I'd traveled with Cyrbus to check on you. But it was a coincidence when I ran into you that night. I nearly collapsed when I saw you come inside."

"And?" I grinned, forgetting I roamed in a land unworthy of such an expression. "What did you evaluate?"

He laughed exquisitely, and I knew if I could bottle it up and echo it throughout Blythe, the land would flourish again. "Well, once I dragged my jaw up off the floor, I noted how different you were." He briefly caressed my cheek and I leaned into his hand. "You stood out so brilliantly in that dingy bar. So out of place. I hated how uncomfortable and reserved you were, and for some reason, I thought it was my responsibility to fix it. It was against protocol to get involved with a case, but I didn't care." He wrapped an arm around my waist while the roaming hills dwindled away, bowing at the feet of the colossal clay formations. "You were so riveting, I couldn't make myself remember who I was. I only wanted to know you."

I smiled, cherishing the memory while I leaned into his hold, confident I would never need to worry that this moment would be our last. Never again would I believe myself to be desperate enough that I'd throw myself on a perfect stranger. If not for Caelum asking me to dance, I wouldn't be here.

"I wanted to leave with you. I didn't know you, but I wanted to stay," I whispered, unable to bravely reveal the depth of my emotions just yet. "I was on my way back to you before Aramis showed up that night. I didn't know what I was doing, but I knew if I crawled back into my house, I would never experience life like that again. I wouldn't truly be alive."

He kissed my hand, giving me no time to appreciate the sweet affection before he casually revealed, "I set a field on fire."

I stumbled over my boots. "What did you say?"

He laughed deeply, running a hand through his sweat-ridden locks. "After you left, I was out of my mind. I was angry I'd let you leave at all, especially with that gaudy ring on your finger. But then I was angry that I'd risked exposing myself to someone I didn't actually know. I planned to burn a little patch—just enough to blow off some steam. But that field was so damn dry, it took off. I managed to smother most of it out before I needed to run."

"You. Did. Not," I gasped in between laughs, as if the smoke I'd smelled lingering in the sky the night we met filled my lungs, grateful Sage had assured me no one was near that night to get harmed. "You are a pyro!" I launched myself onto his back, wrapping him in my laughter as he pulled me around his front, holding me against him. "Are there any more secrets you'd like to tell me?"

Our playfulness diminished when he set me down at the edge of the crimson rocks, not yet braving to enter the narrow slot canyons. His voice was soft, much like his touch to my cheek. "Yes, sweetheart. But first I need you to meet one of them."

Chapter Thirty-Five

Laughter fled when we entered the bare gorge. Where water once flowed, there were only depressed cracks in the surface, as if the gods had slammed their fist against it and eradicated all existence here, leaving not even a dried shrub behind.

I kept my hands crammed in my pockets, resisting the urge to trace the smooth crimson edge, fearing something unalive would emerge from the caves within the towering walls. Hollowed-out homes abandoned after the curse, leaving only a darkness where light wasn't invited to dwell. I shivered, even with the warm breeze bouncing off the walls, carrying whispers of what once roamed here.

Regret coated me like an extra layer of sweat when the narrow gorge opened up to another set of barren plains. Only this time, a gaping ravine lay between them. Internally I shook, despite that I was stiff and frozen, my body refusing to greet the cliff's edge.

"What are we doing?" My stomach sank to the bottom of the pit when Caelum retrieved a thick rope hidden behind a clay slab, no sign of a stallion or anything resembling one. Other than going back through the gorge, our only option now was going off the cliff.

And that was not an option.

But my fear burned to ash when Caelum cradled my face and asked, "Do you trust me, Collins?"

I invited all of Aita to hear as I boldly said, "Yes. I trust you, Caelum."

Caelum kissed me soundly, thoroughly, my nerves on the edge of combustion. He only paused to release a powerful whistle that rattled across the canyon wall. His hands worked quickly, efficiently, while he harnessed the rope between my legs and around my waist, doing the same to his own. A few feet of slack rope separated us before he seized me again, claiming every last bit of my being.

With shaking hands he whistled once more, throwing the high pitch across the lavender sky while he smiled, unable to contain his joy. I couldn't help but indulge myself in his unexplained excitement, grateful he would not only share his sorrowful lows with me, but his intimate highs.

I must've drunk myself silly on him, as I didn't even question his sanity when he said, "Run with me, Collins."

If I wasn't convinced I loved Caelum before, I knew it absolutely when we raced to the edge. My joyful laugh trailed each stride, as we closed the distance to our inevitable death. The winds rose, hollering below in the canyon, beckoning us to accept our fate. We ran hand in hand, not stopping even when we'd nearly devoured all of the sunbaked ground.

Caelum released one last whistle—his last words—before we jumped and plummeted off the edge. In the midst of a free fall, now was the time to utter last goodbyes and plead with the gods to save me. But there wasn't room for fear or even doubt in my full lungs. I was too fixated on engulfing the rich, invigorating air.

Until I caught sight of a shadow, heard a whooshing cry carried up the canyon walls. Caelum eagerly returned the cry, releasing his own soul-shaking shriek. Against my will and succumbing to my awaiting death, I painfully joined their screams, until I collided against a great force—the ground.

Even in death, I shook with my eyes clamped shut, uncertain if I was screaming or not, as I couldn't hear over the rambunctious winds of hell. Death's grip threaded around my waist, adjusting me on the rough, solid ridges digging into my quivering thighs.

"You did it." Caelum's voice beckoned me back while the rope tightened around my waist. A layer of comforting heat pressed against my back, pushing me flat against jagged points thrumming beneath my stomach. "Open your eyes, Collins." I clenched them harder, refusing until he said, "Sweetheart, Ashula wishes to see your beautiful face."

I willed my breaths to slow, to follow his steady chest moving atop my back, and dared a peek. Only now I was on the verge of a stroke when I was welcomed with a pair of slitted silver eyes. Eyes that I swore widened with confusion when I screamed, digging my hands into leathery scales.

"Is that—is that?" I choked out, losing my voice to the thunderous winds ascending through the sky. No, not wind. Wings. Grand, boisterous wings raced through the canyon, their curved structure easily diving and dodging the sharp peaks below us.

Caelum's hold tightened, pressing me back down. His lips danced up my neck, stopping at my ear. "I love you, Collins." My heart stopped at the edge of bursting when a rumble reverberated against my stomach. Caelum laughed, unconcerned about the beast's continuous growl. "I love you as well, Ashula."

"This is not a horse. This is your secret," I hissed while he bowed to the wind, holding on for dear life. "You're telling me that the someone you needed to check on in Aita is a dragon."

She—Ashula—growled again, making me wonder if falling to my death was a kinder fate.

"Isn't she amazing?" My fear shrank, withering to nothing at the gentle awe in his voice. "Before you, she was the only pleasant thing I had. Sometime a year ago, I was wandering through the canyons here when I heard this agonized roar. When I found her, she was badly injured. Never had I been so terrified as I was those few days I ventured through the canyons in the middle of night to nurse her. I have no idea where she came from—her kind is supposed to be long extinct. After she healed, she remained here. It's been her and me since."

I couldn't hold the racing wind responsible for the teams streaming down my cheeks, falling on armored, ebony scales. "You are more than this world deserves, Caelum," I whispered into Ashula's neck, uncertain if it would reach his ears.

His hands covered mine, inviting me to loosen my hold on Ashula. "Look up, Collins. The world is waiting for you." I didn't resist, allowing him to fully lift my arms, spreading them as wide as the glorious wings carrying us. His hands found my waist, steadying me while I forced my spine to straighten and bravely welcome the world with open arms.

Never before had I dreamed with my eyes open. I watched in awe, my mouth gaping, hurriedly trying to absorb every bit of the pure lavender canvas. Up here, the truth of being sold didn't exist. Above, in Aita's crown, I was free of bondage and pain. Freedom to exist for all of eternity, as sure as the solid structures below us who somehow remained after a tragic curse, resisting the deprived lands. A land I realized I'd misjudged, only seeing its faults and not its resilience to continue on, even after all had fled it.

And as it had survived, so had I.

I loosened my arms, allowing them to dance with the racing wind. Ashula craned her sturdy neck to watch me, and I steadily peered into her rare, exquisite eyes. I'd never dreamed of a dragon—only finding them crammed within my dustiest books. But this wasn't one of the cruel, dreadful beasts who lived in fairytales. This one was . . . benevolent. Not because of her gentle, almost-human like eyes, but because of the way she purred beneath Caelum's firm hands as he rubbed her thick midnight skin. It was the deepest black, so deep a hint of blue bloomed within when the sun kissed it just right.

Ashula bared her dagger-edged teeth when Caelum brought my hand to his, letting me trace her smooth wings. They were powerful, unfaltering to the wind while they kept her slender, agile frame afloat.

"Ashula." Caelum chuckled as she growled again. He tightened his hold on the leather reins around her chest where he'd fastened our rope and steered us eastward. "If you can't be polite, I won't invite you to come next time." Perhaps I was high on the pure air, but I was positive Ashula rolled her eyes.

"Is she going to spew fire on me?" I teased, pushing myself further away in case she got any ideas.

"She can't," he whispered solemnly. "When she was injured, one of her glands was damaged." He reached over me, rubbing a soft spot on her rounded head. "Now she's nothing more than a grumpy puppy."

I snorted and leaned back into him, absorbing his unwavering steadiness. "You two make a great team."

"We certainly do." His voice was distant, lost to the air, but before I could ensure he was okay, he tightened his hold on my waist. "Please don't shove me off for this. I assure you, Ashula will believe it to be a game and dive after me, only to drop me again so she might continue to enjoy herself." He laughed quietly in my ear before he asked, "Would you consider remaining with Ashula while I go into the prison? I vow to bring Aramis back to you."

I couldn't help but smile to myself, knowing this was only out of genuine concern, to shield me from the horror he'd once faced, not because he found me incapable. I shifted in his hold, pressing a kiss to his jaw. "We're a team too, Caelum. You and I are in this together."

I steeled my spine when I saw a flicker of fear grow in his eyes, knowing I couldn't allow it to embed into me. Fear that we might not emerge past Cyrbus's wards. Fear of forgetting who we were all over again. But in Caelum's arms and atop Ashula's back, there was no space for such a thing. Not with the world within our reach.

I soaked up the sky, tasting our last moments of genuine peace while Caelum guided Ashula downward, landing us on a flat. "It'll be best to wait until nightfall. We'll need the extra cover if we hope to break Aramis out unscathed." Caelum threaded his hand with mine, assisting me while I jumped off Ashula from where she lay, her back reaching the top of my shoulders.

I smiled as I watched Caelum interact with Ashula, rubbing her small, pointed ears, chuckling when she leaned into his touch for a deeper massage. Her slim, jagged tail urged him closer until he rested his forehead against her bowed head, not afraid of the threatening teeth within grasp of his neck. "I missed you too."

I offered them privacy and turned toward the reverence in the sky, absorbing the mellow, soothing layers of gold and bronze. I smiled while I listened to their inaudible conversation, grateful Caelum had found comfort in the most unlikely of friends.

I searched beyond the horizon, aching for my friend who'd once offered me the same, wishing I could share this experience with Sage. So she too could truly break free and live fully. But she no longer fit within my world. The most I could do was pray she was safe. That she was thriving.

"Collins." I turned around, finding Caelum smiling with his hand extended, suddenly all too aware he stood beside a dragon. *A dragon that's supposed to be extinct.*

What else wasn't truly extinct, but in hiding?

I bit my lip and closed the distance, trusting Caelum every step, even more so when he said, "She won't harm you. She knows you're mine." He grabbed my trembling hand, running it along her coarse, leathery side as she lay on the ground with her muscled front legs crossed, ending in taunting claws. "Do you want to know how I knew I was in love with you?" He guided me along her, rubbing her stout neck. I stared into her silvery eyes, finding nothing but love. "Because after one dance with you, I had to keep reminding myself I couldn't tell you about my pet dragon." Ashula snorted a puff of hot air, as if she understood and laughed alongside Caelum.

"It was probably wise that you didn't," I teased, straining my head back when Ashula rose to her full height and stretched her glorious wings, towering over us. She held my gaze firmly before looking to Caelum. He gave her a curt nod and she leaped into the sky, stirring up a gust of dirt. "Thank you," I whispered when at last the air had settled. "Thank you for trusting me with her."

We lingered at the cliff's edge, watching Ashula dart through the canyon, soaring up and then drifting down. "Do you think Aramis will have his ring?"

"It's possible. If Akira truly helped deliver the note, she may have found a way to slip him his ring. But the wards will prevent him from Drifting out."

"What is this ward? Is it a wall or something?"

"I'm sorry." He wrapped his arm around my waist, pressing his lips to the top of my head. "I need to remember you're still learning the terms of our world. Don't be afraid to call me out on it if I forget, okay?" I nodded for him to continue, grateful for his diligence in protecting my voice. "A ward is created by a protective spell. It keeps unwanted eyes from seeing it, as well as preventing anyone from Drifting inside or out. Think of it like two-way glass. If I'm outside the ward, it'll mirror my surroundings, giving the illusion there's nothing out of place. But if I'm within the ward, I can see through the ward as if it were a window."

"But can we use the rings once we're inside the wards? As long as Aramis is as well?" I asked, hoping to better understand his explanation.

His throat bobbed when he nodded. "Yes—but only within the ward. You need to know there's a real likelihood we're falling into a trap. Even if we're able to Drift instantly to Aramis, it won't be easy to get out. We can't waste a single moment."

"Caelum." I pulled him back from the edge, turning him toward me. "You don't have to do this. I will choose you regardless."

He shook his head. "This isn't a matter of ensuring you won't leave me. This is about doing the right thing, something I should've done long ago. We'll get Aramis out and see if Vidaar made any progress with the Council. If not, we'll force them to listen to you. Cyrbus isn't as untouchable as they believe." His lips kissed my brow. "And then you and I can truly get to know one another again. We can begin a life free of Cyrbus."

I opened my mouth to say what I should've long ago, but the prize confession wouldn't come out. I'd never once uttered those words, never shared something as intimate as this. So instead, I grasped his shirt and pressed my lips to his, showing him in another way.

His kiss was sweet, tender, much like what lay between us. But our connection was also intense, dominating, strong enough to throw worlds off their axes. I leaned into those emotions, letting them absorb me until a different awakening pulsed through me. Any fear I once felt must have been left behind in the sky—my hands were steady when I reached for his belt, certain I was ready to share myself with him.

Caelum groaned while his hand cupped my wrist, stopping me before I could unclasp it. His voice was breathless, ragged like mine. "Not here, sweetheart." My flushed face must've conveyed the brief insecurity pooling in my gut because he quickly pressed a chaste kiss to my cheek. "Believe me, there's nothing I'd love more than to show you how thoroughly I care for you. But I want you to fully know who you're giving yourself to. And when you do, I want the time to memorize every moment with you. To create new dreams while you're in my arms. I don't want Cyrbus to steal another moment from us. I want you to myself."

"I am yours." My voice was sturdy and clear, even as my nerves raced with exhilaration. "Even if Cyrbus wins and I forget you again, I will undoubtedly find my way back to you."

Caelum kissed my hand before backing away, grinning harder with each step. "What are you doing?" I asked, as he stopped at the edge of the cliff, where day and night bickered between who would submit first. "Caelum?"

He grinned, placing one leg in front of him and leaning over it. "If I'm not going to kiss you right now, I may as well ensure you're capable of defending yourself—that way I can kiss you as much as I want when this is over."

I laughed and planted my boots to the ground, raising a hand to beckon him forward. "I think we both remember how well our last training session played out."

He winked. "I won."

Chapter Thirty-Six

No amount of preparation eased the nerves deeply planted within my bones, thrumming as steadily as Ashula's wings driving us eastward. Each time Caelum and I went over the plan, my fear only solidified, confirming this was real. By my own free will, I was going back to where I was once wiped from existence.

"Your name is Collins," I breathed again, grounding myself as I gripped the leather reins.

Caelum's arm threaded around my waist, turning me toward him. "This will end differently than the last time."

I knew he didn't mean from days ago, but years. When we were stolen and sold, obliterated from the world together. But we'd also risen out of oblivion together, offering each other light in the midst of darkness.

"Together." I squeezed his hand, needing him to hear the firm reminder. In our planning beforehand, he'd instructed me to get out as quickly as possible, even if I needed to leave him behind. Even now, a flicker of that same panic, anger, filled my chest. "Vow it to me, Caelum."

Despite the sternness lining my words, he smiled with soft and clear eyes. "I vow to you, Collins. You and I will never be parted again."

It was such a deep intimacy that I forgot where I was, losing myself in the possibilities and love soaring through his eyes. I lost sight of it when he looked away, pulling on Ashula's halter. "Right here, Ashula."

My eyes strained to part night's veil beneath my feet, swallowing Blythe whole as Ashula's wings slowed, gently descending into the utter darkness where Cyrbus hid. "Only lower us to where we can safely jump." He reached over me, rubbing her taut neck. "You must remain unseen. Stay near and wait for my call." Ashula snarled, as if she understood and was as reluctant as I was to leave him. "Please," he whispered tenderly. "I can't have them harm you."

I leaned into his chest, offering silent comfort. The back of his hand grazed my jaw when he said, "One more time, Collins."

I rolled my eyes, secretly loving how protective he was. "You're unsure if there will be guards outside, but we need to act as if there are," I recited for the third time, rolling the sleeves of his jacket up my arms. "If we manage to Drift to Aramis, he'll likely be in a cell. You'll work the lock while I remove his chains. Anticipate being ambushed the moment we step out of the cell." I craned my head back, looking at him as I teased, "Then I'll proceed to kick ass while you stand by and watch."

He smiled, but it didn't quite reach his eyes. He grabbed my hand, tracing the scars branching up my arm. "Remind them that no amount of magic could ever alter your heart. Nor smother the fire within your soul. You do not go softly."

I didn't hide the emotion building in my eyes, letting him see how his words touched me. How he'd instilled feelings in me even on Earth, unknowingly acting as a catalyst, sparking something in me that had long been asleep. And now I was awake.

"You brought me back to life, Caelum. You've given me something worth fighting for."

"You brought yourself back to life, Collins."

I gently kissed him, sealing the words I'd nearly uttered, stopping because those words, that intimacy, deserved to be shared when it was just us. I wouldn't let such an admittance be tainted out of fear of Cyrbus.

Caelum grabbed my hand and together we leaped to Cyrbus's prison below us, hoping this fate would different than the last. But as I fell through darkness and landed on the rough ground, I knew it would be. We were claiming our own fate, together.

I willed myself to focus and absorb my surroundings while my eyes readjusted to the dark. Fear had my veins pulsing faster when I saw the prison encompassed in shadows, leaving me unable to imagine its structure before Caelum grabbed my waist. I reached for my ring, understanding we couldn't dare risk even a whisper. My hand shook while I pressed down on my ring and uttered *Eunoia*—the binding word connecting mine and Aramis's ring—hoping the blood orb emerging from it would truly lead to him. Violet hues kissed the red orb after Caelum whispered *Saudade* and pressed his own, allowing him to trail me while I molded through space and time, translating into a strange, suffocating void.

Caelum gripped my hand as we held our breath, waiting to see if we'd fallen into a trap. Darkness wrapped around us as a thick, frigid blanket. Caelum lift our joined hands to the side, our fingers greeting cruel stone. I found no relief when my eyes adjusted to the parting shadows, not when I saw a figure slumped against the wall, assuring me this wasn't a ploy. But as I inhaled the bitter aroma of filth and blood, I almost wished it was, unable to imagine what Aramis had endured while he hoped I'd come for him.

"Aramis." My voice shook with my hand as I reached in my boot and retrieved my dagger, Caelum unsheathing his two. "Aramis," I rasped from the surety of the wall, hating myself for being too frightened to move. But once the shadow bobbed, I was on my knees, lifting his head from where he was chained. “Aramis, it’s me.” I pushed back his oily locks, willing him to see me.

“Aideen?” he mumbled dazedly, distrusting his eyes.

“I’m here.” I sheathed my dagger and ran my hands over his strained arms, finding his wrists encased in manacles with thick chains attached to the wall. “I’m with you,” I whispered as I blindly followed the knotted chains, searching for the hook Caelum had told me about in our planning. I looked over my shoulder, watching his steady shadow work against the door, making only the quietest of clunks and clicks.

“What are you doing here?” Aramis choked.

“Breaking you out, obviously.”

I smiled when he dryly laughed, urgently running my fingers through the cuts and grooves of the stone, struggling to find the hook. “You’re safe.” The relief in his voice did nothing to steady my nerves. “You’re safe.”

Not yet.

My pulse spiked, fearing we needed a key. I released a breath, choking on the grimy air when I found the hook and lifted it up. I winced when Aramis thudded against the stone, groaning with the chains.

“I’m sorry.” I grunted while I pushed against his shoulders, bearing his weight as he struggled to find his strength.

“I can’t believe it’s you.” His hands roamed up my legs where we knelt together. “I was afraid you wouldn’t understand the message. Or that you wouldn’t be free to come.”

“Of course we’d come for you.” I looked to where Caelum’s shadow was still hard at work. “I wouldn’t leave you behind.” I turned around as Aramis raised clammy hands to my face, his stench encompassing me, his chains resting on my lap. A different set of nerves shook my voice. “Are you almost done, Caelum?”

Aramis’s hands dropped just as a clank filled the room. I shuddered a breath when a steady and warm hand brushed my neck, a stark contrast to the bleak ones holding me moments ago.

"We need to go," Caelum whispered. "Do you need assistance, Aramis?"

Something irrevocable broke in my heart at Caelum's offering, worsening when Aramis only grunted and pushed himself to his feet. I blindly threaded his chain through my fingers. "We'll get these off as soon as we can." I strained to clear the tension fogging the air and teased, "Who knows, maybe they'll come in handy against the guards outside."

"Be ready." Caelum's warmth left me as he returned to the door. I retrieved my dagger from my boot again, clenching the handle as the steel door grinded open. Guilt washed over me when Aramis hissed, cowering from the mild light emanating from the everflames above the cellblock—he must have spent the entirety of his time trapped in the dark.

Sorrow and anger threatened to consume me, but then I was too preoccupied with the man attacking Caelum, biting back my scream when he disappeared through the partially opened door. My shoulder slammed into the steel when I ran out, fearing our escape was abruptly over.

A wave of relief surged over me when I entered the cellblock—as warm as the blood painted over Caelum's hands. I didn't allow myself to look at the near-lifeless body beneath Caelum, his dagger plunged into the guard's gut, and instead scanned the rest of the hallway, anticipating another attack. But there was nothing other than the guttural, wet gasps of the guard.

I claimed the lapse in our escape and ran to Caelum. My hands roamed over his shaking core, checking that not even a scratch lay on his skin, all too aware that his eyes avoided mine, his bloodied hands hid behind his back. I didn't know if he'd killed for Cyrbus before—and even if he had, I knew his soul. Knew how much he hated who he'd been with them.

My dagger clattered to the ground and I reached for his hands. "You are not who they made you to be." I waited until he met my gaze, letting him see I accepted every bit of him while I lovingly rubbed the blood off with my shirt, a small attempt to shoulder his pain.

I broke our gaze and wiped the remaining blood on my hands over Hekate's dried blood on my pants. We remembered ourselves when Aramis cleared his throat. I flinched, not because of the bruises blotching his face, but at the way he sneered. "What is he doing here?" His callous golden eyes reprimanded me from the edge of his cell, his chains dangling over the stone.

"He's helping you. Just like he helped me."

He staggered, hitting his shoulder against the door, and I started toward him in concern. But I stopped mid-step when he spat, "He's the reason we're in this mess."

I sucked in a shaky breath, forcing myself to remember Aramis was in the dark; the last he knew, Caelum had delivered us to Cyrbus. "He's the reason you're out of that cell."

But he clearly wasn't convinced, not even with his stained boots on the brink of freedom, as if he believed his cell was still sealed like the others in this block. And we didn't have time for this. *Get out, and then the Council will help free the rest.*

"He's trash, Aideen. He can't be trusted."

I clenched my fists, disgusted not only by the fact he'd rather remain in a cage than be near his brother, but because of the disdain he openly spewed. "Stop it! We don't have time for this. I don't care what you think, Aramis. Get your ungrateful—"

"We need to go." My anger disappeared at Caelum's steady voice. "Something's wrong. This block should be entirely covered with guards by now."

At last Aramis understood the urgency and left the cell, kneeling while he claimed my discarded dagger and worked on his chains. They quickly collapsed, pooling at his feet. I extended my hand for my blade, only to drop it when he wouldn't meet my eyes.

Caelum pressed one of his own daggers in my hand, and I smiled despite the ache in my chest. His eyes were solemn as his thumb grazed my cheek. "Be ready."

Caelum glanced at Aramis, ensuring he was ready before we took off. I trailed after him, vowing to the locked cells I would be back. I would ensure not one soul was abandoned in this place. Not that there seemed to be a soul here anyway. Caelum quickened his pace and my legs moved faster to match, Aramis's boots sounding behind me. Unease riddled my gut in the dimly lit, narrow hall outside the cellblock with an iron door at the end, offering a glimpse of the night sky through the glass window.

Something felt wrong. This was too easy.

But when Caelum shoved open the door and I sipped the fresh air, for one moment, I believed we deserved easy. After all we'd endured, it was time we got a break. A chance to live our lives.

I hissed out in pain, my shoulder hitting the doorway when Aramis shoved past me, just as Caelum turned his back. Caelum collided with the ground, dropping his dagger out of reach. "Aramis," I screeched as he delivered countless vicious strikes to Caelum's jaw. "Stop it!"

Caelum wrapped his legs around Aramis and flipped him, pinning him to the ground. He delivered one sturdy punch before he bellowed, "I will not have you risk her life because you're an arrogant ass. I was right to leave you to rot."

I was inclined to agree, especially when Caelum had barely steadied himself on his feet before Aramis kicked them out from beneath him again. Savage curses rolled with their unwavering blows until Aramis pinned him down, this time pressing my dagger to Caelum's throat.

I clenched the dagger Caelum gave me, shaking, as Aramis sneered, "Give me one reason why I shouldn't kill you. Why I shouldn't shred your mind like you've done to Aideen again."

Bitter disgust and anger filled my mouth while I watched him threaten Caelum, edging the sharp blade against his pulse—my pulse. I didn't waste another breath pleading with Aramis, succumbing to an instinctual rage. One moment I was frozen beside the prison and the next I was behind Aramis.

I yanked back his grimy hair, baring his throat. Even with the stars reflecting off my blade, the threat I offered brought me no joy. "Because I will kill you if you touch him." A faint part of me quivered at the words, but nothing scared me more than living without Caelum. "I don't want to hurt you, Aramis. But if that's what I need to do to protect my home, then I will. I vow it." The shaking, gripping fear I carried didn't convey to my taunting dagger. "He didn't do this to me. Caelum was harmed like I was. Your brother is only trying to protect you from the same fate."

The truth cracked Aramis's hatred enough he lowered his knife. I'd barely removed my own before Caelum shoved him off, sending one final blow to his jaw.

Aramis looked up at me from his knees, blood dripping down his lips. "Tell me how this fate is any different than the last. How he didn't steal you from me again."

"I was never yours," I whispered the truth as easily as a breath, but breathing wasn't always smooth. It burned to acknowledge, to watch the man who never gave up on me succumb and bow his head. "I'm sorry. I can't will my heart to change—and even if I could, I don't want to. And I have you to thank for that, Aramis. Because of you, I have the freedom to create my own fate."

"No." Aramis bared his bloodied teeth, forcing himself to his feet. Tears freshly lined his eyes when he stepped forward, exhausting my air. "You don't know who he is or what he's capable of. I don't know what he's done to you, but the Aideen I love wouldn't have threatened to kill me."

"Aideen is dead." There wasn't anger or desperation in my voice, only acceptance. I didn't care anymore if I became the lively girl who chased the sun—for once, I had no desire to be her. I was okay existing in the quiet shadows, following the soft beads of light. "She's not coming back."

Aramis towered over me with wild and hard eyes, and I stumbled back a step. He grabbed my scarred wrist, yanking me forward. "No, you're not listening—" His lip curled as he saw the cruel marks on my arm, tightening his hold. "What has he done to you?"

Caelum appeared at my side, his presence alone strengthening me. His voice was tight, his body quivering with restraint. "I suggest you let go of her. Or I will ensure you're unable to touch her again. Or anyone, for that matter."

"Careful, brother. Your threats hold little power when I know exactly how to douse them out." Aramis dared to stare Caelum down, unaware of the shift in him. This wasn't the gentle and meek man who'd kissed my wounds in the forest—this was the one forged with Cyrbus's hands.

But I loved both sides of him.

Aramis dropped my arm, refusing to even glance my way, as if he knew the thoughts roaming my mind. Felt how strongly his brother captivated me. I stopped watching him scan our surroundings when Caelum silently cupped my cheeks. But I didn't need words to understand him. To understand the way he vigilantly searched me, confirming I was safe.

We were safe.

His thumb swayed across my cheek before he lifted his hands to his bloodied mouth, preparing to beckon Ashula. But rather than a whistle piercing the sky, a hiss sliced by my ear before an arrow punctured his shoulder, delivered from the prison behind me.

I turned around, unable to find the source amongst the shadows. All I could hear was his groan as I reached for him, ignoring the warm blood dripping down my neck. Caelum stopped me and gripped the shaft himself, wrenching it out. "Run." His command was the starting gun for a wave of arrows firing toward us, all emerging from above the prison.

My legs moved quickly, grappling to make up for lost time as I followed Caelum's movements and weaved as he did. As if that could change how careless we'd been to waste even a moment of freedom. "Call for Ashula," I gasped while we ran, unable to see more than a few feet of dried grass in front of me. "Caelum! Do it now!"

But as arrows landed among us and pierced our trailing breaths, I knew he wouldn't. He cared too much for her to put her in danger—and now he was doing his best to save us. To save me. "The canyons are up there, we can escape that way."

"What about the wards? Won't we set them off?"

"Something tells me they already know," Aramis shouted from where his long legs strode beside mine. "Once we're through them, we can Drift out of here."

I resisted the urge to scream it was his fault we weren't on Ashula's back, riding to freedom. But I could hardly gasp air into my burning chest, much less scream while my body demanded a break.

My raging, fiery lungs filled with relief when I caught sight of a lapse in the darkness and saw the gaping canyon—our way out, giving me the strength to push forward. I didn't know if Aita's magic laced the air, shielding us from the array of arrows missing us each time and plunging in the dry, grassy ground instead. But even when the arrows ceased to fall, we didn't slow.

But there was no magic to be found, to protect Caelum from the arrow darting straight for him, piercing his thigh. Another one hit him before I had the chance to so much as breathe, to demand my legs to stop. I cried out when Aramis tackled me, shielding me from our attackers—in the shadows before us. I writhed beneath him, inhaling dirt as I struggled to get to Caelum.

A slim shadow emerged, as frightening at night as she was in the day. "You'll forgive me, Caelum. It appears my aim is off tonight." Iveh's voice taunted me, as did the strung arrow docked at her jaw, poised above him. I screamed when it released, his ragged gasps filling the air. "My deepest apologies. I vow I'm aiming for your head."

"Stop struggling," Aramis panted into my ear, dragging me further from Caelum. "We need to leave now. There's nothing we can do for him." It would've been wise to run, as Iveh appeared to not care we were there, too enthralled with punishing Caelum.

But I couldn't leave him.

I dug my nails into the ground, pleading that a drop of Aita's magic remained. But there was no magic in this realm to help me, no friends to assist me—as the only one I had was dragging me from the one I loved. But I couldn't stand by, cowering, while I watched Iveh relish in Caelum's pain.

I had done nothing for too long.

A shock fired through my elbow as it connected with Aramis's jaw. The other hit him in the groin, giving me enough of a lapse to escape his arms. My body led itself and before I knew it, my dagger was in my hand as I tackled Iveh.

We slammed into the ground, her knee wrenched in my gut, fighting as I gasped for air. I fumbled for anything Caelum had taught me, but I could only strain to shove the dagger down towards her chest, her surprisingly strong arms holding me back. Her eyes were wild, almost exhilarated to be tangling with death. She bucked her hips, and my blade slipped, grazing her shoulder. Pain fired down my back as she flipped me over and shoved me against the ground.

I waited for her to plunge Vidaar's dagger into my chest, but her boot only collided with my ribs. I choked for air as she delivered a blow with each word. "That was a surprisingly admirable effort." She put her boot on my rib cage, holding me down with ease, and shrugged. "You should have run while you had the chance."

I wrapped an arm around her leg, ready to pull her back to my level as Caelum had taught me, but a heavy, suffocating darkness pooled over my eyes, rendering me useless. I cried out, screaming when the pain threaded down my spine, tearing me apart, just as a new voice sneered, "That was exciting. I almost believed she had you for a moment."

Conon's crimson eyes pierced mine with purpose, just as an agonizing ache filled my head. It was a twin to the pain I'd experienced on the altar, only this time the herbs were absent, and understanding washed over me. *He's in my head*. Panic coursed through me, threatening to consume me. A flicker of jaws scraped down my mind, and he smiled frighteningly, somehow aware I'd realized what was happening.

Caelitis.

He punished me with a sharp wave, drowning me before dragging me up again. "Get out," I screamed before I was shoved down into the void again. "Get out of my head!" Darkness bowed to my demands and thrust me back into reality. I gasped for air, straining against invisible binds. "Caelum," I cried, afraid he was no longer with me. "Caelum, I'm coming for you."

"Conon, you're draining all the fun out of this." I trailed Iveh's voice to where she frowned at the faint scratch on her shoulder. "Why go through all the trouble of luring them here if you're only going to splatter her mind before we've begun?"

Tears slipped down my temples into my hair while I searched for Caelum, finding him sprawled out on the ground.

Come back to me.

I silently whispered it as if it were a prayer, willing him to hear me. Even with his slowly rising chest, I feared something deeper was wrong. He hadn't resisted, nor put up an ounce of a fight against Iveh.

Aramis collided to the ground beside me, a man with surprisingly gentle eyes holding him down. But the blade he held against Aramis's taut throat, covered in blood leaking down from his mouth, was anything but kind.

Conon clicked his tongue, kicking Aramis in the ribs. "You should have used your chance of escape more wisely."

I didn't have a chance to contemplate his words before blinding pain grasped me again, a burst down my spine. Before, I would've done anything to avoid the kaleidoscope of hallucinations he forced upon me. But I'd gladly beg for them rather than endure this obscured misery. I sagged against the ground as if Conon's invisible hand pressed me down himself.

"That's enough." The man who was restraining Aramis spoke. His voice was deep and firm, much like the sturdy brown arms now tightening around Aramis's neck. "I don't care if she escaped you, that doesn't give you clearance to overstep Alderick's authority."

Conon bared his teeth animalistically while blood trickled down his nose onto his heaving chest. Aramis thrashed beneath his captor as Conon knelt and gripped my jaw with his ghostly hands. "Don't think you and I are done yet, Little Doll. You're far too tame for my liking right now. I've yet to rile you up." I spat my disgust at his sneering face, my mind and body united again. He gripped me harder, digging his nails into my cheeks, and I whimpered, my fingers grasping at the straw grass.

"Get away from her or I'll kill you—" Aramis breathed before the man shoved him face-first against the ground.

Conon rolled his eyes and dropped my face, nudging my ribs with his boots. "I can't help but wonder what you offer in exchange for such loyalty from these brothers." He clicked his foul tongue. "Speaking of—Iveh, could you be a dear and invite Caelum to join us? We wouldn't want him to miss a thing."

I pushed through the lingering pain and rolled to my feet, determined to get to Caelum. I cried out when Conon's hand snared my hair and yanked me back against his bitter, heaving chest. His arm tightened on my neck in warning when Iveh knelt over Caelum and violently yanked out the two arrows wedged in his shoulder before removing the one planted in his thigh.

"Leave him alone," I bellowed when Iveh pulled out a vial and poured it on his wounds, fearing it was the drugs they'd used on me. "I will do anything, just stop. Please."

My plea wedged in my throat when the man atop Aramis said, "This is necessary. She's clearing out the poison and healing his wounds." Conon yanked me with him, twisting my knees as he turned to the deep voice. But before Conon could utter a word, the man shrugged his large shoulders. "You're going to kill her regardless. I don't see the need to further secure your spot in hell by being cruel."

Conon sneered his disgust. "You're delightful, Weylin."

Conon shifted us toward Iveh, digging his nails into my hip. I held my breath as I waited for Caelum to move, to come up for air. My stomach churned with devastation and dread when nothing beyond Caelum's rasping chest moved.

I gasped for air when Caelum did, as if we shared the same breath. He scrambled to his feet with wild and frantic eyes, searching the grounds and settling on me just as Iveh drew her dagger, daring him to take a step.

Even with his still-closing wounds beneath his tattered clothes, he took one anyway, stopping only when Conon pressed a blade to my chest, right above my heart. It didn't matter if Conon stabbed it or not, it broke the moment Caelum pleaded, "Please, let her go. She has nothing to do with this."

I winced as Conon yanked my head back, inviting blood to drip down my ear again, from where the first arrow nicked me. "That's your worst attempt at lying thus far. Even worse than when you said you didn't remember her." His hand slid down the zipper of my jacket, laughing as Caelum followed the movement. "Did you truly believe we would simply let you leave? Let you live a pathetically mundane life with this girl?" He shoved me forward, digging his boot into my back as I fell to my knees. "There are consequences for your actions, Caelum. We can't allow them to go unpaid."

Caelum clenched his fists, shivering with restraint. "Then I will stay and face my consequences. Just let her go. I'll make sure she won't tell anyone of us."

Conon's laugh slithered through my nerves. "It warms my heart to know you believe I possess such mercy." He pulled out a whip, and I started uncontrollably shaking as he circled me. "Perhaps this everlasting love has softened my heart, but I can extend you one mercy, Caelum. I'll allow her to live," he drawled and lashed the whip against the ground, snapping the stalks of dry grass. "If you deliver her ten lashes. But if I do them, I'm afraid she won't have the same fate. You and I both know how thorough I am at it."

Aramis's bellowing faded away, along with Iveh's sneering grin—I could only see Caelum. See the devastation distorting his beautiful face when he realized the future we'd dreamed for was gone, as barren as these cursed lands. I didn't believe Conon's word that they'd allow me to live afterward, but I knew they'd leave Caelum alive. And I couldn't bear for him to live a life where he knew he'd harmed me.

Even if he never truly could.

I didn't allow my voice to falter, to reveal the fear rattling through me, knowing my existence was coming to an end. I mourned silently for what I would miss—but I also solemnly rejoiced. Because not only had I found something—someone—worth living for, but also worth dying for. And what an honor that was. "I'll meet you in the meadow, Caelum." I held his gaze, willing him to hear my silent plea. Even if I died in this moment, I wouldn't cease to exist. I would live on in his dreams forever, live as a piece of his soul. And that was enough for me. "I vow to you, Caelum. You and I will never be parted again."

I shuddered a breath, relieved when Caelum nodded, a single tear descending over his clenched jaw, falling on his torn pants as he knelt.

"Come back to me," he whispered, letting me know he would shoulder this all-too-familiar pain as much as he could.

He didn't leave my eyes, even when Conon cruelly asked, "Is there a brother you'd prefer to remove your clothes, Little Doll?" He chuckled, slashing the whip into the air. "Actually, I'll get a few licks in first. It'll be much more fun to do this in layers."

A piece of me was grateful when Caelum closed his eyes and bowed his head, if only so this wouldn't taint the image he kept of me. I blocked out Aramis's roaring and closed my eyes, inviting the forest of flame to join me. Only this time, I knew it wasn't a dream, but real. I immersed myself in every full moment with Caelum, wrapping myself in our fleeting touches and naked honesty. Stolen kisses and lively laughter settled as another blanket of warmth, shielding me from the fate awaiting behind my back.

I envisioned myself lying in the meadow, when a crack shuddered beside me, a final warning. Anguish slipped past my bravado—I needed one last look at Caelum in peace. But when I opened my eyes, peace didn't exist.

Blythe was on fire.

A fire created by Caelum's hands.

Chapter Thirty-Seven

Daunting flames snaked across the field, igniting the dry grass with a deadly kiss. I only faintly noticed the hands snatching my waist and yanking me up, as I was too enthralled with the dancing flames following their own silent beat. No, not a beat.

Caelum.

The flames rose with his hands, obeying his conductions. Smoke fogged my vision, smothering my view as Caelum grabbed Iveh's bow and melted it with a fleeting touch before encasing her in a sensuous ring of flames. My attention slipped from the majestic copper fire igniting the night long enough to find Aramis brawling with Weylin. I didn't see who held the advantage before I found Caelum amidst the smoke again.

Flames licked at his boots, not daring to crawl up him while they molded with his steps, fire and man moving as one as he closed the distance between us. Pain threaded into my mind—in my daze, I'd long forgotten Conon's cowardly hands around me, shielding himself from Caelum's fury. What if Conon attacked his mind next? But if he had, Caelum showed no sign of it as he steadily continued forward.

I gasped, choking on the smoky air, as ghostly hands grasped my mind. My knees collapsed onto the scorching ground. Screams raked through my mind while a creeping pang slithered through me and consumed my soul, until I was unable to see my surroundings any longer. I writhed in the shadows, struggling to breathe while my insides were wrenched and mangled apart.

An intoxicating, alluring warmth brushed against me, easing the agony when the shadows cowered at its kindling light. A peculiar, yet familiar pressure settled over me, banishing the last drops of misery, and inviting me to emerge through the ebony veil. It parted at my touch when I followed the gentle tug from within, beckoning me forward. I knew nothing of what this was as I slipped out on the edge of unconsciousness, I only knew it felt like *home*.

Tears filled my eyes when they at last opened, burning with my lungs as I found Caelum kneeling beside me. But nothing was quite as ablaze as Caelum's eyes. Eyes that might have been frightening if I didn't love the man within them. They cleared, losing their intensity when his lips kissed my tear-ridden cheeks, leaving rising steam in their wake.

If I hadn't understood before how he'd set the world on fire, I did now. Clarity washed over me, burning me anew as I saw the message within each of his warnings. Understood why Hekate was enticed with him, claiming them both to be forbidden. Why he didn't want me to bear the mark on his arm.

Caelum was a Caelitis.

He lifted me to my feet, only to drop my hands, knowing I'd unraveled the pieces he'd yet to reveal to me. I opened my mouth, straining to say anything to ease the fear I knew was consuming his mind. But there was nothing I could convey when I was unable to smother my own fears.

A Caelitis. The same ones who were banned from these realms after seeking to drain Aita dry, having a mad desire for power.

Anything I could've said dried up when Caelum spun, a flame encompassing his hand. He lowered it when he found only Aramis, his golden eyes burning brightly with rage.

The flames shifted suddenly across the ground, forming a wall between us and the prison, making Caelum stumble a step. "I'll hold them back for now," he rasped to Aramis. "Get her out of here."

"No," I choked, fumbling against Aramis's ash-ridden, relentless hands.

The wall lifted higher, blocking out the three smoky figures on the other side of the coursing flames of copper and gold. Caelum shuddered a breath, not looking at me. "I'll be there in a moment. You can use your ring as soon as you're past the wards."

I didn't resist this time when Aramis wrapped an arm around my waist, pulling me further from Caelum. My legs were heavy and strange while I ran from the fire and raced toward the canyon. I should've felt comforted, safer with every step I put between myself and the deadly flames. But I was cold and lost. I followed the lead of my strained heart and looked back over my shoulder.

Shame burned me thoroughly as I watched Caelum hold the line, protecting us. How was his fire any different than the everflame? The one all of Aita used to offer light. Caelum held the same ability to harm, but he never used it except as a last attempt to protect me.

Caelum had revealed who he genuinely was.

And I ran from him.

I halted at the edge of the canyon, unable to cross the ward. Aramis gripped my hands, stopping me when I tried to go back. "Let me go!" I writhed in his hold as he wrapped his arms around my chest and dragged me away. The flames vanished, the wards blocking them out, dread slapping me in the face. "Stop it, Aramis!" His hands fumbled with mine, desperately trying to reach my ring.

He changed his method and focused on his ring instead, gripping me tight as he clicked his ring six times to the left. He pressed down both on both our rings, no longer needing to click mine as he muttered, "*Eunoia.*"

I stopped thrashing, slowing my breaths, focusing on his heart hammering into my back. Just as the blood orb trickled into the night, I seized the moment and shoved my back into his chest. I slipped out of his hold, his hand pulling my ring off as I went, and reached between my legs, yanking his up between mine. I didn't bother to look back when the orb vanished—Aramis and my ring with it.

I wasn't frightened as I ran back through the ward, but ecstatic, welcoming the thick, smoke-ridden air. "Caelum," I screamed while I ran for him. "Caelum!" The flames faltered when he looked back, but I'd never seen him smile so exquisitely as when he saw me.

Run to me, Caelum.

I'm running to you.

As though my invitation was carried across the desolate land, he sprinted toward me, abandoning the fading flames. Billowing puffs of smoke laced the air like a drug, fueling me as I charged toward him, chasing his rasping breaths, not slowing even as his heat radiated onto me.

But there was no trace of hurt within our embrace as I collided with Caelum, throwing myself around him. His hands were careful and warm, showing no proof of the abnormal power I knew he contained. I buried my face into his neck, inhaling the essence of home and pine among the waves of deep smoke.

I pressed my lips to his ear as I whispered, "There is not a piece of you that I don't love with my entire soul." I pulled back, cupping his jaw while he held me against him. "I love you, Caelum. All of you."

His eyes fluttered shut when he smiled, leaning into my touch as he rasped, "I love you, Co—" His words stopped and he slid to his knees, fumbling for a last bit of strength to keep me from crashing to the ground as well.

"Caelum." His eyes lazily opened in response. I ran a hand across his clammy, charred skin, wiping the blood streaming from his nose. "Caelum, please tell me what's happening."

He rasped a laugh, leaning his head onto my shoulder. "I drained myself dry."

My heart sputtered out when I looked over his soot-covered head and saw the looming figures behind the lingering fire. "How long until your magic is restored?"

"I don't know. I've rarely acknowledged it until now."

Despite the threat behind his flames, it warmed me to know he'd faced this piece he loathed for me. I grinded my teeth, bearing down while I wrapped my arms beneath his armpits, straining to lift him up. "Caelum, you should know I love every bit of your muscles. But it would be really beneficial right now if you were a scrawny twig."

He grunted and forced his knees to straighten, leaning onto me while I wrapped an arm around his panting stomach. His voice caressed my ear, wrapping me in his mist. "Which muscle do you love the most?"

I laughed at the undeniable slur to his words, certain he wouldn't recall this conversation when he was fully himself. But I played along, gasping in between breaths, "Your hands, Caelum. I love your hands the most."

He laughed and relief soared through me, leaving a trail of newfound strength to support him. His voice lowered to a growl. "If only you knew what I wanted to do to you with these hands."

"You're insane." I laughed deeply, as if our lives weren't on the brink of ruin, and stored his words for further harassment later. "Only a few more steps, my love."

"You love me," he rasped with wonder and disbelief.

"I never stopped."

I winced when he shifted and intensified the weight on my back. His steps grew sloppier, dragging on the cracked ground—the canyon still out of reach. I bit my sweaty, salty lip as he said, "I'm sorry. I'm sorry I failed to protect you."

"Stop," I hissed, aware of the fire's glow fading from the canyon, refusing to acknowledge the predators behind us and whether one of them might dare to jump the dwindling flames. "You protected me, Caelum. You always have."

"Go to Irenec once we're past the wards and in the canyon. Even if Vidaar hasn't met with the Council, you can find a way to."

"I can't." My chest tightened with the truth: that freedom wasn't easily within my reach, no matter how close to escaping the wards we might be. "I-I don't have my ring. Aramis does."

Caelum's muscles stiffened beneath my hand, but no trace of it carried within his voice. "It's okay. We can find another way."

I sucked in a shaky breath. "You need to call for Ashula. She can help us."

We passed through the ward and slipped into the canyon. His gasps bounced off the walls, echoing as he collapsed to the ground, wrongly believing us to be safe. "No," he gritted out. "No one can know she exists. They will kill her."

My nails dug into my palms as I looked up at the narrow slits of the evening sky, blissfully unaware of what was occurring in the slender canyon below. "Then you're going to Drift to Irenec and I will find another way out."

He looked up with red-rimmed eyes, flecks of ash falling down his face, blood leaking onto his lips. "No. We can find some cover while—"

"You can't do anything!" I wasn't angry he wouldn't call for Ashula, but that he didn't care for his own well-being. With shaking hands, I knelt beside him and grasped his trembling knee. "You can't protect everyone, Caelum. Especially when you're badly hurt. So if you won't call for Ashula, then you will Drift out of here now. Alone."

I spared one fading moment before I grabbed his hand where the ring lay. Heat lovingly enveloped me as he set his free hand on mine, stopping me. "I'm sorry, sweetheart. I'll call for Ashula." I released his hands, only long enough for him to send a frail whistle into the air, a far cry from the joyful one only hours ago.

I stared at the murky ward behind us, nothing more than a deceitful mirror, hiding the chaos on the other side. It wouldn't be long before Cyrbus stumbled through and seized our delusional escape.

Another weak whistle tasted the air before Caelum brushed a thumb over my cheek. "She won't be long." He closed his eyes, slumping back and resting his head against the parched wall. Exhaustion didn't weigh heavily enough to stop him from tugging on my waist, settling me atop his lap. "Now I'm home."

I rested against his chest, ensuring his heart continued to beat. "What's happening to you?"

He failed to laugh, his chest shuddering instead, ending as a choking cough. "Exactly what happens when an arrogant and inexperienced Caelitis summons magic beyond their capabilities. I shouldn't have been able to form much more than a spark, but Aita must've felt merciful."

"Caelum." I leaned back and trailed a finger up his chest, searching his eyes for the untamed flame, finding only him. "You are sort of a pyro."

He choked on another laugh, clutching his shaking chest before he softly said, "You ran to me, Collins."

"Haven't I always?" I smiled into his chest, leaving a faint kiss there. "Now we can run together. For as long as we'd like."

His fingers tilted my chin up and he kissed me gently while his hands lingered down my face, leaving a trail of warmth. "I love you." He whispered those cherished words onto my lips and grabbed my hands, holding us together. "Would you vow something to me, sweetheart?"

"Anything." I pulled gently on his lips, tasting the intoxicating smoke lining them. "I'm yours."

His fingers tightened on mine, placing them on my lap, keeping me close enough I felt his words move against my lips, tasted his salty tears.

"Vow to me you'll be brave enough to live a life that's true to who you are. One that brings you the utmost joy. *Saudade.*"

I opened my eyes at his plea—at *Saudade*—and saw the vibrant truth in front of me. He held down his ring, the one he'd slipped onto my finger. "Stop," I cried as I fought to remove my hand from his. "Don't do this to me." My voice cracked as our surroundings did, slowly being absorbed by the violet hue extending over me. I writhed against him, sobbing harder when I could no longer feel his strength holding on to me, his familiar warmth that I so desperately needed.

"Please." Tears distorted my vision, his exquisite features washing away in the trickling hue. "You vowed to stay with me." My voice broke with the last bit of my spirit, and there was nothing I could do when darkness claimed me wholly and translated me out of his arms.

But even then, I heard his whisper across the realms. "I'll always be with you."

Chapter Thirty-Eight

The world crumbled with me as I fell, surrendering to a pitiful splat. I gasped for air, choking on tears while water weaved over me, as if the magical fountain foolishly believed it could wash away the tainted slices embedded in my aching heart. Not one bead of water soaked my clothes, nor did it touch the ring lying between my shaking legs as I sat in Mazoe's fountain. My ring. The one Aramis took. The one that was synced to Caelum's. The one Caelum had sent me to when he abandoned me and our hopes of a life together.

I left the forsaken ring and stood, racing through the water shielding me from the world behind it. I leaped over the edge and plummeted back to cruel reality as I cried, "I need help!" The market paid no heed to my pleas, continuing their merry chatter, oblivious that my world was on fire. "Someone help—" I stopped, realizing it was a wasted breath.

I shoved through the crowd, forcing my way through the wagons of merchants towards the busiest one. Slothful, clammy bodies with sour aromas blocked my way, bitter liquid spilling from their mugs. Curses filled the night, erupting when I shoved over the barrels, splashing and splattering among their foul mouths.

"Listen to me!" I pushed over another barrel before I delivered a blow to the merchant reaching for me. Blissful, intoxicating adrenaline filled me as I unsheathed the dagger in his belt, daring him to take another step. He stepped back, retreating as my next words did. Never had I openly acknowledged what was done to me, and I feared by their sneers and drunk heckles they wouldn't believe me. But I only needed one. One person could make all the difference.

"I was sold." They fell silent, quiet as though they cared. "I was sold to a different world and I've barely managed to escape. But those who harmed me are still after us—they're in Blythe!" Their wandering eyes looked among one another as they whispered of the cursed land. "There are people being held there. Their lives are on the edge of being destroyed, but it's not too late to help them! We can help them if we hurry!"

Silence extinguished what little hope I had remaining when they only stared at me. My lungs burned with each rasping breath, deepening when a man at last stepped forward. And my hope grew. I choked on a relieved sob when he smiled softly, believing his kind emerald eyes, glistening off his drink, to be genuine.

But this world was anything but kind.

He doused the last remnants of hope and dumped his mug over my head, summoning the crowd into roaring laughter. Each howl and sneering grin kicked me in the ribs, thoroughly shaming me as I blinked through the bitter yeast drink. The man cackled and threw his mug at my feet, too distracted to avoid the blow to the back of his head.

"Little Flame." Vidaar's copper eyes engulfed me as his arms picked me up, resisting me when I fought against his unwavering hold. Ignoring my pleas to help me face Cyrbus—to bring Caelum home. "I told you, this world has long turned to ash."

I shook violently, struggling to stand as he set me down in the false security of his inn, no sign of his friend, Sander. "I need to get back to Blythe." I didn't let my thoughts sink down that endless pit, certain I would drown. "Caelum was left behind."

He was fine. Ashula had come for him.

I dug my nails into Vidaar's desk when a hollow chuckle from behind me crept down my spine. "I'd say it's up for debate who you truly deserted."

I turned, clenching my stolen dagger, considering how freeing it would be to slice Aramis's glare right off his face. I didn't care if he was angry—I didn't care about him at all. Not only had he discarded my ring in the fountain, but this was all his fault. He was the one who'd carelessly sent that letter, unknowingly sending us into a trap.

I bared my teeth, raising my blade in invitation. "We both know how accustomed you are with deserting your brother."

His eyes darkened cruelly as he seemed to realize Aideen no longer dwelled beneath my skin. Before he could spit his disdain, Vidaar stepped between us. "That's enough. You can have your lover's spat elsewhere."

I rolled my eyes and moved toward the door. "Just because the rest of you have given up doesn't mean I have. I'm going to the Council myself. I'll drag them to Blythe if I have to in order to bring Caelum back."

Vidaar grabbed my shoulder, stopping me when I touched the handle. His fingers dug in, forcing me to turn as he said, "I was in the middle of presenting your case to the Council when whisperings erupted about the perilous fire in Blythe. The Council barely let me finish before they fled for Blythe."

Before they fled for Blythe.

They hadn't laughed in Vidaar's face. They'd gone to Blythe's aid. To Caelum's.

Chapter Thirty-Nine

I hardly allowed Vidaar's words to settle before I Drifted to Blythe with four clicks, landing in the desolate land exactly where I once did with Caelum, racing toward the daunting peaks concealing the prison, not caring if I disturbed the wards. Nor did I slow when I heard Aramis's boots crashing behind mine, refusing to let me be.

But any rage at Aramis departed when I stepped on the plains, leaving me as empty as the land. Not one dry stalk of grass remained, all devoured into ash. Even the ward had fled. Every moment that'd happened here was charred and gone, left to linger only in my mind.

I stared at where Caelum and I had sat—where we abandoned one another—finding no imprint of his frame, not a drip of his blood. Even with hours passed, and the sun rising—oblivious that my world no longer existed—I couldn't bring myself to leave, refusing to believe Caelum wasn't here.

The only undeniable truth remaining was the prison, simple and unfrightening in the daylight. Had I any energy for tears, I would've sobbed when I learned not a lick of flame had touched the prison, firmly believing Caelum had used his magic to keep anyone who might've been inside safe. But I couldn't bring myself to step foot inside to see if anyone remained, not even when six white-cloaked individuals searched it. Searched for the proof that probably no longer existed in the narrow stone building, as if the horrors that occurred inside had all slipped out the single door.

I knelt in the ash, refusing to sink into the cyclone of my mind, and stared at Caelum's charcoal band resting on my finger, much too large for me. I couldn't bear to take it off, even after Aramis had returned mine after retrieving it from the fountain, sparing a moment before he followed me to Blythe.

I tugged Caelum's jacket tighter around my shoulders despite the early-morning heat as a pair of dark boots stopped beside mine. "Hello." It was a man's voice, one that might have been comforting at a different time. "I believe you are Collins?"

I looked up through my lashes and settled on a pair of blue eyes crafted by the sea, a stark contrast to the ones carved from ash that held my heart. He smiled despite my silence and sat beside me, apparently caring little about the soot that would surely ruin his pure white cloak. "My name is Drystan. I spoke with your friend Vidaar." He looked back over his shoulder to where Aramis and Vidaar were—no sign of Sander— lingering closely to the remaining Council members. "You'll forgive me—I insisted questions could wait for a later time, but my fellow members insisted I speak to you while it's fresh."

I narrowed my eyes and studied his flawless pale skin. He appeared much too young to be in a position of authority. "What do you want?" I cleared my throat, choking on the remnants of smoke in the air.

I'd gladly let it burn me if it meant I could taste Caelum again.

He ran a hand through his ebony hair, looking back and forth between me and the ground. His sharp cheeks heated as he said, "From what I understand, you believe that not only were you sold to another world, but that this . . . Cyrbus company wiped your memories with it."

I grinded my teeth at the disbelief in his words. "Yes."

It was hauntingly silent before he released a tight breath. "I want to believe you, Collins. I genuinely do. The moment Vidaar revealed such an atrocity, it was an effort not to race here immediately." I shook my head with my twisting gut, already anticipating his next words. "But when we got here, there were no signs of such a crime. Nothing other than the mysterious flames that came from nothing."

I pulled my knees to my chest and rested my chin on top. There were no words burning in my lungs, no desire to beg for them to believe me. How could I, one simple, spiritless girl, convince them of the corruption in their world? It didn't matter if they believed me or not—I knew the truth.

I'd lived the truth.

Drystan cracked his neck and gracefully rolled to his knees. "Do you have any idea how the fire occurred, Collins?"

"No." I held the challenging gaze of the Council member. One of Aita's leaders, who believed Caelitis—my Caelum—to be uncontrollable and dangerous. "I must have created it in my delusion."

He chuckled as he stood, brushing the ash from his sleeves. "If this Cyrbus you speak of is real, they certainly didn't steal your spirit." He pulled up his hood, concealing himself as he whispered, "There are certain protocols we must follow. I'm afraid my hands are bound. However, I can assure you—if you find proof, I will assist you in persuading the Council to believe your story."

I narrowed my eyes, unable to see how he was any different than the people in Mazoe who'd laughed at my sorrow. "Why?"

He was already walking away when he said, "Because you and I are one of the few who aren't blind to the truth of what Aita has become."

Chapter Forty

I pleaded with the edge beneath my boots to crumble, to send me plummeting toward a different fate. But despite how much I begged, it remained steady and sure. And no matter how many times I raced toward the edge, I couldn't bring myself to jump off the cliff I'd once soared from freely with Caelum.

Because now I was alone.

My hands shook against my chapped, bleeding lips and I released a pitiful whistle. My mouth throbbed from the effort, having done so since I'd left the prison, even as I trekked the sorrowful plains, hoping Ashula would sweep through the sky. That I'd find her loyal rider on her back and everything would be fine. I would be home.

But I was lost.

I'd been adrift the moment I stepped foot in those canyons and saw what I'd failed to understand the night Caelum and I hid outside the ward. He might have called for Ashula—but he knew she couldn't come. Knew her large wings wouldn't fit in the slender crevices of the canyon, and we were out of her reach.

"Please." I trembled while I forced a whistle again, finding it as empty as the breeze brushing my skin. "Come back to me." My chest agonized, suffocating me with the truth—he was gone. I had left him. "Come back to me."

But unlike with Caelum's haunting dreams at the cabin, the unusual and rare invitation didn't cleave through this nightmare. Couldn't offer an end to the terror and dread tattering my mind. Because this was real. And there was no escaping it. This time, Cyrbus wouldn't extend mercy and allow me to forget. They'd left me to writhe and burn in every bit of sorrow and pain.

While they simply disappeared, as though none of it ever happened.

As if Caelum never existed.

But when I looked at the jagged, brutal scar branching up my arm, I knew he had. The mark was insignificant compared to the impression he'd made upon my soul. A soul that was now hollow and throbbing, unable to ignore his absence.

This world had forgotten Caelum.

But I hadn't.

And I would ensure each festive wind, sturdy root, and spirited sea remembered. Not only remembered, but knew the Caelitis who set me on fire. And when I brought him back, I'd help him set fire to Aita, burning it anew.

It was a vow I'd echo throughout all the realms.

ACKNOWLEDGMENTS

Wow. This is almost more overwhelming to write than writing the book itself. I'm beyond blessed with the support I've received throughout this journey. When I started *The Realm of Oblivion*, it was only meant to act as a lifeline as I struggled with depression—never did I imagine I'd publish it. In all transparency, this book started off much different than the story you just read. I often comment on how "embarrassing" that first draft was, but if I'm being honest—that draft saved my life. It solely existed for me, as an outlet to get the not-so-pretty emotions out that I was quite literally drowning in. That book was angry and broken—and so was I. But somehow, with a lot of hard work and patience, I managed to turn it into something I'm proud of—and I'm proud of myself too. So, here's to taking the messy, damaged pieces and creating something worthwhile.

To the chaotic crew on WFA discord: I could not have done this without you. Even though most of our writing sprints turn into GIF and meme wars, I'm grateful for your encouragement and friendship. Long live the squirrels. To my beta readers: Angela, Isabel, Julia, Tessa and Teresa. Thank you for braving a very rough draft, and for your entertaining comments. Your feedback and excitement meant the world to me. To Ashley and Teresa: I'm so grateful for your friendship. We really need to get passports so we can see each other.

To my editors, Liz Lowham and Kara Aisenbrey: Liz, thank you for stomping out what was quite literally a dumpster fire. I am eternally grateful for you taking a chance on me and elevating my book to the next level. You're amazing. Kara, I loved working with you. Thank you for your encouragement and rearranging my sentences to their proper order. And for fixing moments that made Collins sound nude far too often lol! You're both talented gems and if I get to work with you for the rest of my writing career, I'd be so lucky. To Book Blurb Magic: Jessie, thank you for creating my blurb and author bio! You were a tremendous help with putting into words what I couldn't.

To Kody Taylor: Thank you for an outstanding cover. You brought Collins to life in a way I never thought possible. And thanks for not chopping my head off for changing designs on you. You're the best.

To my ARC readers: Thank you for your excitement and hyping this book up. I simply could not have done it without you. To the bookstagram community: Never did I think I'd be thankful for social media—but wow. I am so grateful for the people I've been lucky enough to connect with and the friendships I've built. Thank you for sharing your love for reading and fictional boyfriends, specifically morally grey men. To the readers who picked up this book: Thank you for taking a chance on a little indie author like me. Your support is a gift I'll forever cherish. I hope if you gained anything from reading this, it's that you're brave enough to break free of what's trapping you—who you are now is more than enough.

To the ones who fueled me creatively but will never see this: Taylor Swift, you are an absolute queen and I thank you for blessing the world with *Folklore* and *Evermore*. Sasha Sloan, your music makes me incredibly sad and I love it. "Dancing With Your Ghost" and "House With No Mirrors" played constantly as I wrote Collins's story. To Alani Nu, thanks for feeding my unhealthy addiction to caffeine—you're delicious. And let's be honest, I wouldn't truly be me if I didn't mention Sarah J. Maas—thank you for writing some of my favorite stories and characters that made me feel seen. Aelin was my friend through some of my darkest days.

To Sierra B: Thank you for being a constant support. It truly meant the world to me how often you'd check in, or even just messaging me about the books you were reading. You're amazing and I appreciate you. To Amy N: If I've ever felt a person was placed in my life for a reason, it was you. You started off as a new client, and quickly became one of my most cherished friends. I cannot thank you enough for your support and honesty. You have built me up more than you can imagine. To Mattie B: Thank you for the author photo and helping me feel not so "mom-ish." You're a ray of sunshine and our photographer for life. To the girls at the salon, Alicia, Sasha and Stacey: You might not know it, but all three of you inspire me. Thanks for showing me that it's possible to be a mom, as a well as a boss. To Vanessa M: I'm so glad we reconnected all these years later. Your support and friendship mean so much to me. To Alix and Trish: Oh, how I love the memes and reels we send one another. Thanks for indulging my obsession with particular fandoms. To my clients: Most of you likely had no idea I was doing this, and you may never know, but if you're here—surprise! I appreciate each and every one of you.

To my Good family: Thank you for taking me in as one of your own and supporting me. I am so blessed to have gained two parents, two sisters, two brothers and seven nieces and nephews. Thank goodness for mermaids, sharks, and rainbow dashes. And to Cori: thank you for reading my very first draft and encouraging me on, even though you were delirious from staying up with a newborn lol! We're often sappy with one another, so I'll save the ooey gooeyness for in person. But thank you for holding space for me.

To my family: Thank you for teaching me the value of hard work and showing me just how capable I truly am. For fostering my love of reading and movies and encouraging me to chase my dreams.

To my clone, Kady: We're never mushy with each other, so if this makes you cringe—I'm not sorry. Thank you for being my longest and bestest friend. I could not do life without you. Our late-night phone calls, random texts and reels are my favorite. I love our movie nights, sorry for eating all the cheese popcorn. I know this book wasn't spicy enough for you—but I hope it'll do, at least until we write the barn story. I really hope you like the dust jacket. It's only because of you and Cody that it exists at all. Also: thanks for having the cutest boy ever. Feel free to have twenty more kids. You're my best friend. Let's go to Disneyland and eat a corndog.

To my daughters: Everything I do, is for you. You won't know it until you're older—but it's because of you two that I fought to stay. You're my everything. I love you both more than I could possibly ever say. Thank you for teaching me true joy. And to my fur baby, Butter—you're the best kind of crazy.

To my husband, Brody: This book wouldn't exist without you. Thank you for constantly supporting me and letting me escape to the bedroom so I could write. For not laughing at me when I said I wanted to write a book. For staying up late with me to work through plot holes and encouraging me when I wanted to give up. Your hard work and ideas flow in this book as much as mine do, so thank you. But mostly, thank you for loving me. Without you—I wouldn't know how to write about love at all. Thank you for sitting with me in my darkest days, Brody. For choosing me. You're better than any fictional boyfriend I could ever write. I love you.

And lastly, I must thank my Heavenly Father: I have no doubt that it was your hand that led me to writing in the first place. Thank you for knowing me.

About the Author

Marae Good was born and raised in Arizona, where she currently lives with her husband, two daughters and their sassy Yorkshire Terrier, Butter. After an episode of crippling depression forced Marae to reevaluate her priorities, she found herself returning to an old habit: reading. Mesmerized by the world she could escape to, Marae started creating her own — and *The Realm of Oblivion* was born. When she's not writing, Marae loves to dance with her littles, run and hike in the mountains, or stay up far too late bingeing TV shows (most likely *Vampire Diaries* or *Gilmore Girls*).

Follow her bookish adventures on Instagram: @maraegood.writes

Lightning Source UK Ltd.
Milton Keynes UK
UKHW011837061222
413480UK00004B/140

9 798987 098615